White Hot

Elise Noble

Published by Undercover Publishing Limited

Copyright © 2018 Elise Noble

v6

ISBN: 978-1-910954-71-3

Edited by Amanda Ann Larson

Cover by Abigail Sins

www.undercover-publishing.com

www.elise-noble.com

If you can't stand the heat, get out of the kitchen.
- Harry S Truman

CHAPTER 1

THE MORNING SUN burst through the gap in the drapes, making me squint. I blinked a couple of times as it seared my retinas then focused on the back of the man lying beside me on the bed.

As backs went, it was pretty good—tanned and broad with cords of muscle running along each side of the spine and well-developed shoulders that spoke of a serious gym habit. A tribal tattoo covered the uppermost shoulder, disappearing from view around the front of his body and extending partway down his arm. I couldn't resist leaning forward to trace the pattern with my tongue.

The owner of the tattoo let out a low groan, and as he did so, I felt hot breath on the back of my neck. A pleasant sensation of warmth flooded through me as an arm wrapped around my waist from behind.

I smiled. Who wouldn't? "Good morning, boys."

I had no idea what their names were. Probably they'd told me at some point, but I'd long since forgotten, and to be honest, I didn't really care. After all, I was only interested in one night.

But it seemed as if guy number two was interested in a good morning as well, judging by the rapidly hardening bulge pressed against my ass. I couldn't complain about that. Guy number one decided to turn it into a contest over who could make me happy first, and I couldn't complain about that either. I'd gone beyond happy and was fast heading for delirious when my phone rang.

Not my everyday phone with the number that every Tom, Dick, and cold-calling salesman had. No, this was the one I had to answer.

Groaning, I pushed both men away, rolled over, and picked the damn thing up from the nightstand. "This had better be an emergency."

"Is that any way to greet your best friend in the whole world?"

"You're not my best friend anymore. I have two very good friends with me right now, and they were introducing me to a whole new universe until you interrupted."

My friend, my best friend, chuckled. "You're gonna have to put your boy toys away, you little slut. I've got a job for you."

"What job?"

"It's right up your street. Alley. Whatever. Now, get dressed and come to the office."

"You'd better have coffee waiting."

Dammit.

I hung up and turned back to my entertainment, both of whom waited patiently like well-trained circus animals. They certainly knew all the tricks.

"Sorry, boys. Gotta go."

The one on the left pouted. Kinda cute. How old was he? Twenty-five? Twenty-six? Yes, about five years younger than me.

"Ten more minutes, babe," the one on the right said. "You won't regret it."

Fast-forward half an hour, and I hustled down the street, late as usual. Although I still wore last night's clothes, I'd spent five minutes in the hotel bathroom taming my hair, and I always carried a toothbrush and toothpaste in my purse, so at least I was vaguely presentable—as long as you counted a pair of tight leather pants, four-inch heels, and a red satin bustier as appropriate business attire.

The cab ride to the office took another fifteen minutes, and when I swung my ass through the doors to reception at Blackwood Security, Lottie behind the desk tapped her watch.

"They're waiting. Conference room two."

I went via my office to pick up a jacket on the way. Whistles and catcalls followed me as I strode across the main office floor, but I held my head high. I'd had plenty of practice, after all.

"Hey, Double D! Did you forget to go home last night?"

"Dirty Dan! You living up to your name again?"

I let my middle finger do the talking. The only other answer I could have given was, "yes."

While the men laughed, I grabbed a candy bar out of my desk drawer then shrugged into the tailored jacket hanging over the back of my chair. Heads swivelled as I retraced my steps through the room, fifteen pairs of eyes tracking my ass's progress.

Who cared? Let them look.

Conference room two was right ahead, and I grew kind of curious as I got closer. My diary had been empty when I left last night, and Emmy hadn't said much on the phone.

A job that was right up my street? That meant it was either big or serious, because as the deputy head of investigations at Blackwood, anything run-of-the-mill would have been punted down the ranks to one of my merry men. I had a couple of thousand of those, spread out across the globe everywhere from Abu Dhabi to Zimbabwe.

Security was big business, and Blackwood was one of the biggest.

No, Emmy wouldn't have dragged me in on my day off unless the case was important, especially when she knew I'd gone on a "date." We understood each other. Our friendship had lasted, what, eleven years? Twelve?

I knocked once, pasted a smile on my face, stuck my tits out, and pushed open the door.

What the...?

Okay, that wasn't quite what I'd been expecting. Or rather, who.

The aroma of fresh coffee floated across to me, but only Emmy had a cup in front of her. The other three occupants of the room had glasses of juice.

Emmy sat at the head of the glass table, impeccably dressed as always in a fancy pantsuit. Black, just like her soul. She turned her head as I stepped into the room and regarded me with impassive eyes that gave nothing away.

Hmm.

On the long side of the table, facing me, three boys perched in leather chairs far too big for their small frames. I resisted the urge to check if their feet touched the floor as I tugged my jacket around me and tried to subtly do up the buttons.

The oldest couldn't have been more than fourteen and the smallest maybe nine or ten. More than that, they had a look I recognised. Street kids. Why did I recognise it? Because in the dim and distant past, I'd been there myself.

Emmy had too. I raised an eyebrow at her.

"Boys, this is the lady I was telling you about." She turned to me. "Dan, meet Trick, Vine, and Race."

Three faces looked at me then dropped to my chest. I glanced down. Red lace still stuck out of the gap in my jacket, and I shot Emmy an evil glare. Why hadn't she warned me?

A faint smirk crossed her face then disappeared almost instantly. She was in work mode. Emotionless. Dispassionate.

"The boys have come to us about doing a small job for them."

"Like a job, job?"

Not some sort of charity work? Emmy often helped waifs and strays, but she didn't usually bring them to the office, especially when I was there. Being around children made me miserable—a bad case of wanting what I couldn't have, I suppose—and I tried to avoid them.

Emmy, on the other hand, believed in immersion therapy. If something made her uncomfortable, she kept doing it until it didn't worry her anymore. Which may have worked for public speaking or a fear of spiders but not an inability to have kids. And now she'd invited a gang of them in to chat and possibly more.

"Indeed. A job, job."

I tried to keep the incredulous look off my face. My

charge-out rate was $800 an hour, and Emmy didn't roll out of bed for less than five figures. These kids looked as if they could barely scrape together enough change for their next Happy Meal.

"Okaaaay."

Emmy turned to the biggest of the three, who sat in the middle and wore a jacket at least four sizes too large for his skinny body. "Trick, why don't you tell Dan the same story you told me?"

Oh, this was going to be good. Could Emmy be playing a particularly unamusing prank?

Trick started to speak, revealing a missing front tooth. Had he been fighting? Or did he just have bad dental hygiene?

"See, there's this guy, and he's been arrested, like. But he didn't do it. We know that, don't we?"

Murmurs of agreement came from both sides of him.

"He wouldn't do nothing like that," the kid on his left added.

"He's too kind, you get it? He wouldn't hurt no one. He gives up all his spare time to help us with music stuff."

"We're gonna make it big," the second kid said, emphasising his words with his hands. "He told us we got talent."

The boy might have had talent, but he also had purple hair and a ring through his nose, and someone had shaved lines through his eyebrows so they looked like tiny zebras.

The tall kid cut in again. "We got to get him out, yeah? So he can work with us kids again."

Kid number two—Race? Vine?—spoke once more.

"There ain't no one else who cares. The rest of the grown-ups, they just tell us to shut up and keep out their ways."

"So, what did he do?" I asked. Joyriding? Drugs? Burglary? A bit of petty theft?

"He pays for our instruments with his own money. Otherwise we wouldn't have none."

"I mean, what did he do to get arrested?"

"He's teaching me to play the guitar," said the second kid.

The third kid, the smallest one, stared at me with big blue eyes that didn't match his darker skin, unspeaking. He was kind of cute.

I looked at Emmy, and she refused to meet my gaze. This had to be a joke, surely?

"You in the middle. Trick?" I pointed one black-tipped finger at him. "What's your friend in jail for?"

"Oh. Yeah. Murder."

Emmy looked nonchalantly out of the window, and I reached under the table with my foot. Dammit. She was out of range of my pointy-toed boots. She realised what I was attempting and rolled her chair back another six inches, just to be sure.

Why was she doing this to me? Was this because I accidentally crashed her Corvette the other week? I'd promised to get that repaired.

"Murder?" I asked.

"Yeah, but he didn't do it, and we need him back because otherwise we got no chance of getting a record deal."

A laugh bubbled up in my throat, and I tamped it down. It was too early in the morning for this. Slowly, deliberately, I reached out for the jug of coffee in front of me and poured a cup. Caffeine would help. Caffeine helped everything. I took a sip, scalding my lips before I asked the dreaded question.

"So, boys, who did he kill?"

"He didn't!" the second kid insisted.

"Okay, who have the cops accused him of killing?"

This promised to be a long day, didn't it?

"Just some girl. Don't know who she was," Trick said.

"Even if she was just some girl, Trick, murder is a very serious business."

Oh, good grief, now I sounded like someone's mother. Not mine, obviously. She wouldn't have noticed if I'd held a gang initiation in the kitchen, she was so off her head on crack all the time.

He gave me a sullen look. "Yeah, I know, but it's a setup. Someone else must have done it."

"And we want you to find out who!" the second one said, fidgeting in his seat.

Emmy finally decided to speak. "The boys have got a proposition for us. If we help them find out who the real killer is, they'll pay our fees out of the royalties they get for their first album."

So, basically what she meant was that we'd be working for free, then. Not that I had anything against pro-bono work, but my diary was already crammed full with paying clients.

Her lips quirked up at the corners. "And when I say we, I mean you."

Oh, this was definitely about the car. Yes, it had been a birthday gift from her husband, and no, I hadn't exactly asked to borrow it, but it was only a small crack in the bodywork. Okay, cracks.

"When they told me their story, my mind accelerated straight to you. You're so driven when it comes to these things."

That was it. As soon as I got out of this meeting, I was going to take her damned Corvette and shove it into her fucking lake.

I pushed my chair back.

"Trick, how about you tell Dan who your friend is?"

"Oh, yeah. He's the Ghost."

I stopped my chair mid-wheel. "The Ghost? Are you serious?"

Everyone had heard of the Ghost. Maybe not last week, when he'd just been a DJ-slash-music producer with a fetish for privacy, but since Sunday, two days ago, he'd been all over the news.

According to *The New York Times*, the Ghost was currently the most sought-after producer in the business, and even if you didn't know him, you knew his songs. They were like little earworms that burrowed into your brain and played on repeat. I'd even heard him play live myself once, at a fashion show, although he'd skipped the after-party and disappeared right after his set.

And last weekend, he'd been found unconscious and covered in blood behind the wheel of his crashed car on the outskirts of Richmond. Only the blood didn't all belong to him. In the aftermath, the cops had found the naked body of a young woman in his bed. Stabbed, shot, or strangled, depending on which news channel you chose to believe.

Emmy was giving me this?

That was it. I'd drown her Dodge Viper as well. The Ghost case promised to be a messy spectacle played out in front of the media, and maybe, just maybe, I'd like to actually take some of the vacation I'd been accruing for the past decade.

"Yeah. The Ghost's our friend," the older boy said. "Only we didn't even know it was him until we saw his face on TV. We just called him Ethan, and he's always looked out for us. He used to live on the same block, see?"

"Trick's right," Emmy said. "The Ghost did a lot of good. He ran a music project for the neighbourhood kids."

"Kept us off the streets."

"Crime rates in that area halved after he became involved."

Emmy ran her own charity to assist the homeless. I helped her, but while she worked mainly with children and young adults in Richmond and London, I concentrated on shelters for domestic violence. We each chose what resonated with us the most. Suddenly, her motives for taking on this case became a little clearer—ninety percent revenge, ten percent empathy. And while I sympathised with the boys' cause, Emmy was still a bitch for forcing this on me.

"Did you ever work with him?" I asked her.

She shook her head. "He had his own area buttoned up pretty tight. I met him a couple of times, though. He wasn't what the papers have made him out to be."

Now, that was interesting. The media had turned on the Ghost since his arrest, with the headlines growing more sensational by the day. Yesterday's front page had suggested he could be into devil worship. Last week, they'd been singing his praises, full of news of his five MTV awards and speculating about possible

Grammy nominations, and now they'd demonised him.

I didn't trust reporters, especially after they'd dubbed Emmy the Black Widow when they thought she'd killed her husband, and Emmy was usually an excellent judge of character. She said it came from having met so many assholes in her time. And from the way she spoke, I was working this case whether I wanted to or not.

I sighed. "Give me a few minutes. I need to get my laptop and a notepad."

Emmy grinned at the three young faces in triumph, and they beamed back at her. Four against one.

What had I gotten myself into?

CHAPTER 2

ON MY WAY to find my laptop, I took a short detour via the head of Blackwood's information systems department, who hid out in a cave on the third floor filled with enough technology to give Best Buy a wet dream. My friend and colleague, Mack Cain, leaned back in her chair as she watched a series of incomprehensible waffle scroll up one of her three screens.

The other two displayed a recipe for pot roast and a special offer on manicures at a local spa respectively.

I peered down at the manicure ad. "I like those little stars. Do you think they'd suit me?"

I held up my current colour scheme—black with tiny skulls painted on them in lime green.

Mack looked at my nails then back at her screen. "The stars are kind of cheerful. Are they really you?"

"Thanks. It's good to know you see me as an all-around bringer of happiness and light."

"Why are you here?"

"Can you look up some information on a murder for me?"

"Exactly my point."

Fair enough, murder was a little on the dark side.

"But can you help?"

She groaned and minimised the recipe. "What

murder?"

"That pot roast didn't look so good, anyway."

"I know. But Luke's invited some friends over, and I need to feed them."

"Just call Bradley. He'll sort it out."

Bradley was Emmy's assistant. If you needed something found, decorated, bought, or organised, he was your man.

"I suppose. I just had the vague idea that I could make up for the spaghetti bolognese disaster."

A month or so ago, Mack had decided to try hacking into a foreign government server while boiling spaghetti sauce. She'd done slightly better than anticipated with her attempts to crack the firewall, but the resulting visit from the fire department wasn't something any of us would let her forget in a hurry.

"If you're going to burn things again, give me some warning. I'll come with my camera."

Or perhaps I'd try it myself. I liked a man in uniform. Or even men—I wasn't fussy.

"I didn't exactly plan it the first time."

"Well, maybe you should. All good Girl Scouts should be prepared. We could make an evening of it—dress up fancy, a few appetisers, cocktails, and a visit from hot firemen."

"Will you ever stop thinking with your loins?"

"Why would I want to? So many men, so little time."

I put as much conviction as I could into that statement, but even to my own ears, it sounded hollow. A couple of years ago, I wouldn't have had to consider my answer, not for a millisecond. But that was then, and this was now.

While my two best friends lived in marital bliss, Emmy with Mr. Tall, Dark, and Psycho and Mack with a man who spoke computer better than English, I still maintained my hard-won reputation as a party girl. But the truth was, I'd started to crave what they had. Not the big wedding, the flashy ring, or the joint dinner invitations, but the companionship. I could finally admit that it might be nice to come home to the same dick at the end of each day as long its owner knew what to do with it.

But how the hell did I go about doing that?

The only manhunts I got involved in featured guns and an arrest at the end, and some days, I barely had enough time to eat. What was I supposed to do? Go speed dating? I snorted at the thought, and Mack gave me a funny look.

What could I say about myself?

My name's Dan. I'll answer to "Dirty," though. What do I do for a living? Well, I'm a private investigator. Yes, I drink too much; no, I don't have a goofy sidekick; and yes, I do enjoy my job. Hobbies, you say? I quite like shooting. At targets, people, whatever. Do I have any special achievements? I've tried every position in the Kama Sutra, most of them at least twice, and I once rode a motorcycle at a hundred miles an hour while blindfolded for a dare.

Yeah, I'd get crossed off people's lists pretty quickly.

Dating through work was a no-go for me, despite Emmy and Mack having met their soulmates that way. The prospect of morning-after awkwardness in the office made me cringe. And I'd never get involved with a lawyer again. Last year, I'd even tried internet dating, but after accidentally meeting a man who turned out to have an unhealthy interest in children, getting him arrested, and having to testify against him in court, I got Mack to block that app from my phone in case I ever got tempted to swipe right again.

Unfortunately, Mack and her terrible cooking skills looked like my best shot for meeting a man at the moment, but before she could go home and burn things, I needed her to find me some information.

"Emmy's decided she feels sorry for a trio of street kids, whose good buddy, the Ghost, has landed up in prison. Apparently, we need to take a look at the crime he's been accused of committing."

Mack did a double take when I mentioned the Ghost.

"Do you mean that DJ?"

I nodded.

"But I thought that was cut and dried? I mean, they found the murder weapon in his car, covered in his fingerprints. And didn't he confess?"

A groan escaped as my damned soul protested over Emmy's revenge. "I know all that. And if you think you can talk some sense into our beloved leader, be my guest."

"I'll get started, then. What do you need?"

She knew she had two hopes of changing Emmy's mind. None and zero.

"I'm gonna need everything. It's probably a waste of time, but I have to at least go through the motions."

"Do you want me to check not entirely legal sources as well?"

"I need all the help I can get."

With Mack on the case, I headed back to the

conference room to deal with Emerson and her three little stooges. An hour later, I'd learned that the Ghost was "the shit" and "a lyrical genius, yeah." Fan-fucking-tastic. None of that would help unless he planned to rap his way out of prison. But the kids were growing on me, I'll admit that. When they got up and started beatboxing, they were a lot better than I thought they'd be, and the smallest boy, Race, came alive. He strutted up and down, singing words more suited to Emmy's potty mouth than a ten-year-old child's, even though he hadn't spoken for the entire day. Perhaps the Ghost wasn't such a bad judge of ability after all.

Two hours later, after Emmy's assistant, Sloane, had been dispatched to McDonald's and we were all stuffed full of junk food, Mack finally turned up with a stack of paper and a memory stick full of documents.

"You want a french fry?" I offered. "They're a little cold."

"Or you could have this..." Emmy held out the toy from her Happy Meal. "Uh, I don't know what it is. Disney?"

Mack rolled her eyes. "I've been working my ass off hacking for the last two hours, and this is what you've been doing?"

Perhaps we should have wiped the game of hangman off the whiteboard.

"No, we've been doing other things. Like interviewing the boys."

I waved my hand in their direction then looked over at them. They were staring open-mouthed at Mack.

Okay, so her bright red hair and legs that went up to her armpits were kind of striking, but the boys would need to learn to put their tongues away if they wanted to impress the ladies.

Mack gave us a look that said *yeah, right.* "I've found out a few things, but the boys aren't going to want to see this."

"It won't bother us. Nothin' does," Trick said.

Emmy pulled rank, saving me the trouble. "Look, we've agreed to help, but we have to do this our way. There are some things we're not going to show you. Not because we think you can't take them, but because life is hard enough. We don't want to make living it even more difficult."

"What about you? You're gonna see."

"We'll deal with it. You shouldn't have to."

And we would. We'd each developed our own coping mechanism over the years. Mack went into a quiet room and sobbed her heart out. She tried to hide her tears, but we both knew she did it. Emmy unloaded on her husband, and if he wasn't around, she sleepwalked instead. Or in her case, sleep hit, shot, and stabbed. Believe me, we all breathed a sigh of relief when Black was home.

Me? I found the nearest prime specimen of meat and lost myself in him. Or was it the other way around? Either way, the mind-numbing pleasure gave me what I needed.

"So what do we do?" Trick asked. "We just want to help."

"You've already helped by believing in the Ghost at a time when most people have turned their backs. I'm sure he'll be grateful for that."

"That's it? We just leave?"

"Do you have somewhere to go to tonight?"

"Yeah, Race goes to his foster parents' and Vine

comes home with me. His mom don't care. She's mostly passed out, anyway."

Emmy slid a notepad over to him. "Write your contact details down, and we'll give you a call when we've looked into things."

Trick wrote out a number, his handwriting an untidy scrawl I could barely decipher. Emmy flipped it around and read it back to him, just to be on the safe side.

He nodded. "It's Vine's phone, but the battery's dodgy. Mine got jacked."

"By who?"

"Some kid."

"With a knife," Vine added helpfully.

Emmy shoved her chair back, her mouth a hard line. "Excuse me a minute."

The kids looked at each other, fidgeting. "What did I say?" Trick asked. "I didn't mean to piss her off."

I managed to refrain from rolling my eyes. "Nothing. She's angry that someone threatened you with a knife. Did you tell the cops?"

I had to ask even though I knew the answer. After all, I'd been in that situation as a kid, and I'd kept my mouth firmly shut. Snitching only made things worse.

"Nuh uh. They won't do nothin'."

As I suspected. "Any idea who it was?"

Three heads shook. "It was dark."

"If anything like that happens again, you come to us, okay?"

Emmy marched back in with three Samsungs, still in their boxes. As she broke a phone most weeks, she tended to buy them in bulk.

"Here. One each. Keep them charged, and keep

away from assholes with knives, yes?" Next, she handed out business cards, hers and mine. "And make sure our numbers are programmed in."

As the boys filed out, hugging the boxes to their chests like they were gold freaking bars, I leaned back in my seat and blew out a long breath.

"Why us?" I groaned after the door had closed behind them.

"Because when they googled for private investigators, Blackwood was near the beginning of the alphabet. Apparently, Adams and Abraham didn't answer the phone."

"When this is over, I'm starting my own firm. Zulu Investigations. We'll only be taking cases where the client passes the credit check."

Emmy smirked at me. "As long as you don't put your rates up, I might throw a few bones your way."

That time my boot did connect, and she gave me an evil look before throwing her toy at my head.

"All you need is a pram," I said, referring to one of her favourite British sayings.

"Can we focus on the job?" Mack pleaded. "I've got two of Luke's associates and their wives coming for dinner, and I don't even know what I'm going to cook yet."

She spread her pile of papers out on the table and slotted the memory stick into the data port in the centre console. The crest of the Virginia State Police appeared on the giant screen that took up most of one wall of the conference room. Yes, Mack *had* been busy. I drank in the details as she scrolled through the police report, describing with all the passion of a drive-thru operator the car crash, the discovery of the body, and the Ghost's subsequent arrest. She had to remain detached. We all did, or we'd never get out of bed in the mornings.

"And here's the Ghost, otherwise known as Ethan White."

Mack brought his mug shot up on the screen, and I guessed him to be around my age. I'd just turned thirty-one, or twenty-nine, seeing as I'd decided to start counting backwards from my thirtieth birthday. White's skin didn't match his name. It was a warm brown with golden undertones, and his black hair was cropped closely to his head. He could have been a model if not for the sour expression on his face and his bloodshot eyes. The long cut bisecting his goatee didn't help either.

"This was him two days ago, right after his arrest," Mack said, pointing out the obvious. "And this is how we normally see him."

A new photo flashed up. This time, the Ghost was unidentifiable, his face hidden behind a sculpted white mask that faded into the shadows of a hoodie as he stood on stage behind a DJ deck.

"Looks as if he's a little shy," I commented.

"He's famed for his secrecy. One of the most recognisable faces in music, yet nobody knew what he looked like. I couldn't find a single picture of his face other than those mug shots."

"I'm not surprised," Emmy said. "He hated having his picture taken. The music project the kids spoke about used to be based at the Step-Up Center, same place as the Blackwood Foundation's mentoring workshops. The mayor turned up for a photo op a couple of years back, and I ended up hiding in a storeroom with White until the press disappeared. Of course, I didn't realise who he was at the time."

"Did you talk?"

"Only about our projects. He was preparing to move his kids to a bigger place a few blocks over. Cheaper rent, better acoustics, but needed some repairs, apparently."

"Well, at least we know why he's called the Ghost."

I leaned forward, squinting at his mask. What was it made from? Plastic? Rubber? Whatever it was, it was kind of creepy.

Another click and the picture of White disappeared, replaced with a morgue shot of his victim. Her blonde hair hung in tails around her shoulders, matted with blood, and a thin red line trailed across one cheek. Someone had made an effort to clean her face up, and the cut looked almost as if someone had drawn it on with a sharpie.

"Any photos of the crime scene?" I asked.

"They're not on the system yet. I guess they're in no hurry seeing as they caught White red-handed. Literally."

An ugly vision of bloodstained hands floated through my mind. That poor girl. Nobody deserved to die like that.

"Stabbed," Mack said. "Forty-seven times, according to the pathologist."

"Someone was angry. Who called the police?"

The news channels had been heavy on speculation and light on facts.

Mack brought up a picture of the car wreck. White had driven off a steep embankment, and his black Ford Mustang rested nose-first against a sturdy pine tree, its hood squashed back into the cabin. The doors hung open, and the emergency crews had peeled the roof back like a sardine can.

"White's car was found in a ravine with him unconscious at the wheel. A woman out walking her dog saw it and called 911. The accident happened on a quiet road, and the vehicle was hidden from others passing above. By the time White got to the hospital and the cops got to his house, the coroner believed the girl had been dead for almost a day."

"Long time for somebody to be unconscious," I said.

"He didn't wake up for another two days, at which point they read him his rights. By then, someone had already put two and two together about his showbiz persona and leaked it."

"Who was the girl?" Emmy asked.

Mack glanced down at her notes. "Christina Walker. A junior at the University of Richmond."

"Do we know how they met?"

"According to the interviews, White doesn't remember meeting her at all. The police traced them both to a club called Liquid earlier in the evening."

Emmy made a face. "Ah, one of my competitors." Among her other investments, she owned Black's, a high-end chain of clubs that included Richmond's premier nightspot. "Liquid's door policy's known to be lax, and the owner's a greasy bastard. Just wear something tight when you talk to him, and once he stops drooling, he'll give you whatever you want."

"Noted," I said. "What else do the police have?"

Mack took over again. "When the cops found the car, it took another two hours to cut White free and get him out of the ravine. With the damage to the front end, it wasn't until they brought the car up that they noticed the knife in the passenger footwell, and by then, they'd already found the dead girl."

Four-letter words rattled around in my head, interspersed with others like *guilty*, *evil*, and *monster*. But Emmy laced her fingers together, elbows on the table, and leaned her chin on her hands as she watched me.

I sighed. "So, where do we start?"

Emmy glanced at her watch, not the Tag Heuer one of her ex-boyfriends had bought for her birthday last December, and not the million-dollar white gold Richard Mille Tourbillon her husband gave her for Christmas a week later in a not-so-subtle "fuck off" to the competition. No, this was a cheap-looking digital, and I'd bet what was left of my Porsche Boxster that it had a very, very loud alarm.

"I've got a meeting in five minutes." She was already walking off. "See you later."

"Bitch."

The sound of laughter followed her along the hallway.

CHAPTER 3

I SANK BACK into the leather chair as if it could swallow me up. "Sometimes, I really hate Emmy."

Mack took the seat next to me. "The Corvette *is* her favourite car."

"Where do we start?" I asked again, even though I already knew the answer.

Investigating was my job, after all. I closed my eyes, running through everything we'd gleaned so far in my head.

The Ghost was in jail, and the evidence that put him there sure looked compelling on first impressions. But words on a screen never told the whole story. I needed to speak to the cops and get their take on the case, then I'd have to work through the file, piece-by-piece, and look for any anomalies.

More importantly, I wanted to speak to the Ghost himself. Only two people knew what had happened in his bedroom that night, and one of them was stacked in the morgue.

"Mack, can you find me the details of White's lawyer?"

"Sure. Give me five minutes."

While Mack did her thing, I went off to change. Luckily, I kept a full closet at Blackwood. It was my second home.

When I emerged from the shower in the bathroom just along from my office, wrinkled because I'd stayed under the near-boiling water for almost twenty minutes in an attempt to block out the Ghost and all his baggage, I wrapped a towel around myself and checked my emails. Mack had come through. Or had she?

A public defender?

The Ghost had to have a fat bank account—why hadn't he hired himself a fancy high-priced lawyer?

Lyle Rogers, according to Mack's bio, graduated from law school three years ago in the bottom half of his class. Career highlights included holding the office record for successfully plea-bargaining the most shoplifters in six months and getting held in contempt for arguing with a judge. He hardly looked like a good candidate to win what could be the trial of the year.

Unless the Ghost wasn't planning to fight.

Keeping my fingers crossed Lyle wasn't gay, I selected an outfit I hoped would get me results. A skirt suit with a split at the back that stopped just short of being indecent teamed up with a fuchsia pink silk blouse. I checked my reflection in the mirror then popped open another button. Yeah, that made the most of my assets.

Lyle spent his working life at the Virginia Indigent Defense Commission on East Franklin Street, and it was just after seven when I reached their offices, my high-heeled pumps clicking on the sidewalk. But I didn't stop there. I carried on down the block until I reached The Gavel, a nondescript watering hole that normally wouldn't have warranted a second glance. Elevator music played in the background, and dishes of peanuts and pretzels had been lined up on the polished wooden bar by someone with OCD, perfectly equidistant. Not my type of place at all.

So why was I there?

Well, when Mack had gotten hold of Lyle's credit card statement, she found he stopped off every night at eight thirty for a beer, as regular as a geriatric with a prune juice habit.

I'd settled on a stool at the bar with a glass of Coke when he walked in at nine. His rumpled suit and the dark circles under his eyes suggested he'd spent more than one night working late. Busy with the Ghost? I double-checked the photo Mack had emailed me from his driver's licence just to be sure. Lyle had lost a few pounds and his hair was longer, but it was definitely the right guy.

Now I just needed to fathom him out.

Although The Gavel wasn't busy, most of the seats in front of the bar were occupied. But I'd left my purse on the vacant stool next to me. As Lyle paid for his drink, I picked it up and pretended to rummage through it. Condoms, lipstick, a Beretta Nano.

"Is this seat taken?"

"Go right ahead."

I returned to my pointless search and found the key to Mack's pickup that I thought I'd lost six weeks ago lurking behind a box of tampons. Oops. Still, no time to dwell on it. I slumped over the bar, studying the melting ice cubes in my drink, and let out a long sigh.

"Rough day?" Lyle asked, taking a sip of his Bud Light.

According to his bio, he'd previously lived in Wisconsin, Iowa, and Alabama, and he spoke with a hint of a Southern accent.

"Worse than usual. How about you?"

He pinched the bridge of his nose between his thumb and forefinger. "A nightmare doesn't even begin to describe it."

What do you know? We had something in common.

I reached over and touched his shoulder. "You poor thing. You look as if you could use a break. What do you do to relax?"

He smiled sheepishly. "I like to play computer games."

"Oh, like *Call of Duty*? *Grand Theft Auto*?" I couldn't say I'd ever been into those. I preferred the real thing.

"*Fantasy Farm*'s my thing at the moment."

I turned my snort of laughter into a cough and made my eyes go big. "I've never played—what does that involve?"

"Well, each player has a virtual farm, and you have to plant crops and raise animals and barter with your neighbours. Each time you go up a level, you gain a specialty. Mine's breeding chickens, but what I really want is a tractor repair shop..."

My expression glazed over, and I stopped myself from falling asleep entirely by reliving this morning's adventures with my temporary friends. Tattoo guy and his buddy. They'd given me their numbers, but I wouldn't call. I never did. Eventually, Lyle paused, and I realised he'd nearly finished his drink.

"Sounds fascinating. Perhaps I'll give it a go?" I motioned at his glass. "Can I get you another?"

"Awesome. We could be farming neighbours." He returned my smile. "Let me buy the drinks."

Two beers became three, then I ordered Lyle a double vodka and lemonade. He looked like the kind of guy who'd drink lemonade. As the alcohol filtered through his system, I returned the conversation to work.

"So, what do you do all day?" I moved a little closer until our knees touched, and he choked on his beer. "You okay?"

"Fine..." Cough. "Fine." He swallowed hard and puffed out his chest. "I'm a lawyer."

"You're kidding? What, over at the public defender's office?"

"You know it?"

"I tried to visit somebody there this afternoon, but the receptionist wouldn't let me in."

He chuckled. "LaWanda? She makes me nervous, and I work there. Who were you supposed to visit? Maybe I could help out with that."

"Lyle Rogers. Do you know him?"

His eyes widened. "No way! I'm Lyle Rogers." Then his eyes narrowed. "Wait, you're not a reporter, are you?"

I bet his phone had been ringing off the hook today as the vultures circled. After all, he'd listed the number on his Facebook page.

I quickly shook my head and shuddered for effect. "I can't stand those assholes."

His scowl relaxed, but he stayed wary. "So why were you looking for me?"

"A lost cause, I guess. I hear you're representing the Ghost?"

He gave a wry laugh. "How did I know that was coming?"

"I'm kind of in that position too."

He raised an eyebrow, but his eyes wouldn't quite focus. "Another poor sailor on the sinking ship?" he slurred.

"Something like that. I'm an investigator. An old friend of his hired me to review the case, but it's not looking good."

Poor Lyle. His shoulders slumped, and he looked as if his team had lost at football, his pet dog had died, and his girlfriend cheated, all on the same day.

"I'm trying not to think of the details."

"Tell me about it. I mean, I'm going through the motions, but everything I've seen says it's pointless."

Lyle drained the last of his vodka and signalled for another. Since tonight was quiet, it arrived right away. Or maybe every night at The Gavel was quiet. The clientele didn't look like the type to party into the early hours. The only patron not wearing a suit had on Gucci jeans, and he kept glancing at his leather briefcase as if it contained state secrets.

"I still can't believe the court assigned me this case. I'm gonna embarrass myself in front of the world's media."

"You don't believe the Ghost's innocent either?"

He laughed again, a little hysteria creeping in. "Even he thinks he did it. I said we should at least try for bail, but he said if he'd done what they said he did, they should throw away the key. How am I supposed to defend that?"

"A guilty plea, then?"

Lyle shrugged. "Who knows? Since that day, he's

refused to speak to me."

Hmm. If Ethan White refused to speak to his lawyer, the chances were he wouldn't be too keen on chatting with little old me either.

"What will you do?"

"I don't know. I'm thinking of quitting. Maybe I could work as a cab driver? I love the idea of dropping off my last passenger and going home for the night without work hanging over my head." His head lolled to the right, where the barman chatted with a perky blonde. "Or I could do what he does. Serving drinks and chatting all night. It can't be that hard, can it? Anything's better than this."

He drained his glass and waved his hand to get the barman's attention, easier said than done when the dude was focused on the blonde's tits. I resorted to whistling and got myself a dirty look.

"Whishky, shtraight up." Lyle turned to me, eyes rolling in their sockets. "You want one?"

I shook my head. One of us had to stay sober, and it seemed I'd be the designated sensible person for once in my life.

"Why did you become a lawyer, Lyle?"

"My mom wanted me to. Well, actually she wanted me to be a doctor, but needles make me faint."

"She must have been real proud."

"When I passed the bar exam, she threw this huge party. I didn't go because my boss made me work late, but she saved me some cake and a whole bowl of corn chips and these itty bitty things with sausages, and..."

Lyle downed his Johnnie Walker in one and motioned for another. The barman raised an eyebrow at me, and I laid a hand on Lyle's arm.

"Do you think you should stop?"

He tried to shake his head and swayed alarmingly. "Nope. Thish ish the besht thing ever. I should do thish every day. I feel so happy and free and..."

Lyle reached out for a pretzel and fell clean off the stool. The barman and I both winced as he hit the floor, the crack of his head on the tile echoing over the quiet chatter. All heads turned to look at us.

Well, I couldn't exactly leave him there, could I? And it was kind of my fault. I hauled him up and half dragged him to the door, one loose shoelace trailing along behind him. Good thing I went to the gym every morning.

A cab drove towards us, its light glowing in the darkness, and I flagged it down. The driver peered out, not a hint of a smile.

"Is he drunk?"

"No, not at all. He's just sleepy. It's been a long day."

"He looks drunk. I don't want nobody vomiting in my cab."

"Tell you what—I'll pay you a hundred dollars to drive us home, and if he pukes, I'll pay for it to get detailed too. Deal?"

"Okay."

You'd better believe Emmy would be getting that bill. Once I'd heaved Lyle into the backseat, he slumped against the opposite door, eyes closed.

"Where do you live?" I asked him.

No answer.

I tried shaking him. "Lyle? Where do you live?"

Nothing.

I fished around in his pockets until I found his

wallet. Thirty dollars, a couple of credit cards, no driver's licence, and nothing else with an address. There were no family photos either, which fitted with Mack's belief that he was a bachelor.

What now?

I could call the control room and find out where he lived, which seemed a little stalkerish, my earlier efforts notwithstanding. Lyle began snoring, and I came to a decision.

"Can you take us to Alba?" I asked the driver.

The building I lived in was named after the Italian word for sunrise, and I'd seen some spectacular ones from my penthouse. An extravagance, yes, but I'd clawed my way out of the gutter, and now I liked to sleep as far from it as possible. Tonight, I'd dump Lyle in one of my spare bedrooms. We could finish our conversation over breakfast after he'd sobered up.

When the cab pulled up outside, I grabbed Lyle under the armpits and hauled him up the front steps. The nighttime concierge rushed out to help, taking Lyle's feet and helping me to shove him into the elevator.

"Thanks, Bernard. Uh, this isn't as bad as it looks."

"I'm not sure I want to know, Miss di Grassi."

This was why I liked Bernard—he didn't ask questions, and in return, I bought him an outrageously expensive bottle of Scotch every Christmas.

Lyle's mouth dropped open and he began snoring the instant his head hit the pillow in one of the guest rooms. I backed out, holding my breath because his reeked of alcohol. Even with two closed doors between us, I could still hear a quiet rumble. Thank goodness for earplugs. Although when I thought back to where

I'd been this time last night, the earplugs were of scant consolation. Two hot naked guys versus a drunk lawyer? No contest.

When I checked my email last thing, Mack had filled up my inbox with news articles, music videos, and best of all, the details of a handful of the Ghost's acquaintances here in the city. Literally, three—the guy who helped to run the record label he owned, his manager, and the owner of a grocery store three blocks from White's house who delivered food once a week. How could somebody so famous know so few people?

How could a man go through life like that? I valued my friends more than anything. They celebrated with me in the good times and lifted me up in the bad. I couldn't begin to imagine how lonely the Ghost must have been. How lonely he still was.

A green-looking Lyle stumbled out of the bedroom at nine the next morning.

"Where am I? What time is it?"

He caught sight of the clock over the fireplace in my living area, a burlesque dancer with one nipple tassel for each hand. I'd nicknamed her Dita, because she bore more than a passing resemblance, and she'd come courtesy of Emmy's assistant, Bradley. If you want to get an idea of Bradley's style, pop some acid then take a trip around MOMA. On a unicycle. Wearing 3D glasses.

"Holy crap, I'm late for work!"

I took another bite of my bagel. Toasted with cream cheese, salmon, and cracked black pepper. "It's Saturday."

Lyle sagged back against a pillar. The apartment was open plan, and I had a clear view of him from my perch at the breakfast bar.

"Thank heavens." He took a wobbly step forward. "Although I should probably go into the office later anyway. Read over my notes, cry into my legal pad, redraft my resignation letter, that sort of thing."

"Case getting to you?"

"How much did I say last night?"

"Enough."

Let him make of that what he would.

A low groan escaped his lips. "I shouldn't have said anything. My boss is trying to have me fired as it is."

Sheesh, the Ghost had really lucked out with this one. "Why do you think that?"

"Because last Thursday, he said, 'Lyle, I'll make sure your next career move has you asking whether they'd like fries with that.'"

"Sounds like a nice guy."

Lyle made it as far as the stool next to me and sat on it, head in his hands. "I reported his son for cheating in the second year of law school. He pulled the overprotective father move and sabotaged my degree, although I could never prove that, and three months ago, he transferred in as my new supervisor."

Lyle's luck... Well, it didn't quite rival White's, but it certainly complemented it.

"I'm not gonna talk. In fact, I think we could help each other."

His eyes narrowed in suspicion. "What exactly did you have in mind?"

"You want the Ghost to walk free, and my client's convinced he didn't do it." I refrained from adding that it wasn't a sentiment I shared. "If you help me, I'll help you."

"I'm not sure that's a good idea."

"I'm gonna be working the case anyway. If we team up, it'll make things easier for both of us."

"I can't break attorney-client privilege."

"I'm not asking you to. We could just bounce ideas off each other, talk hypothetically."

Lyle stared out of the bank of glass that overlooked my terrace for a long minute, thinking. A pigeon perched on the railing at the edge, bobbing its head before it flew off. Oh, to have that freedom. Birds didn't have to waste time on impossible murder cases.

"How do I know you're not a reporter in disguise?" Lyle asked.

I took my PI licence out of my wallet and flipped it over to him. "You want references?"

He studied it then shook his head. "The fewer people who know about this arrangement, the better."

I kept my face expressionless, but inwardly, I was grinning wide. I had him! "We'd better get started, then."

A couple of hours, a packet of aspirin, and a gallon of coffee later, Lyle had fetched his files from the office and spread them out on my fancy glass dining room table. It wasn't like I used it for eating. I was too busy to throw a dinner party, and there hardly seemed any point in going formal when I lived alone.

I added my notes to the pile, at least the ones I wanted Lyle to see, and we both read through each other's thoughts. Lyle had given me everything it seemed—so much for a hypothetical discussion. Was he dumb or desperate? The latter, I soon found out. By the time I'd skimmed what he'd gathered, my head was pounding, and I'd learned one important thing: it was worse than I thought.

CHAPTER 4

I DROPPED THE yellow legal pad filled with Lyle's chicken scratches onto the dining table. My coffee mug was still half full, but what I needed was a shot of tequila, preferably served up by a man with abs hard enough to distract me from the task at hand.

"Jay Skinner's prosecuting?"

"The rising star of the Eastern District of Virginia?" Lyle gave a hollow laugh. "Yep, I found out just before I left last night. You know him?"

Oh, yes, I knew Jay. Intimately. Jay had been the solitary exception to my "never more than one night" rule. First Emmy had settled down, then Mack, and Jay had come along at exactly the right time. Or, as it turned out, the wrong time. Asshole.

We'd both been busy and career-driven—still were —but a couple of times a week, it had been unexpectedly nice to come home and find the same warm body waiting for me. Jay understood about my long hours and my need to be on-call twenty-four-seven because he worked in the same way. But ultimately, I'd had to choose between him and Blackwood, and in that contest, there would only ever be one winner.

"I've met Skinner a few times," I told Lyle.

I wasn't about to rake over my disaster of a

personal life with a virtual stranger. Nobody knew the full story, not even Emmy. It was bad enough to admit my lapse in judgement to myself, let alone anyone else. As lapses went, it had been a big one. Huge. And I wasn't referring to the size of his equipment because that had been average at best.

"Does he scare you?" Lyle asked.

Scare me? No. Jay just pissed me off. Looking back, I could see it had been the idea of dating a rich and successful man I'd liked rather than Jay himself, especially as my friends managed it so successfully. Deep down, I was still little Daniela, the child desperate for approval and blinded by success.

I shook my head, trying to get rid of my demons as much as answering Lyle's question. "He's human, just like anybody else."

"Do you think? You know his nickname's 'the cyborg,' right? Jay Skinner's only lost one case in the last three years."

I was well aware of that, and that case was still a sore point for him. But what I really, really wanted was for him to lose another. The biggest of his career.

"Don't think about him. Just think about the Ghost."

"Because that's so much better?"

I had little comfort to offer Lyle, so I opened the nearest file and began to read instead, hoping that I'd spot something new or that the second time around, the details wouldn't be as bad. Two hours later, I vowed never to borrow a car from Emmy again. Not her Viper, not her Corvette, not even the beat-up Ford Focus she occasionally used on surveillance.

"Wanna get drunk with me tonight?" I asked Lyle.

He looked up from his own stack of paper, adjusting the black-framed glasses he'd put on to read. "It's hopeless, isn't it?"

Yes, but I didn't want to be the reason Lyle stepped off the edge of a really tall building.

"We've got some work to do. White remembers nothing?"

"So he says. The doctors thought the bang on the head he received in the accident could have caused memory loss."

Yeah, I'd read that report. The Ghost had been unconscious when he was found, breathing shallowly and suffering from mild hypothermia. A close-up photo of him being removed from the car showed his eyes closed with purple bruising around them, and blood had crusted onto his face before the cut on his cheek scabbed over. He'd been trapped for a while. The next picture showed him on a stretcher, wearing a pair of indigo jeans and a T-shirt that had once been white but not anymore. Instead, it had become a macabre reflection of a girl's death, her lifeblood the logo plastered across his chest.

Except nobody knew that at the time.

The police had traced his car by the licence number, and a pair of officers were dispatched to his home, a large but nondescript two-storey on the edge of town. They'd been hoping to find a relative, but what they got was a closed door. According to the report, the Ghost's bloody handprint on the doorjamb gave them grounds for entry.

Christina Walker's body lay where she died, on the bed in the master bedroom. From her liver temperature, the ME estimated she'd breathed her last twenty-three hours before she was found.

I fingered the corner of one of the pictures of the victim, sliding it closer. Murder scenes always got to me. I didn't want to look at them, but at the same time, I felt compelled to. My job. It was my job. At least, that's what I always told myself.

Emmy would look at those pictures too, but for her, it was a technical study. A lesson. How had the killer snuffed out that spark? Was it quick? Was it painful? And, most importantly, could she learn from it?

For me, it was all about the why. Why, on that particular day, at that particular time, had one person chosen to remove another from this earth? Was it an accident? A crime of passion? Convenience? Or merely a business transaction?

Death also hit me on a deeper level. It reminded me that I was alive.

"Do you think White's telling the truth?" I asked Lyle.

He shrugged. "Who knows? He spent most of the visit staring at the wall."

So, not a lot of attorney-client privilege to break, then.

"Has he seen a psychiatrist?"

"He refused to."

What was White like as a person? Nobody was an average Joe one day then a raging lunatic the next. There was always a build-up and then a trigger.

What was his?

Had there been any signals he was about to snap?

"Have you talked to his friends? His family?"

"I'm still trying to find them." Lyle twisted his hands in his lap. "You can probably tell I'm not very good at this. I've only ever worked on one murder case before."

"What happened to that guy?"

"He got life."

I almost felt sorry for the Ghost. He was screwed.

That little revelation called for a drink. Despite the vodka bottle calling my name, I poured us both coffee and gasped as it scalded my tongue. Stupid.

"How about you?" Lyle asked. "Have you worked on a murder case before?"

Yes, from all the angles—defending, prosecuting, and committing. Best not to admit to the third one, though.

"A few."

"Did you solve them?"

"About ninety percent."

I'd always been proud of my record. Sure, there were a handful of cold cases on Blackwood's books, but we never gave up on them. Never. Only last month, we'd retrieved a missing child from the wilds of Canada, five years after his father snatched him in Mississippi.

Lyle yawned and stretched his arms over his head. "Well, thank goodness one of us knows what we're doing."

"If you're going up against Skinner, you'll have to change your attitude. If he smells blood, he'll eat you alive."

"Do you have to remind me?"

"Yes."

I dropped Lyle back at his apartment with an instruction to get some rest while I headed into the office. Not that I didn't need sleep too, but I had cases to catch up on where the clients were paying in something other than dubious quality demo tapes.

With no new developments on Sunday, I went to the gym, then to Emmy's place. She had a shooting range out the back, and I took the opportunity to put a few hundred rounds through my guns, imagining her face on the target every time I pulled the trigger. Bitch, bitch, bitch.

"So how's the new case going?" she asked. She'd come out to join me for a bit of sniping practice.

I gave her my best glare. "I'm holding a gun."

"I have a bigger one."

So she did. I set my Sig Sauer on the table in front of me and sighed. "Skinner's prosecuting."

She gave a low whistle. "Ouch."

"Tell me about it. It's a high-profile case, and he wants the glory."

Jay had always been ambitious. He didn't so much step up the ladder as clambered over the pile of bodies he left behind, their careers in tatters and their spirits broken.

Emmy grinned at me. "I'm putting fifty bucks on you."

And that was why she was my best friend, despite her reluctance to overlook my small prang in her beloved car. No matter how long the odds, she always believed in me.

"The thing is, I'm not sure I want either side to win. There's a hell of a lot of evidence against the Ghost, and if I can help to get him off on a technicality, do we really want him on the streets?"

"Has his attorney considered an insanity plea? That way both sides lose," Emmy said.

"He figures White's got a screw loose, but the dude hasn't let a shrink near him to find out for sure."

"Are you gonna see him?"

"I'm trying, but he won't even talk to Lyle at the moment."

"We could always break in. It would be an interesting challenge."

"You should put in your own insanity plea."

"Just sayin'."

"I think I'll exhaust the conventional routes first."

On the way home, the county jail popped up in my mind—the location, entrances, exits, and known security. *Stop it, Dan.* Damn Emmy and her crazy ideas.

Lyle had said he was going to visit the Ghost first thing on Monday, and by noon, I'd shredded the stress toy Bradley had left on my desk and clicked my pen so many times Emmy's husband had stomped over and replaced it with a pencil. The second my phone display flashed with Lyle's number, I snatched it up.

"Well?"

"Uh, good morning. How are you?"

"It's afternoon now." By five minutes. "What happened?"

Life was short enough without wasting it on small talk.

"Don't get excited. It was the same as before."

"Nothing?"

"He asked how long he could stay in solitary, that's all."

"He's scared?"

Usually, solitary confinement was a punishment, not a choice, although the Ghost did seem to be a loner.

"Hard to tell, but I don't know why else he'd want to be there."

"And what was your answer?"

"The whole time. They're transferring him to Redding's Gap tomorrow. Segregation's the norm there."

They were *what?* Redding's Gap was a super-max prison with the worst reputation in the whole of Virginia. When a man went to Redding's, he came out one of three ways—as a monster, as a broken man, or dead. That was if he got out at all.

"How the hell is he going there before he's even been convicted?"

"The jails are full. The county did a deal with the state, and one wing at Redding's Gap is housing remand prisoners. It's supposed to be temporary, but with crime rates rising the way they are, I don't see it being reversed. Rumour has it Skinner brokered the arrangement."

Why didn't that surprise me?

"You didn't fight it?"

"White wouldn't. I asked if he wanted me to try for bail, and he shook his head. Besides, the detentions officer said White was going to end up at Redding's eventually, so why postpone the inevitable?"

What kind of man would choose to stay on his own in a cell if there was a chance, however small, of him getting out? Especially at Redding's Gap, which would have been a perfect candidate had Dante ever needed a tenth circle of hell. Did the Ghost have money problems? I made a note to ask Mack, just in case, but my gut said that wasn't the answer. The house in the crime scene photos hadn't been flashy, but having spent the last decade around Emmy and Black, I knew understated elegance when I saw it.

"Can White have visitors?"

"Only if he agrees to see them." Lyle's sigh came through loud and clear. "I've never had a client so unwilling to defend themselves before. Every other person either swears blind they didn't do it or wants to know how short I can get their sentence. I don't understand."

"It's guilt. He's already convicted himself."

"Skinner's gonna slay me. I'd better start drafting my obituary."

"No, you'd better start doing your job."

While I did mine.

First, I reviewed my list of cases and delegated everything I could. I'd never admit it to Emmy, but I found the Ghost's case kind of fascinating. What had caused him to turn like that?

Then there was Lyle. Normally, the men in my life fell into two categories: those I wanted to fuck and forget, and those I became good friends with. Lyle appeared to be a previously unknown third type, a doleful puppy dog I needed to defend against a good kicking.

And if I could stuff one of my size-five boots up Jay's ass in the process, so much the better.

Sorting out my caseload took the rest of the day, but

at least that left me with relative freedom to work on the White case over the next few weeks. Emmy might have assigned it to me as a joke, but she didn't realise how much time it had the potential to take up.

After a day in the office, I couldn't be bothered to cook—or rather, reheat—so I went to Emmy's for dinner. Her house, Little Riverley, had just been rebuilt after an unfortunate incident involving a fourteen-man assault team and a fire, but I'd already moved a closet full of stuff over there. If the office was my second home, then Little Riverley was my third.

As usual, I wasn't the only person who'd decided to stop by. Every night was open house, and it was a rare evening that the place was empty. Tonight, Emmy had gone out, but Xav, a friend and colleague, was watching TV with his girlfriend, Georgia, and Emmy's pseudo-sister, Tia, was slumped on a couch nearby with her boyfriend, Eli.

"What's for dinner?" I asked.

"Cannelloni," Georgia told me. "Mrs. Fairfax left it in the oven."

Mrs. Fairfax was Emmy and Black's housekeeper, and she'd been a fixture at Riverley for as long as I could remember. I helped myself to a plateful of Italian goodness and carried it through to the living room. Having company sure beat dining alone.

Baby Libi slept on Georgia's lap, wrapped in a fleecy pink blanket. Motherhood suited Georgia. She'd been positively glowing ever since Libi's slightly dramatic entrance to the world, and even Xav had embraced being a parent. I sometimes wondered whether I'd have made a good mom, seeing as I hadn't exactly had the best role model. Once, I'd thought I'd have the opportunity to try, but fate had kicked me in the teeth. Or rather, the stomach. An emergency hysterectomy had followed, and now I'd never know.

Today, I smiled through the pain that had once been almost impossible to bear. If Emmy hadn't stopped me from doing something stupid, I'd have been with my son now.

"She looks so peaceful."

"Oh, she does at the moment," Georgia said. "Half an hour ago, she was wailing like a banshee. I thought we'd have to call an exorcist."

"Good thing I got stuck at the office, then."

"On that Ghost thing?" Xav asked.

Wow, didn't good news travel fast? "You heard about that? I thought you'd been too busy playing daddy to keep up with gossip."

"Everyone knows. Besides, I like to go to the office for a break."

That I could understand. "Yeah, a bit. Mostly shuffling my diary today, but tomorrow Ethan White takes over."

"*I* didn't know," Eli said. "You're working the Ghost case?"

Had he been locked away in a bunker? Oh no, silly me, he'd been with Tia. It was most likely a bedroom. They were still at that loved-up stage that left the bitter taste of saccharine on my tongue.

"The one and only."

"I can't believe he did it."

Not another one. "Evidence doesn't lie."

"I get that. It's just he never seemed the type. Most producers I worked with were arrogant assholes, but not him. He was always down-to-earth."

"Hang on—you met him?"

Eli had spent his teens in the music business before retiring from all that hoopla at the grand old age of twenty. I should have thought to ask him about the Ghost.

"A few times. Yeah, he used to wear that mask out in public, but apart from that, he was a normal guy. Shy, though. He hated having an entourage."

"Did you speak to him much?"

"Only about music." Eli stole a nacho off Tia's plate and munched away. "Except one night when we broke for pizza. That was the last time I saw him, and he'd thawed out some by then."

"He was eating pizza? With his mask off?"

Eli shrugged. "He didn't make a big deal of it or anything. It was just us in the studio by then. Twelve hours, we'd been there, trying to get the last few lyrics right. The other guys in the band had given up and gone home, but Ethan stayed with me to re-record my part."

"What did you talk about?"

"Cars, mainly. If I remember rightly, he was thinking of buying a Mustang."

Eli was the first person I'd come across, either in person or the police reports, who admitted to seeing the Ghost mask-less while knowing who he was. His manager must be another, I suspected, but so far, my attempts to speak to the elusive Harold Styles had failed. His PA kept giving me the runaround.

"I talked to him as well," Tia piped up.

"Seriously?"

Was I the only person in this household who hadn't? I raise an eyebrow at Xav, and he gave his head a little shake. Okay, that made me feel slightly better.

"Yes, when I was in New York working for Ishmael. That time the Ghost did the music for his runway show."

"And what did you think of him?"

"Nice, I guess. He didn't say much. But his manager's an arsehole. He sent this crazy rider for the Ghost—white this, white that, even a framed poster of a white flipping tiger for the wall—and berated me when I couldn't get the right bloody candle. Then the Ghost showed up and said he didn't care about any of it."

"Then why have the list in the first place?"

"I reckon his manager liked the power trip. All the Ghost wanted was a bottle of water."

As well as the kids, that was three people I trusted who thought the Ghost was an okay guy. And one of those people was Emmy, whose judgement you could multiply by ten.

Curiouser and curiouser. More than anything, I wanted to meet Ethan White and his manager myself and form my own opinions.

The question was, how?

CHAPTER 5

LYLE HAD PROMISED to get me more information on the crime scene, but waiting for my requests to materialise was like watching a glacier melt. I got Mack to take another look, but as the cops were convinced the Ghost was guilty; they hadn't put a rush on the forensics, and a lot of the samples were backed up at the lab. For a moment, I considered calling in a favour and having someone bump the testing up the line, but ultimately, I decided against it. Favours were like currency in my world, and I didn't have many stored up with the forensics team. Better to save them for cases that weren't open-and-shut and where the clients were actually paying us.

Cases I desperately needed to catch up on, even with my efforts to delegate.

Three days later, with my regular work on track once again and little hope of seeing those lab results any time soon, I cleared some time in my diary and dug deeper into the human aspects of the Ghost's mess, starting with the man himself. Ethan White sure didn't make that easy. His friends, if you could call them that, were split into two categories—the superficial acquaintances who'd gone running to the tabloids at the first sniff of money, and the true friends who'd kept well out of sight. The first group proved easy to find—I only had to open the trashiest news websites and there they were, spewing secrets that smelled more like lies. The second group? Ghosts, much like the man himself.

And it was them I needed.

While Mack trawled the dark recesses of the internet, I decided to focus on two of the people we'd found already: the Ghost's manager and Ronan Pearce, the guy who ran his record label, Spectre. They must have had more contact with White than anybody.

According to an email Mack intercepted, Styles had taken a trip to California, representing one of the other acts he looked after—a four-piece boy band with a rock edge called Elastic Trickery. A scan of their website revealed that the Ghost had discovered them playing in some underground bar in New York, and his backing had led them to the big time. Ethan White was a regular Good Samaritan, wasn't he?

The airline reservation system showed ol' Harry wasn't due back for two more days, a fact I confirmed by finding his favourite hotel via his Instagram account and calling the front desk. Rather than chase him across the country, even though I could have used the sun, I concentrated on the record label guy.

"What have you got?" I asked Mack, dropping into the seat beside her.

She eyed up the bag I was carrying. "Are those cookies?"

"Freshly baked."

I held my stash out, and she took a white chocolate chip with raspberry.

"Bribery will get you everywhere," she mumbled through a mouthful.

"How was your dinner the other night?"

She brushed crumbs off her lip and groaned. "Don't ask. Luckily, I convinced Claude's to deliver."

My second favourite restaurant. French, with a mouth-watering menu and eye-watering prices. I went as an occasional treat—my old penny-pinching habits died hard, and I was more of a Taco Bell kind of girl—but seeing as Mack had married an English guy who'd made a fortune selling computer security products, shelling out for a fancy dinner wasn't a problem. Her husband, Luke, enjoyed hacking almost as much as she did, so it really was a match made in heaven.

"Look on the bright side, at least nobody got food poisoning this time."

She made a face. "Next time, I'm not even going to attempt cooking. I threw the pan away in the end. The burnt bits wouldn't come off."

I couldn't help laughing. "So, how about this case? Can you get me a home address for Ronan Pearce?"

"I've got it already. I'll email it to you."

"And could you find out how much money the Ghost has? I'm curious."

She gave me one of those, "what do you think I've been doing all day?" looks.

"Seven million dollars in cash, stocks, and bonds. Plus his house, a recording studio, and the record label. That's not huge, but it's profitable and it's growing."

"Thanks, Mack."

Her expertise at ferreting out information made my job so much easier, and all those backdoors she'd built into government and private databases also allowed her to revoke my speeding tickets. On second thoughts, you didn't hear me say that last part. Or the first part.

But she'd answered my question about whether

White could afford bail if it was offered. He most likely could; he just didn't want to.

Ronan Pearce lived in a tidy duplex on the outskirts of town. The place was easy enough to find, which was unfortunate, because a crowd of the local press had located it too. I parked my car—okay, Mack's car—down the block, got my camera out of the trunk, and slung it around my neck. Time for a little chat.

"Bit late to the party, aren't you?" one old-timer said as I walked up.

He, on the other hand, looked as if he'd arrived a week ago and not taken a shower since.

"I'm from upstate. There's not much else on, so my boss sent me to take a look at this Ghost thing. It was either that or another dog and pony show."

"Wasting your time here. We all are. Two days, I've been waiting, and all the man's done is drive out of the garage in the morning and drive back into it in the evening. Keeps the drapes closed too."

"You know if anyone's tried his office?"

"Went there first. Security won't let us within twenty yards of the place. Pearce goes in via the underground parking garage and nobody can talk to him."

I let out a huff, but only for show. At least that meant Pearce wasn't being harassed by the paparazzi.

"Looks like my boss sent me on a wild-goose chase. Figure I'll spend a couple of hours having lunch then head back again. Any recommendations?"

The old guy chuckled, no doubt amused by us

young 'uns and our lack of tenacity. With fewer reporters on the scene, he had more chance of getting a scoop.

"Sure, try Bessie's. It's three blocks in that direction, straight up. You can't miss it."

He was right about Bessie's. The lady herself must have been well into her seventies by now, but she still made the best chocolate milkshakes in the whole of Richmond. They'd been my favourite treat as a child on the rare occasions my mom had money in her purse to steal. Today, I couldn't resist stopping off to buy one before I went back to my car. And perhaps a donut too. I'd spent two hours in the gym this morning—surely that earned me some rights?

Back in the office, I slumped at my desk in a food coma as I worked out a plan. I was speaking to Ronan Pearce whether he liked it or not.

"How's it going?" Emmy asked, pausing by my desk to liberate a cookie from the collection I kept in my drawer. I swear that woman could sniff out any junk food within a ten-mile radius.

"About as well as expected." I explained my strategy. "What do you think?"

"Could work. But I'd take someone with you. Make it look more official."

"Not a bad idea. Any suggestions?"

Her eyes alighted on a guy sitting on the far side of the room. He'd only arrived a couple of days ago, a transfer from the New York office, and last time I saw him, he'd been working at a fashion show and wearing considerably less than he was right now.

"Take Cade," Emmy said. "He's tough in combat, but I'm not sure of his finesse."

"With that ass, who cares about finesse?"

"Dan, stop harassing the staff. He wants to work in Special Projects, and he'll need brains as well as brawn. I'd be interested to see how he does."

Emmy ran the Special Projects department at Blackwood, that crazy band of people who dealt with all the shit nobody else wanted to touch. If it was tricky, insane, or otherwise unusual, Emmy ran with it, often with spectacular results. She only worked with the best, and if Cade wanted on her team, he had a lot to prove.

And the first thing he needed to work on was his attitude.

The next morning, he stood with me beside one of the company pool vehicles, grumbling.

"What kind of job is this?"

"When you came to Blackwood, you wanted a gun. Now you've got a gun and a calculator."

He still wasn't happy. "What if somebody asks me difficult questions?"

I patted him on the cheek. "That's where your pretty face comes in. You smile to distract them until Georgia tells you what to say."

Georgia had majored in accounting at college, and although she'd taken a break from the subject while she was married to an asshole, she now worked part-time in Blackwood's forensic accounting team. Cade was miked up and wearing an earpiece, and she was on hand via radio to help out.

I wasn't kidding about the smile, either. Cade may have lacked enthusiasm for the job, but he sure as hell had the looks to make up for it. My gaze dropped to his ass before I could stop it, and I gave myself a mental slap. *Too young, Dan.* At twenty-four, Cade was a year under my self-imposed limit—my age less six—and I'd put that in place for a reason. Any younger, and things tended to be over faster than I liked. Older was fine, because with age came experience.

Even so, I might have been tempted to relax that rule with Cade if not for my other rule, the one that trumped everything. I didn't fuck anyone I worked with. No colleagues, no clients. Ever.

Emmy might have worked out the logistics of sleeping with her friends and somehow staying on good terms with them afterwards, but I didn't need that awkwardness. There were enough anonymous warm bodies in the clubs and bars of Richmond without having to shit in my own house.

Which meant this morning, I was strictly window-shopping. At my request, Cade had dressed in a suit—not made to measure, but it was tight enough in the right places that it didn't matter. I'd gone for the business look too, in a pencil skirt that almost reached my knees. Demure indeed for me.

A few fans hovered outside Spectre Productions, Inc., one wearing a Ghost mask and another holding up a placard proclaiming White's innocence. Somebody had faith; it just wasn't me.

Gentleman that he was, Cade waited for me to climb the steps to the front door first, but I gestured for him to go ahead and lagged a couple of steps behind. My gaze dropped. Just one last treat before the real work started. The buzzer had an "out of order" sign taped to it, so Cade rapped on the door with his knuckles.

Two minutes passed before a glowering security guard cracked it open.

"What?"

Good morning to you too. I stepped forward and held out my genuine fake ID, carefully created by our company forger.

"Danielle Russo, IRS. We've had reports of false accounting, and we're here to do an inspection."

"Nobody said nothing about that."

"It's a surprise inspection. That's the whole point."

"I'm not sure about this."

"Well, I suggest you find a way to get comfortable, because if we have to go away and come back again, the fine's only going to go up."

Fine. One word, and it worked like the modern-day version of "open sesame." The door swung open, allowing us into the inner sanctum. A bead of sweat popped out on the back of the guard's neck as we followed him along the hallway.

"Who do you need to speak to?" he asked.

"I need the manager..." I pretended to consult my diary. "Ronan Pearce. And my assistant here needs the payroll department."

"Payroll's over there. Sandra! Can you help these people?"

I left Cade with three ladies gawking at him while the guard escorted me to Ronan's office. I didn't bother knocking.

"Ronan Pearce?"

He'd been sitting at his desk with his head in his hands, but at the sound of my voice, he sat up so fast I wondered if he'd got whiplash.

"Who the hell are you?"

I turned to the security guy, who hovered in the doorway. "That'll be all, thanks. I can take it from here."

He got the message and backed away, pulling the door closed behind him. Papers crackled under my ass as I dropped into a vacant chair, a modern orange thing designed for style rather than comfort.

"You didn't answer my question," Ronan growled.

"I'm here with a few questions about Ethan White."

Pearce reached for the phone, one of those fancy consoles with six lines and a hundred buttons. "And you won't be here for much longer."

It only took a second to reach down the side of his desk and unplug the cable. "Hear me out."

If looks could have killed, I'd have keeled right out of my chair.

"Give me one good reason why I should."

Chapter 6

PEARCE MENTALLY WRAPPED piano wire around my neck while I studied him. What was the best approach to take? Planning these confrontations in advance was almost impossible without first-hand knowledge, but as Ronan sat there hoping I'd choke on my words, I decided to take a chance. Everything I'd heard said the Ghost was a good guy, apart from the teensy issue of him committing murder, and I was betting he hadn't been a bad boss either.

"Why should you hear me out? Because I'm one of the few people working to get Ethan a better deal, and I need all the help I can get." Ethan, not White. Build rapport.

Ronan's eyes narrowed. "And why should I believe you?"

I flipped over my real ID card. "I'm a private investigator. My client believes Ethan's innocent, and if he is, I need to prove that."

"Who's your client?"

"Afraid I can't disclose that."

I wasn't about to admit I was working for a bunch of kids.

"There aren't many people left who believe in Ethan."

"Are you one of them?"

The last tendrils of hope leached from his body in a long sigh. "Yes, I am."

Finally, I was getting somewhere. I stuck out my hand and smiled to break the tension.

"In that case, I'm pleased to meet you. Dan di Grassi."

He leaned forward, half out of his chair, and shook. "Ronan Pearce. Except you already knew that."

"So..."

"So?"

"Will you help me?"

I watched, silent, as he waged an internal battle. Did he hold on to his secrets and leave White to fight alone, or take a chance on me? Ronan's eyes closed, and another sigh drifted from his lips. A minute passed, and he focused on me again.

"What do you want to know?"

Everything. I wanted to know everything. "To start with, I'm trying to work out what kind of person Ethan is and what might have caused him to snap and kill a girl. My research says it was totally out of character."

"If you find the answer, let me know, because I can't work it out either. Have you spoken to him?"

"He won't see anybody."

"Figures. He's always been wary of strangers."

"How did you meet?"

"Music." He shrugged as if to say, "how else?" "When Ethan first came to Richmond, we played in a band together."

"A successful one?"

My research hadn't turned that up.

"Before he joined, we did okay. The odd gig in a bar to make a few bucks, that sort of thing. But Ethan was the one with the talent. If it made a noise, he could play it, everything from a pipe organ to a harmonica. With him involved, we were booked every night. Top venues too, not dives."

"I thought he was always on the other side of the mixing desk?"

"Now he is, and even then, he preferred to stay in the shadows. He didn't wear the mask, but he always kept a hood over his face. And once we started getting bigger gigs, he refused to play the guitar in public anymore. Said women always went for the guitarist or the singer."

"Which one were you?"

"Lead guitar."

Figured. Ronan had to be pushing forty, but even with frown lines marring his forehead, there was still something appealing about him. Dirty blond hair, a dimple in his chin—I could imagine women screaming when he got on stage.

"And Ethan?"

"Keyboards mainly. Sometimes the drums."

"What happened to the band?"

"People kept asking to buy our tracks, so we decided to lay down an album. Except when Ethan got into the recording studio, he never wanted to leave. The guy who owned it was looking for an assistant and hired him on the spot."

"That must have stung for the rest of you."

"Not as much as you might think. The band started off as a hobby, and when it grew, let's just say there were some pissed-off wives and girlfriends. We kept on as a four-piece and played a couple of gigs a week until kids started coming along, then we quit."

"And Ethan?"

"He bought the studio when the owner retired. By then, Ethan had discovered DJing and turned himself into the Ghost. He always loved the buzz of being on stage, but he hated the fame. People think when he puts that mask on, he becomes somebody else, but they're wrong. He becomes himself."

"And he hit the big time."

"Knockout punch."

Too right. He'd even got his own brand of sneakers.

"Ethan kept in touch with you, but what about the other band members?"

Ronan chuckled. "We still talk. Our singer fell in love and moved to Albuquerque, and our bassist headed back home to Tennessee and became an architect. Floyd, the main drummer, moved to LA to try his hand at acting."

"Has he been in many movies?"

"Nothing memorable, at least in front of the camera. He's a sound engineer now. We still get together once a year to grill a few steaks and reminisce over the old times. Or at least, we did. Guess we won't anymore now Ethan's locked up."

"What about family? I haven't managed to track any of Ethan's relatives down."

Ronan's face clouded over, and his knuckles turned white as he gripped his pen, a silver ballpoint engraved with Spectre's logo, a stylised mask. "Ethan doesn't have any family."

Okay, so that subject was obviously off-limits. Mental note: Avoid mentioning Ethan's family for the time being, to Ronan at least.

"How about friends? A girlfriend?"

Ronan's grip relaxed. "Until a couple of months ago, he hung out with a guy called Ty."

"Why'd he stop?"

"Ethan never told me, but I got the impression they'd had a fight."

"And did he have a girlfriend?"

"Again, he never shared much. I think he was dating one girl for three or four months, but she faded away."

"What about Christina?"

"The girl they say he killed?"

I nodded.

"I never saw her before, but that doesn't mean much. Even when he was young, he'd pick up the occasional woman in a club. Never groupies, though, and never from our gigs. He liked to compartmentalise. Always kept women and music separate."

Which fitted with the video Mack had shown me this morning—shaky footage from a camera phone. It showed White and Christina in Liquid, hanging out near the club's main bar. Their body language said they hadn't known each other before. A later clip showed them on the dance floor, closer this time, but not all over each other. A cab driver had come forward to say he'd dropped them both off at White's place, and in his opinion, the pair had been tipsy rather than full-on drunk.

What happened after that was anyone's guess.

"You know the name of the girl Ethan was dating?"

Ronan shook his head. "I can't even say for sure that he was. But on a couple of days, he quit work early and said he was going to dinner or a movie. Those aren't the sort of things you do alone."

Or with a one-night stand. I knew that from experience.

"How about Ty? Do you know his surname?"

"Sorry. He was just Ty to me. Sometimes, he hung out in the studio when Ethan was working."

"What did he look like?"

"Black guy, about Ethan's size and age. Had a tattoo of an eagle on his left biceps."

Not a lot of information, but I'd found men with less. "I'm curious. If nobody knew Ethan's identity, how did he get anything done, business-wise? Booking gigs, signing contracts, that kind of thing."

"Harold. He always had Harold." Ronan's tone suggested he didn't care for the man much. "He was the publicist at the studio when Ethan started working there, and when he realised how much potential Ethan had, he took over as his manager."

"So Ethan was reliant on him?"

"Yeah."

Ronan missed the word "unfortunately" off the end, but his grimace said it all.

"And what about you? How did you go from the band to working here?"

"Via a brief stint as a high school music teacher." He gave a wry laugh. "A very brief stint."

"It didn't work out?"

"I didn't have the patience for it." He looked around at his walls, covered from floor to ceiling in framed album artwork and gold and platinum-selling discs. "Although some of the celebrities aren't much better than the kids. But Ethan was a different story. You know about his work with the Music Matters Project?"

I nodded.

"He spent hours teaching those youngsters, even the ones who were tone deaf. Said as long as they were enjoying themselves, it was worth persevering. People can say what they want now, but that's how I'll always remember him."

How did a man like that snap so dramatically?

"You sound as if you're writing him off."

"Isn't everybody?"

When I first met Emmy, she gave me one very important piece of advice. It was something she lived by, and I'd taken it to heart over the years. *Never, ever give up.*

"I'm not."

I might have been losing my mind, but I wasn't writing him off. Not totally. Not yet. Too many little things didn't add up about this case. Ronan closed his eyes for a second and sighed again. That seemed to be a habit of his.

"So, what now?" he asked.

"Honestly? I don't know. The evidence I've seen so far is strong, but even if Ethan does get convicted, character witnesses can certainly affect the sentence. We need to help him in any way we can."

"I've thought over and over about that poor girl's death, ever since I first heard the news. I don't get why he'd do something so out of character. His life may not have been conventional, but he had everything he wanted. Why ruin it?"

"I can't answer that at the moment."

"Good luck with finding out."

Ronan gave me his card, which at least meant future meetings would be easier, and I went to collect Cade.

Judging by the number of women clustered around him, he certainly was learning a lot about figures. I shoved through the crowd and pulled him towards me.

"Time to go, fast fingers."

There was a collective groan.

"Sorry, people, this turned out to be a misunderstanding. It's all sorted out," I told them.

"But we only got through six months' worth of records," whined a blonde in an overly tight shirt.

"You're doing an excellent job, ladies," Cade told them, giving them a panty-melting smile. "Maybe I'll be back next year."

"We're gonna have to make a mess of the taxes," I heard one whisper as we walked away.

"You get what you needed?" Cade asked.

"I got some useful stuff. You?"

"All of their phone numbers and a crash course in social security deductions from Georgia." He paused. "You think Emmy'd be okay with it if I called the blonde one?"

"She's laid back about things like that, as long as you give it your all at work."

Now I got the smile. "Perhaps this morning wasn't so bad."

It was lunchtime before we got back to the office, and we made an emergency stop at a diner on the way to pick up proper food. Toby, Emmy's nutritionist, was on another of his health kicks, and he'd stocked all the kitchens at Blackwood with green stuff and vitamin pills—no cookies or chips or soda in sight.

"Any luck?" Mack asked.

I gave her a chocolate bar, and she looked around surreptitiously before shoving it in her desk drawer.

"Toby's around?" I asked.

"He just had a bust-up with Emmy when he caught her eating a cheeseburger. She tried to convince him it was much-needed protein."

"Did it work?"

"He put it down the garbage disposal."

I had to laugh. Emmy would take on the Taliban without a second thought, but Toby could bring her to her knees. "I'd better hide the rest of this candy, then."

"Emmy's stashed hers in a biohazard container in the basement."

"Good plan." Mine could join it. "I've got a couple more leads for you to look into." I told her about Ty and the possible girlfriend.

"So that's why you brought me chocolate. Fine, I'll go through White's phone records and cross-reference. Have you been to see him yet?"

"That's what I'm struggling with. I need to have a chat with Emmy about it."

"She's suffering from sugar withdrawal at the moment. Take junk food."

Emmy was not only a devious bitch, she was a devious bitch with contacts. Over the years, she'd become a master at the political game, trading favours left, right, and centre, although she was more elusive than the Ghost when it came to pinning down her whereabouts. After a fruitless search, I got Mack to track her phone and found her on the roof, sitting cross-legged beneath a satellite dish with the remains of a burrito in her lap.

I tossed a Milky Way bar at her. "I need a favour."

"How did I guess?"

An hour later, she sauntered into my office and

took a bow.

"Are those jelly beans?" she asked.

I pushed the package towards her. "Tell me you've got good news."

"Blackwood is now the unofficial sponsor of the Redding's Gap staff Christmas party. You get two hours a week with the Ghost, split into two sessions."

"Alone?"

She nodded. "Your first visit's tomorrow. He'll be shackled at all times, and they'll have video but no audio. And they're insisting on searching you before you go in." She gave me a one-shouldered shrug. "Sorry, best I could do."

I'd have to take it. I made a mental note to wear matching underwear.

"What if he refuses to see me?"

Emmy smiled, the devious smile she always wore when she knew things were going her way. "The warden assured me that wouldn't be a problem."

CHAPTER 7

REDDING'S GAP STATE Prison was a monstrous grey scar on the landscape named after its nearest town. Even that was an hour away. The prison itself had been built on the site of an old copper mine in an area devoid of any civilisation. Virginia's most dangerous inmates had only deer and squirrels for company.

Life in a seven-by-twelve cell, if that could be called life.

I called it a slow death.

Conditions at Redding's Gap were reputed to be the harshest in the country. Segregated prisoners stayed in solitary confinement for twenty-three hours a day. Their cells contained only a steel slab with a thin mattress for a bed, a steel desk and shelf, and a steel toilet/basin combo. Meals were served through a slot in the door, and the cells were arranged so inmates couldn't see any of their fellow guests.

Five days a week, the prisoners got an hour in the yard, watched over by armed guards, and every other day they were allowed the luxury of a shower.

The life of an animal.

Actually, worse—most caged animals got more human interaction than the inmates at Redding's Gap. The only reason the suicide rate wasn't higher was because the poor sods had nothing to kill themselves with. Last year, the death of an inmate who'd achieved the feat by repeatedly bashing his head against the concrete wall of his cell had made the news.

And Redding's Gap was the Ghost's new home. Oh, how the mighty had fallen.

According to SatNav, the prison was a six-hour drive from Richmond. In my world, time was money, so I borrowed Emmy's helicopter for the trip and cut that to three. And when I say borrowed, I mean I sent her a text message once I was in the air. After dropping this case in my lap, she damn well owed me.

Leah, my assistant, had arranged for a car to meet me at the tiny airfield in town, and as I settled Emmy's shiny new Eurocopter into its assigned landing place, I spotted an ancient Ford saloon parked up by the hut that masqueraded as a terminal. My ride?

Yes, it turned out, and Otis, my driver, spent the entire journey moaning about everything from the weather to the state of the roads to the prisoners who'd had the misfortune to end up so near his town. By the time we arrived, I'd have gladly swapped my seat for a not-so-comfy cell.

Inside, I suffered the indignity of being strip-searched by a woman more butch than most of the men were. She'd probably been on her high school wrestling team as well. While I shimmied out of my matching set from Victoria's Secret, the Ghost would be going through the same thing on the other side of the wall. Only his search would culminate with his hands being cuffed to a waist belt and his legs being shackled together before a guard with an Ultron II electronic stun device led him to the room where we were to meet.

Five minutes later, I got my first look at the Ghost.

White was already seated when I got there, and I peeped under the table to check the situation. The guards had secured his leg shackles to the metal chair, which was in turn bolted to the floor. A steel table stretched between us, and he fixed his eyes firmly on its scratched surface.

I sat down opposite him. "Hi."

No answer, so I tried again.

"I'm Daniela."

Nothing. So, this was how it was going to go.

"Would you prefer me to sing a song or tap dance? I should warn you, I'm not a great singer."

Finally, White looked up. He hadn't shaved for a while, and his once tidy beard had grown into an unruly black fuzz. What was the policy on razors in here? Worry lines marred his forehead, much like Ronan's, only White's eyes had dark circles underneath them. They never turned the lights off completely at Redding's Gap, but I doubted the prison's electrical policy was what had caused White's sleepless nights.

But despite the beard and the wrinkles and the lack of rest, I couldn't deny White was attractive. If I'd seen him in a bar, I'd definitely have given him a second glance. Those aqua eyes were clear but with a depth that spoke of hidden thoughts and secret dreams. Turbulence lurked under the surface, a whirlpool of fear that sucked me in and held me captivated. It was all I could do to tear my gaze away.

I sucked in a breath and held it. Was White going to say anything? Or would silence be his only answer?

"I don't care."

The words came out low and husky. In any other situation, they'd have liquified my insides, and as it was, I went kind of mushy. *Get a grip, Dan.*

"What *do* you care about?"

A whisper of a sigh escaped his lips, and his gaze dropped to the table again. Thank goodness. No photo did those eyes justice.

"What do you want?" he asked.

"To help you. I'm a private investigator assigned to your case."

"By who?"

"Your lawyer." More or less.

"Let me save you the trouble and him the money. Go home."

"It took me six hours to get here."

"Well, you wasted your time, didn't you?"

"That's a matter of opinion."

White lapsed back into silence, and as dead air stretched between us, I felt an uncontrollable urge to speak. What was wrong with me? Usually, I liked keeping my interviewees on edge.

"I can't do anything if you won't talk to me."

"Then don't. I've got nothing to say."

I began to understand why Lyle was so pessimistic about the whole case. White was so damn negative I wanted to shake him. I might have reached out and done so if it wouldn't have got me clapped in a pair of handcuffs and escorted off the premises.

I bit my bottom lip to stop my sigh of exasperation from escaping. How could I get him to talk? The kids? Maybe, but *I* didn't want to talk about the kids. What had I learned from other people? Eli's voice popped into my head, telling me he'd spoken with White about music and cars. A normal conversation, he'd said.

"Look, I'm here for the next hour, and my boss will

give me hell if I leave early." The bitch with the rubber gloves had confiscated my watch, so I only had the clock on the wall to go by. Fifty minutes left. "So if you won't discuss the case, could you satisfy my curiosity about something?"

White's head tilted up slightly. "What?"

That one word dripped with suspicion.

"I always see those music desks on TV, you know, the ones with all the little knobs and buttons?"

He stared blankly, no doubt wondering what the hell I was talking about. I carried on regardless.

"Anyway, I've always wondered how they work. I mean, how do you remember which bits to adjust? There must be hundreds of settings."

"Are you serious?"

I shrugged and tried a smile. "Might as well fill the time in. Silence drives me crazy."

His look said he thought I was quite mad already, but as I'd hoped, he started speaking.

"It's not as complicated as it looks. Sure, there're a load of buttons, but they're really just the same ones repeated over and over, one set for each track. You know what a track is?"

Vaguely from Eli's chatter, but I shook my head.

"When you record a piece of music, it's not just one mash-up of all the sounds. Each part's split out into a different track. So you might have one track for the drums, another for the guitar, a third for the voice. Get it?"

"I think so."

"Each track has its own set of controls, arranged vertically on the console. They change the volume, adjust the balance between the base and treble, distort particular notes, that sort of thing."

"It sounds straightforward when you put it like that."

"It is. You might have two thousand knobs and buttons, as you put it, but what you've really got is the same twenty buttons a hundred times over. Well, ninety-six, in my case." His voice fell to a whisper. "Or at least, that's what I had."

He faltered in the middle of that last sentence, and I cursed myself inwardly for being so insensitive, pushing him when he didn't want to talk. But at the same time, I couldn't pass up the opportunity to carry on.

"Ninety-six? Still sounds like a lot to me."

"It's a good number. Mixing desks come in banks of twenty-four, but when you get above a hundred, it's just showing off. A contest over who's got the biggest dick. There's no real reason for it, only ego."

"So ninety-six is the musical equivalent of eight inches?"

White cracked a grin. "Try nine."

His smile quickly faded, reined in as if it had escaped unbidden. Yet his sense of humour had shown, just for a second. And for that brief moment, I wished we could have met under different circumstances—a coffee place, his music project, a concert. Anywhere but a super-max correctional facility.

Dan, don't even go there.

The man seated opposite was more than likely a murderer, no matter how pretty he looked or how cute he acted. My job, my goal, was to help Lyle get White the most appropriate sentence under the circumstances.

What would that be? Life? Or an insanity plea? Because the guy sitting across from me hadn't shown any signs of being nuts.

Yet. There was still time.

Those blue-green eyes studied the table again. Ronan was right—despite White's former occupation, he was incredibly shy.

"I hear you used to play the keyboards," I said. "And sometimes the drums?"

"Have you been talking to Ronan?"

"I saw him yesterday."

White nodded slowly. "Yeah, I did. Back then, I played for money, but now it's just for my own amusement. Well, not now, but before I ended up in here." He paused to compose himself. "Did he tell you what the band was called?"

"No, he didn't mention it."

"King. Our singer was a big fan of Freddie Mercury, so it was a play on Queen. We used to kid about turning up with gold, frankincense, and myrrh."

"Did you cover their songs?"

"Sometimes, but I preferred when we played our own. I always liked to create the music, not just copy it."

"Who wrote your stuff?"

"Me. The other guys would chip in occasionally, but mostly they were happy to let me get on with it. They were more interested in performing."

The conversation kept flowing, and tempted though I was to steer it back to the investigation, I thought it was more important to gain his trust. Eli was right—White did open up more about music, everything from Handel to hip-hop. Hearing him speak, it was clear a soundtrack ran through his soul, and being in Redding's Gap was torture for him.

"I'm not even allowed a radio here. Too dangerous, or so they say."

"There's no music at all?"

"Nothing. I tried humming to myself, and they sent the shrink in to talk to me."

Some prisons had education and rehabilitation programs, but Redding's Gap seemed to prioritise extra razor wire and fresh batteries for the guards' stun guns over cultural enrichment. Imprisonment here must be worse than death for a man like Ethan.

A knock at the door made me jump, and a sour-faced guard opened it seconds later.

"Time, Miss di Grassi."

"Right." I turned back to White. "I'll come back, okay?"

A quick nod. "Will you say hi to Ronan for me, I mean, if you see him again? His wife's pregnant, and she's been real sick. It wasn't an easy time for him even before...this."

More evidence of White's good side. Or was he just a great actor?

"I'll call him."

And I'd get Leah to pick up a little gift as well.

"Thank you."

White's gaze met mine again, but only for a second. As the shadow of the guard fell across the table, he looked away. I tried to push my chair back then remembered it was bolted to the floor. Guess they weren't taking any chances. I slid out sideways instead, cursing under my breath as I snagged my pantyhose on a sharp screw. Shit. This place was the fucking pits.

As the guard herded me from the room, I took one glance back at White, head bowed, shoulders slumped in defeat.

Who was he, really? The mild-mannered musician I'd seen today, passionate about his work, tongue-tied about everything else? Or the monster who killed a woman in a frenzy then tried to flee the scene?

Right now, I couldn't answer that question, but I did know one thing for sure. I was going to find out.

CHAPTER 8

WHEN I ARRIVED back late that Thursday afternoon, I settled Emmy's helicopter behind Riverley Hall, the larger of the two Virginia homes she shared with her husband. Their other house, Little Riverley, lay right next door, a starkly modern contrast to the gothic palace that Charles Black had inherited from his parents as a teenager.

Why did they have two homes? Well, that was another story, but in short, the arrangement worked for them.

This time last year, the helipad had been a utilitarian grey slab, but one sunny summer's day when Emmy and Black weren't looking, Bradley had got out his paintbrush. Now it looked as if a florist had thrown up over it. Bad enough in daylight, but at night, the whole thing glowed in the dark like an otherworldly funeral. Of course, Black had issued orders to repaint it, but Bradley kept finding excuses not to. Fifty bucks said the flowers were here to stay.

I stepped out onto a giant tulip, and as the rotor blades stopped turning, Emmy and Ana half ran, half stumbled across the lawn, pursued by a large man on a dirt bike.

"Pick your feet up!" he yelled.

Ana swore over her shoulder in Russian, and Emmy

gave him the finger.

"Afternoon, Alex," I said.

He paused next to me and gave what passed as a smile. "*Privet*, Dan. You have good day?"

"I'm not sure."

He chuckled and accelerated off, already shouting instructions at the two girls again. Rather them than me. I trained with him occasionally, but mostly I stuck to the gym.

Inside the cavernous kitchen, I'd made myself a delightfully healthy peanut butter and jelly sandwich by the time Emmy reappeared, her hair damp from the shower.

"Good run?" I asked.

"I can't believe I pay that man money."

"Me neither. If you want to be tortured, why don't you just get kidnapped by a dictator with a dubious human rights record and save yourself a few dollars?"

"Because Black would say I'd got off easy. How was your trip?"

Hmm. How *was* my trip? I mulled it over, even though I'd thought of little else on the flight back.

"Question too difficult for you?" Emmy asked.

"It was funny."

"Funny ha-ha or funny strange?"

"Strange."

"In what way?"

"White wasn't how I imagined. Everyone I spoke to said he was a good guy, but with what he supposedly did, I guess I didn't believe it." I paused again. "I expected a touch of arrogance with a veneer of nice over the top, but that wasn't what I got."

"Interesting. Supposedly?"

"Huh?"

"You said 'what he supposedly did.'"

"Did I?" Dammit, I did.

"Whenever you spoke about him at first, you were quite certain he was guilty."

"He refused to discuss the case. But I've met enough crazy people in my time. Sociopaths, psychopaths, and sundry freak show participants."

"Me."

"Yes, you. But I didn't get any creepy vibes from Ethan. The only thing he'd talk about was music."

"He's Ethan now, not White?"

Shit, she had me again.

"Now I've seen him with the mask off, I've realised he's human after all."

Just as I finished my sandwich, Mack called. I swallowed down the last mouthful and quickly answered.

"I've got that info you wanted from White's phone bill."

"Ty and the girlfriend?"

"For the girl, I'm gonna go with Melinda Frame. A couple of calls and messages a day from August to October last year, then they fizzled out."

What happened five months ago? "Fizzled out? They didn't end with a bang?"

"Seems not. There's been the odd call since, once a week, then once every two weeks, and only one in the month before the murder."

"That doesn't fit with a big bust-up."

"Nope. And while the initial calls originated in the Richmond area, Melinda's phone is now located in North Carolina."

"You figure she moved away?" I asked.

"If I was a gambling woman..."

"You *are* a gambling woman."

Last week, she'd bet me fifty bucks I couldn't go an entire morning without chocolate. The Hershey's wrapper that fell out of my back pocket at a quarter to twelve had given the game away. I'd been so, so close.

"Only because you're so easy to beat."

"Can you get me Frame's address?"

Mack gave a little, "what do you take me for?" harrumph. "Check your email."

"And the guy?"

"Ty D'Angelo. He's still in Richmond, working at a bar downtown."

"The call pattern?"

"Every day, every other day for the two years back I analysed, mostly D'Angelo calling White. Stopped abruptly two months before the murder."

Now, that was more interesting.

"Thanks, sweetie, I owe you one."

"I was hoping you'd say that. Dinner at my place, three weeks from Tuesday."

Oh, crap. I'd walked right into that invite. "What's the occasion?"

"Luke's mother's in town, and I need all the moral support I can get. Carmen and Nate are coming, but I can't exactly ask Emmy."

I could see her point there. The last time those two had crossed paths, the argument had ended with Emmy asking Mrs. Halston-Cain who her late husband had been fucking behind her back. No, it was down to another of Blackwood's directors, Nate, to take one for the team along with his wife. Although if Emmy did come, the meal might not be quite so boring.

I swallowed down my sigh of doom.

"Sure, I'll come. You gonna find me a hot date? With all this shit going on, I won't have time to look for my own."

She laughed. "I'll see what I can do."

Research showed that Melinda Frame lived in a small town just east of Fayetteville, North Carolina. An interesting move from downtown Richmond, but when I dug a bit deeper, I found out the insurance company she worked for had transferred her there to set up a new branch office. She may have landed in a hick town in the middle of nowhere, but it was a step up for her, career-wise at least.

I pencilled her in for a visit tomorrow morning. With the amount of spare time I didn't have, I'd need to use one of Emmy's jets and land at Fort Bragg. Oh, the hardship. But hey, she was the one who gave me this damn case. As I called the pilot, I mentally added up the fuel costs. Those kids had better hit the big time.

Melinda Frame lived on the third floor of a shabby walk-up. It looked as if the insurance industry didn't pay so well. Weeds grew through cracks in the sidewalk outside, trash blew in the breeze, and mustard-yellow paint peeled from her door. More flakes dropped off when I rapped on it with my knuckles.

Nothing.

I knocked again and waited. And waited. I'd almost given up hope of anybody answering when the door inched open, big brown eyes peering through the gap above the security chain.

"May I help you?" a polite voice asked.

"Melinda Frame?"

She nodded, her knuckles pale where they gripped the door jamb.

I plastered on my most benign smile. "My name's Daniela, and I'm a private investigator. I was hoping you might answer a few questions about an important matter."

"Ethan?"

I nodded, and Melinda stared at me in silence for a whole minute, thinking.

"Whose side are you on?"

Good question. Before I trekked to Redding's Gap, I'd have said the dead girl's, but now? Nothing about this case made sense.

"I've been hired by a friend of Ethan's. He doesn't believe everything the police are saying, and he wants to find out the truth."

Well, that wasn't a complete lie.

Melinda let out the breath she'd been holding. "Thank goodness. You'd better come inside."

After she'd fumbled with the door chain, I followed her into a tiny living room filled almost entirely by a flowery couch and a mismatched armchair. Paperwork lay scattered across a small coffee table, and a black-and-white movie played in silence on a TV in the corner.

"Excuse the mess." Melinda fidgeted from one foot to the other as she motioned me to take a seat. "Can I offer you a drink? Coffee? Water?"

"Coffee would be great. Cream, no sugar."

Sometimes I took cream, sometimes I didn't. It depended on what mood I was in. Right now, I wasn't even particularly thirsty, but doing something familiar often calmed people down. And Melinda looked flighty as hell. She bustled through a door opposite the TV, and I heard running water followed by the clink of cups. Melinda wasn't what I'd been expecting. The murdered girl, Christina, had by all accounts been a party girl, outgoing and popular. In my mind, I'd painted a picture of Ethan's "type," but Melinda didn't fit it. Her shyness, her nervous, bird-like mannerisms... She still hadn't made eye contact. In some ways, she reminded me a little of Ethan himself.

Five minutes later, she came back with a tray. Silence reigned as she poured out two cups of coffee from a cafetière, and I breathed in the rich aroma. She added a splash of cream to one before looking up at me to see if that was okay, seeking approval.

I nodded, and she sat in the armchair, holding her own cup and saucer, her feet tucked underneath her. The china rattled as her hand shook.

"Have you lived here long?" I asked her.

"A few months."

"How have you settled in?"

"Okay, I guess. I mean, the people seem friendly."

"It's a big move, from Richmond all the way out here."

"I needed a fresh start." A nervous giggle. "Things weren't so great back in Richmond."

"With Ethan?"

She shook her head, and coffee slopped into her

saucer. "Ethan was the only thing that kept me there for so long."

"So what was the problem?"

"I moved to Richmond with another guy. My ex. All those sweet words... The promises... But he turned out not to be so good for me."

That I could understand. "And how did you meet Ethan?"

"I was standing on the edge of some bridge over the Potomac. I don't even remember which one. Ethan was the only person who stopped."

Holy shit.

"He talked me down."

I'd been expecting Melinda to say their paths had crossed in a club, or a bar, or possibly the studio. Not that. A lone tear rolled down her cheek, and I wanted to give her a hug, to tell her I'd been there too, but I didn't dare.

"What..." My voice came out as a croak, and I tried again. "What happened next?"

"I was soaked through from the rain, so he took me home with him. Yes, I've seen what they're saying on TV. I've thought 'that could have been me.' But deep down, I don't believe it. Ethan was nothing but gentle."

"What did he do?"

"That night? Wrapped me up in a blanket and made me a hot drink. I couldn't stop shivering, so he got one of those portable heaters, you know the type with the fan?"

I nodded.

"He set that in front of me until I dried out, and then we talked."

"What about?"

I felt guilty having to pry, but at this point, I didn't have a lot of choice.

She laughed, a thin, reedy sound with no joy behind it. "Me. Well, I talked and he listened. Nobody ever did that before, you know? Listened. I'd split with my boyfriend, and I was sleeping on a friend's couch, only her man was getting pissed because he didn't want me in their space. I had no money and nowhere to go."

"And talking to Ethan helped?"

"More than I ever thought it could. The next day, he drove me to pick up my stuff, and I stayed with him till I moved here. One of my girlfriends from high school lives in the next town, and she told me it was real nice." Melinda wrinkled her cute little ski-jump nose. "It's not quite what I imagined, but it's better than what I had with my ex."

"Hold on—you lived with Ethan?"

"Only for a couple of months. He said I could stay for as long as I wanted, but he refused to accept any rent money, and I always felt kind of guilty, you know? For the way I'd intruded in his life."

"What was he like in the house?"

"Easy to be around. Quiet."

Inside, I was buzzing. Aside from Ronan, Melinda was the first person I'd found who'd interacted with Ethan outside of business. And she was yet another of his acquaintances who didn't have a bad word to say about him.

"Did you spend much time together?"

"Not really. I worked during the day, and he was always out in the evenings. He never told me what he did. I mean, I knew he was into music, but finding out he was this famous DJ... That was a surprise."

"How did you know he liked music? Did he talk about it?"

She paused to blow across her coffee then took a tentative sip. "Ethan never spoke about himself. But he always had a song on in the background, and sometimes he'd play the guitar or the piano. And he had, like, a recording studio in his basement. Just a small one, but sometimes he'd disappear in there for hours at a time."

"You say he *never* mentioned anything personal? That's unusual for a man."

I forced a laugh, thinking back to the time I'd spent with Jay. He'd always loved to drone on about his favourite subject—himself—but boy he did struggle with listening. Case in point: I hated Brazil nuts, and I'd told him this over and over, yet he still bought me an entire box of the little bastards coated in chocolate for my birthday. Oh, and then he'd skipped the birthday dinner Emmy arranged because he had to work on a case. Prick.

Melinda shook her head. "No, I can't remember Ethan ever getting personal. Not once."

There was a long pause, and I didn't rush to fill it. If Melinda wanted to say something, I'd give her the space to do so.

She stared off into the distance and her voice dropped to a whisper. "You know he's broken, right? Broken inside? He spent all his time trying to fix me, but I couldn't fix him."

Her eyes glistened, and she wiped at them with her sleeve. A tear escaped, followed by another, and another. Oh, fuck it; she needed a hug.

I gathered her up in my arms and held her tight as

she wept, her tears soaking into my cashmere sweater. I'd dressed for work today, and I couldn't help wishing I'd stuck with my leather jacket. At least it was waterproof.

"What do you mean, broken?" I asked, once her sobs had subsided to sniffles.

"It's hard to describe. He's got this air of sadness, and there's this barrier between him and the world. I don't think he has many friends, and not once did he mention his family."

"Did he ever do anything that worried you?"

"You mean to me?"

"Or anybody else?"

She shook her head so hard a barrette flew out of her hair and skittered across the floor. "No, never! Ethan was the kindest man I could have ever hoped to meet."

"Didn't you think of staying with him?"

"Yes, but I know deep down it wouldn't have worked out. Two damaged souls like us? We'd only have ended up hurting each other."

"Did you sleep together?"

I felt like a bitch for even asking, but I had to know.

"No, but if he'd ever wanted to, I would have."

That told me a lot. Melinda had spent more time than most with White, and she wouldn't have hesitated to get closer.

"Can you think of anyone else Ethan knows who might have more information?

"Sorry. Like I said, he wasn't very social." Her lips had gone dry, and she flicked out her tongue to moisten them. Stress, probably. "Are you going to see him?"

"Yes, next week. He won't talk about the case,

though."

"Will you... Will you tell him I'm thinking of him?"

"Yes, I'll tell him." I offered her a card, and she reached out slim fingers and took it from me. "Call me if you think of anything else?"

She nodded. "If there's any way I can repay him for the kindness he showed me, I'll do it."

"Believe me, you'll be the first to know."

My stomach grumbled as I climbed into a cab outside Melinda's place, but I didn't have time to stop and eat. We kept snacks on the plane—a protein bar and an energy drink would have to do.

"Where to, ma'am?" the driver asked.

"Simmons Army Airfield, Fort Bragg."

He pulled away from the kerb, and I fished out my amber phone. I usually carried three phones, designated red, amber, and green. The red phone never got turned off, but that one was for emergencies only. I silenced the amber phone when I was busy. The green phone, the one every asshole and journalist had the number for, was turned off on my desk back at Blackwood today.

And now I groaned as I looked at the amber phone. Twenty-one missed calls? One from Trick, which I ignored, and sixteen from Lyle. What the hell had happened now?

CHAPTER 9

LYLE ANSWERED ON the first ring, breathless. "Dan?"

"Either that, or someone's stolen my phone. What's the problem?"

"I just met with Skinner."

And he was alive to tell the tale? That was a good start. "I can't imagine that would have been much fun."

"He's going for the death penalty."

I narrowly managed to stop my fist before it slammed into the back of the seat in front of me. That son of a bitch!

"How is this even a death penalty case?"

"Because of the forensics. He told me it was rape as well."

"Unless there's a whole bunch of evidence I haven't seen, he can't prove that."

"He says the signs of a struggle indicate it."

"That's tenuous."

But Jay would run with it anyway, the bastard.

"It's what he's saying."

I was so angry I risked exploding if I tried to speak, and besides, it wasn't a conversation I wanted to have in front of a cab driver.

"I'm flying back. Can you meet me later?"

"When and where?" Lyle's relief that he'd be getting

help with this mess came through in his voice, which had lost a little of its shakiness.

I gave him directions to Riverley and hung up. Never in my life had I wanted to kill somebody as much as I did right then. Jay wasn't doing this for Christina, the good people of Virginia, or womankind, no matter how he might try to dress it up for the TV cameras. He was doing it for himself.

The election for the commonwealth's attorney for Richmond County was due to take place next year, and I'd heard a rumour Jay had his eye on the top job, which didn't surprise me in the slightest. He'd always been ambitious to the point of ruthlessness. But he had strong competition, and what he needed was a big case to put himself on the map, something to make Jay Skinner a household name among the voters.

The Christina Walker murder certainly had the power to do that. But if White pleaded guilty, the drama would fade away after a few days on the front pages, and Ethan would be left to fester in Redding's Gap until he went mad or died. No, Jay wanted to showboat in front of a jury, and the only guarantee he had of doing that was to seek the death penalty.

The fucking bastard.

An hour passed before I got back to Riverley. To add insult to injury, the weather gods were hurling down sheets of rain, and I got soaked just running from my car to the front door.

Emmy took one look at me when I walked in and stepped backwards. "Bad day?"

"I want to punch somebody."

"Would you like to borrow Alex?"

"I've got an anger management problem, not a

death wish. Anyway, when I said 'somebody,' I meant Jay Skinner."

"Ah, the whole death penalty thing?"

Why didn't it surprise me that she knew? I swear she had a battalion of tiny drones whose sole job was to round up juicy titbits of information and report back to her. "How did you find out?"

"It was on CNN."

Okay, that too.

"Lyle called. He's freaking out, and I told him to meet me here." I hadn't seen his car outside, which meant he hadn't arrived yet. "Do you have any Valium? I suspect he's gonna need it."

"He's a trial lawyer. Shouldn't he be injecting testosterone instead?"

"He's tried four cases. The only one he won was for cheque fraud, and he only managed that because the main witness for the prosecution didn't turn up."

As usual, Emmy and her warped sense of humour found that funny, but I wasn't laughing.

"So, the only chance he'll stand is if we chop Skinner's tongue off."

"That's not the only thing of Skinner's I'd like to chop off."

"How long did you date him for?"

"Too long. It was the most stupid thing I ever did."

"Even stupider than the time you drank six margaritas and decided to slide down the bannister?" She waved at the polished walnut slope behind her.

That had hardly been my finest hour. Not only had I spilled my drink, I'd ended up with first degree burns on my ass before I fell off the end.

"Even worse than that."

She grinned. "A grudge match. I like it."

"Hell, this whole thing is a disaster waiting to happen."

Emmy took my elbow and led me into the nearest living room, a gloomy room panelled in dark wood with oil paintings of her husband's ancestors glowering from the walls. She dropped onto an overstuffed leather couch, and I followed suit, trying to get comfortable. It proved to be an impossible task. Whoever designed the furniture didn't understand the concept of relaxation.

"Break it down," she said. "What's your goal?"

"I'm not even sure anymore." Damn Emmy and her logic. Sometimes, I thought her perfect exterior hid a robot. But I sighed and did as she said, taking a mental step back and thinking things through. "At first, I was only going through the motions. And by the way, I'm still pissed you gave me this case."

"Learn to drive, Dan."

I stuck my middle finger up at her. "But now Skinner's involved, it's become personal. More than anything, I want to see him lose on his big day in court, but I can hardly side with a criminal, can I?"

"It's a difficult one."

"You're telling me. All I've got so far is half a dozen people telling me what a great guy White was, Tia and Eli included."

"And Ishmael."

"Ishmael? You spoke to him about this?"

"Bradley did, him and his big bloody mouth." Ishmael was a world-renowned fashion designer as well as Tia's ex-boss and an old college buddy of Bradley's. "Ishmael's fucking nuts, but like Bradley, he's a good judge of character. His only complaint about Ethan was his dress sense."

"What about his dress sense?" I'd only seen him in an orange jumpsuit so I couldn't really comment.

"Ishmael reckons if a man can bounce quarters off his ass cheeks, it's only right for him to wear tighter trousers and show them off. Apparently, the Ghost prefers a looser fit."

I snorted, and Emmy gave me a strange look.

"That's the worst he could come up with?"

"Yeah, and they did a few shows together. What do you think of White now that you've met him?"

The first word to come into my head was sexy, but that was clearly a malfunction of my synapses. Brought on by the stress of this case, no doubt. "Quiet. Shy. Sad. And he'd only talk about music."

"And how did you feel inside?"

I knew what she was asking. We'd both met enough assholes in our time—murderers, rapists, thugs, gang members, thieves—and there was usually something "off" about them. Maybe an arrogance they couldn't help or a glibness that hid their true intentions. And with practice, you could *feel* when something was wrong, a sixth sense, if you like. Alarm bells had rung with Jay, and I'd ignored them. I shouldn't have.

But with Ethan, I'd got nothing.

"He didn't ping my radar."

Emmy sat in silence for a full minute, mulling things over. Once, she'd been crazily impulsive, but she'd developed new habits over the years, encouraged by Black. He'd always been a thinker.

"What would Skinner get if he won? If Ethan got the death penalty?"

"Glory."

"A little birdie told me that Mayor Poulter, who happens to be a golfing buddy of Skinner's, is pushing him too. Poulter reckons there've been too many high-profile acquittals, and he wants to prove the Eastern District hasn't gone soft."

See? Emmy knew everything. "So he gets political favour as well. That's not going to hurt when it comes to the election for the commonwealth's attorney."

"And what would Ethan get if Skinner lost?"

"A lot of years inside. I still think he'll plead guilty."

"So for White, you've got death versus a living death, and for Skinner, he either basks in the Office of the Commonwealth Attorney or he crashes and burns in court. You need to pick a side and go all out. Who's it to be?"

When she put it that way, the decision was easy. "White."

"What did Skinner do to you, anyway? It's not like you to get so riled up."

I groaned and buried my face in the arm of the couch. "He played me. The asshole played me."

"Played you how?"

I'd always kept it to myself, but with Jay's involvement in this case, I needed to come clean, even if it left me embarrassed as hell.

"He made me think he cared. Not totally hearts and flowers, but enough that I let my guard down. Then one night, I woke up thirsty, and when I went to get a glass of water, I found him at my dining table going through one of my case files. He tried to make out I'd left the folder right there, but I know damn well I'd locked it in the filing cabinet. The fucker took the key out of my bag."

"I take it he had a vested interest in that particular case?"

"I found out afterwards it had been assigned to him after his squash buddy broke his arm."

She grinned. Not a normal reaction, but nothing about Emmy was normal. "Well, when Skinner interfered with your case, he interfered with my company, and by extension, me. So I'm looking forward to fucking him over."

"That makes two of us."

Lyle arrived a few minutes later, and he looked as if Death was hot on his heels, scythe in hand. Bradley answered the door and ushered him into the hallway, rolling his eyes at Lyle's overly short pants.

"The press was waiting for me when I came out of my office," Lyle said. "They wanted a statement. What should I say? What on earth should I tell them?"

Bradley closed the front door and Lyle began pacing, his heels clicking on the tiled floor. I couldn't think with the noise, so I steered him into the lounge where he could walk up and down on the Persian carpet instead.

"What did you do?" I asked.

"I ran back into the building and got a taxi to pick me up at the rear."

Nothing like confronting a problem head-on, was there?

Mind you, I didn't intend to do that either, not when I could sneak in sideways and catch Jay by surprise. But Emmy was right—I couldn't afford to procrastinate over my next move because the outcome would be a solid victory for my prick of an ex. If I had to look at his ugly mug on the news for a four-year term, I'd be tempted to pick the death penalty myself.

No, I'd fight, and I'd fight hard. It was only my professional reputation on the line as well as Skinner's. No biggie.

CHAPTER 10

THE FOLLOWING MORNING, Lyle paced the living room at Riverley again. Up and down. Up and down. Up and down. At this rate, Emmy would need a new carpet. I glanced out the window to the helipad where the sleek black Eurocopter was being refuelled. *Hurry up.*

Or not.

Because we'd soon be on our way to Redding's gap to visit White. At least, Lyle would be speaking to him—we weren't both allowed in.

"How do I tell a man he's going to die?" Lyle asked.

From the way he spoke, anyone would think he'd be the one facing the firing squad.

"Well, you don't put it quite like that." Lyle sniffled, and I felt guilty for snapping. "Come on, why don't you sit down until we're ready to go?"

I steered him over to the couch, and he sat where I pointed. Fuck. Today promised to be hell.

"You need to break it to Ethan gently. At the moment, the death penalty is far from certain, just something the prosecution has indicated is a possibility. Before it gets that far, he'd have to be found guilty, and then a jury would need to unanimously agree that capital punishment was the best option. And even if that does happen, there's the appeals process."

Lyle began shaking, and I wondered if I should get him removed from the case. It would be easy enough, even without the Ghost's cooperation. A short bout of sickness, a little accident... But keeping him also had advantages—Lyle was easy to manipulate, and whoever took his place might be worse.

"I-I-I never thought I'd have to do something like this. I'm much better at dealing with misdemeanours."

I gave him a reassuring pat on the shoulder. "And when this is over, you can go back to your misdemeanours. But first, you've got to man up and give your all to helping Ethan. He's depending on you."

Lyle bolted from the couch, and a few seconds later, I heard the bathroom door slam along the hallway. Fantastic.

"He doesn't handle stress well, huh?" Emmy said from her perch on the window seat.

"Ten out of ten for observation. I got Mack to research him, and he's never had to deal with this kind of pressure before. The closest he's come to death was getting held up by some punk on campus at Samford."

"Stanford? He went to Stanford?"

"No, SAM-ford. It's in Alabama. And when the cops caught the mugger, it turned out he had a banana and not a gun. The police report said Lyle needed to change his pants."

"Good grief."

Several times on the flight to Redding's Gap, I nearly told Lyle I'd talk to the Ghost instead of him, but I held back. My visits were limited to two single hours a week, but as White's attorney, Lyle could visit more often. I needed to save my time in case of an emergency.

I was almost as nervous as Lyle when we got to the prison. What were the chances of him not fucking this up?

Not good, it turned out.

He was inside for half an hour while I alternated pacing in the parking lot and perching on the hood of Otis's car, willing myself to relax. I hadn't smoked since I was a teenager, but for the first time in years, I craved a cigarette to calm my nerves. Yes, I'd spent ages going over what to say with Lyle, coached him on how to develop a rapport with Ethan and dig a little deeper into his psyche, but I didn't have a whole lot of confidence that he'd follow through.

And as soon as I saw Lyle leave the building, shoulders hunched, I knew it hadn't gone well.

"Lyle?" He kept his gaze fixed on the ground. "How did it go?"

"Well, White didn't shout at me."

Understandable, since that would have got him thrown straight back in his cell.

"What did he do?"

"Nothing. Just stared at the table."

"That was it? He didn't speak?"

"I suggested he might want to hire a more qualified attorney, and he shook his head."

Bloody idiot, as Emmy would say. I'd picked up a few of her expressions over the years. If my life was on the line, and I had the kind of money White did, I'd buy my own fucking law firm.

"Did you explain we're going to do everything we can for him?"

"I told him what you said, but I might as well have been speaking to the wall."

And I felt like punching one. Why wouldn't White fight for himself? Whoever murdered Christina Walker had the fires of hell burning in him, but now Ethan was more like a wet blanket. Any flames had long since fizzled out.

Chapter 11

LYLE BARELY SPOKE on the way back from Redding's Gap. I didn't care, just as long as he refrained from throwing up in the helicopter. His greenish tinge was kind of concerning, and the thing was a bitch to detail. Halfway to Riverley, angry clouds gathered above us and it began drizzling, turning a black day even darker.

I spent the trip thinking, and by the time we landed, one thing was clear—whatever White wanted, I wasn't leaving Lyle to handle the legal aspects of this mess. He needed help, and he needed it badly.

I left the hapless lawyer slumped over the breakfast bar, staring into a cup of coffee as if it held the answers to life, and went to look for Emmy. I found her in the gym, running on a treadmill where, according to the display, she'd been for the last two hours. Seemed she'd settled in for the day, what with the iPad propped on the front and the Bluetooth headset stuck in her ear. Yes, Emmy was the queen of multitasking as well as the Queen Bitch.

"I'll ask her and text you later, okay?" she said. "Just make sure you keep out of trouble."

A roll of the eyes.

"Go see the blonde lady in Blackwood reception, and I'll get her to give you twenty bucks. Just make sure Vine eats something healthy. Got it? ... Good." She hung up and raised one perfectly plucked eyebrow at me. "Let me guess, we need Oliver?"

"We need Oliver."

Theoretically, Emmy's lawyer, Oliver Rhodes, headed up the firm of Rhodes, Holden and Maxwell, but his corner office in downtown Richmond may as well have been another branch of Blackwood. Emmy had Oliver on permanent retainer.

"Can you grab me a bottle of that green shit Toby put in the fridge?" she asked, tapping away at her iPad screen.

"Who was on the phone?"

"Trick. He said he left you a voicemail, but you never returned his call."

"I've been busy."

"They're not bad kids, even if Vine does live on chips and Twinkies. You should talk to them."

"You know why I don't."

And what was wrong with Twinkies? They'd been one of my staples as a kid, seeing as they were easy to shoplift and the electricity at home got cut off every other week so I couldn't actually cook anything.

"I do know," Emmy said. "But, honey, it's been over a decade. I get that it hurts like fuck, but you can't let your past ruin your future. Hey, look at me—I had the childhood from hell, and I turned out okay."

I just stared at her. She grinned. I stared at her some more.

"Emmy, you're an assassin."

"Yeah, but I only kill bad people. The green shit Toby made—can you get it?"

No doubt about it—my best friend was insane.

I meandered over to the mini fridge by the door.

Judging by the vase of tulips on the top, Bradley had struck again. I found a bottle of swampy liquid, unscrewed the lid, and sniffed.

"Ugh! You drink this stuff?"

It smelled like seaweed mixed with compost.

"It's good for me. Allegedly." She took a mouthful and grimaced. "I must be psychic, because I've already spoken to Oliver. He'll be here within the hour."

The only change when I got back to the kitchen was that Lyle's coffee had gone cold. He looked like a man with the weight of the world on his shoulders, and I didn't know whether to feel sympathetic or pissed off that he was so out of his depth with this case.

"Help's coming," I told him.

He looked up, eyes bloodshot. "What?"

"I've got another attorney coming to assist you. Give you some pointers, that kind of thing."

"Another public defender?"

"No, somebody who's had more practice with trial work."

Lyle brightened a little. "Has he ever won a case?"

"Yes, quite a few of them."

Just then, Oliver strode in. His made-to-measure suit made Lyle's badly fitted off-the-peg number look even scruffier, hardly surprising since Oliver's attire probably cost several months of Lyle's salary.

My old friend leaned down and kissed me on the cheek, and I couldn't help smiling inside. At thirty-four, Oliver only looked better with age, and the same charisma that allowed him to command a courtroom left a trail of disappointed ladies in his wake.

Next, he held out a hand for Lyle to shake, and the younger lawyer's jaw dropped.

"You're Oliver Rhodes."

Oliver smirked. "Well, I guess that saves me from introducing myself."

"Holy crap. You're, like, a legend."

"I'd like to believe I'm not old enough to be a legend."

"Man, you won every case you ever defended."

"Actually, I lost one. The third I ever tried, and not an episode I care to remember."

"I can't believe you quit. You were my role model all through law school."

Oliver had the good grace to blush. "I'm sure you could have found someone better."

"No way. So, are you going to defend the Ghost?"

He shook his head. "I don't do trial work anymore. I'm just here to assist."

"Why not? You're a mastermind in the courtroom."

"I felt I'd achieved everything I could. It was time to take a step back."

A lie, though few knew the truth. Oliver quit after defending a murderer whose victim's family didn't share Lyle's admiration of Oliver's skills in front of a jury. Oliver's win-at-all-costs mentality meant he got his acquittal, even though he knew his asshole of a client was guilty as fuck, but the sweet taste of victory was soured by having to attend the funeral of someone he cared deeply about three months later.

A case of mistaken identity, the cops said, but Oliver didn't believe it. Neither did I when I was hired to investigate. A month after that, the killer's body turned up on a building site, and Oliver's alliance with Blackwood formally began.

Even now, six years later, there was still a sadness in Oliver that he couldn't quite keep hidden. It lurked just under the surface, showing up when his thoughts strayed from the present to the past. In fact, when I thought about it, Oliver reminded me a little of Ethan.

But Lyle shook his head in disbelief at Oliver's answer. "If I could win the way you did, I'd never quit."

"Then you need to learn that there's a time to fight and a time to yield." Oliver turned back to me. "Tell me, why am I here? Emmy sounded remarkably vague on the phone. All I know is that there's a problem with a case."

"Two problems, actually. All the evidence and the defendant."

Oliver took a seat on the stool furthest from Lyle. "Those sound like fundamental issues."

"Oh, and the prosecutor's Jay Skinner."

"Nothing like making it easy, is there? Go on, fill me in."

I gave him a brief précis of the events so far and threw in a few of my thoughts as well. Oliver took notes on a yellow pad, twirling his Montblanc fountain pen around in his fingers as he listened. While Lyle's writing was an illegible scrawl, Oliver's was neat and controlled, and I couldn't help thinking their penmanship reflected their characters.

When I'd finished, Oliver rolled his eyes. "Dan, how do you always manage to get these cases?"

I shrugged. "Just lucky, I guess."

"We have to get a good look at that evidence."

"I know. We should have more details by Monday,

and I've got Bay on standby."

Blackwood had a forensics lab at its main facility, a purpose-built complex on a sprawling estate thirty miles east of Richmond. Its director, Bayani, was a genius at spotting things that other people missed. I wanted him to go over the police reports with me, just in case anything in there could help.

"Good." Oliver sighed and reached for his pen once more. "In the meantime, I'll review these files with Lyle."

"You need me here? I could do with catching up on my other cases."

"No, we're good."

He said that, but when I finished my final conference call two hours later and returned, frustration showed in both attorneys.

"But defending this case is impossible," Lyle said.

"Nothing's impossible. Some things are more difficult than others, but impossible? Never. You've got to change your attitude. If you go into a courtroom thinking your client's going to lose, they sure as hell will."

Oliver tried to conceal the exasperation in his voice, but I'd known him for too long to miss it. Part of me wished he'd take over the case. I'd even considered trying to convince him to do just that, but in the end, I'd decided against it. Quite apart from Oliver's self-imposed courtroom embargo, I didn't want to tip our hand to Jay yet. If Skinner thought he was up against Lyle, the chances were he might get complacent.

Like a cute little clownfish protecting its anemone home from predators, Lyle would go through the motions of mounting a defence, but against an advancing stingray such as Jay, he wouldn't stand a chance. Oliver was a great white shark.

But I had to admit I shared Oliver's frustration.

"How am I supposed to mount a defence when my client won't even speak to me?" Lyle asked.

"First, you need to gain his trust, and at the same time, go through every detail of this case until you can recite them backwards in your sleep. Then you need to do the same with similar cases, so when Skinner challenges you, you can answer like that."

He clicked his fingers, the sharp snap a contrast to Lyle's silence.

"Why didn't I become a realtor? Or a shoe salesman? Or a bartender?"

Oliver's expression said he wondered the same thing himself. "Because somewhere inside you is the man who wanted to stand up in court and convince a jury he was right. We just have to find him."

CHAPTER 12

ON SATURDAY EVENING, I stared out my bedroom window on Riverley's third floor, waiting for darkness to fall. I wanted to speak to Tyrone d'Angelo, seeing as he was the only person we knew White had fallen out with, and one of my contacts said he worked the night shift in a bar called The Firefly on the outskirts of Richmond. As bars went, it was only one shitty wine menu above a sawdust-on-the-floor joint, certainly not somewhere a dude would take a lady if he wanted a second date.

But at least I wouldn't look out of place in leather, my fabric of choice. For tonight, I picked an old favourite, a scuffed biker jacket Emmy had given me not long after we met. It looked a little the worse for wear now, but its battle scars told the story of my life.

I teamed the jacket with skintight jeans and a pair of cowboy boots, a sort of unofficial uniform, plus a purse big enough to fit my Glock into. And my pepper spray and a pair of handcuffs—life's little essentials. The handcuffs came in useful for all sorts of adventures, not just the criminal apprehension kind.

In front of the mirror, I adjusted my boobs so the knife I'd stuffed into the front of my bra didn't show. A touch of dark red lipstick, a swipe of mascara, and I was good to go.

"Nice outfit," Oliver said when I stopped by the dining room to say goodbye.

It even got me a half smile, the equivalent of a grin from Mr. Oh-So-Serious. He and Lyle had papers spread all over the table, and a handwritten sign taped to the door said *War Room*. Emmy had stuck it up months ago because little dining ever got done in there.

When Lyle caught sight of my chest, his eyebrows rose so high they could have painted the ceiling. Good. I'd made the right clothing selection.

"Everything going okay?" I asked.

Lyle turned bright red and mumbled something unintelligible, while Oliver rolled his eyes.

"Brilliant. Just fucking brilliant."

The body shop hadn't repaired all the panels on my Porsche yet, and being honest, I had my doubts they ever would. That meant I could take one of the pool vehicles or borrow a car from Emmy's garage instead. I looked longingly at the keys to her Dodge Viper hanging in the lock box then opted for a company Explorer. I didn't want to risk landing another case like this one.

The parking lot at The Firefly was full, but as I circled, a pickup pulled out of a slot in the far corner and I shoehorned the Explorer into it. Fingers crossed it would still be there when I wanted to leave.

Mack had sent me a photo of Ty, and he wasn't hard to spot. The eagle tattoo covered most of one arm, and he showed that and his muscles off in a white vest, Die Hard-style. I hoped it wouldn't come to that.

Eyes tracked me across the dimly lit room as I walked towards the bar, and not content with staring, some of the assholes felt the need to catcall as well. I ignored them all and parked my ass on the cracked red leather of a wobbly barstool.

By then, I had Ty's attention too, and he raised an eyebrow.

"Gimme a beer."

I didn't plan on drinking much, and this wasn't the sort of establishment where a girl ordered sparkling water. He slid a bottle over to me, and I passed him ten bucks.

"Keep the change."

A crowd of people came in, rowdy and already well past tipsy, and fifteen minutes passed before Ty spoke to me again.

"Haven't seen you in here before."

"Never had a reason to visit."

"And you do now?"

I took a swig of my drink, my hand left wet by the condensation running down the bottle. "I do."

He smiled, and I had to concede he wore it well. On another occasion, it would have aroused my curiosity, maybe even other things as well, but tonight was business.

"Care to let me in on the secret?" he asked.

"I came to talk to you."

His smile faded. "What about?"

I caught myself picking at the label on my beer bottle and made myself stop. "Ethan White."

Now he turned ugly. "Not interested in that conversation."

"Ten minutes."

"No."

I reached into my pocket and took out a couple of hundred-dollar bills. Working in this place, I bet he wasn't made of money.

Indecision showed on his face. I added a third note.

"Ten minutes," he growled. "Kemal, I'm taking a break."

I followed Ty through a door behind the bar, into a staff area that made front-of-house look upmarket. A small office on the far side was barely big enough for the desk and chair it contained, but Ty motioned me in there and pushed the door closed. He didn't offer me a seat, and even if he had, I wouldn't have put myself at a disadvantage by taking it.

"Clock's ticking," he said. "Who are you, anyway?"

Might as well get straight to the point. "I'm an investigator working for White's lawyer."

"I thought you were a reporter."

"Yeah, I get that a lot." Not that the revelation made much difference. Ty still glowered at me. "I hear you fell out with Ethan a few months back."

"So what if I did?"

"I'm trying to get a handle on what kind of person he was."

Ty perched on the edge of the rickety-looking desk. It creaked under his weight, and I took half a step back. I didn't want to get my toes squashed if it gave out.

"Ethan was a two-faced bastard, that do ya?"

Interesting. Ty was the first person I'd come across who had anything bad to say about Ethan. An anomaly? Or was Ethan good at hiding his true colours?

"Care to elaborate?"

"Ethan was seeing my girlfriend behind my back."

Bitterness seeped through Ty's voice, cloying and slick. Perhaps this *was* a new side of Ethan I hadn't seen.

"How do you know that?"

"I saw them having dinner together. Some fancy Italian place. Pricey."

Ty spat the last part, his tone saying what his words didn't. White went out to impress. He'd taken Ty's girl to a restaurant Ty couldn't afford.

"You followed them?"

"I got better things to do than stalk a woman."

"Then how did you find out?"

"A brother of mine waits tables there. He sent me a picture."

Lucky or unlucky? Nobody wanted to find out about a betrayal second-hand, but better to know than to remain ignorant. I'd learned that all too well from my experience with Jay Skinner.

"Did you confront White about it?"

Ty's expression said, "What do you think?" as did his snort. "He said it was just dinner. That nothing went on. But it sure didn't look like that in the photo."

"Have you still got it?"

Ty scowled as he scrolled through the pictures in his phone. A minute of my allotted time passed. How many photos did this dude take? Finally, he handed it over and sure enough, there was White sitting at a table. A brunette sat opposite, their joined hands resting next to a basket of breadsticks. But for a man on a date, White looked surprisingly tense. Yes, he was smiling, but through clenched teeth, and there was a tightness around his eyes that spoke of stress.

"See?" Ty asked.

"Are you sure this is your girlfriend? I mean, you can only see the back of her head."

"Yeah, it's her. She admitted it, and so did Ethan."

"You spoke to her about it? What did she say?"

"Same as Ethan—that there was nothing going on. But you don't take a chick out for an expensive dinner and hold her hand like that if you're not looking for action later."

He had a point. At least, I thought he did. I hadn't been on enough dates with men to be sure. For the most part, I just skipped the small talk, the dinner, the getting to know each other, and went straight to the sex. The only time I had a cosy dinner with a guy was for work, and that could involve anything from hand-holding to full-on tongue action if we needed to maintain our cover. But White was a DJ, not a secret agent, so he didn't have that excuse.

"And how did White react when you confronted him?"

"Said he was sorry I was upset. That it was just dinner, not a big deal. But he knew I liked her, man. I'd been hooked on her for months. And when I called him an asshole, he just shrugged like he didn't care."

So White hadn't got heated, even in a volatile situation? Hmm. "And your girlfriend?"

"Oh, she yelled back. Always did have a pair of lungs on her. Told me I was overreacting and that I was the asshole for... Well, I punched Ethan."

"You ever consider that maybe she was right?"

"You ever consider that maybe your mouth's too big?"

Ty pushed up off the table, towering six inches above me as he stood straight.

I gave him a wink. "Most men think that's an asset."

He settled back again, tension broken. "Look, he

deserved that punch. There's a code, and he broke it. I don't need friends like that."

"I get where you're coming from." That's what I said, but to me, it sounded as if they were both in the wrong. And I'd still only heard one side of the story. Had White's halo really slipped, or was Ty lying to me for some reason? "What's your girlfriend's name?"

"Why do you want to know?"

"Like I said, I'm trying to build up a picture of White. Any input I can get would be useful."

"Well, you're not getting hers. We might not be together anymore, thanks to that piece of shit, but I'm still not gonna let the likes of you bother her." He checked his watch. "Ten minutes is up. Time to leave, sweetheart."

"I'll pay you an extra hundred for the name."

"She's not for sale."

When I didn't move fast enough, Ty grabbed me by the elbow and pushed me towards the door. I nearly—so nearly—laid him out, but I took one of those deep, calming breaths Black had drilled into me and shook Ty off instead.

"I can walk."

"Walk faster."

Jeers came as I strode through the bar, plus one offer of a date and two for a quick trip out to the parking lot. Some greasy dude shoved what I assumed was a phone number into my back pocket and narrowly escaped losing his fingers as I turned on him.

"Get your fucking hands off me."

"Feisty. I like that."

"I bet your mouth is bigger than your balls."

"You wanna find out?"

"Only if you want to lose them."

I marched through the door, reaching for my car key. So. Many. Assholes. I'd had enough, at least for today.

As I stepped outside, a cloud of tobacco smoke engulfed me, thick enough to make my eyes water. Through the blurriness, I saw a glowing end and recognised one of the men I'd seen hanging out by the bar.

Lightbulb moment. "Want to earn a few bucks?"

He considered my offer for a nanosecond. "How?"

"A couple of months back, I went on a date with the dick behind the bar in there, and I left a necklace of mine at his place. I want it back, but he said he gave it to the girl that came after me."

The guy blew out another lungful of carcinogens and coughed. "Doesn't surprise me."

"He still won't tell me her name." I softened my voice a little, pleading. "The necklace belonged to my grandma. I don't want to cause trouble; I just want it back."

"How does that get me cash?"

"I need to know who the other girl was."

"That's it?"

"That's it."

"How much you offering?"

I held out a hundred. This was all going on my expense account. If Emmy was going to give me a bullshit job, she could damn well pay for it.

"Two months ago, you say?"

I nodded.

"That was probably Lisa. You must have dated Ty when they were on a break. They've had their ups and downs over the last year or two, but I think they finally split for good. I haven't seen her around for weeks."

"Lisa. You have a surname?"

"Never knew it, but she works in the nail salon two blocks down. Tall girl, wears a lot of earrings. That enough?"

"That's enough."

I handed the bill over and walked back to my car. In the dim glow from the courtesy light, I checked my nails. There were a few chips, and the polish was growing out at the bottom. Yeah, I could probably use a manicure.

CHAPTER 13

IN DAYLIGHT THE next morning, my nails looked even worse, and one snapped off completely when I used it to clear a jam in my AR-15 out on the shooting range. Oops.

Emmy was in New York, but Mack and I got into a contest over who could shoot five into the centre ring the fastest. Then Ana came out and did it twice as quick without even warming up. Then Carmen stopped by and matched Ana's time, but from twice the distance.

At times, I felt like the poor relation, especially beside Emmy and Ana. Neither of them deliberately tried to make me feel as if they were superior, they just...were.

Emmy had always done her best by me, even when I fucked things up by crashing her cars and falling out of my heels in her clubs. She'd always be my best friend, no matter what. Ana, I still wasn't sure of. She was damaged, like all of us, but I hadn't fathomed out to what extent. The only person who truly understood her was Emmy, and she didn't share.

I suppose that was partly why I wanted to crack this case. To prove that I could get thrown to the wolves and come back leading the pack, just like they did.

And to do that, I needed to speak to Lisa.

File 'n' Style was the second in a row of five ageing

storefronts, crying out not for a coat of paint but for demolition. As I walked along the cracked sidewalk, a panhandler shook a paper cup with a few coins in it at me.

"Spare some change?" he croaked.

I leaned down and dropped twenty bucks into his cup, earning a toothless grin in return.

"You're an angel, darlin'."

Nothing could be further from the truth, but at least I'd made one person happy today.

A faint buzzer sounded as I walked into the salon, a last gasp from its dying batteries. A girl with vivid pink hair sat at the back, her feet soaking in a basin while a middle-aged black woman worked on her fingernails. It wasn't long before a second nail technician meandered over, and this girl fitted cancer guy's description of Lisa.

"Are you looking for an appointment?"

No, lady, I'm looking for a lost dog. "Yes, please."

"This morning?"

"If you have a slot available."

Looking around the almost empty room, it was hard to see how they could be fully booked, but she made a show of paging through the diary anyway.

"I can fit you in right now if you want?"

She was pretty when she smiled. It transformed her face. But working in this place and dealing with a guy like Ty, I bet she didn't have much to smile about. She led me over to a vacant chair and fussed around, setting my fingers to soak in a bowl of fragrant water.

"Do you have anything in mind?" she asked.

Yes, I did, but I was going to wait until my nails were done until I broached that subject. I didn't want to end up on the street with half a manicure.

"I'll leave that up to you. Something funky. And can you fix up the broken one?"

"Sure."

She decided on tiny sunsets, shades of purple, peach, and yellow set behind the sea with a palm tree outlined in black on each of my thumbs. Not a bad job. If she was still speaking to me after this, I'd come back again for sure.

"Anything else?" Lisa asked as she put on the final touches.

"Actually there is. I understand you know Ethan White."

She sucked in a breath and the brush skidded across my nail, leaving a black streak in its wake.

"Oh shit," we both said at the same time. Well, Lisa said "shoot" because she was politer than me.

"I'm not talking about him," she whispered harshly, dabbing at my nail with a cotton ball. "What are you, a reporter?"

"Just somebody who's trying to help him, but I'm not having much luck at the moment."

"He's beyond help from what I understand."

"He is if everyone takes that attitude."

She glanced sideways at her colleague. "Will you keep your voice down? Look, Ethan's in my past. I've got a new boyfriend, and he doesn't know about that part of my life. I want to keep it that way."

"I don't want to make your life difficult."

"Then leave me alone."

"Five minutes. Just give me five minutes."

"Who are you, anyway?"

"I work for Ethan's lawyer."

"I'm not sure anything I know would help."

"Why don't you let me be the judge of that? We only want to find out what drove Ethan to do what he did. You know the prosecutor's going for the death sentence? Finding a motive could mean the difference between Ethan living and dying."

"If I talk to you, do you promise it stays between us?"

"Scout's honour."

Not that I'd ever been a Girl Scout, but it was better than swearing on a half-empty vodka bottle. Drinking had been my favourite pastime at that age. Lisa fell silent, for an entire minute according to the dusty clock on the wall behind us. Finally, she came to a decision.

"Do you know the park three blocks down?"

No, but I'd find it. I nodded.

"Meet me there at one, by the snack bar. I'll talk to you while I eat lunch."

I squeezed her hand, causing another smudge on my long-suffering nails. "Thank you."

Two hours to kill. I headed to the Richmond office to catch up on my regular work. You know, my actual job before Emmy decided to make my life hell? My team had closed a couple of cases and made progress on others, so I had to be thankful for that at least.

At one o'clock, I sat waiting in a plastic lawn chair next to a grubby table. I'd bought myself a hotdog from the van behind a shabby-looking basketball court, but I wasn't sure I wanted to eat it. I'd had better-looking food on survival training in the jungle. What were the green bits?

Lisa shuffled along ten minutes late, looking like she'd rather be at an appointment with her gynaecologist. She plopped into the seat next to me and looked at my meal.

"Want one?" I offered.

"Yeah, I'll get something. I know the guy who runs this place."

She waved a finger at him, and he smiled and nodded.

Great. Now, I was going to have to take at least a bite or I'd seem rude. Actually, it didn't taste too bad. I just hoped it wouldn't give me the shits.

"So..." I said.

Lisa looked at me.

"What's the story with Ethan? I spoke to Ty, but I wanted to hear your side of things."

"Ty's an asshole, that do ya?"

"I was hoping for something a little more concrete."

She sighed. "Fine. Ty saw me out with Ethan and laid into me about it. It was none of his business. We were on a break, and after that I made it permanent. Ty was a control freak. He got pissed if I so much as looked at another man."

The guy from the snack bar came over with her food, a stacked burger dripping with grease. Boy, she must have some metabolism.

"Ty made it sound like you were still dating."

"We weren't, we're not, and we won't ever be again."

So, she wasn't cheating as Ty had made out. White's halo had remained intact, at least at that point. "You said you've got a new man. What happened between you and Ethan? Did you split with him as well?"

She laughed, a cross between incredulity and humour. "I wasn't dating Ethan. He doesn't do the girlfriend thing, which is a crying shame. *Was* a crying shame. We just had dinner. He asked me to go with him as a favour, and I couldn't say I was too upset about it."

Didn't do the girlfriend thing? That was news. What *did* he do? The boyfriend thing? How did that fit in with Christina?

"What kind of a favour?"

"There was some weird woman following him around. Everywhere he went, she'd be there. He hoped if she saw him out with another girl, she'd get the message and back off."

White had a stalker? Why hadn't he mentioned this?

"Did she turn up that night?"

"Only briefly. She saw me there and left, which I guess was the plan."

"What did she look like? Could you identify her?"

"I didn't see her. I had my back to the door. Ethan looked up and told me she was there, and a minute later, he said she'd left."

"Nothing else? Did he say where he first saw her? How long had it been going on?"

Lisa gave a quiet moan as she bit into her burger, and I wondered if I'd been too hasty in my judgement. I took another mouthful of hotdog, chewing slowly.

"Ethan never used to say a lot. He always was quiet." She thought for a second, looking into the distance. "But he mentioned she left him notes. Slushy notes. He got embarrassed when I asked what they said and changed the subject."

Hmm... The stalker couldn't have been Christina, could it? She'd been pretty and willing, after all.

Perhaps Ethan had needed some action and gave in to the temptation following him around?

It was a possibility, and one I needed to consider. I knew firsthand how crazy stalkers could be. My friend Nick's girlfriend had almost died at the hands of hers. Maybe when Ethan invited Christina into his house, he didn't realise how deep her issues ran and something went wrong?

"Do you know if the woman kept hanging around after she saw you and Ethan together?"

Lisa looked away, embarrassed. "I kind of lost touch with Ethan after that. When Ty punched him, I didn't know what to say. I mean, I felt like it was my fault, being as their disagreement was over me. I should have made it clearer to Ty that I wasn't interested anymore."

"You never saw Ethan again?"

"Just once, in a club. The music was deafening, so we didn't get a chance to talk."

"Was he alone?"

"I didn't see anyone with him." Her eyes widened. "Hey, come to think of it, that was the night the Ghost played a set. I didn't realise back then that they were the same person."

"I guess he kept that quiet."

"None of my friends knew either."

Despite being liked by everyone I'd met except Ty, Ethan seemed to have kept people at arm's length. Did he go home most nights alone, his only company a stalker?

"You said earlier that Ethan didn't do the girlfriend thing. Was he gay? Bisexual?"

"I don't think so. I saw him talk to women

occasionally, flirt a bit, but I never saw him do the same with guys. Plus my gaydar's pretty good, and he never registered on it."

"Did he ever date anyone?"

"Not that I know of. And when I made it clear I was interested, he didn't bite. Guess that turned out to be a good thing."

"In all the time you were friends with Ethan, did he ever get angry? Or violent?"

"The opposite. Even when Ty gave him a black eye, he just walked away."

"You saw it happen?"

"No, I but I heard the story from half a dozen people afterwards."

"Would you be willing to talk about Ethan in court?"

"I already told you I can't. My new guy's sweet. A family man. Looks after his grandma, goes to church on a Sunday. I don't want him finding out I used to hang with the likes of Ty and Ethan."

"It could be the difference between Ethan getting sentenced to death or life in prison."

She stared down at the remains of her burger then pushed it away.

"Look, I don't want to, but if it comes to that, I'll do it. The Ethan I knew was a kind man. I don't want him to die."

With that small victory, we parted company, and I knew what was next on my list: taking a closer look at Christina.

Up until now, everyone, myself included, had assumed she was collateral damage. A victim of circumstance, the object of Ethan's violent outburst, a simple case of being in the wrong place at the wrong time.

Nothing in the evidence we'd unearthed so far suggested she and Ethan had met before that night. But what if they had? What if she'd been a contributor to what happened rather than the passive victim everyone thought?

CHAPTER 14

ON MONDAY MORNING, the forensics report finally got uploaded to the police network, and Lyle got his hands on copies of the lab work. I strongly suspected Jay had engineered the weekend delay, just to give Lyle two fewer days to go over everything. He was considerate like that.

The mere thought of Skinner made me clench my teeth. How had I let myself get taken in by him? He'd seemed so charming when we first met, and it took me months to realise his outward respectability hid a pool of slime.

Mack and Bay were with me in the lab when details of the crime scene started to arrive. Mack could be overly sensitive at times, and I told her she didn't need to look at the photos, but she still insisted on helping. I glanced over at the door. Yup, there was a trash can next to it, complete with a fresh bag. I had a feeling Mack would be using that before the morning was over.

"Where do you want to start?" Mack asked.

"Let's check out the pictures first."

Not only did they have the potential to tell us the most, but there was also an element of getting the worst over and done with. Having to look at the moment someone's life was snuffed out then break it down in excruciating detail was never a pleasant job.

Bay loaded the photos up onto the big screen, one at a time. While three forensics assistants studied the technical details, I blocked out their mutterings and concentrated on the overall scene.

To say it wasn't pretty was like saying Jabba the Hutt wasn't quite a supermodel.

Christina lay broken on the bed, her arms and legs sticking out at awkward angles. No care had been taken over the arrangement of the body—it was as if she'd been shovelled onto the mattress and left there. Trails of blood ran from her torso, pooling underneath her and soaking into the cream sheets. Jackson Pollock would have been proud.

"Forty-seven stab wounds," read out one of the assistants.

"If you're going to stab somebody, it's worth doing it properly, yes?" Bay said in his clipped tones.

English wasn't his first language—he was originally from the Philippines—but he'd managed to adopt a sense of American gallows humour perfectly. And he was right about the level of effort. This wasn't a burglary gone wrong or some kinky sex game that ended in tragedy. This was anger. Pure anger. Christina had been stabbed with a passionate fury I'd rarely seen.

A fury hard to reconcile with the quiet man I'd met in prison.

Emmy picked that moment to stop by. "Whoa, someone was pissed."

"Sure looks that way."

She picked up a copy of the detailed crime scene report and glanced through it. "And all so unnecessary. The wound to the heart alone would have done it, and the ME reckons that one came first."

I took the file out of her hands and read it for myself. Christina's left ventricle had been pierced by a single stab wound as the knife blade slid up under her sternum.

The frenzy of slashes, slices, and punctures led to a patchwork quilt effect, and in the good doctor's opinion, the killer had carried on after Christina was dead, otherwise there would have been more mess. The bleeding had slowed after her heart stopped pumping, according to his notes, but in my opinion, the room still looked like a slaughterhouse.

Bay clicked on to the pictures of the autopsy. We all took a step forward, except Mack, who went rapidly sideways and grabbed the trash can. I heard her retching in the hallway.

"You could have warned her," I told Bay.

"Oops."

The new photos showed the damage to Christina's chest and heart. A dark gash marred the muscle, and close-ups showed the severed blood vessels.

"They say the way to a woman's heart is through the stomach, past the liver, and right a bit," Bay said, coming over to stand beside me. "And it's certainly quicker than waiting in line to buy chocolates."

"He still had a crack at the traditional method, though."

"What do you mean?" Emmy asked.

I thumbed through the file and pointed out the open bottle of champagne sitting on White's nightstand, a single glass next to it, still half-full.

"Just one glass?"

"The other's smashed on the floor," Mack said, wiping her mouth as she walked back in.

I peered more closely. The bottle was still three-quarters full, and the glass left intact had lipstick marks on the rim.

"Doesn't look like she drank much. Although the cab driver said she was tipsy before she went to Ethan's place."

"Blood alcohol was point zero five percent," Bay said. "She'd have been slightly intoxicated but nowhere near drunk."

"And Ethan's?"

"Zero, but it was twenty-four hours at least before they drew a sample. If he'd only had a glass or two, it would have been metabolised by then."

"So we don't know whether he was driving drunk?"

"Nope, but something impaired his ability to handle a vehicle, seeing as he wrapped it around a tree," Emmy pointed out.

I imagined driving in a blind rage could have contributed. "They found the knife in the car, didn't they?"

Bay nodded. "In the footwell on the passenger side. Not until they'd dragged the car back up the slope, though."

Why did he take it with him? Why not just leave it with the body?

"Blood spatter's interesting," one of the lab techs piped up.

"In what way?" I asked.

"None of it's clean. The blood all over the body's been smeared, like someone pulled something over the top of her."

"The blood wasn't just on the bed either," Bay said, tapping key areas with his finger. "There are a couple of pools here, but they've been smudged as well."

"Any footprints?"

"Yes, but apparently there were some issues with preserving the integrity of the crime scene. The first officers to respond walked through most of it before they realised Christina was beyond saving."

"Anything that matched Ethan's shoes?"

Bay called up more photos. "It's hard to tell. The whole scene is in chaos. I've never seen anything like it."

"What do you think these marks are?" an assistant asked, pointing at some dark but faint smudges leading towards the bedroom doorway.

"I don't know." Bay scanned the report again. "And there's nothing in here about them."

"It almost looks as if someone dragged something," I said. "Did the police note anything missing from the room?"

"No, but how would they know? The only person who could have told them is the Ghost, and by all accounts, he's not talking."

I put that on my list to ask him tomorrow if I was allowed to take a copy of the photo in with me. Not that I honestly expected to get an answer.

Tomorrow... I wasn't looking forward to the visit. When I first started working on the case, I'd been apathetic. Could you blame me after the way it landed in my lap? Then, as things progressed, I'd viewed White through the eyes of the witnesses I'd spoken to, and the apathy turned to curiosity, even a little sympathy.

But now, having seen the crime scene in graphic detail, I only felt disgust. White might be benign most of the time, but he had evil hidden inside. I looked back up at Christina's broken frame. Satan himself would have been impressed with that job.

Bay scrolled to the next photo, this one of Ethan after he was extracted from the car. I'd already seen it, when Mack pulled it from the police system, but that didn't make it any less shocking. Blood covered him from head to toe. It couldn't have been much worse if he'd rolled in it.

While I thought about what I was going to say to the Ghost the next day, the geeks read over the rest of the lab reports. I'd looked at a few of them, but to me, they were written in code. Interpretation was best left to the experts—that was why Blackwood paid them the big bucks.

I was staring into space when Emmy sat down next to me.

"Dollar for them?"

"My thoughts are barely worth a cent."

"Try me."

"I just don't get it. Everyone says White was a kind, gentle guy. Then this." I swept my hand over towards the pictures.

"Insanity defence?"

"At the moment, there isn't any kind of defence. The Ghost won't speak up, and Lyle's incapable of making him. I'm at a loss."

"What outcome do you want?"

"Does that matter?"

"Sure. You pick one then you make it happen. We already spoke about this, remember?"

"Well, either he gets life at Redding's Gap, death, or if he's found insane, locked up in a secure hospital. It's like choosing between Coke, Pepsi, or RC Cola."

"Just playing devil's advocate, what about the fourth option?"

"What fourth option? Red Bull?"

"He walks free."

"You can't be serious? Even you couldn't contemplate putting someone who stabbed a woman in a frenzy like that back onto the street. The guy's so unstable he could explode at any moment."

"You're sure he did it?"

"You're not?"

She shrugged, and then her phone rang. I recognised the opening bars of Pearl Jam's "Black." Her husband was calling. She stood and headed for the door, already reaching into her pocket.

"Think about it," she said over her shoulder before she disappeared.

I did. I didn't want to, because that would mean opening up a whole new can of worms, but I did think about it.

When Bay and his team finished talking among themselves, I broached the subject.

"Did you find anything new in the report? Anything strange?"

"They'd had sex before she died. There was a used condom in the bathroom trash can."

"He definitely used it with Christina?"

"DNA traces on the outside matched her and the semen matched him."

"Any sign it was non-consensual?" Because that was what Skinner was angling for.

"Some bruising around the vagina and slight tearing inside. But if he wanted to hide the evidence, why didn't he just flush it?"

"Maybe he wanted to be environmentally friendly?" an assistant suggested.

A killer who cared about pollution. Yeah, right. "Could somebody else have had sex with her after White and also used a condom?"

"I guess that's possible, but there aren't any defensive wounds. If an intruder suddenly appeared, wouldn't she have fought back?"

"What if the rape happened post-mortem?"

"No, it wouldn't have bruised like that. This looks more like rough sex."

"Okay. What else?"

"The blood evidence is useless to either side. It's been contaminated, both at the house and in the car. Too many people were there, and procedures weren't followed as they should have been."

"And what's your opinion of it?"

"What I've seen is conclusive with Mr. White having killed the girl, but I can't say with certainty that he did."

Interesting. "What makes you doubt it was him?"

"Not doubt, per se, but there are a few unexplained anomalies. Those marks on the floor, for instance. There was also a smudge of Miss Walker's blood in the trunk of the car, and nobody has been able to work out how it got there."

"What else?"

"A stray hair on the carpet beside the bed. Light grey, just over an inch long. It clearly didn't belong to the victim or the suspect."

"Could they get DNA from it?"

"There was no follicle attached." Bay sighed,

running his hands through his hair. "Apart from all the mess, it's not a particularly exciting murder. The weapon came from the suspect's kitchen. Eight-inch paring knife. Effective but unoriginal."

"That's it?"

He paused for a second. "I'm not sure whether it's important, but nobody's found Mr. White's house keys. He could have dropped them somewhere, but it's a loose end."

I felt weary as I left the lab. Sometimes my job made me want to go home and drink a bottle of whisky, but today that wasn't an option. Not when I needed a clear head. No, I needed a different distraction.

A warm body.

Tonight, I promised myself, I'd find one.

CHAPTER 15

MY NEXT STOP was the coffee place next to the police station in Richmond. Blackwood employees tended to have a love-hate relationship with the local cops. If we believed we were on the same side, we'd go all out to support them, but there were also occasions when our interests didn't align, and our tendency to ride rough-shod over their procedures had ruffled more than a few feathers.

I checked my watch. Officer Tenlow was running late. I ordered his usual—a cappuccino and a granola square, his pretence at being healthy—then snagged a table in the back corner, out of sight of curious eyes.

Tenlow, who his buddies at training college had immediately nicknamed Highfive, was one of the few members of local law enforcement I hadn't managed to piss off at some point or another. I'd also helped him out a couple of months back on a burglary case, so he owed me a favour.

It wasn't long before he walked in, his slumped shoulders speaking of the stress he encountered daily. He slid into the seat opposite me and took a sip of his drink before he'd even said hello.

"Sorry." He paused to wipe the foam from his lip. "I got caught up in an interview. I thought we were getting somewhere, but then the kid's lawyer shut it down."

If there was one thing the cops liked less than a Blackwood employee, it was a lawyer. Good thing I didn't have Lyle in tow. Or worse, Oliver. They detested Oliver.

"Lawyers do have a habit of doing that."

Tenlow took a bite of his granola square and sat back, stretching out his legs. "Why did you want to see me?"

"I'm working on this Ghost thing."

He groaned. Good to see I wasn't the only person this case was getting to. "I'm not supposed to talk about that."

"You're not supposed to talk about any of the things we discuss, but you still do."

"This is different. Everyone's watching."

"Tell me something I don't know. I feel like I'm in a goldfish bowl at work. Everyone keeps asking 'How's it going, Dan? Have you cracked the case yet, Dan?' It's driving me nuts."

We're in the same boat here, buddy.

"Our switchboard operator's gone off sick with stress. Fans keep phoning in death threats. What case have you got to crack, anyway? Everybody knows he did it. He still had the girl's blood on his hands when we caught him."

Well, I guess that answered my question about how much time they were spending looking at alternative theories.

"Skinner's trying for the death penalty, and I'm not convinced that's appropriate. Everything I've seen suggests White a straight-up guy who suddenly snapped, not a cold-blooded killer. I think he needs help, not a lethal injection."

"He also has the option of electrocution."

I stared sharp, pointy implements at Tenlow. "How did last month's sensitivity training go?"

"Shit, I didn't mean it that way. I was just saying... never mind. Look, I guess I can understand where you're coming from. I saw White at the station when we had him in for questioning, right before he got transferred. The guy was zoned out."

"You were at the scene, weren't you?"

"Yeah. Crazy, just crazy. What kind of guy fucks a woman then goes to the kitchen, gets a knife, and kills her? It must have been one hell of an argument."

And the crime scene report said there were no signs of a struggle away from the bed itself.

"How far was the kitchen from the bedroom? That was where the knife came from, right?"

Tenlow paused, tracing his finger along the table. "Along the landing, down the stairs, along another hallway, and the knife block was on the far side. It was a big house."

"How long do you think it would have taken him to walk there and back?"

"A minute? Maybe a minute and a half?"

"So White and Christina had some sort of argument, and then she lay back on the bed and waited calmly for a couple of minutes while he stormed off?"

I didn't buy it. If I'd been in that situation, I'd have been half-dressed and preparing to run by the time he came back.

Tenlow shrugged. "Stranger things have happened."

Not many, I was willing to bet. The more I delved into it, the more this whole case felt off.

"What did he say when he was at the station? Did he admit to the killing?"

"Nope. Just said he didn't remember anything then refused to speak again. He was kinda...compliant. No trouble. We still took him everywhere in leg irons, though. Like you said, there's no knowing what set him off."

"What about the girl?" I asked.

"What *about* the girl?"

"Did you look into her? Her background? Why she was there that night?"

"She was just some college girl. White picked her up in a nightclub from what I've heard. Could have happened to anyone."

Including me. If I'd met White in a bar, I'd have gone home with him. After all, how many times had I headed back to a man's apartment without knowing more than his name? It was a sobering thought. Suddenly, my planned excursion for that evening didn't seem quite so appealing.

I blew on my chai latte, took a sip, and asked a few more questions, but I'd exhausted Tenlow's usefulness. Talk turned to baseball—his son played Little League and Tenlow coached in his spare time. He left smiling, while I left more confused than ever.

Tenlow's words hadn't shed much light, other than to tell me that the cops had taken the simple option— no other suspects, an easy arrest, an open and shut case. Or so they thought.

If there was any way of helping White, it was Lyle and me against the world.

CHAPTER 16

NOW MY THOUGHTS had been sent off down a different path, I wanted to find out more about Christina. The cops hadn't looked into her at all, Blackwood hadn't done much more, and yet the feeling she was a bigger part of this puzzle than anybody realised grew stronger and stronger.

In my head, I kept seeing her broken body lying on the bed. I'd also seen the "before" pictures. Twenty-one-year-old Christina had been pretty and popular, on the cheerleading squad in high school and the dance team in college. Her roommate had told the police she couldn't imagine why anybody would want to kill her, but didn't everyone say that?

I wanted to do a bit more digging.

Once I'd picked up extra muffins for Mack and Emmy, I headed back to the office. Emmy was nowhere to be seen, so I ate hers, but Mack was stationed in front of her computer.

"You're not thinking of cooking again, are you?" I asked, looking at the quiche recipe on her screen.

"What's wrong with that?"

"Honey, some people were born to cook, but you weren't one of them."

"I just want to make one meal without it being a complete disaster. Is that too much to ask?"

In her case, it probably was. "Here, have a muffin instead. Can you give me a hand with something?"

"How did I guess?" she asked, brushing crumbs off her top as she took a bite.

"I want to know more about Christina Walker."

"You think there's something more to be found there?"

"I'm not sure, but I want to check just in case."

"Leave it to me."

With Mack taking care of the initial searches on Christina, I could spend an hour or two catching up on my other cases. Or so I thought. I'd barely set foot inside my office when my phone rang.

"Dan?"

"Yes, Lyle?"

"I'm stuck in my apartment," he hissed.

"What do you mean, stuck? Did the door jam or something?"

"No, it's not the door. The press is camped in the lobby. I tried to leave, and it was like being attacked by the zombies in *Dawn of the Dead*, except with flashbulbs going off. I managed to run back inside, but now I can't get out."

"Have you tried the fire escape?"

"They're down there as well." His voice held a hint of panic. "I'm supposed to be meeting Oliver at Riverley in an hour. What should I do?"

If it had been anyone else, I'd have told them to grow a pair and elbow the reporters out of the way, but I couldn't imagine Lyle forcing his way through the mob. A sigh escaped before I could stop it.

"Give me a minute."

Nick Goldman's office was next to mine, and we

shared an assistant. He ran the protection division of Blackwood and had a whole array of bodyguards at his disposal.

"Knock knock."

He glanced up from his desk. "What do you want? You want something, right?"

I smiled sweetly. "Could I borrow a couple of your people? Not for long."

"What for?"

"I've got an attorney and a pack of paparazzi, and the two aren't mixing well."

"Is this the guy Oliver was grumbling about yesterday?"

"Very likely, yes."

"Oliver would rather you sacrificed him to the baying hordes, I'm sure."

"And that would mean the Ghost got appointed another equally incompetent public defender in his place."

"Sounds like you're having fun with the case. It's a good thing you didn't borrow *my* car—I'm not sure I could have come up with a punishment to rival this one."

"I hate all of you. Just go get Lyle, would you?"

I heard him chuckling as I walked back to my office. After this was over, I was strongly considering buying another vehicle of my own. Borrowing was so last year. I could get a Hummer. Or maybe a tank. Even I couldn't break a tank. How much did one cost, anyway? I opened up Google to consult, dialling Lyle's number at the same time.

"Someone's coming to rescue you. And pack a bag, yeah? You'll have to stay at Riverley until this is over."

"Is there a swimming pool nearby? I have to swim every morning or I get really stressed."

"It's got a pool and a gym. And a tennis court. And a movie theatre."

"Maybe this case isn't so bad after all."

At least one person was happy. It was just a shame that person wasn't me. As the activity in the office wound down for the evening, with the administrators going home and the investigators on the evening shift heading out on the streets, I picked up my purse, borrowed a pool car, and went back to my apartment.

The stop was only temporary, though. I had a mind to lose.

CHAPTER 17

I'D REHEARSED THIS routine so many times before. Strip, shave my armpits and my legs, then check my bikini-line wax was still good. Take a shower. Moisturise and put deodorant on. Blow-dry my hair. Brush my teeth. Do my make-up. Make sure I had condoms and lube in my purse.

I could have done it in my sleep.

So why, tonight, did it feel so awkward?

The girl staring back at me from the mirror as I brushed on mascara wasn't looking forward to going out, and when she touched up her lipstick, she didn't relish the thought of somebody else sucking it off.

What's wrong with me? This was what I did. This was how I got through my life, from one week to the next. It was my drug, my fix.

Why wasn't I craving it like the lifeblood it was?

On my way through the living room, I paused and knocked back a finger of whisky. Then another. That gave me enough courage to go out the door. My destination, Black's, was a few blocks down. Easily walkable, even in heels. I bypassed the line, one of the perks of Emmy being the owner, and slid past the velvet rope, raising a hand to the doorman in greeting as I went.

Inside, the music was thumping as usual. I headed

straight to the bar.

"Double vodka and coke, please."

The barman raised an eyebrow because I never normally drank double anything. I nodded a confirmation and he shrugged, pouring my drink with agonising slowness.

Meanwhile, I scanned the crowd with a practised eye for likely targets. I spotted a couple—men attached to small groups, perhaps with a girl or two at the same table. If they were in a pair, I steered clear, as far too often they turned out to be gay, and I avoided the ones on their own at all costs. Ethan White was a perfect example of why picking up a loner was a bad idea.

I headed for the first of the possibles, but before I could get there, another woman swooped in and landed on his lap. Dammit. I veered in the direction of man number two instead.

He was available. He made that clear within three seconds of meeting me. But when he slid his arm around my waist and asked what I wanted—and he didn't mean just a drink—I felt nothing. Not a flutter in my belly, not a throb between my legs. I was dead from the waist down.

When the same thing happened with the third man, and then the fourth, I felt something all right—a sliver of fear brushing against my ribcage. What was my damn problem?

These men ticked all my boxes. They were well-dressed, hot, drinking the good stuff, and friendly. On any other night, I'd have been in a cab with one of them or maybe even two.

I returned to the bar, weary, and got another drink. I had a tab here although I never had to pay it. Emmy may have bitched about me borrowing her cars, but she was always generous with the drinks budget.

I'd just leaned forward to pick up my glass when someone pressed against me.

"Can I buy that for you?"

I twisted around. "I already paid."

"Shame. I'll get the next one."

The guy was gorgeous by anyone's standards. Six inches taller than me with smooth, light brown skin that made me want to lick it. I felt a ripple of heat in my belly as I studied him more closely. Close-cropped black hair, muscled shoulders—if it hadn't been for his eyes, which were filled with confidence instead of sadness, I could have been looking at... No. I wasn't even going to go there.

"Dance?" he murmured in my ear.

I let him lead me over to the dance floor, and by the time the intro to the first track had played, I knew this would be my warm body for the night. Half an hour, six songs, and another drink later, his confidence had turned to lust and my panties were wet.

Then one of Ethan's songs began playing.

It was like someone had got out a fire hose, turned it on full blast, and hit me in the chest with it.

"Daniela?" my new friend asked. "You okay?"

"Can we just go?" I muttered.

I didn't need to ask him twice. He steered me out of the club and into a waiting cab, and twenty minutes later, we pulled up outside his place.

Any heat between us had turned tepid, at least from my side, but I wasn't backing out now. This was how I worked. This was what I needed.

At least, that was what I kept telling myself.

All the way up to his apartment, through his living room, and into his bedroom.

When a man peeled off my clothes, it was as if he was peeling away the layers of stress and loneliness and self-loathing. When he thrust into me, he pounded the monsters that lived inside me into submission. When he came, it was an affirmation that somebody wanted me, that somebody cared enough to give me a little piece of himself, and I used that energy to get through the next day. Two or three days if I was lucky.

I fucked to remember, and I fucked to forget.

Only that night, it didn't work.

I half-heartedly faked an orgasm, and when he rolled off me, all I could do was mumble an apology and pull my dress over my head. I didn't even bother with shoes. I could run faster barefoot.

And run I did. I raced along the sidewalk until I saw a cab, then I leapt into it.

The driver twisted around, his face a mask of concern. "You want me to call someone? The police?"

"No, no, I'm fine," I choked out, even though I was far from it.

I managed to keep it together until I got home. It was only when I crawled into bed that I allowed myself the luxury of tears. And I didn't even understand why I was crying them.

Normally, sleeping with a man left me satisfied, refreshed, even happy at a push, but not today. When the sun shone through the full-length window over my balcony, I just felt...dirty. Like I'd been used and tossed aside, although in reality, it was me who'd done the tossing.

In the morning, I tried to get out of bed, and the

instant I moved, I clutched at my temples. The pounding in my head didn't come from a hangover, though. Instead, it came from the realisation that in just a few short hours I had to visit the man whose face had haunted my dreams the night before.

The man whose face I'd seen as a stranger pounded into me the previous evening.

The man who, in all likelihood, had murdered a girl a decade younger than me in a vicious rage.

As ice flooded through my veins, I realised I was fucked again but in a very different way.

CHAPTER 18

THE THUMPING OF the rotor blades as I flew up to Redding's Gap didn't help my headache. Neither did Otis's incessant moaning on the last hour of the journey. If I had to make many more visits, I needed to seriously consider getting my own vehicle here because, otherwise, the town would have another murderer on its hands.

I posed for my strip search, feeling an uncharacteristic twinge of embarrassment at the hickey on my left breast. I didn't even remember getting it, but then again, my mind had been on other things—okay, people—last night.

As I expected, the prison officer was mighty interested in the photos of the crime scene, and not at all keen to let me keep them.

"Why not?" I asked. "What's he going to do, give me a paper cut?"

"We're not supposed to let you take anything in."

"His lawyer's allowed to take them in."

"That's different."

I plastered on a sickly smile. "How?"

"Because... I don't know, he's a lawyer."

"And all that would happen is that I'd write down the questions for him to ask and he'd write down the answers. This just cuts out the middleman."

The officer looked at his watch and sighed. Yup, break time was coming up. "Fine. Keep them. Just don't tell anyone it was me who let you."

This time my smile was genuine. "Thanks."

Ethan was already in the room when I arrived. His legs were shackled to the chair, and each hand was cuffed to a corner of the table. He looked up at me with a mixture of sadness and trepidation. What would I put him through today?

I wasn't even sure myself yet.

I settled myself onto the metal seat, the chill from the surface seeping through my jeans. Not even a little bit comfortable. At least I hadn't done anal last night.

Ethan's beard was longer this time, the lines on his forehead deeper. It seemed like being in here accelerated the ageing process. I guess it did, really. Because unless I figured out a way to help him, his life expectancy could be significantly shortened.

"How are you?" I asked.

It was a stupid question, but I didn't know where else to start. For all the time I'd spent thinking about what to say, it hadn't helped the words to come any easier.

He gave a tiny shrug. "Not good," he said, so softly I had to lean forward to hear.

Had I honestly expected any other answer?

"Have you been getting the time out of your cell you're entitled to?"

An hour a day in the yard, five times a week, plus three showers, each under the watchful gaze of a prison officer. It wasn't much.

"Yeah."

I noticed a cut on the edge of one eyebrow.

"What happened to your eye?"

Nothing. Silence.

"Ethan?"

"Someone hit me during rec time."

Fuck. He wasn't cut out for a place like this.

"Did the guards sort it out?"

He paled a shade. "They shot at him. From up in the towers."

High concrete walls topped with razor wire surrounded the exercise yard. Guards were stationed up there at intervals, and this was one of the few prisons to allow the use of live ammo.

"Did anything hit you?"

He shook his head, bottom lip trembling. "I didn't want to go outside again, but they said I had to."

Ethan might have been emotional, but so was I, and that only made things harder. He didn't belong here. Whatever temporary insanity had caused him to kill Christina, that wasn't who he truly was.

"Ethan, I want to help you, but I can't do that if you won't help me."

"I'm beyond help."

"I don't think you are."

"You don't know me."

"No, but I've spoken to people who do, and they're worried about you."

"Who?"

"Melinda. Lisa. Ishmael. Eli. Ty."

At the mention of Ty's name, his face clouded over. "Me and Ty don't get on so well now."

"I gathered that. But he hit you and you didn't retaliate. That says something about your character."

"Then why did I kill that girl?" Ethan's voice came

out as a strangled whisper, and the agony was plain to hear.

I turned the question back on him. "Why do *you* think you killed her?"

He looked away from me. "I don't know. In here, I've thought of nothing else, and I don't know."

With little to lose, I decided to push him. Either he'd open up or shut down, but this pissing around was getting us nowhere.

"What do you remember about that night?"

He shut down.

I forced myself to wait in the painful silence, hoping he'd fill the void, but he didn't.

What next? I could talk about something lighter, just to get him speaking again, but what would that achieve? Ultimately nothing. He'd still be stuck in here, waiting for Skinner to do his worst.

How could I convince a man who had nothing, and to whom I could offer nothing, to talk? In the end, I realised there was only one thing I could take away from him: myself. It might make him hate me, and that hurt me more than I cared to admit, but I had to do it anyway.

I got to my feet.

He looked up. "Where are you going?"

"I'm leaving. I can't help you if you won't make any effort to help yourself. I'm done."

His eyes burned into my back as I moved towards the door, the heels of my boots tapping out a slow beat on the concrete floor.

I'd raised my hand to knock, signalling to the guard that I wanted out of there, when I heard Ethan's voice.

"Dani, I don't remember anything."

Thank fuck. Not that he didn't remember but that he was talking. I erased my smile before turning back to him.

"Nothing. It's all blank," he said.

The door cracked open behind me.

"Are you coming out?" the guard asked.

He must have seen me through the viewing window.

"No, I'm staying."

I headed back to my seat, trying to hide the elation that I'd chipped away a tiny bit of Ethan's shell.

"You talk, or I walk."

"I don't know what to say."

"What's the last thing you do remember? Anything at all on that day?"

"I picked lunch up from the deli down the road. A meatball sub. I always liked those. I know I was supposed to play a gig that evening, and I guess I must have gone because that was where they said I met the girl. But I don't remember it. The last thing in my head is that I was in my studio at home, sorting out records to take with me. After that, it's all blank."

"Had you played at that club before?"

"A few times."

"I'll admit I'm kind of surprised you'd play a venue like that. How many Grammys have you won?"

"Six. But I enjoy playing the smaller places. They've got their own kind of energy, and I'm right there with the crowds. Liquid was easy because it was close to home."

"So assuming you went, what time would you have left your house?"

"My set was at nine, but I'd have had to get ready

first. Probably about seven."

"And what would you normally have done after you packed your stuff, before you left?"

He shrugged. "Nothing much. Maybe hung around in the studio. Played the guitar, messed around with some new mixes."

"The studio you ran with Ronan?"

"No, that's the commercial place. I've got my own in the basement at home. Nobody records there but me."

"There's a video of you in the bar with Christina, and you weren't wearing your mask. Why not? I thought you always wore it?"

"That must have been after my set. Sometimes when I've finished working, I'll pack up and leave then sneak back in again. Just to enjoy the music and the atmosphere without people asking for autographs or trying to shove demo tapes in my hand. Not for long, usually. Maybe an hour or so. That was the beauty of the mask. I never wanted the fame or the fortune the Ghost had, the screaming groupies, the hero worship. I look at some celebrities and they can't walk down the street without being harassed or followed. That's its own kind of prison. Your life doesn't belong to you anymore. But when I took the mask off, I was just me again. Just Ethan. I could go where I wanted and live a normal life without all the bullshit that came with the Ghost's name."

"Why do the job you did, then?"

"An accident, really. I believed in the music, and I liked to share it. More and more people started to listen, and the only way I could give everyone what they wanted was to become someone else."

"And how about women when you were just Ethan

again? Would you talk to them?"

"Sometimes." He looked away. "If they were pretty and sweet."

"And you'd take them home?"

"Sometimes," he said again. "Not often. Not if I thought they were going to want more."

We weren't so different after all, him and me. Neither of us wanted the burden of a relationship. Neither of us wanted to let anybody in.

"What about Christina? Is she someone you'd talked to in the past?"

I slid a photo of her over. Not one of the morgue shots, but a candid snapshot taken at college.

"The police already asked me that. I never saw her before. If I talked to her that night, I don't remember it."

"Is she the kind of girl you would have taken home?"

He shrugged. "Maybe. It would depend on what she was like to talk to. I may have been taking her home because I planned to sleep with her, but I still would have wanted to be able to have a decent conversation."

At least he had some standards. I'd have been disappointed if he'd admitted to fucking anything in a skirt. I sensed we weren't going to get any further with Christina at that moment, and my time with Ethan was short, so I switched to a different tack.

"You said earlier that with the mask off, you didn't get recognised, but Lisa said you had a stalker. Is that true?"

"Yeah. Lavinia."

"You know her name?"

That surprised me. Most people didn't tend to get

that close to the people following them, at least not until the police got involved.

"She wrote me letters, and that's what they were signed."

"How do you know they were from her?" I asked.

"She gave them to me."

"Hang on. Can we back up a bit here? Start at the beginning. How did you meet her?"

He fidgeted in his seat, trying to get comfortable, but it was an impossible job. "I played at Liquid a few months ago, but when I left, I wasn't as careful as I should have been. She must have followed me home, because the next day she showed up on my doorstep with a pile of CDs she wanted me to sign."

"And did you?"

"I tried to say I didn't know what she was talking about, and that was when she said she saw me play. I figured I might as well sign her stuff, and I asked her if she'd mind keeping my identity quiet."

"And I take it she did?"

"She seemed to like knowing something that hardly anybody else did."

"And the stalking?"

"She used to show up now and then. Sometimes she'd try and talk to me; other times she'd give me a letter or a gift. One week she'd hung around outside the house every day, and that was when I took Lisa for dinner. Lavinia backed off after she saw us together."

"So you were never on bad terms with her?"

"No. I used to feel sorry for her sometimes, standing outside in bad weather, but I didn't tell her that in case it encouraged her. She was an irritation more than anything."

"I'd be interested in talking to her as a character witness. She saw you at times nobody else did."

"I don't know how to find her," Ethan said.

"Do you still have her letters?"

"They're in my house, or at least they are if the police didn't take them."

"They probably didn't. Their investigation's been somewhat superficial so far."

Ethan described how to find the letters, which were in one of his desk drawers in the study. I'd seen nothing about them in any of the police files Mack had found so far.

"I'll take a look."

"Won't my house be sealed off still? By the cops?"

"Don't worry about that." I'd had plenty of practice with both lock picks and avoiding law enforcement officials—my shitty childhood had given me some advantages in later life. Then I had another thought. "Do you have any idea what could have happened to your house keys? The police report said they were missing from the scene of the accident."

"I always put them in the same place, along with my car keys. It's a habit so I don't lose them. I don't know where else they'd be."

"And where's that?"

"The table in my hallway has a hidden drawer underneath. If you press the front of the right-hand end, it pops out."

"Why hide them? Were you worried someone might steal them?"

"No, it was just convenient. Right next to the front door. But what have my keys got to do with anything?"

"I'm not sure," I admitted. If they were hidden in

the house, the cops could have missed them. "But if you opened the drawer to get your car keys, wouldn't you have picked up your house keys as well so you didn't get locked out?"

"On any other day, yes, but if I'd just killed a girl, I was hardly thinking logically, was I?"

No, but he was now. The conversation we'd just had was about as coldly rational as you could get, even though Ethan was stressed as hell. I could tell from the way he'd balled his hands tightly into fists, the skin stretched thin over his knuckles, and the quiet cough he gave to clear his throat before speaking. The pulse of his carotid artery when the light hit it at the right angle showed how fast his heart raced.

I tried to force a laugh, but it came out as more of a choking sound. "You've got a point there." I checked the clock. Ten minutes left. "Ethan, I've got something else I need to ask you."

At least he didn't go silent on me again. He just looked resigned. "What?"

"In your bedroom, it looks as if something was moved across the floor, but we can't work out what. I need you to look at the photos and tell me if anything's missing."

"Fuck." He bit his bottom lip, leaving dents in the flesh. "I was sick when the police showed them to me."

"These ones were taken after the body was removed."

"I doubt they're much better."

"Will you do it? Please?"

He let out a long sigh. "Fine. It's not like my stay in here could be much worse."

I spread out half a dozen pictures in front of him,

covering all angles of the room. He was right. Even though Christina was gone, the outline of her body on the bed in blood didn't leave much to the imagination.

Ethan glanced at the array, then a second later, he looked up, focusing on a spot behind my head as he tried to compose himself. His breathing quickened, the opposite of mine as I held my breath, waiting to see what he'd do next.

After two agonising minutes, he bowed his head and studied the pictures. Another minute passed before his eyes met mine again, and a tear ran down his left cheek. He tried to wipe it on his shoulder, but with his hands attached to the table, he couldn't quite manage it.

"I can't see anything missing. I didn't have a lot of stuff."

Another tear fell, and this time I couldn't help myself. I reached forward and wiped it away with my thumb, his cheek warm and soft under my touch.

A second later, the door opened. "No contact with the prisoner," the guard informed me. "Your time's up, anyway."

Ethan's other cheek was wet now, but there was nothing I could do. Times like this, I really hated my job. I gathered up the photos and leaned as close as I dared.

"I'll be back in a couple of days, okay?"

His lips quivered as he tried a smile. Tried and failed. "I'm not going anywhere."

CHAPTER 19

I WALKED OUT of Redding's Gap feeling pretty damn mixed-up. *Don't think of the last few minutes, Dan.* I pushed Ethan's tears to the back of my mind and concentrated on the good parts instead. I'd got Ethan to talk!

Now I just had to work out what everything he said meant. Were the letters still there? How about the house keys? What would Lavinia have to say when I found her? And I *would* find her.

As soon as the chopper touched down on the helipad at Riverley, I leapt out full of enthusiasm and ready to start digging, then realised Emmy was standing to the side, watching me.

"What?"

She handed me a bulletproof vest. "We're getting straight back into that."

"Where are we going?"

"A mall to the north that we've got the security contract for."

Ana ran up, dressed in black, and I eyed up the gun on her hip and the duffel bag full of equipment she carried.

"I'm guessing this isn't a shopping trip?"

"Nope. This is far more entertaining."

Great. Just great.

I spent the rest of the afternoon assisting with a tense hostage negotiation, which is to say I was the eyes out the front while Wonder Woman and her psycho sidekick snuck around the back and disabled the hostage taker.

All that drama because the guy behind the counter at Starbucks served someone close to the snapping point the wrong kind of coffee.

At least the deadly duo was cheerful on the way back.

"What did you think of the new Taser?" Ana asked.

Emmy crinkled her nose. "I'm not sure I liked the way he flopped around like that."

"Nothing is ever going to be as neat as a .22 round to the head."

Jeez, I was glad those two met up. They were both as crazy as each other. Although I had to admit, normally I'd have joined in with the banter. Instead, I tuned out their conversation because all I could think of was the afternoon I'd wasted helping them rather than Ethan. It was another afternoon he'd spent inside a cell while I'd been free, and I was growing more and more convinced he didn't deserve to be there.

First, I needed to get into his house. Was the police guard still there? Not that a sentry would stop me, but it would give us one less thing to work around.

"How do you feel about a bit of breaking and entering?" I asked Emmy as we exited the helicopter.

"I'm always up for that. When and where?"

"Ethan's place. I'll have to plan it."

"See? I told you this case would be fun."

"Fun. Right."

Emmy nudged me, grinning, still high on

adrenaline from earlier, no doubt. "You always love a challenge."

"Right now, I'd rather flip burgers."

"Liar."

I'd diverted my calls to Leah while I was out, and when I returned to the office, I found I had a message from Ronan. Ethan's manager was back, and he'd be at Spectre tomorrow morning if I wanted to speak to him?

Did I ever.

Harold Styles was the person who'd spent the most time day-to-day with Ethan over the past few years, not to mention one of the few who'd known the Ghost's true identity, and I couldn't wait to get his take on things.

I sent Ronan a text to let him know I'd be there then tried to get some sleep. Tried being the operative word. Sleep wasn't being kind to me at the moment. Over and over again, I wiped Ethan's tears from his face, and by the time the world finally went black, I was crying my own.

The next morning, I stifled a yawn as I walked into Spectre Productions. At least this time I didn't need to go under false pretences, although four of the women stopped me on the way through to ask whether Cade would be coming back.

Ronan instantly became my new hero when he pushed a cup of coffee over to me. "Here, I just got this, but you look like you need it more than me."

A strong Americano? Boy, did I ever.

"Thanks. You're a lifesaver."

"How's Ethan?"

"He's holding up, but being in that place is taking its toll."

"How's...you know, the case?"

"A few interesting things have cropped up."

"But you can't talk about them, right?"

I shook my head. "Sorry."

I barely knew Ronan, and I was wary of discussing specifics with anyone involved in an investigation. Especially this investigation, where I had a feeling things weren't as they seemed.

He shrugged, accepting. "It's okay. As long as you're doing your best for Ethan, that's fine by me. Harold's just got in, but he's on the phone." Ronan waved at a red light on his own console. "I'll take you through as soon as he gets off it."

I sipped my coffee while Ronan took a call of his own, and after fifteen long minutes, the light next to Harold's line blinked off. About time. Having to be patient was the thing I liked least about this job.

The instant Harold opened his mouth, I knew I wasn't going to like him. Probably because the first words out of it were, "My, aren't you a pretty little thing."

The comment was addressed at my chest, and believe me, there was nothing little about that.

I stuck out my hand, trying not to cringe openly when Harold took it in his and kissed it.

"Daniela di Grassi. It's good to finally meet you," I lied.

"Likewise. Ronan tells me you've got some

questions about Ethan. Such a terrible business, that. It just goes to show how you can know someone for years yet not really know them at all, doesn't it?"

So Harold thought Ethan killed Christina? Strange that the man who'd probably seen more of him than anyone had a different opinion to everybody else.

"I guess it does. I understand you were closer to Ethan than most?"

Harold preened a little. "I always believe in representing my clients to the best of my ability."

Good non-answer. "Do you have many other clients besides Ethan?"

"Elastic Trickery, plus a couple of solo artists. Did Ronan tell you about the band?"

"He said Ethan discovered them."

Harold smiled at me, as if he was surprised my tiny brain had managed to remember that fact. "He did. And since this mess began, their bookings have gone through the roof. No publicity is bad publicity, eh?"

Unless of course you were stuck in a super-max like Ethan.

"So, I take it you've been busy, then?"

"Oh, yes. Meeting after meeting after meeting. I've spent so much time on planes it's played havoc with my skin."

He stroked a dry patch on his face to emphasise his point.

Asshole.

"But what about Ethan? Have you been in contact with him?"

Not that Harold would have got very far if he *had* tried to call, but I was interested in his answer. I had a feeling I knew it already.

He shifted in his chair. "I didn't think that was a good idea."

"Why not? Don't you think he could use some support?"

"I can't be seen to be condoning murder."

"So you think he did it?"

"From what I've heard on the television, the evidence speaks for itself."

"But you know Ethan. Didn't the news surprise you?"

"Well, of course. But you never can tell, can you?"

"Can I ask you a few questions about Ethan's behaviour before the incident?"

"I guess, but I'm not sure what the point would be. I didn't see him on the day that poor girl died."

"I'm trying to build up a picture of who he was so I can work out what might have made him act so out of character."

Harold reached out and ran his fingers along my arm, making me want to chop them off. "All right. Since you asked so nicely."

Half an hour later, the only new thing I'd learned was that Harold Styles was an even bigger prick than I initially thought.

He managed to turn every facet of the conversation to himself. How worried he'd been about his career when Ethan got arrested. The hurt he'd felt that Ethan had been so stupid and broken their partnership. His fear that his earnings might drop as a result of Ethan's antics.

And he did all that while sitting close enough for our knees to touch.

What surprised me most out of the meeting was

that if Ethan had indeed decided to kill somebody, it hadn't been his manager. Ol' Harry was lucky it wasn't Emmy asking the questions because she'd have plotted his murder by now.

He sat back in his chair and stretched his arms over his head. "I must say, that wasn't a bad little discussion, was it? Can I interest you in joining me for lunch?"

Only if I had time to shoot back home and pick up some arsenic first. "Sorry, I have to get to my next meeting."

"Maybe another time, then?"

"Maybe." Right after me, Satan, and Osama bin Laden all went ice skating together.

A little bit of sick came into my mouth as he leaned down and kissed me on the cheek, then I escaped back to Ronan's office.

He laughed when he saw my face.

"Dare I ask what you thought of Mr. Styles?"

"Not unless you're fond of expletives. My only question is *why*?"

Ronan knew straight away what I meant. "When Ethan first met him, he wasn't so bad. Harold had contacts, and he got him some decent gigs to start with. I don't think Ethan's ever forgotten that."

"But now?"

Ronan gave me a wry smile. "As Ethan developed his talent, Harold developed his ego."

"What did Ethan think of that?"

"He didn't like it, but he put up with it. More than once I hinted that he should dump Harold, but he didn't. Ethan's non-confrontational."

I was beginning to understand that, and I didn't bother to hide my grimace. "I couldn't work with that guy."

"Most of the time, I find it difficult, but as long as Harold kept getting bookings and organising shows, I didn't have a reason to push for change. But now? I'm worried about where Ethan being away will leave the business. Harold essentially controls it at the moment."

"Is he a shareholder?"

"No, but he and Ethan are the only directors. And one of the girls in accounts told me Harold's already given himself a raise."

I hated the man more with each passing second. "I'll talk to Ethan, see if I can persuade him to do anything."

And if that didn't work, I'd speak to Emmy. She'd probably be easier to convince.

CHAPTER 20

YOU KNOW WHEN someone gives you a surprise gift, and you get all excited, and then it turns out to be shit? Well, that was what happened to me on Thursday.

"I got you security camera footage from the club, the night Ethan met Christina," Mack informed me, sounding chipper.

I would have been thrilled if it hadn't been ten past five in the morning. Damn Mack and her crazy work hours. Not that she woke up early. No, Mack was practically nocturnal at the moment and hadn't yet gone to bed.

"Can you send it over?"

"The link'll be in your inbox in a few seconds."

I couldn't function without coffee, and since I was awake now anyway, I went to the kitchen and fired up the machine. One double espresso later, and I'd rejoined the land of the living. I meandered over to the couch, turned on the big screen, and pressed play.

The picture quality was better than I'd hoped for. Not as good as the top-of-the-range system in Emmy's club, but when I zoomed in, it was easy to make out people's expressions. The camera was mounted high up on the wall, and after a minute or so, I saw Ethan walk into frame, his arm around a blonde.

Christina.

A pang of something hit my chest, making my breath hitch. No way. That was *not* jealousy.

Neither of them seemed in a hurry as they sauntered over to the bar. Ethan leaned down and whispered something into Christina's ear, and she laughed, her face open and happy. As they waited for drinks, Ethan tucked her against him protectively, and she rested a palm against his chest. How the hell did that night end in carnage?

I watched as they had a drink, then another, and after that, they hit the dance floor. Fuck me, Ethan could move. It was hard to reconcile the shy guy I'd met with the man on film, shaking his hot ass while a crowd of girls gave Christina icy stares.

And it wasn't just the girls. Men were watching Christina too. She had the looks and she had the moves, and every time she flicked her long hair back, more heads turned. There was no doubt they were the sexiest couple in there that night.

The pair of them kept it up for almost an hour. I fast forwarded through some of it, firstly because I didn't think it would help me much and secondly because I couldn't bear to watch the happiness before the storm hit. I slowed the tape again when they left the dance floor, hand in hand, and headed back towards the bar.

Before they got there, Ethan pulled Christina tight against him and kissed her. Not a sweet kiss, not a gentle kiss—it was an "I want to rip your clothes off" kind of a kiss.

Holy smoke.

I thought they'd been going for another drink, but it seemed as if they'd changed their minds. They veered towards the door, arms wrapped tightly around each other's waists.

The last steps of a dead woman.

The last steps of a condemned man.

I stopped the film, their shadows still on the screen, my eyes fixed on the image.

I didn't get it. I genuinely didn't get it. They'd been so into each other, and Ethan looked out for Christina whenever strangers came near. Why would he hurt her himself?

I was still puzzling over it when Mack called again.

"You are never going to believe what I've found."

I could tell from her breathless tone it was something good. Mack rarely got excited over anything but computer code, and I doubted she'd be calling me about that.

"Emmy ate pineapple on a pizza?"

Normally if she caught sight of that topping, drastic measures were taken. Last time someone put a slice in front of her, she blew it up with one of Nate's explosive pens.

"Nope."

"Ana sat through an entire episode of *X-Factor*?"

Ana's attention span for reality television was even shorter than her fuse.

"Guess again."

"Black's Aunt Miriam's signed up as a volunteer at the animal shelter?"

The only thing that bitch hated more than dogs was showing compassion to any living creature.

"Getting colder. For a detective, you're not very imaginative."

"I give up. Just tell me already."

"Fine." She sounded a little disappointed. "Christina was a hooker."

"Sorry, come again? For a moment there, I thought you said Christina was a hooker?"

"Otherwise known as Crystal."

"Holy shit!" I whispered. "How the fuck did you find that out? And how the fuck didn't the police?"

"I guess they didn't look that hard, although it wasn't the easiest thing in the world to find. I ran her face through that image recognition program that Luke wrote and it trawled the internet for me. She popped up on a website catering to the higher end of the market. It's called 'Rubies are a Man's Best Friend', the rubies in question being the girls they're hiring."

A hundred thoughts flew through my mind, and none of them were pleasant. Had Christina been working on the night she died? Had she and Ethan met in the club, just two lonely hearts out for a bit of fun, or had he booked her in advance?

"What's her going rate?" I asked Mack.

"The girls on the site are rated one to five rubies. She's a four. I got Logan to call, and that means her rates start at four grand a night."

"We're in the wrong profession."

"That's just for the company. Apparently, any extras are agreed between the girl and her 'friend.'"

I guessed straight sex would add another thousand, maybe two. Ethan certainly had that kind of money; I just hadn't imagined him spending it on prostitutes. Had I been wrong about him?

"I wonder if they could have had a row over money?"

"Or perhaps exactly what these 'extras' would

entail."

"It's possible. The complete lack of motive is something that's been puzzling me, and this could give him one."

I'd almost convinced myself that everyone else had misjudged Ethan, but this new information made me look at him in a different light.

What if Mr. White had another side to himself that he kept hidden?

One that he didn't show to Ronan, Melinda, or Lisa? Or me?

Right now, I didn't know the answer, but since I'd been sucked into this mess, I was damn well going to find out.

Chapter 21

STUPID O'CLOCK IN the morning, and the helicopter door rattled as I slammed it shut. Fuck this shit.

I was furious with Ethan because he'd kept his penchant for prostitutes from me and angry with myself for having the wool pulled over my eyes. No, not just wool. A whole fucking sheep.

How could I have been so blind?

Otis was waiting for me when I landed in Redding's Gap, the car engine running and the air conditioning on full.

"Back again, eh? Waste of time, if you ask me."

"Good thing I didn't ask you then, isn't it?"

What I didn't admit was that I was beginning to think he was right. My short tone gave him pause, and we spent the rest of the journey in silence. Thank goodness for small mercies.

At the prison, the grim-faced wench whose job it was to search me was in a temper as foul as mine, but I wasn't in the mood to take any of her shit.

"Strip," she commanded.

"Go on, take a good look. I bet it's not often you get to see thighs without cellulite."

That got me a cavity search.

And the cavity search earned her a BOLO for her personal vehicle. I'd get Mack to add it to the police database later. Suck on that, bitch.

Ethan looked up at me when I stomped into the room, a tiny smile playing on his lips. Two days ago, I'd have found it endearing, but now I wanted to slap it right off his face. Maybe I would have if it hadn't been for the eyes I knew were watching.

I'd barely sat down before I started. I couldn't help myself.

"Did you forget to tell me something?"

The light in his eyes faded, replaced by confusion. "What?"

"When you said you took women home to fuck, you didn't think it might be pertinent to mention that you paid them?"

"What are you talking about?"

"Christina. Or did you know her as Crystal? She was a fucking hooker."

He shook his head, the only part of him that wasn't secured to something. "No. No way. I wouldn't have paid her."

"Don't lie!"

"Dani, look at me." An urgency in his tone made me pause. "I've never paid a woman for sex. Not once. Believe me when I say I haven't needed to."

"Girls like that don't work for free, Ethan. Not when they can earn four thousand bucks a night by spreading their legs."

"She didn't get four thousand bucks from me."

"You don't know that. You already said you don't remember."

"I remember what I was doing earlier in the day, and at no point do I recall thinking, 'Hey, maybe I'll hire a girl for the night and have her meet me in a nightclub.' I wouldn't even know where to start."

"The internet?"

"I didn't even have a computer. The screen on my laptop failed, and it was at the repair shop. They've probably still got it. If you don't believe me, get them to check my search history. You won't find any sites full of half-naked girls."

The thing was, I almost did believe him. And I could certainly understand the bit about not having to pay girls to sleep with him.

"Some men get a thrill out of it," I tried again.

"I wasn't one of them. When I'm with a woman, I want her to feel pleasure from my touch, not because I'm gonna slip her a couple of large afterwards."

"What if you'd got her home, and then she asked for money? If she'd led you on?"

"I'd have shown her to the door."

"How about if you were turned on? Aroused? If you wanted to get your rocks off and she was right there?"

"I've got a hand and an imagination, Dani. And, believe it or not, some morals."

The stubborn side of me wouldn't give up. "Well, I still think somebody had to have paid her."

"It wasn't me."

We looked at each other.

"What if...?" I started.

My words fizzled out as my brain went into overdrive.

What if somebody else had hired Christina and told her to pick up Ethan for the night? The tape didn't show their initial meeting. What if instead of him approaching her, it had been the other way around?

But how did he end up killing her? That was the bit

that didn't fit in all of this. I could only think of two possibilities. Drugs, or...

"Ethan, did you ever touch drugs? Indulge in a few recreational pharmaceuticals?"

"I took Molly once, years ago. Scared the shit out of me. Nothing since."

...he didn't.

Was that possible? Could somebody else have been in the room with them?

I thought of the stray hair. The police had assumed it came in on Christina's clothes, but what if it hadn't? Then there was the messed up blood.

Could something as vile as that be staged? How? Don't get me wrong, I'd taken lives before, but on the rare occasions I did it in cold blood, everything was neat and tidy. Same with Emmy. I wasn't sure where to start with a scene like the one in Ethan's bedroom.

But I knew several people who'd have a better idea.

"Dani?" Ethan's voice cut into my thoughts. "What if someone else hired her?"

Way ahead of you there, buddy.

"That's what I'm wondering. What if she was working that night, and you didn't realise?"

"Why would someone do that?"

"To make it look like you killed her."

His eyes widened. "That's crazy."

It was Sir Arthur Conan Doyle who said, "When you have eliminated the impossible, whatever remains, however improbable, must be the truth." I had that quote framed over my ornamental fireplace as a reminder to keep my mind open.

While I couldn't quite say the other scenarios were impossible, none of them fitted with the man sitting in front of me. What if there was another option? A big ol' can of worms just waiting to be opened?

Well, I always did like fishing.

"Crazier than you killing her yourself?" I asked Ethan.

"I don't know." Desperation crept into his voice. "The cops told me I did it, no question."

"It wouldn't be the first time they've been wrong."

"But why was I in the car? The police said I was on the run, trying to escape from what I did."

"Maybe you were trying to get away from whoever was in the house instead? If there was a nut with a knife in my bedroom, I'd have run too."

"I guess." Ethan paused as he turned that over in his mind. "I thought I deserved to be in this hellhole if I could kill someone like that."

"Perhaps you should be trading places with somebody else."

For the first time, I heard a new note in his voice. Hope. "What the hell should I do now?"

I thought for a minute, then gave him an answer he probably didn't want to hear. "You do nothing. If there *is* a murderer running around out there, I don't want to tip our hand. I want him to feel safe while I hunt for him. Or her."

"Her?"

"I'm not ruling anything out."

Women were every bit as dangerous as men, sometimes more so. The Blackwood team was living proof of that.

He closed his eyes. "Dani, what if someone tries to hurt you as well?"

"I'm tougher than I look."

"Why are you doing this?"

A good question. I could say it was because Emmy was a bitch, but deep inside, I knew that wasn't true. She dumped the case on me to make a point. Once she'd made it, I could easily have palmed it off on one of my team when she lost interest. But I didn't.

The truth was, I was intrigued, first by Ethan's apparent breakdown, and now by the realisation that all might not be as it seemed. The little girl in me, the one that always asked "Why?" wanted answers.

And although I didn't want to admit it, there was another reason. And that was Ethan himself.

"Because I believe in justice."

"Thank you." His voice was hoarse. "I wish I could say more, or do more, but I can't. Just thank you."

I itched to reach over and squeeze his hand, but I couldn't. Instead, I tore my eyes away from his and forced myself to stand.

"I can't come back until next week, but if I have more questions, I'll send Lyle. Talk to him, yeah?"

"Okay. Stay safe. Nothing else matters. I don't matter. Just stay safe."

That was a lie. Ethan did matter, and more than I wanted to let on.

Instead, I gave a half-hearted nod. "I'll do my best."

CHAPTER 22

MY FIRST CALL when I escaped from prison was to Mack.

"Is there any more footage from the club? I want to know if Ethan had been expecting Christina, or if he approached her in there." Or maybe something else.

"You mean whether he'd pre-booked?"

"Exactly."

"Sorry, that was the only film on the server."

There had to be more cameras. *Had* to be. No club the size of Liquid had only one. They needed to stay alert for theft, drugs, and assault, and that meant having eyes everywhere.

"I did find out something else, though," Mack continued. "You know Christina's roommate?"

"Stefanie?"

Her details had been in the police file. She'd been interviewed after the body was found, although the transcript consisted mostly of sobbing.

"Stefanie is also known as Sable. She gets three rubies."

Holy hell. "Nice one, Mack. Can you get me her address? I think I should head over for a little chat."

"Sending it now, and I've got another piece of good news."

"What is it?"

"Luke's mom's delayed her visit, so you get a stay of execution on dinner. She got through to the next round of some tennis tournament, which takes precedence over her son."

Sad, but on balance, I had to be happy for Luke because his mom was a bitch. And it also gave me more time to work the case.

Two roommates, two call girls, one murder. Were they involved in something together? This puzzle had more pieces than I ever could have imagined.

According to Mack, Stefanie lived in an apartment block on the edge of the city. A nice enough area, but when Christina was alive, the pair of them could have afforded something better with all their rubies. Was the rest going to their education? A drug habit? Fancy vacations?

Mack had helpfully included Stefanie's class schedule, and I saw she had a business lecture until five. In the meantime, I decided to confirm my suspicions. My next call was to Emmy.

"Have you been to Liquid recently?"

"Getting bored of Black's? Is it time for a refurb?"

"No, I just need to find out how many cameras they have, and I thought you might know."

Emmy noticed things like that. Black, her husband, had trained it into her since she was a teenager.

"Oh. Yeah, there's loads. If you keep your head down and hug the right-hand wall, then cut across by the first pillar, you can get to the manager's office without being spotted. Other than that, you'd better smile."

I didn't even want to know. "So if I was looking for a camera covering the area beyond the bar, I'd be in luck?"

She thought for a second. "There are three."

"What do you think the chances are that they'd still have the tapes from the night Ethan was there?"

I did some sums in my head, but Emmy did them faster. "Twenty-three days since the murder? You should be good. If they haven't changed in the last couple of months, they'll be on a thirty-day loop."

Again, didn't want to know. "Thanks, bitch."

"Always happy to be of service. Are you on your way back?"

"Just climbing into the helicopter."

The trip to Riverley couldn't go fast enough for me. The instant I touched down, I was out and jogging across the lawn.

"Why are you running? Is there a shoe sale on that I haven't heard about?" Bradley called.

He was over by the back terrace, standing next to a pink swan taller than he was. There were going to be words about that, I was sure.

"I need to get to a nightclub."

He looked at his watch. "Bit early for that, isn't it?"

"It's for work."

"That's what they all say. Do you want me to do your make-up?"

"No time for that."

I blasted through the kitchen, startling Emmy's housekeeper. Normally I'd hit a midday slump and coffee would be calling out to me, but today I was wide-awake as I ran past the espresso machine. I needed keys, any keys—I didn't care which ones. I punched in the code to the key cabinet and pulled out the first set that came to hand.

Oh joy, it was Emmy's Corvette again, the car that started all this. I guess that was kind of poetic. A minute later, I was in the driver's seat and flooring the beast out of the driveway. The driver of the truck I just missed laid on his horn, but I just gave him a wave and mashed my foot to the floor. Right now, I had more important things on my mind.

Liquid was dark in the day, a contrast to nighttime when it was lit up with enough bulbs to rival the Las Vegas Strip. I rattled the front doors. Locked. Never one to give up, I meandered around to the service alley to find the smoking door. Every establishment like that had one, and it was usually unlocked. Heaven forbid people should have to fiddle with a key before they could get their hourly fix of nicotine.

Yup, there it was, a nondescript grey door wedged by a folded-up pizza delivery flyer. I pulled it open and headed into the gloom.

My shoes squeaked on the concrete as I walked down the hallway, listening out for any employees. A cleaner shuffled by pushing a cart, but I ignored him and he ignored me. That wasn't who I was looking for.

The place was almost deserted, and I managed to get all the way to the manager's office without seeing another soul. The door was ajar, and a man I vaguely recognised as the owner sat at a desk, bent over his laptop.

"Knock knock," I said.

He looked up with a start. "Who the hell are you?"

Slimy, Emmy had said, and the man's little piggy eyes roamed over me as I handed over a business card and explained. It felt like I was doing that a lot lately. Explaining. Perhaps I could save time by having some flyers made up? Dan di Grassi, specialist in impossible investigations, difficult questions, and crashing cars. Although I didn't mention the hooker part. Some things were better kept to myself.

"Blackwood, you say?"

"Yes. You really should consider securing your fire exit."

"You'd better not be here to spy on the competition."

I almost snorted; Black's had Liquid beaten hands down. But I managed to refrain.

"Not at all. I'm only here because of the murder, and nobody wants to see Ethan White get the death penalty."

"I spoke to him a few times when he played here. The Ghost. Always seemed like a straight-up sort of guy. Packed the place out too."

"He played good music."

"More than that. He could read the crowd. They'd respond to each other, and the atmosphere he'd create was electric. None of my other acts manages to do that. Shame he's not around anymore."

I didn't want to get stuck discussing the past. I was more worried about the future. "Actually, I'm looking for information on the last night he was in here, the night he met the victim. Did you talk to him?"

"Sorry. My kid was sick, so I had to leave early."

"I've seen a tape of White by the bar, but I was hoping you might have something more."

"Yeah, I was surprised the cops didn't ask for those. Although I watched them myself after the story broke and there's nothing earth-shattering. He's minding his own business, the girl comes up and talks to him, and she persuades him to go with her. She was real pretty. I mean, what man would have said no?"

"Hang on, she approached him?"

"Yeah. He was sitting at a table, nursing a beer, and she went over to him."

"Like she knew him?"

"No, not like that. I'd say they'd never met before. He didn't want to get up at first, but as I said, she was pretty."

"Can I take a look?"

"Sure."

Son of a bitch, he was right. Unless they were acting out some weird stranger fantasy, they'd never met. When Christina first went up to Ethan, he shook his head and turned away. Only when she persisted did he start to talk. It was her who'd instigated their meeting, not him.

But why? Could it be because she simply liked Ethan, or did someone put her up to it? What the hell did it all mean?

Chapter 23

AS SOON AS I left Liquid, I drove straight to the address Mack had given me for Stefanie's apartment. The building was well kept but not ostentatious, the kind of place young professionals on a reasonable salary tended to gravitate towards.

There was no doorman, just a panel full of buzzers, and I pressed one after another until somebody let me in. I didn't want to announce myself to Stefanie just yet. It was a lot easier to get someone to talk to you if you had your foot blocking their door, and I couldn't do that from outside.

And it was a lot easier to get someone to talk to you if they were in. After I'd waited for twenty minutes, I came to the conclusion that Stefanie wasn't.

She was probably out working. The bills weren't going to pay themselves, and now she had nobody to help with the rent.

I felt like kicking the door, but it was a glossy white and a black mark left by my biker boot probably wouldn't go down well. Instead, I walked back out to Emmy's car, only to find a bird had shit on the windscreen. And when I say shit on, I mean covered. The perfect end to a perfect afternoon.

Following a trip to the car wash, I detoured past Ethan's house out of curiosity on my way back home.

Even now, several weeks after the murder, a patrol car was still parked outside. The officer at the wheel looked bored as hell, but I imagined he'd wake up fairly sharpish if I turned into the driveway.

Back at Riverley, I spent the evening catching up on my normal caseload, which I had to admit was suffering. Although I worked with a team, I was lead on several of the trickier investigations—two murders, a complicated web of fraud, and a spate of robberies, plus I had to oversee everyone else's work. If something didn't give soon on Ethan's case, I'd have to consider seconding another manager over to the Richmond office to assist with everything I was neglecting. Emmy would be thrilled. I'm sure it wasn't what she'd had in mind when she gave me the case but tough luck.

As I lay awake that night, staring at the ceiling, I couldn't help thinking of Ethan. While I was on a memory foam mattress with thousand thread count sheets, he was on a steel slab with a thin blanket.

I needed to get him out of there.

The next day was a Saturday, and according to Stefanie's schedule, she didn't have any classes. She had no job either, apart from Rubies, at least not one she paid taxes on. I only hoped she'd gone home the previous night rather than staying out with a client.

I knocked lightly on her door just after eight and was rewarded by it cracking open. A face I recognised from Mack's picture peered out at me over a security chain.

Although it was the same girl, she looked to have

aged five years since the photo was taken. I didn't know if that was because she'd been in the business a long time, or because the last few weeks had taken their toll.

"Can I help?" she asked.

She wouldn't meet my eyes, and she kept her weight behind the door, ready to push it shut. Good thing I'd worn steel toecaps.

"I was hoping to have a chat about Christina."

There it was. The door thunked against my foot, and shock registered on Stefanie's face when she couldn't close it.

"W-w-who are you? Are you a reporter?"

"I've been hired to investigate her death."

"Why? We all know who did it."

"There are a few loose ends, and the prosecution wants to get them tied up before the case starts. Nobody wants a killer to get off on a technicality."

Her frown lines smoothed a little. "Oh, so you're working with Mr. Skinner, then?"

"Jay and I go way back."

"Hold on while I take the chain off."

At some point, I was going to have to give this girl a lesson in safety. She didn't even ask for ID.

The home Stefanie had once shared with Christina was far nicer than anything your average college student could hope for. Bright and modern, it still managed to have a homely twist. A red corner sofa covered in colourful cushions was the focal point of the living room, and Stefanie motioned me over to sit on it.

"Would you like something to drink?"

"A coffee would be great. Black, no sugar."

China clinked in the kitchen, and she came back with a couple of mugs and a package of cookies, which she placed on the coffee table in front of me. Polite but nervous.

"Sorry, I've only got butter cookies. Nothing with chocolate."

"I love butter cookies."

Stefanie picked up her own drink and cradled it in her hands as she took a seat facing me, legs tucked up underneath her.

"What can I do to help?"

"I've been doing some research, and something's come to light about Christina's, er, profession that might not be looked upon too favourably by a jury."

Her colour paled a few shades, and she reached forwards to put her mug down. Even then, she still splashed coffee all over the table because her hands were shaking so much.

"I was hoping nobody knew," she whispered.

I shrugged apologetically. "These things do tend to emerge once an investigation gets underway."

"Oh, hell. Are her parents going to find out?"

"That's quite likely. Once the questions start, witnesses are fair game."

She closed her eyes for a second before focusing them on mine. "Do you know about me?"

I nodded.

"My family will never speak to me again if this gets back to them."

"I'm not going to say anything, but I can't guarantee they won't find out through other channels." I paused, pretending to think. "If you can point us in the direction of anyone else who might be able to help, maybe we could keep your name out of this."

"You really think so?"

"I'll certainly do my best."

She took several deep breaths to compose herself before speaking again. "Then what do you want to know?"

"I'm trying to work out how Christina and Mr. White met. Whether it was through her work or whether she just met him on a night out."

"I'm sure it was work. I mean, Ethan White wasn't her type. Besides, she said she was going to give someone a birthday surprise."

A birthday surprise? I knew for a fact that Ethan's birthday wasn't for another five months.

"Did she say who?"

She shook her head. "No, but it had to be the Ghost, right? I mean, that was who she met."

I decided to go along with it. "More than likely. Did she elaborate on what kind of surprise?"

"She said it was a massage, and maybe a bit more, for a guy who liked kink."

"A massage?"

"You know, like the sensual kind. She almost forgot the massage oil and the gloves. She went out, then came back again five minutes later because she'd left them in her room."

"Gloves?"

"Leather ones, long, right up to her elbows. Apparently, he had a fetish for them. The person who booked her put the gloves and the oil in a silver gift box, but it wouldn't fit in Chrissie's purse, so she took them out."

I'd read the crime report at least ten times by now, and nowhere in it did it mention a bottle of massage oil or a pair of gloves. Could they have been overlooked?

And was Ethan really into that sort of thing? It didn't really jibe with his "pick a girl up in a club and take her home for the night" habit, but perhaps I was just projecting my own expectations onto him.

"Do you still have the box?"

She looked at her feet. "I threw it out."

"Did it have a label on it?"

"No, just a bow on the front and tissue paper inside."

"Do you have any idea how this surprise was arranged? Would it have been booked through the Rubies site?"

A tear leaked down Stefanie's cheek. "I think so. Chrissie only worked through Octavia, no other places."

"Octavia?"

"She runs Rubies. All the calls are fielded by them, and the guys don't get the girls' numbers. Unless…"

"Unless what?"

"I think Chrissie may have booked some of her regulars directly. We're not really supposed to do that, it's in our terms and conditions, but Octavia takes twenty percent."

"Christina wanted to cut down on the commission?"

"Maybe. I noticed a few months back she had a second phone, a cheap one. I don't know why she'd have needed it unless it was for them to call her."

"Do you have the number?"

Stefanie shook her head. "She never even told me about the phone, not officially. I just saw it in her purse."

Two phones. Neither of those had been found in Ethan's house, either. A brief footnote in the police report said Ethan was assumed to have disposed of

Christina's phone somewhere on his drive, and the search for it was ongoing.

And that second phone was the one I needed to find.

"So, her regulars, do you know who any of them were?"

"Not the specifics. One of them was a soccer player. She used to joke about him knowing what to do with his balls. And then there was the stockbroker who couldn't get it up half the time. She said it was a good thing his wallet was bigger than his dick, or she'd have to start calling in sick."

"Anyone else?"

"An older guy. Mr. Grand, she called him, like a play on Mr. Big from *Sex and the City*. He bought her gifts—perfume, flowers, that sort of thing. I think she secretly hoped it would lead to more."

"Any idea of his real name?"

"Sorry. We never spoke much about the details of work—not the people—just stupid stories sometimes. For me, once I'd finished a job, I didn't even want to think about what I'd just done, let alone discuss it over breakfast. Maybe one day I'll see the funny side like Chrissie did, but not now."

"So you don't enjoy the work?"

"Look, I grew up in a small town in Georgia. My family didn't understand why I wanted to leave, but if I'd stayed, they'd have smothered me. Then I had an accident and landed myself with big medical costs. Bills were mounting up everywhere—tuition, rent, my credit card—so I did it." She looked beyond me, her eyes fixed on a pigeon preening on the window sill. "I did it, but that didn't stop me from hating every single second. No matter how many showers I took, I still couldn't get the feel of them off me."

I saw the pain in her eyes as she spoke and heard the rawness in her voice. The Rubies website may have made her lifestyle look glamorous, but this was the reality.

"And Christina? How did she feel about it?"

"Chrissie was a business major, and that's how she approached the job. Her goal was to have enough money in the bank to buy her own house free and clear once she graduated, as well as paying for all her tuition. She worked out how many clients she needed to see each month and made damn sure she achieved it. The last few weeks, she was working almost every night— she was getting close to her fifth ruby, and she was determined to get it by her twenty-second birthday."

"No boyfriend then, I take it?"

Stefanie stared at me like I was crazy. "What kind of man would touch us? Girls like Chrissie and me? We're tainted goods."

"You mentioned earlier that Ethan wasn't Christina's type. What sort of man would she have gone for if she had the choice?"

"She liked sugar daddies. Mature men, powerful ones with money, the kind who gave her fancy gifts and paid her the big bucks."

"You sound like very different people."

"We were. That doesn't mean she wasn't my best friend. We could talk about anything apart from work, and she was just so damn cheerful all the time. Every day, it was like waking up to brilliant sunshine."

Until the storm came over.

"Did she have any enemies?"

"Nobody that I knew of." Another tear fell. "Everybody loved Chrissie."

I spotted a box of tissues on the sideboard and got up to fetch it. Stefanie took a handful and wiped her eyes.

"Dammit, I'm such a mess."

"It's only to be expected. This can't have been easy, and I appreciate you taking the time out to help."

"It's okay. I want justice as much as you do," she said, making me feel like a complete shit for lying to her.

"Can I leave my number in case you think of anything else?"

"Sure."

"And if I need to call, when's the best time to get hold of you?"

"Evenings, I suppose. I have classes in the day, and I quit work."

Which didn't particularly surprise me. "It sounds like that was the decision you wanted to make."

"It was. I only wish I'd done it sooner."

I smiled and squeezed her hand. "Even if you just want someone to talk to, call me. I'll always listen."

She gave a little sniffle and suddenly pulled me into a hug. "Thank you. You're really sweet."

Sweet? No. I was just hungry for justice.

CHAPTER 24

ONCE I'D LEFT Stefanie's apartment, I called Mack again. I was going to owe her a lot of favours when this was over.

"Mack, Christina had two phones, and they're both missing. Can you find out the call histories for either one?"

"Luke's better at the phone stuff than I am. I'll get him to take a look."

"And it looks like Christina met Ethan for work rather than pleasure. Stefanie says she only took clients through that one website, and I need to find out who booked her."

"I'll do that one myself."

I pictured Mack's lips pressing together in a thin line. Nope, she wouldn't want Luke browsing a website that was only a few scraps of lace and satin away from being porn.

"Thanks, sweetie."

As I climbed back into my car, I thought through the next steps. I had a nasty feeling the hard work was just beginning. Not only that, we now effectively had two cases: firstly, prove Ethan was set up, and secondly, find out who did it. And how.

The how part bothered me. Creating that scene hadn't been an easy job, especially with two victims adding an edge of unpredictability. Time to call in the experts.

"Emmy, can you do me a favour?"

"I might consider it if you bring my car back intact."

Hmm. She sounded kind of grumpy.

"I haven't even scratched it yet. Anyhow, I need to know the best way of staging the murder at Ethan's."

"You've decided that's the right path?"

I gave her a quick recap. "There are too many gaps in the evidence. The police dropped the ball in a lot of areas. But for me, the biggest issue is the lack of motive. Nobody, Ethan included, can work out why he'd want to kill Christina, but if someone wanted to frame him and she was just collateral damage, that makes more sense."

"If somebody wanted him out of the picture, why do it this way? Why not simply shoot him? This wasn't just assassination; it was character assassination."

That thought had crossed my mind as well. "Someone had a problem with him personally. They wanted him to suffer."

"Sex, money, revenge. It's always one of those."

And so far, all the evidence pointed to the first of those motives. Which made me focus on the other two.

"Apart from Ty, Ethan doesn't seem to have any enemies."

"Money, then. He's got plenty of that."

"And right now, he can't spend any of it." But somebody else could.

"Dan, whoever did this was angry as fuck as well as unstable. Whether he had a grudge against Ethan, Christina, or life in general, I don't know, but tread carefully."

"I'm on tiptoes."

"Good."

With Emmy working on the logistics side of the murder, all I had to do was not crash her car. Oh, yeah, and make a list of suspects.

Number one had to be Harold, partly because he was an asshole and partly because he'd gained from Ethan's incarceration in some ways, namely his self-imposed pay raise and the publicity for his other clients. But he'd also lost his headline act. Would he have risked everything on an uncertain outcome? Elastic Trickery's success was by no means guaranteed. And ol' Harry had said himself he'd been worried before the extra bookings started to roll in.

Then there was Ty. He'd been angry enough to hit Ethan, and his animosity was obvious when I spoke to him, but did his blood still run hot? Now he'd lost Lisa for good, would he have sought further vengeance?

The stalker puzzled me too. Could she have been involved somehow? More than once, obsession had led to insanity, and just last night, the news channels had broadcast the story of an Oklahoma woman who'd accelerated into the side of her ex-fiancé's car when she saw him riding with his new girlfriend. The girlfriend died, the guy was left paralysed, and the spurned woman lost a leg, and all because she'd decided that if she couldn't have him, neither could anybody else.

What crazy thoughts lurked inside Lavinia's head? I needed to track her down and find out.

Who else would stand to gain from Ethan's absence? Although I liked him, I couldn't discount Ronan. He'd been in the shadow of his ex-bandmate for years. Perhaps he wanted another shot at hitting the charts, this time as a producer rather than a musician? What would happen to the studio with Ethan out of the picture? Like Harold said, no publicity was bad publicity.

And what about Christina? Why her? Why not Stefanie, for example? Was it simply a case of Christina being in the wrong place at the wrong time, or was she part of the plot? Could she have been double-crossed and turned into an unwitting victim?

Another possibility, however remote, was that Ethan had been the victim of a random attacker. Some psycho, high on drugs and his own fantasies, a freak who got off on violating women.

So many questions, so few answers. I needed a damn vacation. Tahiti, Bermuda, the French West Indies. A month of sitting on a beach with palm trees and cocktails and half a dozen bare-chested waiters, string bikinis and flip flops, and Ethan beside me to rub in my sunblock. Fuck! *Dan, stop thinking about him that way.*

But there was no rest for the wicked. I needed to start with what I had. Speaking to Ethan would have been the best option, but that wasn't possible for a few days, at least not in person. I could send Lyle, but... yeah. Lyle didn't understand nuance. Instead, I turned the car towards Spectre Productions.

Even though it was a Saturday, the place was still busy. The receptionist recognised me from my last visit and smiled.

"Are you here to see Ronan again?"

"Is he around?"

"He's in a meeting, but he'll be finished up in just a minute. Would you like a drink?"

"I'll never say no to coffee. Black, no sugar."

Two minutes later, she came back with my Americano and a cappuccino for herself. At least Spectre had invested in a decent coffee machine.

"Ronan said you were trying to help Ethan?" she said, settling back into her seat.

I didn't particularly want my involvement to be broadcast to the world, but since she already knew, I wasn't going to lie. "That's right."

"Well, good. It's about time somebody did. Everyone who's ever spent five minutes with Ethan knows he'd never have killed that girl."

"So everybody liked him?"

"Well, not everybody. This is the music industry— there's always drama going on, and it's usually blown out of all proportion."

"What drama was going on with Ethan?"

She looked around furtively then lowered her voice. "He came in with a black eye a couple of months ago, and he wouldn't tell anybody what happened."

"I already know about the altercation."

"Oh." She sounded a little disappointed. "I suppose Ronan told you about the lawsuit too?"

Lawsuit? What lawsuit? "No, he didn't mention that. Somebody was suing Ethan?"

"I'm not sure if it had gotten that far, but I overheard him discussing it with Ronan." She clapped a hand over her mouth. "Maybe I shouldn't have told you."

"No, you were absolutely right to share. It might help."

"Could you not tell Ronan you heard about it from me? I'm not normally one to gossip."

Yeah, right. "Sure, I won't let on. Who's suing him?"

"Uh, some DJ, I think?"

"Do you know his name?"

"Sorry."

Never mind. I'd just have to convince Ronan to tell me. "Anything else I should be aware of?"

She turned pink and shook her head just as Ronan walked through the doorway to her left.

"Daniela, this is a surprise."

He grabbed my hand and shook.

Yes, it was. I just loved surprises. Unannounced visits always got suspects more flustered, so I tended to drop by without notice a lot.

"I hoped you might have a minute?"

"Of course, come on through."

I drained the last of the coffee then followed him into his office. Music played quietly in the background, and he turned it off as I sat down.

"Just listening to some demos," he explained. "Ethan used to do most of that, but in his absence, those decisions are falling to me."

"Do you enjoy that kind of thing?"

"Truthfully? Yes, but I don't have time to do that and my day job. We need to hire extra help."

"Not an easy pair of boots to fill, I imagine."

"No, but I've got an old acquaintance who's interested. It'll be a good fit."

Convenient. "Is he anyone I've heard of?"

"She, actually, and I doubt it. Reena's talented, but she never quite managed to crack the commercial scene."

So with Ethan gone, Ronan was going to install a friend of his into the job. Just how close of a friend was she?

"What name does she perform under?"

"Reena Cassidy, pop with a folk edge. She mainly sings covers, but her own tracks are better."

"I'll make sure to look up some of her stuff."

Reena Cassidy. Someone else for Mack to delve into, just in case she was getting bored.

Ronan reached behind him and pulled a bottle of water out of a mini-fridge. "Want one?"

I shook my head.

He unscrewed his and took a swallow. "What can I do for you today? I assume this isn't a social visit."

"I've got a few people on my radar, and I'm trying to get a feel for them. I'm hoping you can help me out."

As well as giving me more of an insight into the man who is Ronan Pearce.

"Sure. Who do you have in mind?"

I'd already spoken to Ronan about Harold, so I skipped him. "Ty D'Angelo for starters."

"Ty was a hanger-on. Ethan's too nice; that's his problem. Ty was using him for his contacts and his studio, but he couldn't see it. Although the bust-up wasn't pretty, I'm glad he's not around anymore."

"Can you see him harbouring a grudge?"

Ronan stroked his chin while he thought. "In all honesty? No. I'd imagine him as the type to move onto his next victim rather than wasting time on the past."

"Have you seen him around recently?"

"He called a month or so ago, wanting to use the studio. He asked for a discount, but I told him no. We're fully booked, and even if we weren't, I wouldn't have given it to him."

"Nothing apart from that?"

"No."

"How about Lavinia? Have you seen her around?"

Ronan's brow furrowed in confusion. "Lavinia?"

"Ethan said she'd been following him around?"

"Oh, you mean bird woman?"

My turn to look puzzled. "Bird woman?"

"Black lady, small, kind of sad looking? Late thirties, early forties? The first time I saw her, she was wearing a sweater with canaries on it. I turned to Ethan and said, 'Look, bird woman,' and it stuck."

"He didn't tell me about that. Just that he saw her around, and she wrote him letters."

"Yeah, that's her. Ethan always got letters from crazies—most celebrities do—but bird woman was harmless. Every so often, she'd talk to him or give him a little gift, but mostly she just stared. One day when it was cold, he bought her a cup of coffee."

Well done, Ethan, you sure know how to deter a stalker.

"Did she ever seem upset? Do anything hurtful?"

"Not that I saw. I mean, she had to be sprung in the head, but not in a nasty way."

If Ronan was right about Ty and Lavinia, I was fast running out of suspects.

"You mentioned letters from crazies—did any of them stand out to you?"

"Ethan liked to open his own mail. Every so often, he'd tell me about a problem, but he didn't seem worried by anything recently.

"I also heard rumours of a lawsuit. What's happening with that?"

"Which one?"

Damn, there was more than one? "How about you

give me details on all of them? Why didn't you mention them before?"

"Lawsuits happen every week in this business. There's always some greedy asshole out to make a quick buck off the back of somebody else's success. It's nothing unusual."

"So what was happening with Ethan?"

"The most recent claim came from another DJ. He accused Ethan of stealing parts of his song."

Ronan's chuckle and shake of the head told me what he thought of that accusation.

"But you don't believe it?"

He turned to his computer. "Here, listen for yourself." He pushed a few buttons. "This is from DJ Steel."

A song played out through Ronan's tinny speakers. The beat was something I'd dance to in a club, but the drums were too heavy, and there was an annoying chirp every few seconds.

"And this is Ethan's."

This track was different, more urgent and definitely catchier. It was a song you'd hum along to on the radio then curse about all day because you couldn't get it out of your head. It was smooth, polished, and light-years away from DJ Steel's track.

"They don't sound anything like each other."

"Exactly. There's maybe a few notes in there that are the same, but that's just coincidence. I was with Ethan when he wrote it. He tried out all sorts of tweaks before he settled on that."

"So DJ Steel doesn't stand a chance?"

"None. I've seen his type before. All he wants is a blast of publicity from having his name associated with the Ghost's. By the time the suit gets thrown out, people will know who he is. Like they say, no publicity..."

"Is bad publicity," I finished. "So with Ethan being all over the news, whatever claims this asshole makes are going to get even more column inches?"

"That's possible, but don't you think murder's kind of a drastic marketing tool?"

"To any normal person, yes, but people have been killed over far less."

"In the paper last week, some teenager shot another in FoodLand over a donut. A damn donut."

I'd read that story, too. There was something seriously wrong with society when a sixteen-year-old kid couldn't even buy a snack after school without taking a bullet to the chest.

"Sometimes, I think the world's gone mad."

"You're not wrong. Do you want copies of the paperwork for the lawsuit?"

"I'd be much obliged."

"I'll email it over. Avoids printing out a ream of paper—got to save the planet, right?"

I was more concerned about saving Ethan, but email worked for me.

When I left, I'd added one more suspect to the list but taken several steps back with two others. And Ronan himself? He hadn't rung any alarm bells.

This fucking case was gonna be the death of me.

CHAPTER 25

WHEN I GOT home, I called Mack, but she was in a restaurant, about to chow down on a steak dinner. Slacker. No doubt she'd be having Luke for dessert, so I wouldn't get anything useful from her until tomorrow.

That meant I was reduced to doing my own searches at my kitchen counter while I ate instant noodles washed down with a bottle of beer. No, they didn't go together, but I was too tired to cook and too edgy not to drink.

I found several blogs where DJ Steel had accused Ethan of plagiarism, but so far, they'd been overshadowed by all the stories on the murder. Bummer for him. What was he planning next?

After that, I googled the Ghost. What did the mainstream media have to say about him? Well, he didn't get drunk, he didn't flout the law, he didn't fall out of clubs, and he didn't get into fights with other celebrities. There was the odd page of puffed-up, speculative bullshit, but they were few and far between until the story of the murder broke. No solid facts, no dramatic photos. The Ghost had certainly lived up to his name.

Even after Christina died, the articles had little personal information on Ethan. The same photos cropped up over and over—a grainy snapshot of him on stage with King, his mug shot, and one of him in court with Lyle just after he'd been arrested. Nothing on his early years, and Mack hadn't found anything so far either. To all intents and purposes, his life had started at sixteen when he met Ronan and joined the band.

He'd materialised rather than grown up.

Curiouser and curiouser.

As I slept that night, Ethan took centre stage in my dreams, and not in a good way. In a *very* good way. A way I shouldn't be thinking about him. My subconscious needed a reminder of my number one rule—I didn't screw around with clients.

Except the devil on my right shoulder had clearly been having words with her counterpart on Emmy's because she reminded me that technically, Ethan wasn't my client. The kids were. I was going to have to gag her, the little bitch.

Still flustered, I woke early and couldn't get back to sleep, so I decided to get back at Mack for her ridiculously early phone call the other day.

As the hands on my bedroom clock crawled past 5:00 a.m., I hit dial.

"Is it an emergency?" Mack croaked.

"Define emergency. I'm dying for coffee—does that count?"

"What do you want, Dan?"

"Just wondering how your research went yesterday."

There was a clatter as she dropped the phone. Sleepy Mack wasn't very coordinated.

"You still there?" she asked a few seconds later.

"Yup."

"Right, okay, I checked the Rubies website.

Whatever Christina was doing that night, she wasn't booked through them. They had her marked down as unavailable, but when I looked at the IP logs, she'd added that notation to the calendar herself."

Interesting. Was Stefanie right about Christina going it alone?

"Did you have any luck with her phones?"

"I've got the call history for her main number, but if she had another, it wasn't in her name."

"Anything good on the one you did find?"

"The odd call from an unregistered phone, but not much recently and nothing that looks like a pattern. The only regular callers were Stefanie and one Octavia Jackson, who—"

"Runs the Rubies website."

"Right. Her office screens the clients, makes the bookings, and emails the details to the girls."

"Did you look at the messages?"

There was a pause, and I imagined Mack putting on that indignant little pout of hers.

"Give me some credit, please. I went back six months, which is all that was available. Their hosting company had a server failure before that, and it turned out their backup policy wasn't as robust as it could have been."

Fucking great. One step forward and two back again. What if there had been a clue in the missing information?

"Did you find anything?"

"I'll send over a summary, but the only thing that jumps out was a couple of rendezvous with a congressman from Minnesota."

"Married?"

"Of course. But he was hosting a fundraising dinner at the time of the murder."

He could always have hired someone, but how did Ethan fit in? I shoved him down the list.

"Could you also run checks on a singer called Reena Cassidy and a DJ Steel?"

"Are you paying overtime?"

"I'll cook you dinner when this is over."

"If that's supposed to incentivise me, it's not working."

"How about I promise not to cook you dinner, ever?"

"That's more like it."

Although it was still early, I decided to head to Riverley. I needed to return Emmy's car before I broke it, and besides, her gym was better than the one in my building's basement.

When I arrived, I found out Emmy wasn't home.

"Something urgent came up in Florida. She flew out in the early hours," Oliver told me.

At 6:30 a.m., he was already working, scribbling on a yellow legal pad at the breakfast bar, dressed in yet another made-to-measure suit.

His attire didn't surprise me—Oliver didn't do casual—but the sight of Lyle sitting next to him made me raise an eyebrow.

"What are you doing here?" I asked Oliver.

"I figured somebody needed to turn Lyle here into a trial lawyer, and it's not the work of five minutes."

Lyle gave me a sheepish smile, his mouth full of cereal. He finished chewing then swallowed. "I'm learning a lot. Oliver's, like, a trial guru."

Oliver's expression didn't change, save for a tiny

quirk at one corner of his lips. "I wouldn't go that far. But you're learning. By the time the trial starts, you'll be ready."

At least they were getting along. More than that, I noticed a spark in Oliver's eyes that hadn't been there in a long time. Not since he suffered his own tragedy six years ago. I'd worried about him ever since, and even though Emmy invited him to hang out at Riverley, he rarely turned up. He avoided relationships too. Like me, he preferred one night of oblivion over anything lasting.

Would this case be the catalyst that finally brought back the old Oliver? I sure hoped so. And while he was here, I could pick his brains about this whole DJ Steel thing.

"Oliver, can I ask a..." I paused mid-sentence as my phone rang. Unknown caller. "Yeah?" I'd got my monosyllabic greeting from Emmy, she of few words.

A breathless voice greeted me. "Daniela?"

"Who is this?"

"It's Stefanie. We met yesterday?" she added, as if I might not remember.

I could barely hear her words. Her voice was a whisper, hindered further by a crackly connection.

"I remember. Are you okay?"

"Yes. Well, no. I don't know."

"What's happened?"

"S-s-somebody just tried to run me over. In the parking lot outside my building."

"What do you mean tried to run you over?"

"A car. They drove a car straight at me."

"Are you sure it wasn't an accident?"

"Yes. No, I mean, I don't think so. The car

accelerated as it came towards me, and when I jumped to the side, it swerved and tried again."

"Are you hurt?"

I heard a sniffle as she choked back tears. "Bleeding. My hands and knees are bleeding from where I dove out the way."

"Where are you now?"

"In a coffee shop down the street. In the bathroom. What if the Ghost hired someone to kill me because I knew Christina? What if he thinks I know something?"

She was dead wrong on Ethan—he wasn't even allowed a phone call—but she could be right about the motive. Poor girl. She'd been through enough already.

"Stay there. I'll come and get you."

It looked as if I'd be needing Emmy's car again after all.

I abandoned the Corvette in the tow-away zone outside the front door of the coffee place and strode inside, heading straight for the bathrooms and ignoring the shouts of the barista that they were for customers only.

There were four stalls, and only the furthest one was occupied. I knocked gently on the door.

"Stefanie?"

It cracked open, and her tear-streaked face peeped out. The instant she saw me, she started crying again.

"Hey, hey... It's okay."

I reached past her and grabbed some tissue for her to wipe her eyes.

"Thanks," she sniffed, sinking back onto the closed toilet bowl.

I took in her appearance. Her hands were filthy and covered with dried blood, and she'd scraped the knees out of her pants. Fucking marvellous. Another innocent person caught up in this mess. When I caught the piece of scum behind it, he was getting one in the knackers from me, to borrow another of Emmy's British phrases.

Meanwhile, I put an arm around Stefanie's shoulders. "Can you walk? We really should get those cuts cleaned up."

"I-I-I think so."

She trembled as I helped her to her feet, her tears still falling. The barista gave us a dirty look as we walked to the door, and I flipped him the bird. Didn't he know there were more important things in life than coffee? Although coffee ran a close second, I had to give him that.

Outside, I ripped the parking ticket off the windshield and stuffed it into the glove compartment. Emmy wouldn't even notice it in the pile she accumulated every month. I swear the officers followed us around, just waiting to see where we left our cars next.

Once Stefanie was settled in the passenger side, I hopped into the driver's seat. "Did you see the licence plate on the car?"

"N-n-no."

"Make? Model?"

"I think it was black. Or maybe dark blue. It all happened so fast."

"Never mind. We'll check for camera footage and see if we can find any other witnesses. Where do you want me to take you?"

"I don't know. I can't stay at home. Whoever tried

to hit me knows where I live, and I'm not waiting for them to come back and try again. I guess I'll have to go to a hotel."

I sighed. Riverley had plenty of spare rooms. Emmy wouldn't mind one more guest, right?

"I know somewhere you can stay."

"You do?"

"Yeah." But that also meant I had a little confession to make. We'd see whether she'd still want to be anywhere near me afterwards. "But I wasn't entirely honest with you before."

She blinked a few times, and I thought she was going to break down again, but she pulled herself together. "Why? What weren't you honest about?"

"I don't work for Jay Skinner. I'm on Ethan's team."

She reached for the door handle. "Get away from me! I don't want anything to do with that monster."

"He's not a monster, and I don't believe he killed Chrissie. He's as much a victim in all this as you are."

"But the police said—"

"The police are assholes. They just want to close the case and bask in the publicity. Skinner too. But there are so many things about this that don't make sense."

Stefanie hesitated, hand still on the door.

"When I started looking at this, I thought Ethan did it as well. But I've changed my mind. And whoever tried to run you down this morning is probably the real culprit."

Stefanie's hand fell back into her lap. That was a good sign.

"What am I supposed to do?"

"Help us, then as soon as this is over, you can go back home."

"You think you can catch the person?"

"The fact that they came after you this morning means they're worried. Chances are we're getting closer."

She leaned back against the headrest and closed her eyes. Another tear rolled down her cheek.

"Then I don't really have a choice, do I?"

CHAPTER 26

BACK AT RIVERLEY, my phone rang as we walked up the front steps. Leah calling.

"Dan, we need you in the office. Jorge's been watching the suspect in the Hawkins case, and the guy's packing a suitcase. We think he's gonna run."

Talk about bad timing. Who could I palm Stefanie off on? Bradley? Mrs. Fairfax?

I was just considering the options when Lyle meandered through from the kitchen, and the look in his eyes said, "Cha-ching!"

Perfect.

He stared at Stefanie, shuffling from foot to foot until I introduced them. Then he blushed pink as he shook her hand.

"Stefanie's going to be staying with us for a little while. She's got a small problem that means she can't go back home."

"Oh, me too! My lobby's full of reporters. Want me to show you around?"

She smiled shyly. "I'd like that."

Aw, sweet. "Play nice, guys. I've got to run into the office."

Five hours, it took, but the fact that the dude was packing and his one-way ticket to Ecuador gave us the extra evidence we needed to convince the cops to arrest our suspected rapist. Now he was in custody, waiting for us to tie up the loose ends, and Officer Tenlow owed me another favour.

I was dead tired by the time I got back to Riverley. As the world, his dog, and the dog's pet hamster seemed to be staying there at the moment, I figured I might as well join them. Good thing Emmy's husband was overseas, or he'd have been wearing his grumpy face because of all the noise.

"Lyle has a girlfriend?" Emmy asked me over breakfast the next morning.

"She's Christina's roommate."

"He can afford her prices? I didn't think they paid public defenders that much."

"He's not paying her. Someone tried to run her over yesterday, so I said she could stay here for a while."

"At this rate, I'm gonna have to move into my other house."

Just a slight exaggeration. Riverley had eighteen bedrooms.

"At least then I won't need to look at your ugly mug over breakfast."

She glared at me over her new glasses. "I take it you don't need my help with this case?"

I did. She knew it, I knew it, and she knew I knew it.

Damn.

"As it happens, I could use a hand, oh beautiful one. What's with the glasses, anyway? You look geekier than Mack."

They were cute, black plastic frames with thin purple stripes on the arms, but Emmy had twenty-twenty vision.

She passed them over. "Nate made them. They've got a camera built into the bridge. Neat, huh?"

Yeah, they were. I peered closely, and unless you were looking for the camera, you'd never notice it was there. Oh, I wanted a pair of these.

I handed them back. Reluctantly.

"So what do you want help with? You mentioned breaking and entering?" she asked.

"I want to get into Ethan's house, but the cops are still sitting out front."

"Any particular reason?"

A shadow passed behind her. Ana, Princess of Darkness, carrying a machine gun. She put it down on the breakfast bar and helped herself to a banana.

I tried to ignore her eyes on me as I answered Emmy. "There are a few things I want to look for. Some letters from Ethan's stalker, a set of house keys, a pair of gloves, and a bottle of massage oil."

I'd double-checked the reports again, and the massage oil definitely wasn't mentioned. Ditto for the gloves.

"I'm not even going to ask. Does he have a security system?"

"Mack hacked into the monitoring company. It's disabled at the moment."

"Are we having an outing?" Ana wanted to know.

"Yeah," Emmy answered for me. "Dan wants us to break into Ethan's house, only the police are guarding it."

I stifled a groan. Ana could make a man keel over

and die just by staring at him the wrong way, and having her tag along made me nervous. But I couldn't argue with her qualifications for the job.

"How many of them?"

"Just one, I think," I answered.

"Pfffft. One is easy. Are we going tonight?"

Emmy raised an eyebrow at me, and inwardly, I shrivelled up into something that looked like chewed gum. "Sure, why not?"

By the time darkness fell, we had a plan, and we also had Mack. She didn't want to be left out.

"I feel like I should have a lip piercing," Emmy said.

Emmy, Ana, and I had got dressed separately, but we'd all come out in various shades of black and purple, heavy on the mascara and light on morals.

"If you pass me a pin, I can do it," Ana offered.

I wasn't sure whether she was kidding or not, but Emmy laughed.

Mack was the sunshine to our gloom. She wore a pale-yellow scoop-neck top, a red spandex miniskirt, and high-heeled pumps. Oh, and a hidden earpiece and microphone—we all had those.

"Ready to go?" she asked. "These shoes are pinching."

I nodded. Might as well get this over with.

Mack borrowed a cherry-red vintage Mustang from Black's stable of cars, and the rest of us piled into one of the company Explorers. The way Emmy drove, it wasn't long before we parked in the shadow of an old maple tree a couple of streets away from Ethan's place.

Emmy radioed through to Mack. "Where are you?"

"About ten minutes away."

"But we left at the same time."

"I wanted to have some rubber left on my tyres."

The seconds slowly ticked by as we waited. Emmy tapped her fingernails on the steering wheel while Ana flicked her knife open and closed.

Snick. Click. Snick. Click. Snick. Click.

I tried to block out the noise and instead focused on why we were doing this. Ethan would be resting in his cell right now, the lights dimmed down to their nighttime glow. They were never turned off entirely, so the guards could keep a constant watch. Was he getting much sleep? I doubted it. This case kept my mind churning, but his turmoil must be a thousand times worse.

Mack's voice broke into my thoughts, loud and clear in my earpiece. She'd gone back to her Southern roots tonight, a proper damsel in distress.

"Oh, officer, thank goodness you're here. My car quit on me a block away, and my phone's dead too. Can you help me?"

I imagined her fluttering her eyelashes and thrusting out the chicken fillets she'd stuffed in her bra. That picture couldn't have been far from wrong because the cop replied, "Of course, ma'am, that's my job. You can borrow my cell."

I listened as Mack called her assistant, who we'd briefed earlier, and pretended to order a tow truck.

"An hour? That's crazy! I'm all alone, and it's dark. Can't you send somebody faster?"

The answer was obviously no.

Mack could cry on command—she even practised.

And I'd bet a hundred dollars she'd turned on the waterworks.

"Is this a safe area, officer?"

"If you're concerned, ma'am, why don't you wait right here with me? You can return to your vehicle when the tow truck comes."

"Oh, really? You're too kind."

I had to mute Mack as she started with the sort of inane chatter that made my ears bleed. Her assistant would carry on listening and interrupt us if anything important came up.

As we slipped out of the car, the calmness I worked hard to maintain before a job gave way to the first trickles of adrenaline. My heart began to beat a little harder, and my senses sharpened up. I was alert to the tiniest sound, the slightest movement as we hugged the shadows that led to Ethan's back wall.

Emmy went first, running up eight feet of bricks as if it was a single step. Ana followed, and then it was my turn. While the other two had taken to parkour with an easy grace, I looked more like a penguin climbing a tree. But my practice paid off, and I got there.

We dropped down on the other side, our steady breathing the only sound in the cool evening. Emmy raised three fingers then spread them, signalling us to split up.

As we'd planned back at Riverley, I got the left side of the house, Emmy took the right, and Ana had the back. I started at the front, cursing silently when the security light came on and hoping that Mack was giving the cop an eyeful of her tits.

I paused. Nothing nasty came over the radio, so I carried on.

The windows on my side were all double-glazed and locked—nothing easy to break into. The only possibility was a balcony on the second floor, which had a handily placed tree within jumping distance. I was preparing to shin up and take a look when Ana's voice sounded in my ear.

"I don't think we're the first to try this."

"Elaborate," Emmy said.

"There are steps down to the basement, and the window beside them has been forced open."

I tiptoed away from the tree and crept around to the back of the house. Emmy materialised a few seconds later, and we stared at what Ana had found. Sure enough, when she slid the blade of her knife under the window frame, it moved easily upwards, completely unsecured.

I peered through and took a chance with my flashlight, covering most of the beam with my thumb. "The catch is broken."

"The question is when and by who?" Emmy mused. "It's not obvious to look at, only if you push it."

"Somebody could already be in there," I whispered.

Unlikely, but possible.

"What do you want to do? Abort or carry on?"

"If somebody is already in there, it would save us the trouble of looking for him," Ana pointed out.

Oh, that made me feel much better. This house had already seen one murder; it didn't need another.

I weighed up the risks. If someone *was* in there, he or she could have a weapon, or worse, a camera. But there were three of us, and I wouldn't rate anyone's chances against Emmy or Ana on their own. When the two of them acted together, I actually pitied their enemies.

"Dan, what's it to be?" Emmy asked.

"We carry on."

CHAPTER 27

THE WINDOW SET high in a basement storage room was big enough for us to climb through easily. Ana went first, moving silently around boxes and a dusty mountain bike to cover the door while Emmy and I slid inside. Rather than stick with our initial plan, which had called for Emmy and Ana to give the house a quick once over while I searched for the keys and letters, we had to waste time clearing each room to start with.

Guns in hands, we stacked up outside the first door, Emmy taking point, then Ana, then me. Then we were through, and Emmy broke left, Ana right, then me left again. We'd spent hours training for this. Blackwood headquarters had a specially built "kill house" behind the main office building that allowed us to practise every scenario from rescuing a hostage to raiding a meth lab. So our moves were instinctive, a perfect flow as we moved from room to room.

Fifteen minutes later, we knew we were alone.

"Time for plan A?" Emmy whispered.

I nodded, and we split up, searching by the light of the full moon and occasionally clicking on a muted flashlight if the need arose.

Ethan said the keys would be in the hallway table, which was covered with black powder where the forensics team had dusted for prints. I reached out a gloved hand and pressed on the front as he'd described. Sure enough, a hidden compartment popped out.

And in it were two sets of keys.

I picked up the first. Those were the house keys, surely? I tiptoed over to the front door and studied the locks. A deadbolt and a nightlatch. According to the police report, the deadbolt had been open when the cops arrived, with only the nightlatch engaged. I tested it with one gloved hand—it was a standard type, one that could be opened from the inside without a key and would automatically lock when the door was pulled shut. I tested the keys, and they both fitted.

A blue Ford logo graced the fob of the other set, and the only car Ethan owned was his Mustang. The one he'd been found in. But if his keys were here, what had been in the ignition? A spare? It must have been. But if he was running for his life from a lunatic, why would he have dug out the spare? Why not grab this one as he ran for the front door?

"Thirty minutes," Emmy murmured, reminding me we'd used half our time.

I couldn't stop and think right now. That would have to come later.

The letters came next. Following Ethan's directions, I found the key to his desk in his pen holder and opened the second drawer on the pedestal. The top folder was labelled "Kooks." Inside, the first sheet was pink and decorated with little hearts, drawn in felt-tip pen and coloured in red. The overall effect was childlike. The faint smell of cheap perfume still lingered on the paper, a residue of the person who wrote it.

But further investigation would have to wait. I

shrugged off my slim backpack and slipped the folder inside, together with the keys. Time to hit the mother lode.

"The cops haven't done much in the rest of the house," Emmy said.

"Just some fingerprinting and a cursory search," Ana agreed. "They might as well not have bothered. There was blood on the wall in the kitchen pantry they don't even appear to have noticed."

Good to know my tax dollars were hard at work. Which reminded me, how was Mack getting on outside with Officer Hapless? I switched channels on the radio for a second and heard him dictating a recipe for cinnamon rolls. Yup, hard at work.

Beside me, Emmy pushed open the door to the master bedroom. Even now, the metallic tang of blood still hung in the air, a grim reminder of the girl it had once given life to. Under that permeated the musky scent of the man who'd once slept inside. Two lives had been lost in this room, not one.

A fine layer of powder covered every hard surface. I only hoped none of us needed to sneeze. The sheets had been removed, but a vague outline of Christina still remained, stained into the mattress like a modern-day version of the Turin Shroud.

"Gloves and massage oil," I muttered as I bent to look under the bed.

There was nothing there. Or indeed anywhere else in the room.

Ethan's clothes hung neatly in his walk-in closet, rows of jeans and the world's largest collection of hoodies. I opened a drawer, revealing a selection of masks.

Emmy picked one out and held it up to her face. "Does it suit me?"

Ana snatched it from her. "Not when you're supposed to be using your eyes to search."

She harrumphed and carried on looking, but it was pointless. Apart from a safe built into the floor that looked untouched, we found nothing of interest. I'd have to ask Ethan what was in that. There was no time to start safe-cracking tonight, and we'd need a specialist in any case.

"Are you sure Christina's massage client was Ethan?" Emmy asked. "Could she have had two jobs lined up that evening?"

"She didn't have enough time. The time stamp on the video from the security camera says she got to the club an hour after she left home, and we've checked the time stamp's correct. There's only half an hour missing, and no girl of her calibre would get a man off that quickly. Four thousand bucks, remember?"

"Well, it's not here, and Mack's probably gone hoarse by now."

"I know. We should leave."

Fuck it. I'd hoped to at least find the bottle of oil, which would have validated Stefanie's story, but it wasn't to be. What if Stefanie was lying? That was a possibility I needed to consider, but at least we had the letters.

Back in the car, we called off a bored-sounding Mack and started the drive back to Riverley.

"Find anything good?" Emmy asked.

"I got the letters and the house keys. But the house keys were next to another set of car keys, right in the hallway. Now I need to work out what keys Ethan used when he drove off and why."

"The keys you found were hidden, yes?" Ana said.

"Yeah."

"Then it's simple. Ethan wasn't the one driving the car." She made it sound so straightforward.

"But he was found behind the wheel."

Ana waved her hand dismissively. "That's easy to do. All you have to do is park the car at the top of a slope and shove the victim in the driver's seat, then take off the parking brake and jam their foot on the gas pedal. If you get lucky, the car explodes at the bottom."

"That's always the fun part," Emmy chipped in. "I've only had one go up properly, but he was an arsonist. I thought someone up there was looking down on me."

"The key is to make sure the tank is full and the engine is running," Ana said. "That way it's about fifty-fifty. Or if you have more time, you can rig the airbag igniter to blow."

"Guys, enough talk about how to kill people."

Ana swivelled around in her seat. "I thought you wanted to know how to kill people. Emmy said so. We've been discussing it."

I sighed. "Yeah, I do, but only one. Christina. And if you figure someone else was driving the car, that must mean Ethan was in one of the other seats, or the trunk."

"The trunk," Emmy said. "If he wasn't complicit in this, he must have been unconscious or tied up, and there were no rope burns on his wrists."

"Unconscious, then." And wasn't there a smudge of Christina's blood in the trunk? That could have been transferred as somebody hefted him inside. "But the medical report only reported one head injury, and that was consistent with him hitting his head on the steering wheel."

"Did anyone screen him for drugs?" Emmy asked. "GHB? Rohypnol?"

I was sure they hadn't, but it wouldn't have made a difference anyway. "No, but he wasn't found until a day later. Club drugs like those have a really short half-life. He'd have metabolised it out of his system by then. They screened Christina, though, and they found nothing."

"How would it have got into his system, anyway?" Ana asked. "It didn't happen while he was at the club, or he'd never have made it home."

"There was a bottle of champagne in the photos," Emmy said. "Maybe it was in there?"

If only it were that straightforward. "But Christina was drinking that as well. There was a half-empty glass with lipstick on the rim."

"Was there any other food or drink in the room?"

I shook my head. "And if there was, there was no guarantee that Ethan was going to touch it."

"Maybe Christina gave him something?"

She took both hands off the wheel and snapped her fingers. The car lurched to the side, and I grabbed at the door handle. Thank goodness I was wearing a seatbelt.

"Will you hold on to the damned wheel? Otherwise, someone's gonna be investigating *our* car crash."

"Stop being so nervous. Anyway, what about the oil? The bottle we conveniently can't find? Maybe there was something in that? Stefanie said Christina wore gloves, which would have protected her from touching it."

"I'm not sure that would work. GHB and Rohypnol aren't absorbed through skin. He'd have had to drink the stuff."

Emmy screwed her face up in the rear-view mirror. "Yuck. What if it wasn't massage oil in the bottle? Could Christina have tipped something in his drink?"

"Not if she was an unwilling participant like Stefanie believes."

"Okay, then what about something else in the oil? Another drug?" She tapped at her phone, and a dial tone filled the cabin. "I know just the person who can help us."

And I knew exactly who that would be.

Three rings, and a woman picked up. "Yes?"

"Fia, got a question for you, honey."

Fia Darke, Emmy's ex-girlfriend and a walking, talking, breathing encyclopaedia of poisons and other deadly substances. Which was more than could be said for her victims. She'd just moved to Virginia with her new boyfriend after spending three months in the Cayman Islands.

"Shoot."

"If you wanted to knock a guy out, what would you put in a bottle of massage oil to accomplish that?"

"Are we talking temporarily or permanently?"

"Temporarily. An hour or two."

As she paused, I pictured the corner of Fia's mouth twitching the way it always did when she was deep in thought.

"I'd try scopolamine."

"Scopolamine?"

"It's absorbed through the skin, and in low doses,

it's used in patches to combat motion sickness. But in high doses? Night-night."

"You're certain that would work?"

"Well, I've never tried it."

"Hmm..."

"Only one way to find out. We'll need a willing volunteer."

I leaned back and closed my eyes. This was so fucked up. But then again, what was new?

"How about Jed?" I suggested. "He's a little taller, but close to Ethan in terms of build."

"I'll talk to him," Emmy said. "Fia, you want to come watch? We can have dinner afterwards. Mrs. Fairfax has a new recipe for beef casserole."

"I love her beef casserole."

"It's a date, then."

CHAPTER 28

IF EMMY AND Ana were right, this case was even worse than I'd imagined. It hadn't just been Ethan's reputation that Christina's murderer wanted to trash. If they'd pushed him off the edge of the road in his car, they'd been trying to kill him as well.

This whole mess was a contradiction from start to finish. The calculated planning, the red-hot anger of the stabbing, then the coolness as the killer walked away from the crash scene and disappeared. We were still missing something—we had to be—but I couldn't quite grasp what it was.

I could only carry on pulling at loose threads until things began to unravel.

When I'd got back to Riverley last night, I'd started reading Lavinia's letters. Ethan and Ronan were right. They weren't horrible or threatening, more like the ramblings of a lonely woman who'd found some joy in watching a man from afar. I still wanted to track her down, just to be on the safe side, but I just couldn't see her being involved in this plot.

Finding her shouldn't be too difficult, at least. She'd signed one of her early letters with her full name, Lavinia Dixon, and in another, she'd mentioned her hometown, half an hour outside Richmond. I'd get Mack to cross-reference the two and find her address.

More interesting were the other letters in the bundle. Among Lavinia's descriptions of the Ethan-shaped cookies she'd baked and the T-shirt she'd had screen-printed with his face on it, there were notes from someone else entirely. Two of them, both typed on plain white paper.

They'd arrived care of his record label, according to the envelopes, which were postmarked Norfolk. The first called the Ghost every name under the sun and vowed to put him out of business. The second threatened to wipe the mask off his face personally. They were hate on a page, pure vitriol. The kind of anger that could stab a woman forty-seven times.

There was no indication of the sender, and I needed to speak to Ethan about them. My next visit to Redding's Gap was scheduled for the day after tomorrow, forty-eight long hours away, and the thought of waiting had me fidgeting at my desk. Should I bring it forward?

An email pinged on my screen, and I scrolled through it. Jed was free tomorrow, and if I promised to give him a massage, he'd help us out. Times like this, I was glad he was such a man-slut.

I replied in the affirmative, oddly nervous about what the outcome would be. Was it really possible that things had happened as we suspected?

Only twenty-four hours until I found out.

That still gave me today, and what better way to spend the afternoon than to visit my favourite music manager again? Apart from the mystery letter writer, Harold Styles was the person in this affair who raised my hackles the most.

Time to shake him up a bit and see what came

loose.

Harold had bought a new suite of office furniture since I saw him last. The desk was bigger, the chairs were leather rather than fabric, and he'd treated himself to some ugly artwork to hang beside all his gold and platinum discs.

Once again, he held onto my hand too long. In the end, I pulled it away and wiped it on my jeans.

He was oblivious to the insult.

"How can I help you, little lady?"

I had a feeling "crawl into a hole and die" wasn't the answer he was looking for, so I smiled sweetly. "I just wanted another chat about Ethan."

"I'll give you a friendly piece of advice. Let it go. There are plenty of other worthwhile causes you could be spending your time on. I'm organising a charity luncheon for next Thursday, and we're looking for pretty girls to sell raffle tickets."

"Sorry, I'm busy cleaning my gun that day."

He stared at me for a second before forcing a laugh. "Oh, I do like a sense of humour. Just say the word if you want to help."

"Yeah, sure. Anyway, about Ethan..."

He walked around his desk and put a hand on my back, gently pushing me towards the door. "Forget him. It's the best thing for everyone, yourself included."

Was that a veiled threat? Because that would only bump Harold up my suspect list. I decided to play along—who knew what he might let slip in future if he thought I was dumb?

"Maybe you're right. I think I might go and get my nails done instead."

He rewarded me with a flashy smile, and the light glinted off his gold tooth. "That's more like it."

I stomped over into Ronan's office and slammed the door. "Asshole."

He looked up from a pile of papers. "What did I do?"

"Not you. Harry."

He sat back and sighed. "Yeah, he's getting worse. Did you see the new furniture?"

I nodded.

"He bought it from some fancy designer in New York, and yesterday his new company car arrived. It's a Rolls Royce."

How much more of Ethan's money had he spent? I didn't know, but I wanted to find out. As Emmy said, most murders came down to sex, revenge, or money, and Harry certainly seemed fond of the latter. Ethan ending up in jail proved to be a nice little earner for him.

"A pretentious car for a pretentious driver. It's a good match. Look, is there any chance you could get me a backup of Spectre's accounting system? I'd like to see what else he's been buying."

"I'm not sure I'm allowed to give that kind of information out. Ethan—"

"Ethan's not here."

"Even so..."

"You want to sit around and watch Harry move into his company mansion with room for a company helicopter and company pony?"

He grimaced. "Not really." A thin sigh escaped his

lips. "Okay, I'll get you the data. It might take me a couple of days, though."

"I appreciate it."

I was still seething about Harold when I walked out to my car. Well, Emmy's car. The fact that he wanted Ethan to stay in jail made me even more determined to get him out.

And when I arrived at the office, I found Mack had another piece of information that might help me with that.

"Come and look at this." She grabbed me as soon as I walked in, almost making me spill my coffee.

On her screen, she had a picture of two Mustangs. Ethan's car after the crash on the left, and a shiny new version on the right.

"Watch this."

A 3D avatar walked across the screen and sat behind the wheel of the good car, settling himself into the seat and stretching his legs out.

"What am I looking at?"

"The man is Ethan. I took his dimensions from the photos I have of him. And if the seat in his car was set in the position it was in when it met the tree, he'd have had to really stretch to reach the pedals. I peered more closely at reconstruction. Sure enough, there was an inch of air between the soles of Ethan's feet and the gas. No way would Ethan drive his car like that every day. He'd move the seat forwards.

"Son of a bitch. Someone else was driving the car. Ana was right."

"Ethan's five feet ten, and I'd say your mystery person was at least three inches taller."

"Mystery man. It's got to be a man. A woman that

size with enough strength to manhandle an unconscious Ethan? I haven't come across anyone in this case who fits that description."

But Harold and Ty did. Ronan was too short, and I had no idea about DJ Steel. Yet.

Another piece had just been added to the puzzle, but it was still far from complete.

Chapter 29

AT ELEVEN THE next morning, Team Blackwood was ready to film a movie. Bradley had recreated Ethan's bedroom in one of the spares at Riverley with a bed, nightstands, and a couch in the same place. We had the set, we had the cast and crew, we even had a bottle of scopolamine-laced massage oil concocted by Fia. But what we didn't have was a script.

Instead, we had three directors, who were currently having a heated discussion over the first scene.

"Can't he just stay still?" Xav asked.

"No way," Ana argued. "This has to be convincing. Unless we drug him properly, we don't know if this will work. It's all just a theory."

Jed lay on the bed in a pair of boxer shorts, hands behind his head. "I'm not sure I want to be unconscious. What if Emmy shaves my eyebrows off again?"

"That was ages ago, and I only did that because you decided to host a naked pool party at my house."

"It was fun. Besides, I invited you to join in."

"I didn't want to join in. It was three in the morning, and I wanted to sleep."

"You need to lighten up."

"Guys!" I interrupted. "Stop arguing. Jed, I promise I won't let Emmy shave any part of you. And we've got the doctor here to monitor things."

"Okay, then get on with it."

Blackwood's physician, Kira, sat on a stool in the corner, fiddling with her phone. I'm pretty sure she thought we were all insane, and that wasn't far from the truth. Oliver was beside her with a legal pad and his fancy fountain pen, and Bay sat beside Mack, Fia, and Emmy on the couch, ready to point out any inaccuracies in our reconstruction.

And now Emmy clapped her hands together. "Right, let's go."

Thanks to Bradley, I was wearing a dress similar to Christina's, although she'd ended up naked by the end. We knew she'd had sex with Ethan because of the condom in the bin and the traces of semen inside her, but the condom showed no blood. The ME's report said there was tearing in her vagina, so we worked on the assumption that either she and Ethan got rough afterwards and he disposed of the evidence, or the killer did it instead.

Bay gave everyone a quick recap, and Jed grinned.

"I'm looking forward to this."

"I already told you, we're skipping the first bit, and I'm only going down to my underwear."

"Spoilsport. If I'm getting knocked out, the least you could do is put out."

There was a point in Jed's life when he might have been serious, but love had blindsided him, and he no longer chased anything with tits. He was only kidding.

"No can do, big boy."

I dropped the zipper on the dress and stood there in boy shorts and a sports bra.

He groaned. "Darlin', you could have made an

effort. Lace, silk, something crotchless... You look like you're going to the gym."

I cracked my knuckles, slipped on a pair of elbow-length leather gloves, and held out one hand. "I'll make an effort, don't you worry."

Fia passed over the massage oil—scopolamine mixed with a carrier—and I poured some into my hands.

"Ouch, that's freezing," Jed whined when I touched his skin.

"Wait a few minutes, and you won't even notice."

Emmy kept an eye on the time while I attacked Jed's back and shoulders. Thank goodness he'd flipped onto his front, because I didn't want to see what my back rub was doing to *that* part of him. After a couple of minutes, his lewd comments began to slur, and then they stopped altogether.

"Twelve minutes," Emmy announced.

I picked up his arm and let it flop limply back to the bed. "I'd say that worked."

"Next step," Emmy said while Kira checked Jed's vital signs. "Xav?"

"We're assuming the killer was close by," he said, stepping across from the doorway. "And that Christina recognised him, otherwise she would have tried to run or fight."

Xav stepped close enough for me to feel his body heat. "Hey, baby," he murmured, then stabbed me under the ribs. Or at least, he pretended to. We had a plastic cover on the knife blade for safety.

I went limp, and he held me up.

"I'll leave the knife in. Less blood that way." He leaned closer, his lips brushing my earlobe. "Struggle, sweetheart. You still have some strength left."

I shivered involuntarily. Even though this was all an act, Xav scared the fuck out of me. I wriggled a bit more, and he easily held my hands behind my back in one of his. I'd had years of combat training, but against Xav and his kind, it was wasted. Useless. If the killer had even half his strength, Christina wouldn't have stood a chance as the life leaked out of her.

Xav half pushed, half lifted me over to the bed, laid me down, and pinned me in place with his body weight. I could barely move, and that was without having a genuine knife stuck in my chest.

"So if he did rape her, my guess is it would be at this point," he said. "She's running out of energy, but with the knife still in her, there's not too much mess."

"It fits with the ME's report as well, where the lesser wounds came after the fatal one," Bay said.

That was sick. And if it really had gone down that way, I'd bet my favourite leather jacket Christina wasn't the freak's first victim.

"Mack, I want you to expand the database search this afternoon. Anyone who was raped around the point of death and died from knife wounds."

She paled and nodded.

"You don't have your hand over my mouth. I could scream," I said to Xav.

"Nobody to hear. Probably turned him on. I'm not putting my hand near your mouth because I don't want to get bitten."

Emmy checked her watch. "The bastard would have been excited, so let's give him two minutes to shoot his load."

Kira poked at Jed again while we waited and gave

us the thumbs up.

"Now he stabs her," Xav said, sitting up and miming the movement.

"No, no, no," Bay cut in. "He couldn't have been sitting on her legs like that. There was blood on them. He must have been beside her."

Xav hopped off the bed and stood next to me, leaning over. Now he had to switch the knife to his left hand to get the right angle.

"Interesting," I said. "Unless he was sitting on Ethan when he stabbed Christina, he must have been a southpaw."

"It wouldn't be natural for him to attack with his other hand," Xav confirmed.

"You're dead now," Emmy told me.

For emphasis, she emptied a bottle of theatrical blood all over my chest. It smelled sweet and sickly, and I touched a drop to my lips.

"Tastes like corn syrup."

Now it was time for Xav to earn his money. Well, not money exactly. I'd promised to babysit Libi, his daughter, while he took Georgia away for a grubby weekend, even though the prospect filled me with dread. Immersion therapy, right?

"You need to get Jed dressed. And smile—you're on camera."

We tried not to laugh as Xav squashed Jed into a pair of jeans and a T-shirt, which was what Ethan had been wearing when he was found. Jed's arms wouldn't behave, and he kept flopping about. It took almost ten minutes for Xav to finish dressing him, sneakers included.

"Jed's got no blood on his front," Emmy said.

"Ethan was covered in it. So much it soaked through to his skin."

Bay consulted his iPad. "It was smeared on the shirt. Like someone wiped it on him."

"I don't want to get covered in it myself," Xav said. "I still have to get home unnoticed." He picked me up and dragged me on top of Jed. "How about this?"

Bay shook his head. "Christina didn't move. It would have to be the other way around. You'll have to get another shirt and try again."

I wriggled back to my original position while Xav re-dressed Jed with Emmy's help, then Xav pulled him over on top of me.

"Any good?" he asked, shoving Jed back to his side.

Bay checked the photos again, comparing them to Jed. "Close enough. He probably smushed Ethan around more, but it'll do."

"Okay, what's next?"

"The car," Emmy told Xav. "But you can't find the keys. You run around the house looking in the obvious places."

"And finally find them on a hook in the kitchen cupboard," Ana said. "The blood I saw in there was above an empty hook."

"Okay, so let's assume delay of, say, ten minutes? We've already used five while we re-dressed Jed."

We waited some more. Emmy poked Jed with her foot, but he didn't stir.

"Now I need to get him downstairs," Xav said.

He pulled Jed off the bed with his hands under his armpits and started dragging him across the room.

"Do you reckon that corn syrup will come out of the carpet?" Emmy asked.

"I doubt it," Bay said. "But those marks are similar to the ones on Ethan's floor."

He was right. It wasn't anything Ethan owned that was dragged out of the room; it was Ethan himself.

Xav bumped Jed down the stairs and into the hallway, leaving him in a heap while he opened the front door.

"Gonna have to carry him for this last bit, or he'll get dust and shit on him. That wasn't in the report, right?"

He looked to Bay for confirmation, and Bay shook his head.

Xav leaned down and picked Jed up, slinging Jed's hundred and seventy-pound deadweight over his shoulder. I couldn't see anyone much smaller than Xav managing that, not unless they spent a serious amount of time in the gym.

He went to drop him in the trunk of Georgia's Mustang, but Bay stopped him.

"Hold on. Either there would have been more bloodstains in there, or our victim must have been wrapped in something."

"There was a bed sheet missing from one of Ethan's spare rooms," Ana said. "I noticed when I checked under the mattress."

Emmy ran back inside and fetched one, then Xav wrapped Jed up like a mummy.

"He was found, what, a five-minute drive from his house?"

"About that. Let's see if the blood seeps through."

It was into this little scene that Emmy's husband drove, fresh from a trip to Europe. He paused his Porsche Cayenne and rolled down the window, his eyes settling on me as I stood there in my underwear, drenched in fake blood.

"Do I want to know?"

Emmy leaned forward and kissed him. "Probably not."

He rolled his eyes, wound up the window, and drove off. If only all men were that understanding.

"Five minutes is up," Ana announced.

I peered in at Jed. "No blood on the outside of the sheet."

"It'd dried a bit before Xav wrapped him," Bay said. "Plus some rubbed off on the carpet."

Xav leaned in and unrolled our pseudo-victim. "Last challenge. I need to put him in the front."

Between the pushing, shoving, and cursing, it was no wonder the killer had forgotten to readjust the seat position. Xav had just strapped Jed in when he started to stir.

"Perfect timing," I said. "Welcome back."

Fia nodded and smiled. Job well done. When I'd asked how she worked out the dosage, she'd spouted figures and lost me, but I should have known to trust her. Ethan had been out for longer, but the trauma of the accident probably had something to do with that.

"How'd I do?" Jed asked.

"I'd give you an Oscar."

Once Jed came around properly, we sat in the conservatory and had a conference. Emmy's housekeeper served us afternoon tea—crustless sandwiches, scones with jam and cream, and petits-fours. So jolly civilised for a discussion about blood and murder.

"You reckon Christina put the drugs in the oil

herself?" Emmy asked.

I shook my head. "Whoever booked her to give Ethan the massage supplied her with the goods. Now all we need to do is find him."

"*All* we have to do..."

"Yeah, I know, the hard part's only just beginning. You don't need to tell me that. At least things are moving now. We know more than we did yesterday."

"Indeed," Oliver said. "We know staging the scene is possible, likely even, but the question is, how do we prove it actually happened?"

"Step one," Bay said, "is to test Ethan for scopolamine."

"Isn't it a bit late for that?"

"In his blood and urine, yes. But you can test a hair sample a month after the incident, and we're just coming into that window. It won't give an exact date, but it would show whether Ethan had it in his system recently."

Oliver scrawled across his pad. "It's going to be a fight to get the police to do that. Skinner won't want to jeopardise his case." Oliver's lips curved into a half-smirk, half-smile. "I look forward to watching the proceedings."

"And if the test comes back positive? Then what?"

His smile widened. "I vote we go for bail with the circumstantial evidence. It'll be high, but Ethan's got the money.

"Skinner's gonna be furious."

A fact that made me oddly happy.

"Then we'd better get Lyle fitted for body armour."

CHAPTER 30

ON MY DAY to visit Ethan, I woke with the same anticipation kids have on Christmas morning as they hurry downstairs to see what Santa's brought. Or at least that was what I imagined. The most my mother gave me on that special day was a black eye and a cigarette burn. I still had the scar.

My excitement was purely because of the case, you understand. The prospect of getting justice, of seeing the real killer locked up in Ethan's place. Then I pictured his blue-green eyes locked on mine and my traitorous pussy throbbed. Fuck. I slammed the shower door shut behind me and turned the water on cold. *Ethan's off limits, Dan.* Just thinking of him that way was a sure recipe for disaster.

Be a good girl for once in your life.

I felt upbeat as I landed the helicopter at Redding's Gap, and I even managed a polite nod to Otis. Today, the old man's constant moaning couldn't put a dent in my mood because for once, I had some good news for Ethan.

The bitch who searched me regarded me through slit eyes. My smile obviously gave her grounds for suspicion, because she made me strip completely and examined me in minute detail. I bet she got a kick out of it, too, the pervert.

That delayed me getting to Ethan, and he looked nervous as a lamb in a slaughterhouse when I arrived, his hands shackled to the table once again.

"I was scared you changed your mind. I've been in here for half an hour," he said.

"I'm not going to change my mind. I'll always come. How have things been?"

He shook his head, unable to speak at first. "Not good," he finally got out.

"Did anyone try to hurt you again?"

"No. It's just spending so much time on my own; it's driving me crazy. I was always a solitary person, but now... There's nothing to do but stare at the wall. I asked again if I could have a radio, and they said I couldn't because I was a suicide risk. How the hell do they think I'm gonna kill myself with a radio?"

He slumped forward, defeated.

"Don't lose hope."

"Easy for you to say. In less than an hour, you'll walk out of here and get on with your life. This *is* my life."

He rattled the cuffs against the table, and the metallic clang echoed around the tiny room.

"I'm working on things. Don't get upset."

"Sorry, Dani. I'm not upset with you. You're the only good thing in my life at the moment. If you didn't come, I'd...I'd... I don't know."

His eyes glistened, and I willed him to hold it together.

"Things are happening; I promise. We want to run a test on you, but we have to get the judge to authorise it first."

"What kind of test? A lie detector or something? I'll

take it, but what happens when I say I can't remember? I won't even know if anything they ask me's true or not."

"No, not a lie detector. This is a test on your hair. We're working on the theory that you were drugged on the night of the murder, and it'll show us if anything unusual's been in your system recently."

His eyes widened. "Drugged? Like with roofies?"

"Not roofies, but something similar."

"But I'm always careful in clubs. I drink out of a bottle, and I keep it with me."

"We think it happened at your house."

"By the girl?"

"Sort of. Well, yes, but she didn't know she was doing it. We know she was hired to give you a massage, and we think whoever booked her gave her the oil to use. It was laced with a sedative that took effect through your skin."

"Are you serious?"

"Unfortunately, yes."

"A massage?"

"If she'd offered, would you have taken her up on that?"

"Probably. Like any other red-blooded male. But you said someone hired her? Who in hell would want to do that?"

"That's the part we're struggling with. Someone carried you out of your bedroom and all the way down to your car, so most likely a guy was involved. And we think he was taller than you. The cops found a short grey hair on the bed." I shrugged. "That's pretty much all we have right now."

"He wanted to ruin my life. Don't forget that part."

"We haven't. Trouble is, you don't seem to have pissed that many people off."

"Quality over quantity, huh?"

"You got that right. I did find two nasty letters alongside Lavinia's, though. Whoever wrote those seemed pissed with you."

"And everybody else."

"What do you mean?"

"Half of the people in the music industry got those letters. The guy seemed to hate anyone with lyrics about sex, guns, women, money... The list went on."

"Did you report it to the police?"

"Along with fifty other people. They just asked for scanned copies, and a few weeks later, a cop called to say they'd arrested somebody."

Ethan smiled at me, just for a second. A proper smile, eyes and fucking dimples. It was the first time I'd seen those baby blues look anything other than haunted, and my heart did an involuntary flip even as another lead faded away.

"I'll check into it, but..."

"When will they be able to do the test?" he asked.

"Lyle's sorting out the court application as we speak."

His mouth twisted. "Is Lyle capable? When I thought I did it, I couldn't see the point in hiring a different lawyer, but he seems kind of...nervous. He never says much when he's here, just looks at his hands a lot."

"I've got the best trial attorney in Virginia giving him legal lessons."

"Can't I hire *him* to represent me instead?"

"If only. Oliver doesn't do trials anymore, but he's

agreed to help Lyle out as a favour. It's your decision if you want to change, but I'd suggest keeping Lyle until after the bail hearing. At the moment, Skinner thinks he's up against an inexperienced public defender. He doesn't realise Lyle's speaking for Oliver, and I'm hoping Skinner'll underestimate him."

"What do you mean, bail?"

"If this test comes back positive, that's what we're going for."

Ethan's next words were shaky, as if he didn't dare to hope. "Do you think there's a chance it'll be granted?"

"We're doing everything we can to make it happen."

"You know, I never used to pray, but I think I'm going to start."

"Another question... What's in your safe? Anything interesting?"

"Nothing much, just some cash. The safe came with the house; I didn't install it."

"And where did you keep your spare car keys?"

"On a hook in the pantry. Why?"

Fuck. Another point to Ana.

"They're not there now." I glanced at the clock. Ten minutes left. "Can we go through a list of your associates? Anyone big, over six feet two, and strong."

I scribbled with a blunt pencil on a prison-supplied notepad as Ethan spoke. As well as Harry and Ty, there were guys from the gym, security staff, musicians who used the studio, a couple of volunteers at Ethan's music project. The only thing they had in common was that Ethan had no beef with any of them.

With five minutes to go and Ethan looking visibly stressed, I switched the topic to music. Just once this week, I wanted him to have a normal conversation, one that didn't revolve around court or suspects or murder.

"I hear from Harold that Elastic Trickery is doing well. He said you discovered them?"

"Yeah, in a club in Queens..."

If it hadn't been for the orange jumpsuit and the shackles, not to mention the complete lack of ambience, we could almost have been on a date. *No, not a date.* Just a chat over coffee. Minus the coffee, of course. *Hell, what was I doing?* Now Ethan had lost his initial shyness, he became more animated talking about a subject he loved. I wanted to ask him about the music project, his time with King, the studio... But our precious time flew by, and my heart sank when the door opened behind me.

"Time," the guard informed us.

My eyes locked on Ethan's as I got up from the table. "I'll see you soon."

"I'll be waiting." His lips flickered. "Got nowhere else to go."

Fuck, that husky voice did bad things to my insides.

As I walked out of the room, I knew Ethan wasn't going to be the only one who started praying.

CHAPTER 31

A CHAMPAGNE CORK whizzed past my ear and hit Jed square in the chest, but I'm not sure he even noticed. Pecs of damn steel.

"I can't believe it!" Lyle screeched, swigging from the bottle. "I actually managed to win a case. Well, not win, exactly, but it was better than getting laughed out of court."

"You did good," Oliver said.

He'd been watching the hearing from the public gallery, hidden in amongst the throng of reporters. There'd been gasps when the judge set Ethan's bail at $12 million.

"Skinner was furious, wasn't he? And did you hear me? I made an objection and it got upheld!"

Bless him, he was like a kid in a candy store. With a shopping cart. His smile got even wider when Stefanie walked over and gave him a hug. She looked far happier than when we'd first met as well.

"We're all so proud of you," she said, giving him a kiss on the cheek.

He promptly turned tomato.

Now that she'd seen the evidence we'd gathered, Stef had switched allegiance to Team Ethan. Yesterday, when Skinner had phoned to ask if she'd pop in for a chat, she'd told him she'd come when the devil installed air conditioning. We were all proud of *her* too.

Of course, we still had to deal with the small matter of Ethan's actual release. The bail paperwork was in progress. With everything Ethan owned, he'd managed to raise $10 million of the total needed. And when Lyle had called me from outside the courtroom to say none of the bondsmen wanted to put up the rest, I'd taken a deep breath and said, "I'll cover it."

I had no idea what the fuck I was doing. Even Emmy raised an eyebrow.

"I know that spacey look," she said.

"No, you don't."

"Yes, I do. You got it when you started dating Jay, before you realised he had a black belt in asshole."

"You're seeing things."

She just chuckled and walked away. Sometimes I hated her.

I was brought back to the present by Oliver, who thrust a champagne glass into my hand. "Is this Cristal?" I asked.

"I think so."

"Shouldn't we be waiting until Ethan's actually acquitted before we break out the good stuff?"

Bradley waltzed past, another bottle in each hand. "If now isn't the time for a party, I don't know what is. Besides, Black's got cases and cases of this stuff in the cellar."

Trying to stop Bradley from throwing a party was like trying to dam up a river using a box of toothpicks. I gave in and knocked back my drink.

"That's more like it," he said. "Another?"

I shook my head. "One's my limit for tonight."

Heads swivelled and jaws dropped. Yeah, yeah, I

know, it was out of character for me. I usually had a glass in each hand, and they were constantly full.

But tonight, I was staying sober because tomorrow, I needed to pick Ethan up.

Redding's Gap was a six-hour drive, and I was taking my car instead of the helicopter because I refused to inflict Otis on Ethan. The poor guy was getting out of prison. Put him in a car with Otis, and he'd be begging to go back in.

Yes, I'd given in and bought a new car. My third in three months. As well as the Boxster, I'd accidentally left my parking brake off and let the Audi that came before it roll off a small cliff. So much for having a good crash rating. It looked like a caricature of its former self by the time it had concertinaed at the bottom.

My new Chevrolet Camaro was yellow with black go-faster stripes. Not exactly the most subtle car in the world, but I'd got the souped-up version so I could just outrun trouble instead. And sound good while I did it. The V8 engine was sweet music to my ears, and the fact that I'd get to spend six hours listening to it alone with Ethan was merely a happy coincidence.

Totally.

Bradley had sucked in a breath and muttered dire warnings about the environment when I mentioned the 6.2-litre engine, so yesterday afternoon I'd been forced to purchase two hundred hectares of Brazilian rainforest as an offsetting measure to appease him.

"I hope it's got monkeys," I muttered as I signed the paperwork.

"Mine's got monkeys," Emmy said. "And snakes and spiders and a fuck load of biting insects."

"Bradley sent you on a guilt trip too?"

"My seven hundred hectares is right next to Black's four thousand. His has an uncontacted tribe living in the middle of it, which we thought was kind of cool until some dude shot an arrow at us."

"You visited?"

"A couple of years back. We were in Rio, someone opened a bottle of cachaça, and it seemed like a good idea at the time."

"Maybe I'll just fly a plane over my bit."

"Think of the carbon footprint. Bradley'll make you buy another fifty hectares."

"Or I could just stay home."

"Good plan."

After my single glass of champagne, I retired to bed. Four in the morning and me didn't get on, but we'd have to call a truce tomorrow with coffee acting as mediator. I was due at Redding's Gap at ten, and I didn't plan on being late.

CHAPTER 32

I MADE IT to Redding's Gap with half an hour to spare after three stops for coffee and one minor delay for a speeding ticket. Despite that, my cheeks ached from the grin I'd been wearing most of the way. My new Camaro rocked.

And the thought of having Ethan beside me in the passenger seat for the return trip felt pretty damn good too. There, I admitted it. Are you happy now?

Even though I'd arrived early, the bitch that had searched me on my previous visits made me wait on a metal bench outside the entrance for almost two hours. For a moment, I wondered if she knew it was me who'd somehow obtained the login details for her Twitter account and tweeted about her fetish for taking it through the backdoor to her 172 followers. If she didn't let me out of here soon, I'd be doing her Facebook tomorrow.

Just before my ass cheeks went totally numb, a weary-looking Ethan emerged into the sunshine, blinking as he stepped from the gloom. He looked from side to side, and when he spotted me, his grin matched mine and his steps quickened.

They'd given him an oversized denim shirt and a pair of ill-fitting khaki pants, and he still wore the prison's standard-issue lace-less canvas shoes.

"Nice outfit," I said.

"The irony is, if I'd worn this two months ago, I'd have started a new fashion trend."

"You'd better believe it. I was on Twitter yesterday, and you've got twelve-year-old kids parading around in orange jumpsuits and Ghost masks."

He groaned. "You're kidding?"

"Nope. I brought you some clothes, though. I figured they weren't gonna give you anything snappy, and if you get spotted, that isn't a look you want on the front page."

"I'm surprised there're no reporters hanging around at the gates."

"Lyle's holding a press conference as we speak, telling everyone you're getting released tomorrow."

He'd come up with that idea all by himself. Thanks to Mr. Rhodes, his devious side was developing nicely.

"I guess I need to thank him. He did better than I thought he would in court."

"He surprised me as much as anyone. Oliver's taught him a lot."

"I just hope he does as well in the trial."

"He will. Have faith."

"I'm trying, but it's been sorely tested over the last few weeks."

I reached over and squeezed his hand, something I'd been aching to do for days. "It'll be restored."

He didn't let go, and I knew then that everything Emmy said was right. I was in trouble. Big trouble. I tried to speak, but it came out as a croak. Dammit. I swallowed and tried again.

"We should get going. It's a long drive back."

With one last stroke of his thumb over my knuckles,

he released my hand. "You're right. Is this yellow monster yours?"

"Yup. I've had her for two days, and she's still scratch free."

"You sound surprised. Should I be worried?"

"My crashes aren't usually serious. I specialise in small dents."

"Fuck," he said as he pulled open the passenger door. "Maybe I should have stayed back there."

He jerked his thumb at the ugly grey building.

"Nah, this is much better. And I'm going to try really hard not to get pulled over on the way back."

He was still shaking his head as we peeled out of the lot. Soon, Redding's Gap was nothing but a dust cloud in the mirror.

"Can you make yourself useful and play DJ?" I asked him, pointing at the radio.

He laughed, deep and throaty, and goose bumps popped out on my arms.

Huge. Fucking. Trouble.

"I think I can manage that."

Soon the car was alive with the sound of rock, and Ethan leaned back in the seat with his eyes closed, enjoying the music. I stole glances as I drove, feeling some of my own tension seep away as Ethan's jaw relaxed.

Once we'd gotten ten miles along the road, I pulled over next to a stand of trees. "You wanna change?"

"Can't wait."

I handed him the bundle of clothes from the backseat and checked my emails while he changed behind the car. Okay, so I snuck a peek in the mirror. I was only human. Then I may have watched while he stripped off the shirt, stretched, and pulled on the hoodie I'd brought for him. Damn, the man had muscles—the perfect bumps of a six-pack and deliciously lickable pecs. Hey, just looking wouldn't hurt, would it?

"Better?" I asked when he climbed back in beside me.

"Much." He gestured at the pile he'd thrown behind him. "Those deserve to be burned."

"I'm sure I can dig out some matches."

We drove on in silence for a while. Ethan had pulled his hood up over his face, so I couldn't try to guess what he was thinking. But despite that, the atmosphere wasn't tense. It was the peace of two people comfortable in each other's company.

Eventually, Ethan was the one who spoke. "Dani, I don't know how I can repay you for everything you've done."

"You don't have to."

"I do. If it wasn't for you, I'd still be in a concrete box and I'd probably die there."

"Don't think like that. You're not in there, and if I've got anything to do with it, you're not going back."

"Lyle said you put up the rest of my bail money," he said quietly.

"Yeah, I did."

"Why?"

"Because..." Because every time I fell asleep I saw Ethan in my dreams? Because when I heard his voice, it sent shivers through me? Because I struggled to keep my pulse steady when I was around him? "I don't know why. I just did."

"I'm not gonna let you down; I promise."

"Yeah, I know."

He sighed and shifted in the bucket seat. "Lyle may be sketchy when it comes to court, but he knew what he was doing when he hired you."

How did I tell him this? "Uh, it wasn't Lyle who hired me."

"He didn't? Then who did? Ronan?"

"Not Ronan either."

I told Ethan about the three boys and how Emmy had given me the job as a punishment for crashing her car. I'd finally given in to her badgering yesterday and called them after the hearing with an update, and they'd been so fucking happy it made me go mushy inside.

Ethan was shaking his head by the end of my story. "Those kids are something else. I've missed working with them. Every week they'd turn up, and they've got this enthusiasm that most professionals are missing. I only hope I can work on the project again in future. And I swear, I'm never gonna criticise your driving, no matter how bad it is."

I grimaced. "We'll see whether you still feel the same way when we've got back."

"Back... yeah." He sighed, a long exhalation that tugged at my heart.

"What?"

"I was so focused on getting out of Redding's Gap, I never really thought about what would happen after. Lyle said my house is off-limits, and I'm not sure I ever want to set foot in there again, anyway. I don't even have the cash for a hotel because it's all with the court. Can I borrow your phone to call Ronan?"

"Uh, I kind of arranged something already."

"You did? Where?"

"A friend of mine has a place near Richmond. The security's good, so there won't be any reporters around."

When I'd broken the news to Emmy that I wanted Ethan to stay at Riverley, she'd just rolled her eyes and said, "What's one more?"

"Are you sure your friend won't mind?"

"Nah, she's fine about it. Besides, as it was her who gave me the job in the first place, it's only fair that she chips in. Lyle's staying there too. He got chased out of his place by the paparazzi. And, er, Stefanie."

"Who's she?"

"Christina's ex-roommate."

Ethan put his head in his hands. "Shit, she's gonna hate me."

"No, she isn't. She knows it wasn't you, anyhow. Somebody tried to hurt her the other day, and we figure it was the same person."

I hadn't told him that part while he was in prison because I didn't want to add to his stress, but now he needed to know the full story.

"Hurt her? How?" His voice shook.

I told him about the attempted hit-and-run. "I think whoever's behind this is worried what Christina might have told Stefanie. Trouble is, she didn't say much at all."

"How many more people are going to get caught up in this? It's a living nightmare."

He wasn't wrong about that.

Halfway back, all the coffee I'd drunk on the trip down caught up with me, and I pulled into the next gas station.

"I need the restroom, and the car needs gas," I told Ethan. "You want anything from the store?"

"A coffee would be good. I haven't had one since I've been inside, and I didn't get any breakfast this morning either. You want me to pump the gas?"

"Thanks."

I got out of the bathroom just in time to see my car pulling away from the pump. Shit, shit, shit! I ran halfway to the door, heart pounding, until I realised Ethan was just moving it out of the way so a woman in a pickup could fill her tank. He parked neatly outside the kiosk and turned the engine off.

Phew. I needed to trust my gut, and my gut told me to trust Ethan.

When I headed back to the car, laden with supplies, Ethan was back in the passenger seat. I handed him a latte and took a sip of my own.

"They didn't have a lot of choice. I got chips and a couple of candy bars."

"Breakfast of champions."

A few miles down the road, I pulled over again. Food. I needed food.

"I didn't want to hang around at the gas station. Too many people coming and going."

Ethan nodded, mouth full. "I never thought a Twinkie bar could taste so good." He swallowed then paused before he took another bite. "Want me to take a turn at driving?"

My first instinct was to say, "No way." I was a terrible passenger, and I had an argument with Emmy every time we got into a car together. Last year, she'd got one of my exploded airbags framed and given it to me as a Christmas gift. But I'd been driving for nine hours already today and tiredness was fast catching up with me.

"Maybe I'll just take a short break."

I was having a rather dirty dream about a certain music producer when a hand on my shoulder woke me up. Tell me I hadn't moaned in my sleep?

"We're just outside Richmond," Ethan said. "You're gonna have to help me out."

I looked up and saw the city limits approaching. Had I really been asleep for two-and-a-half hours? I checked my watch. Fuck, I had. I must have been more tired than I thought.

"Okay, take a left here. We need to head east."

At long last, the huge iron gates of Riverley appeared, and Ethan let out a low whistle when we turned into the drive. "When you said a house, I was expecting something on a street with other houses, not this."

"I felt kind of awed when I first saw it too, but I guess I'm just used to it now."

"Do you spend a lot of time here?"

"Probably as much time as at my own place."

"Where do you live?"

"I have an apartment in Richmond, not too far from Liquid, but I'm staying here at the moment."

"That's... What are all those balloons for?"

Oh, Bradley. He'd decorated the stone columns at the front of the house with a whole array of foil balloons. When we got closer, I could see they had a musical theme—guitars, pianos, music notes, even a tuba.

"That'd be my friend's assistant. He gets excited about new guests."

Bradley must have been waiting for us, because the instant the car pulled to a halt, he bounded out of the door. This morning, he'd done his hair up in green and silver stripes, which matched the feather trim on his sweater.

"Okay, I've set up a room and arranged new clothes. I wasn't totally sure of the sizes, so I just ordered extra and I can send the rest back." He bounced around to Ethan's door. "What do you like to eat? Mrs. Fairfax hasn't started dinner yet. Oh, I'm Bradley by the way."

I recognised the look in Ethan's eyes. The shutters had come down, the same way they did when I first met him. His head dropped so he looked at his feet, his face barely visible under the hood.

"Bradley, leave him alone. I'll bring him down to the kitchen when he's had a chance to settle."

"I'm only trying to help."

Bradley may be pushy, but he had a heart of platinum. I put an arm around his shoulders. "I know, and believe me, we both appreciate it. It's just that today's been a bit overwhelming for Ethan."

"I suppose I can understand that."

"Why don't you ask Mrs. Fairfax to surprise us with dinner? Anything she makes is going to be delicious."

"Okay, I will."

He shuffled back into the house, a little deflated.

"Is he always like that?" Ethan whispered once he'd gone.

"Yeah. You'll get used to him. He means well."

"I guess. I'm not used to this. I've only ever lived on my own before. Well, at least since I was twelve."

Twelve? He'd been alone since he was twelve years old? "What about your parents?"

This time it was me who got the shutters. "I don't talk about them."

I put a hand on his arm, feeling hurt when he flinched. "Sorry, I didn't mean to pry. I won't ask any more questions." Not when they upset him so much. "Let's go inside."

He followed me meekly, his earlier good spirits evaporated. Why had the mention of his parents upset him so much? By the sound of it, the issues were all in the past, but that didn't stop me from burning with curiosity. I needed to have another chat with Mack.

Chapter 33

NOW THAT ETHAN had been released, I had a little bit of breathing space, and I needed to catch up on some of my other cases. This morning's team meeting had been a marathon of reports, planning, decisions, and briefings that lasted four-and-a-half hours, but I'd survived it, and before I started work on the stuff I couldn't delegate, I deserved an iced caramel macchiato.

Ethan had made it through dinner last night and even managed a smile when Bradley brought out a cake shaped like a miniature jail with a hole blown in the wall. By Bradley's standards, that ranked as tame on the scale of offences against taste.

This morning, I'd left Ethan in the kitchen talking to Lyle and Oliver over breakfast. Mrs. Fairfax had the day off, so Stefanie had made them all scrambled eggs.

All that meant I was on my own as I walked out of the coffee place next to Blackwood's Richmond office, juggling a to-go cup and a bag containing a chocolate muffin. I deserved that too.

"What the hell do you think you're playing at?" a voice behind me growled.

Fuck. I'd forgotten he knew about my coffee habit. "Care to elaborate?"

"You're sabotaging my case."

"No, Jay, I'm looking at the evidence objectively, which is more than can be said for you."

"Bullshit. You're just trying to get back at me for whatever you imagine you saw the winter before last. Talk about holding a grudge."

"There was no imagining necessary. You were going through my files."

"Yeah, yeah, you always did believe what you wanted to believe, and now you're doing it again."

"You're the one who's talking bullshit."

"Ethan White's a murderer, no matter what your so-called forensic expert says. He was covered in a hooker's blood, for heaven's sake."

"That was circumstantial."

"Daniela, did your ceaseless partying finally kill off the last of your brain cells? Or is there another reason you're defending a madman?"

Jay peered closely at me, and I forced myself not to wither under his gaze. He was a tall man, and he used his size to dominate, both in court and out of it.

"Ah, I get it," he continued. "You're fucking him, aren't you? You got seduced by a celebrity and that's blinded you to the truth."

"No, I'm not fucking him. You have no clue what you're talking about."

Even to my own ears, my words lacked conviction, because while I may not have fucked Ethan, as Jay so eloquently put it, I found it more and more difficult to deny that I wanted to.

"If I'd known that was all it took to get you on my side, maybe I'd have dragged you into the sack a few more times."

He caught my fist half an inch from his face. The

muffin bag hit my foot and bounced away.

"Now, now, there's no need to be so hot-headed. You always were a feisty one, weren't you?"

"I hate you."

He laughed at me, and a drop of spit hit my cheek. "Just wait until the end of this case. I'm going to send your boyfriend to the chair, and that'll give you something to really detest me for."

It was a good thing I'd left my gun in the office, because threatening to shoot a prosecutor wouldn't be a great career move. Instead, I forced myself to speak calmly.

"Ethan's not going near the inside of a jail cell again."

"What are you going to do? Smuggle him to a non-extradition country?"

If it came to that, yes. "I won't have to."

Jay took a step closer, then another, until we were toe to toe. "If you do anything to fuck up my election chances, little girl, I'll rip you apart."

"All you've got is words, Jay, and they've got no power over me. We'll see you in court."

I refused to let him have the last word, so while he took one of his customary dramatic pauses, I turned on my heel and strode off, making myself walk steadily rather than sprinting like my feet wanted to.

But a few steps out, anger hit me and I swivelled around, wound back my right arm, and hurled my coffee at him. It hit him dead centre in the chest, a perfect bull's-eye. I resumed my tactical retreat while it dripped down his custom-made suit, ignoring the obscenities he shouted after me.

Fuck.

I was still shaking when I got back to Blackwood. That bastard. That utter, utter bastard.

"Is everything okay?" Leah asked.

"Would you be a doll and get me an iced caramel macchiato and a chocolate muffin from the place down the street?"

"But I thought you just went... Sure."

She grabbed her purse and ran out as I slammed my office door behind me.

Why did I let Jay get to me so much? I knew what he was like by now. He wound people up to breaking point then waited for them to snap.

The last time we'd spoken was over a year ago, after he lost the case we'd split up over. My evidence had swung the acquittal, so the defence lawyer told me, and Jay was far from happy about it, something he'd made quite clear in the parking lot afterwards.

A bit like today, really.

I'd wondered if time might have mellowed some of Jay's bitterness, but clearly it hadn't, just as it hadn't lessened mine. It looked as if we'd be going up for round two.

Maybe I should just avoid parking lots.

My door cracked open, and I was about to tell my unwanted visitor to piss off when I realised it was Emmy. Might as well save my breath. She wouldn't listen, anyway.

"What's up?"

"I just had a run-in with Skinner."

"Ouch. Is he still the same twisted prick he always was?"

"I think he might have got marginally worse."

She walked around my desk and gave me a hug.

"Just ignore him. That man's so full of shit his eyes are brown."

"I'm trying, but he knows which buttons to push, and he keeps fucking pushing them."

"Want me to have a chat?" Which translated as, "Want me to tear him a new asshole?"

Tempting though it was, this was one battle I had to fight for myself. I was the one who'd been stupid enough to get involved with Jay, and I was determined not to drag others into my mess.

"No, it's all right. I'm just going to ignore him."

"Well, you only have to say the word if you change your mind."

And that was another reason Emmy was my best friend. She may be irritating as hell and so damn good at everything it sometimes made me want to scream, but at the end of the day, she had my back. She'd had it for the last decade, and she'd held me up through the worst times of my life.

I hugged her back as hard as I could. "Love you, bitch."

"I know."

Chapter 34

THE CONFRONTATION WITH Jay left me in a shitty mood for the rest of the day. Rather than biting people's heads off in the office, I went out with one of my teams. Yes, I know I was technically the second-in-command of the entire division, but paperwork bored me, so I often hit the streets. Today, we were hunting for a bail jumper who'd been charged with robbery, and he'd already gotten away from us twice.

"Third time lucky, do you think?" Isaiah asked.

"Damn right."

We found him in a bar downtown, drinking beer as he chatted up a skanky blonde. Evan shouted from inside before our jumper skidded out the front door and took off down the street. I'd worn sneakers, but it was amazing what desperation could do to a guy. He sprinted three blocks like an Olympian then turned left into the park. Through the trees we went, then he spotted Isaiah coming from the left and cut right, splashing through an ornamental stream and heading for the trees. Fucking fantastic.

I followed him through the wooded area, branches clawing at my face and clothes. The asshole was still ten yards ahead when he vaulted the perimeter fence into a building site, and I vaguely remembered Mack's research notes mentioning he ran track in college. Next time I decided to chase a criminal, I'd pick one too fat to run. Fuck this shit. We dashed past a half-built wall, and the jumper glanced back and stumbled. I seized the chance, leapt forwards, and rugby tackled him. Even then, he didn't give in and began kicking and screaming until we both fell into a bloody great hole.

Isaiah hauled me out, and between us, we dragged the prick's unconscious body into a company Explorer, shackled him to a ring in the floor, and dropped him off at the precinct.

"Well, that was fun," Isaiah said. "Are you coming back to the office?"

I'd had enough. Of everything. "Just drop me back at Riverley, would you?"

"Sure thing."

No matter how bad my day had been, I still smiled when I saw Ethan. His face lit up when I walked into the kitchen, but the light in his eyes quickly dimmed when he looked me up and down.

"Dani, what the hell happened?" He reached forward and picked a piece of twig out of my hair. "Your knees are bleeding."

"Oh, that's nothing. Occupational hazard."

"It's not nothing. Is there a first aid kit here?"

"Uh, yeah."

I led him over to the cupboard off the hallway where Emmy kept the supplies.

He did a double take. "What are these people trying to do, equip their own hospital?"

"Emmy believes in being prepared."

Even more so since the incident with an assault team that resulted in the death of one of her employees and the serious injury of another.

"I can see that. Do you want to change your pants?"

The slut in me wanted to do my hair and slip into a dress, but then common sense overruled and I put on pyjamas instead. I was planning to go to bed right after I'd eaten, and nobody stood big on ceremony in this house. *And I absolutely did not want to impress Ethan.*

I rolled the legs up and tried not to wince as he picked gravel out of my knees with a pair of tweezers then doused me with antiseptic. Hell, that stung. He taped dressings over the top and stood, knees cracking.

"Now all you need is for your momma to kiss it better."

"The only thing my mom ever kissed was a crack pipe."

Might as well get that out there. If Ethan was going to be around for a few months while we fought this case, he'd most likely find out anyway.

"Are you serious?"

"Yeah. I was the thorn in her side."

"What about your father?"

"What father?" I hoped if I told him a bit about my family, he'd reciprocate. "He left two months after I was born and never paid a cent in child support."

But Ethan didn't say a word. Instead, he dropped to the floor in front of me, dipped his head, and placed a soft kiss on each of my knees. Goose bumps worked their way up my legs and across every bit of my skin, and my family, his family, and anybody else who might have happened to roam the planet slipped clean out of my mind.

In fact, the only words on the tip of my tongue were, "Could you go a little higher, please?"

I bit them back. Totally inappropriate.

Ethan got to his feet again, cheeks flushed. "I'm sorry."

I wasn't sure whether he was apologising for what he'd just done or for my shitty childhood. Either way, it didn't matter.

"You've got nothing to be sorry for."

Nothing but giving me another sleepless night, anyway.

My phone rang in the dark, vibrating and flashing as it played "Trouble in the Message Centre" by Blur.

Shit.

I jumped out of bed in an instant, the first trickles of adrenaline already running through my veins. No matter how tired I was, I followed the same routine every night: brush my teeth, check my gun was in my purse, ready and loaded, put my shoes next to the purse, then lay out my phone and headset on the nightstand.

That meant I was always ready for an emergency, and the late-night invasion by a team of mercenaries at Riverley two years ago left me the tiniest bit on edge whenever I stayed there.

Headset on: check.

"Perimeter breached in the gallery. One of the French windows," a voice from the Blackwood control room told me.

"Dan here, heading downstairs now."

"Diamond to control, armed and ready."

"Ana's already on her way," the control room said.

"She's on radio silence now."

Of course she was ahead. Ana was always ahead. Sometimes, I doubted she even slept. She was like a vampire—permanently out for blood.

Since I didn't have anywhere else to put my gun, I kept it in my hand as I hotfooted it down a hidden staircase. Emmy, also known as Diamond, met me in the hallway complete with her Walther P88 and wearing one of her husband's T-shirts.

"Do we have visual?" she asked.

The control room linked into Riverley's entire security system, cameras included. "One target identified, looks like a male, wearing dark clothes and a hood. He's heading for the barn."

A hood? Could it be...? No, surely not.

Emmy's hand tightened around the grip of her gun. Nobody messed with her animals, although if anybody paid a visit to her horse, Stan, and didn't bring either fruit or extra strong mints, the grumpy bastard would probably kill them himself.

"Let's go."

A wide gravel path led to Emmy's barn, but we stuck to the grass at one side so we didn't make any noise. And I use the term "barn" loosely. Because Stan came from Spain, it looked more like a fancy villa, complete with stucco walls and a terracotta roof. That was what happened when Bradley was left to renovate unsupervised.

I heard the *crunch, crunch, crunch* of footsteps ahead, and a figure came into views, hands in pockets and head down. Dammit, what was he doing out here? I put a hand on Emmy's arm, stopping her, and she raised an eyebrow.

"Ethan," I mouthed.

The other eyebrow came up, and I shrugged. No, I didn't know why he was out there either. My heart rate slowed as the danger receded, only to stutter when a black-clad figure materialised from the trees ahead.

"Stop. Raise your hands. Slowly."

"Ana! It's Ethan."

Her gun didn't waver.

"Why are you out here?" she asked him.

His hands were above his head by now, and they didn't look too steady.

"Ana, put your fucking gun down," I told her.

Good grief, was that a grenade on her belt? Unlike yours truly, she was fully dressed, wearing black from head to toe. She'd also brought night vision goggles, two knives, and enough ammo to take out an army battalion.

Me? I was in my underwear.

Emmy lowered Ana's gun for her and patted Ethan on the shoulder "You'll have to excuse my friend here. She's a little touchy." She held a hand out. "Emmy Black. Interesting to finally meet you."

He shook her hand but stayed silent.

"Seriously, why *are* you wandering around in the dark?"

Nothing.

Oh, Ethan.

"I'll deal with it, okay? You two go back to sleep."

Ana stalked towards the house, pausing next to me on the way. "You should handcuff him to the bed if he's going to keep walking off."

"I'll take that under advisement."

And try damn hard to resist the temptation.

Once Emmy had followed Ana, I took a deep breath. "Ethan, why are you out here? It's one o'clock in the morning."

"I just needed air." His eyes widened as he turned and took in my attire, or rather the lack of it, and he struggled to take off his hoodie. "Here, have this."

"Thanks." I shoved my arms into the jacket and zipped it up. Now that the excitement had died down, it was kind of chilly outside. "You can't just go in and out at night, not without deactivating the security system. Everywhere's monitored. The second you opened the window, an alarm rang in the control room."

"Sorry, Dani. I didn't even think. I'm so used to being on my own, and..." He held out one hand in the moonlight. "Fuck, I'm still shaking. Who was that woman? Not Emmy, the other one."

"Probably best to pretend she doesn't exist. Come on, let's go inside."

I couldn't go straight back to sleep after that, and I bet Ethan would struggle too. It wasn't every day a man got accosted by a heavily armed ninja. Rather than heading upstairs, I led him through to the kitchen to get a drink. It was either hot chocolate or alcohol, and it would be best if I kept a clear head for the next day.

"So," I started. "One in the morning?"

"I couldn't sleep."

"The case?"

"The case, work, being here... Plus my body clock's never functioned so well. Before when I got restless, I'd go to the studio and mess around with a few tracks, but I can't do that now. Or sometimes, I'd go for a run. Have you ever been out running in the moonlight?"

"Only when I'm chasing somebody."

He eyed up my gun on the counter. "Right. How are your knees?"

Itchy, scabby, and stinging like hell. "Not too bad." I spooned cocoa powder into two mugs. Riverley had one of those taps that did boiling water, so at least I didn't have to wait for the kettle. "Most of us here get up at odd times. Mack, our computer expert, is practically nocturnal this month. Have you ever tried anything to help you sleep?"

"Like pills, you mean?"

"Pills, meditation, one of those funny light clock things that's supposed to reset your circadian rhythms. When I was a kid, I'd stay up all night then sleep when I was supposed to be at school. If I didn't drop off, I'd just drink my mom's vodka."

"Dani..." He used a warning tone.

"What?"

"I know what you're doing, and I won't talk about it. I can't. Just know that as far as I'm concerned, my life started the first time I climbed on stage with a guitar in my hands."

Dammit. The nosy little bitch who lived inside me fidgeted like she'd rolled in poison ivy, but I had to tread softly.

"My life started the day I met Emmy. Sometimes, I think I'd rather have had a guitar."

"Now I've met her too, I can understand that."

I studied Ethan as he sipped his drink. We were similar and yet different. Neither of us wanted to talk about our early years, but we'd survived our childhoods and now we overcompensated with work. Both of us escaped through music and alcohol, although Ethan was better at the former while I specialised in the latter.

But we were also different. Ethan hid away behind his walls, both physical and metaphorical, while I spent my days building my networks, person by person. He hated accepting help, whereas I'd learned to work as part of a team.

Both of us were products of our pasts, but how would the future shape us?

Oh, fuck this. I'd been spending too long with Black and his psychobabble, and it was too late for this shit. Or too early.

"Let's play a game."

Ethan looked suspicious. "What sort of game."

"Scrabble."

"Huh?"

"You're awake, I'm awake, and neither of us wants to talk about anything that means something. So, let's play Scrabble."

"Are you crazy?"

"Do I really need to answer that?"

Georgia had a thing for board games, and she'd stashed a whole bunch of them in a cupboard in the living room. I dragged out Scrabble, wrapped a blanket around my legs, and set it up on the coffee table. Ethan looked at me expectantly.

"Tell me you've played Scrabble before."

"No."

"Not once?"

"Never had anyone to play with, Dani."

Of all the things Ethan had ever said, those were the words that shot me straight through the heart. My chest seized as I imagined a small boy, a boy much like Race, but one who didn't have a single person he could call a friend. As a kid, I'd put up with perverts and assholes, but I'd never been totally alone. In many ways, I thought that would have been much, much worse.

I forced a smile and hoped my eyes weren't watering too much. I was meant to be the strong one here, but Ethan chipped little parts of me away inside.

"Okay, so each player starts off with seven letters, and the aim is to make a word out of them and place it on the board."

"And if you've already put a word there, can I use those letters too?"

"Yes, and then there are the extra point values..."

Ten minutes after I'd explained the rules and we started playing, Ethan slammed me with *yakuza* on a triple word score. We should have played Jenga.

"That's good, right?" he said.

His cute little smirk said he knew damn well it was.

"I hate you. If we're going to keep playing, I need a proper drink." To hell with the hangover. I'd had enough practice at dealing with them. "Want one?"

"I needed one right after GI Jane pointed a gun at me."

"Vodka?"

"Yeah. Better stick with a single."

"Belvedere, Grey Goose, or...actually, I don't know what this is. Ana brought it back from Russia so it's probably vicious."

"Ana?"

"GI Jane."

"In that case, I'll have Grey Goose. One encounter with Ana is enough for any night."

"That's probably sensible."

Two hours later, I fell sideways on the couch,

giggling. My glass was empty. The bottle was empty.

"*Shart* is not a proper word."

Ethan squinted at the board. "Yes, it definitely is."

"Merriam-Webster doesn't agree with you."

"It didn't agree with you for *derp* either, Dani. But I still let you have it, even when you spelled it with two p's."

"But the rules..."

"Earlier, you said you hated rules."

"I do. Rules, schmules." When he leaned closer, I stroked his face. "I like your beard. Did I ever tell you that you're really pretty?"

"Let's make a deal. You let me have *shart*, and I'll carry you up to bed, because I'm quite sure you can't walk."

"Okay, but you still have to add the points up."

"Don't worry about that. Let's just say you won."

Oh, if Ethan was going to carry me, I'd definitely won. He scooped me into his arms, blanket and all, and I breathed him in. A hint of cologne, courtesy of Bradley, no doubt, and a lot of man. His hoodie still smelled all Ethan-y too. Yup, I was totally, one hundred percent wrapped up in Ethan.

And Scrabble was my new favourite game.

CHAPTER 35

THE NEXT MORNING, Mack called while it was still dark. I rolled over and looked at the clock. The numbers floated around a bit, but when I squinted, I saw it was just after five. Hurrah—I'd gotten a whole hour of sleep. We really needed to have words about this.

"I'm still ash...asleep."

"You sound drunk."

"I will neither confirm nor deny that rumour."

"Well, I found your stalker woman. Her claim to fame is having restraining orders from three different celebrities. I think she's collecting them."

So, Mack had found Lavinia. Did it really matter now? Unless she was six feet tall and popped steroids like candy, she wasn't going to be our culprit. But a tiny voice inside me that wouldn't shut up said *what if?* I should visit her, just in case.

"What's the address?"

I scribbled it on my hand as Mack recited it, hoping I'd be able to read my own writing when I woke up properly and hopefully sober.

"Oh, and one more thing. DJ Steel's five feet four and looks as if a squirrel could take him down."

Fan-fucking-tastic. "Then I guess we can rule him out. Is that everything?"

"Get some rest, Dan."

"Absolutely. I can do that."

Stefanie was making breakfast when I did eventually make it downstairs. She'd fried a stack of bacon and covered it in maple syrup, and now she was busy with pancakes. The aroma permeated through the house like a tractor beam, drawing the inhabitants towards the kitchen.

Emmy was in her gym clothes, munching her way through a plateful while Alex glowered at her over his smoothie. Oliver chewed absentmindedly as he studied a pile of documents, and Lyle's food was getting cold since he was paying more attention to Stefanie than her cooking. It was kind of sweet, the way he mooned over her. Every girl deserved a man to look at her like that.

Ethan had chosen a spot at the far end of the table, and he watched the others through wary eyes. He really didn't do well with crowds, did he? I piled my own plate high and took the stool beside him, beyond grateful when he slid a package of headache pills in my direction.

"Feeling all right?" he asked.

"No worse than usual. You okay?"

He gave me a delicious little smile. "Mmm hmm."

Oh, hell. Ethan was tastier than bacon.

And the bacon was pretty damn delicious.

"Thanks for helping me last night. Usually, people just leave me on the couch."

"Anytime. What are we doing today?"

"I need to go visit somebody, and you need to keep a low profile. Before I go, I'll give you a proper tour of the house and a rundown on the security system so we don't have a repeat of last night."

"Some parts of last night weren't so bad."

"You want a rematch?"

Out of the corner of my eye, I saw his hand inch towards mine, but then he seemed to have second thoughts.

"At drinking or Scrabble?"

"Both?"

"Okay." He chewed for a few moments. "Do you think I could go to Spectre today? I need to speak to Ronan and Harold, and I'm missing my guitar like crazy. It's in the studio there."

I thought of inviting them over to Riverley, but if Harold had any part in this whole affair, I didn't want him near Emmy's estate. Nor did I want Ethan at Spectre. Last I'd heard, there were more reporters waiting outside than at the local newspaper's offices.

I was also curious to see where Harold called home. Mack had already gotten me aerial photographs of the mansion, hidden behind towering walls amidst beautifully landscaped grounds.

"I don't think visiting Spectre's the best idea. How about you get Ronan to pick up your stuff and we meet at Harry's place?"

"That works too. I'll make some calls and set it up."

While he did that, I went to get my visit to Lavinia over with. According to Mack, she was thirty-nine years old and lived alone in an apartment over her parents' garage. Mack hadn't been able to find any record of her being employed, so I had high hopes of finding her at home.

And I did. She cracked open the door and peered up at me through the gap. Yes, up. She was even smaller than me, and judging by the skinny arm holding onto the door, she'd struggle to carry her groceries let alone a fully grown man.

Still, I was here now, so I figured I might as well ask some questions.

"Lavinia Dixon?"

She nodded. "Are you the police?"

"Were you expecting them?"

"No. Well, kind of, I guess."

"About Ethan White?"

She looked down at her feet and nodded again.

"I'm not the police, but I am working for him. Could I have a little chat with you?"

"You're working for Ethan?"

"Yes, I'm a private investigator."

She slowly swung the door open, and I followed her inside. The apartment was basic, furnished in thrift shop chic and neat as a pin. Unremarkable, except for the collage of Ethan pictures that covered an entire wall of the living room. Newspaper clippings, magazine pages, hand-drawn portraits, and even a lopsided needlepoint. Wow.

"Please, sit down."

She motioned me towards a lumpy couch and took the seat opposite, perching right on the edge of the mismatched armchair as if she planned to take off at a moment's notice. That was okay, though. I had my running shoes on again.

"Are you investigating the murder?"

"Yes, I am. I don't think Ethan did it."

I watched her carefully to gauge her reaction, and her head wobbled back and forth like a bobblehead doll. Her expression? Relief.

"Oh, yes, I know. Ethan would never hurt anybody.

It was that other man, wasn't it?"

She clapped a hand over her mouth.

Come again? "What other man?"

Silence.

"Perhaps I shouldn't have mentioned him."

"No, you really should."

Nothing.

"Please, Lavinia. I promise you won't get into any trouble. What other man?"

"The one who was outside that night."

My heart started beating a wild tattoo. Was she telling me what I thought she was?

"Hang on, you were there? On the night of the murder?"

She hesitated a beat then nodded.

"Whereabouts? What did you see?"

More silence.

"Lavinia?"

"You promise I won't get into trouble? Mom gets upset every time I get a restraining order."

Good grief. "I promise."

She glanced at the door and cleared her throat.

"I've got this little spot in Ethan's garden, see? Sort of behind the bushes. Sometimes I see him walk past the windows."

Oh, that wasn't creepy at all.

"And what did you see that night?"

"Ethan brought a girl home. You know, the one who died? I saw her on the news, real pretty she was."

"They were alone?"

Lavinia nodded. "They went inside, and the lights came on upstairs. I thought they were...you know..."

Jealousy flashed through me, sharp and red. Stupid

considering how the evening had ended. *Focus, Dan.*

"And after that?"

"The man arrived. I thought it was strange because he parked out on the road instead of in Ethan's driveway."

"What did he do?"

"Stood in the shadows for a minute or two, then he disappeared around the side of the house and appeared in the living room. I guess he must have gone in through the back door."

Or the cellar window.

"Did you see him come out again?"

"Maybe five minutes later? He put a bag in Ethan's car, and then he looked straight at me. I could hardly breathe! He was only a few feet away, and I swear I thought my heart would stop beating."

"But he didn't see you?"

"I don't think so. He went back into the house, and I ran all the way to the bus stop on Montrose."

Fuck. So near, yet so damn far. But I'd found an actual witness who could place the suspect at Ethan's house that night. Jay was gonna shit boulders.

"So you didn't see anything else?"

"I was terrified he'd catch me and tell Ethan. I know I shouldn't have been there, but Ethan's the light of my life." She waved at her stalker-wall. "See?"

"I totally understand." Perhaps not totally, but I could relate to finding Ethan attractive. "What did he look like?"

"Big."

That was it? Big? I already knew that much.

"What about his face? His hair colour? Was he old or young? What race was he?"

She shrugged helplessly. "I don't know. He was wearing one of those hoods like Ethan normally does, and gloves."

"That was all you saw?"

"I think he was a white man. In the house, under the living room lights, I caught a glimpse of his face as he turned, and he looked kind of pale. And his top was by Nike. I saw the swoosh."

So we were looking for a white, Nike-wearing big dude. That didn't narrow it down much. I suppose at least it ruled out Ty.

"You said he parked out on the street. Did you see what car he drove?"

"I'm not sure. There was a dark-coloured car a little way up that wasn't there when I arrived."

"What sort of car? Do you know the make or model?"

"A BMW. You know, with the blue and white badge? Kind of big."

"I don't suppose you saw the licence plate?"

She shook her head no.

Okay, so she didn't give me anything concrete, but she had confirmed a lot of my suspicions. Couldn't the dark-coloured car outside Ethan's place be the same one that tried to run down Stefanie? We hadn't found any camera footage of that incident yet, but Mack was still looking.

"Why didn't you tell the police about this?"

"I thought they'd arrest me."

"They won't. I'll make sure of it, and Ethan won't be angry. Would you be willing to testify in court if he needs you to?"

"Will it help him?"

"Yes, and I'm sure he'd be eternally grateful." Just like I was sure he'd be installing motion sensors all over his next property.

She clasped her hands together and smiled. "Then of course I'll do it."

Chapter 36

OLIVER LOOKED HAPPIER than I'd ever seen him when I told him about Lavinia, and Lyle, well, I thought he was going to turn cartwheels.

Ethan, on the other hand, looked shell-shocked.

"You know, up until now, I always had that bit of doubt in my mind, that maybe I did do it. I can't believe there was somebody in my house and I didn't notice."

"You were probably unconscious by that point."

"That's even worse."

I squeezed his arm. "Neither scenario's great. Did you get the meeting with Harry and Ronan set up?"

"Yeah, for tomorrow. Harold's wife's having a dinner party tonight. Just don't call him Harry to his face—he hates it."

I made a mental note to call him Harry every single time we spoke.

"I feel sorry for his wife." Especially when I thought back to the way his fingers had crawled up my arm when I was in his office. "I get the impression Harry doesn't keep his dick in his pants."

Ethan chuckled. "I wouldn't feel too bad for her. I accidentally walked in on her balling her tennis coach last year. We've been avoiding each other ever since."

My embarrassing snort only made Ethan laugh louder. "They're perfect for each other."

"You don't like Harold?"

"Honestly? No."

Ethan sighed. "I don't know what to do about him. Ronan wants me to find someone new, he did even before that poor girl died, but it's difficult. Harold's been with me since I started. I still remember the old days where we'd drive to gigs together, and he'd go in and sort out the arrangements while I slept in the backseat of his car. I'd play, and afterwards we'd split a pizza on the way back to the hotel. Neither of us had much money back then. He may have turned into a bit of a prick, but I couldn't have made it without his help."

"I understand your loyalty, really I do. But I just think it might be misplaced."

"Once this is over, maybe I'll look into my options."

"I think that's a good idea.

I met Harold's wife briefly when we arrived at the Styles residence the next day. Ethan rode behind tinted windows in the back of a company Explorer, and I got him to lie down as we approached Harry's house when I spotted a couple of reporters hanging around outside.

April Styles opened the door for us and looked at Ethan like he was dog shit. Her Botoxed forehead didn't move; it was all in the eyes. Ice blue, flat and cold. Then she aimed her gaze in my direction and checked me out from head to foot, assessing.

"You must be Ethan's new toy. I've heard about those women who go for criminals, but I've never quite understood why."

I smiled sweetly at her. "In Ethan's case, it's mostly

to do with his enormous cock."

We left her choking as I took Ethan's hand and pulled him further into the house.

"I can't believe you just said that," he whispered.

"I have problems keeping my mouth shut sometimes."

He gave me a cheeky smile. "Good to hear."

I couldn't believe he just said that.

Ethan took the lead and steered us through the hallways until we reached Harry's den. Ronan was in there already, seated on a wooden chair while Harry lorded over a desk even bigger than the monstrosity in his office.

He looked pointedly at his watch. "Glad you could join us."

Asshole. We were only two minutes late. Ethan took over the discussion, and I tuned their voices out as they started talking in minute detail about recording contracts and a charity gig Styles wanted to arrange.

Ol' Harry had a nice house here. It was sure as hell more expensive than Ethan's. I knew what Ethan's net worth was, but how much money did Harry have? And more to the point, how much of his lifestyle did Spectre fund?

I needed to give Ronan a nudge about those accounts and also chase Mack up on Harry's personal finances. Did this place have a mortgage? How did his credit cards look? Harry had certainly gained financially from Ethan's incarceration if Ronan was to be believed.

What would happen now Ethan was back?

I tuned into the conversation again. Ethan spoke quietly but confidently about his business, and I noticed Harry's cockiness had subsided since we first arrived. He still got his points across, but he was almost deferential when Ethan had a difference of opinion. They talked for a few more minutes, and Ethan spent a little longer reading through some contracts before signing them.

"I've brought your guitar," Ronan told him as we got up to leave.

"Thanks, bro."

Ronan waited until we were outside in the hallway before leaning close and passing me a memory stick. "And I got this for you."

"The accounts?" I whispered.

He nodded and stepped back as Harry came out behind us. I guess no nudging was required, then.

Ethan picked up his guitar case, and I followed him down the hallway. I was dying to see exactly what was in there—electric or acoustic? And I was even more impatient to hear him play it. It was true what Ronan said—girls went for the guitarist.

We'd parked further up the drive than Ronan, well out of sight of the gates. I didn't want any photos of Ethan going public. I bleeped the locks on the car, but before we could climb inside, a man sprung out of the bushes next to it.

A reporter? No, not without a camera. This dude had nothing in his hands and a crazy glint in his eyes. He smelled pretty bad too, like he hadn't showered for a week or washed his clothes for a month.

"I knew you'd show up here eventually, you piece of scum," he hissed.

Ethan tried to get in front of me, but he obviously didn't understand how this worked. I shoved him behind me instead and faced up to the guy, hands on hips.

"Who the fuck are you?"

"I'm nothing, not now. Just the man whose sister he murdered." He fixed his dead stare on Ethan. "Why did you do it? That's what I want to know. Why?"

"I didn't kill Christina."

"You're lying!"

So, this must be Kevin Walker, according to Mack's file. He flew at Ethan, arms outstretched, and I swept his feet out from underneath him.

"Don't," I warned.

Ethan stared at me, open-mouthed, while Kevin screamed blue murder into the dirt. I held him down until the yelling subsided.

"If I let you up, are you going to keep back?"

There was a muffled response and he went limp. I took that as a yes.

I'd misinterpreted.

The instant Kevin got to his feet, he came at us again with the same result.

"One more chance," I said. "You don't get a third."

I let him stand again, and this time he stayed back, screaming obscenities at both of us.

I balled up my fists, tempted to make him stop, but Ethan snaked an arm around my waist and held me steady.

"Leave it, Dani. He's lost his sister, and he's got a right to be upset." Ethan didn't sound angry, only sad.

"But he's blaming you."

"Because right now, I'm the only person who looks guilty."

"He shouldn't—"

"Dani..."

"I have questions for him."

"Not now. Let's just get out of here."

Fury pulsed through my veins, but the rational part of me, the part that wasn't angry a misinformed hobo had just tried to attack the guy I refused to admit how much I liked, knew Ethan was right. Kevin had as much fault in this as Ethan, and lashing out was natural.

I took a step back.

Ronan had appeared beside us, and his colour didn't look great. He bore more than a passing resemblance to one of Ethan's masks. I gave him a little wave.

"Nothing to worry about. Just an occupational hazard."

His expression said he thought my occupation was insane, but he tentatively waved back.

"Well, that's the entertainment over for this afternoon," I said to Ethan as Kevin stomped away.

"You have a lot of occupational hazards, don't you?"

"A few."

"Have you ever considered getting a nice, normal job? Hairdressing? A secretary?"

"What, and miss all this fun? No way."

CHAPTER 37

THE INSTANT HARRY'S gates opened, I blasted out of them, sending the reporters scattering for cover. I hoped they broke their stupid cameras. At least one got crunched under the wheels.

Ethan sat up a few streets later. "I know I promised not to criticise your driving, but..."

"It's okay, I didn't hit anything."

I saw him roll his eyes in the mirror. "What did Ronan give you?"

"A set of your accounts."

"What for?"

"I don't trust Harry. Something's off about him."

Everything was off about him.

"True, he's grown into a bit of an asshole over the years, but I'm not sure he's dishonest."

"Well, let's find out for sure, shall we?"

"But—"

"Do you trust me?"

Ten seconds passed, twenty, thirty, before Ethan softly answered, "Yeah, I trust you."

Good. We were making progress. "Then let me look into this."

The next morning, with Ethan and his guitar safely ensconced in the music room, I called in my two secret weapons. As well as Georgia, I had Nick's girlfriend, Lara, who happened to be a genius at math. With Mack on hand to trace wire payments, I was confident we'd dig out anything suspicious.

That left me with the rest of the investigation. Ha.

I tried cross-referencing all the names on my list with car registrations, but nobody drove a BMW. Then I did the same with the list of similar crimes Mack had dug up, and although I found seven hits, none of those led anywhere. Two of the perps were still in prison, one more had died, and the remaining four cases were colder than a refrigerator in the Arctic.

Three days, wasted. Three days of staring at a computer screen and walking the streets. Three days of smoky clubs and dive bars and blank stares and shrugs that left me tired as fuck and twice as irritable. I barely saw Ethan. With his strange sleep patterns and my even stranger work patterns, we were like two ships passing in the night.

He did email me, though. Memes about vodka and Scrabble jokes and stupid words from the urban dictionary. His messages were the only thing that made me smile.

"You look like shit," Emmy helpfully told me after breakfast on day four.

"Thanks, sweetie. You too." I wasn't kidding. She had a black eye and a bandage on her left forearm. "What happened?"

"Black took me out to La Mesa. You know, the new Spanish place?"

"The service was that bad?"

"Service was good, food was excellent. But that armed gang that's been targeting upmarket restaurants paid a visit after the main course."

"Shit."

There had been eight robberies so far in and around Richmond. Four men on motorbikes would burst in, threaten diners with guns and knives, take whatever cash and jewellery they could get their hands on, and disappear into the night.

"The score was Blackwood four, robbers nil."

"What happened to your eye?"

"One of the assholes cracked me with an elbow while I was relieving him of his pistol. He'll probably be awake now. They had to surgically remove a fork from his thigh."

"And your arm?"

"A waiter spilled coffee on me. On the bright side, our meal was free."

"Trouble follows you around."

"Must be my natural charm. Anyhow, why do you look so rough? How's the Ethan thing going?"

"It isn't. That's the problem. Nobody knows anything."

"Sure they do, you just haven't found them yet. Why don't you take the day off and regroup? You're not doing anyone any favours when you're run into the ground like this."

I sighed and poured more coffee. "Maybe."

Emmy pushed the mug away from me. "Do it. Go back to bed." She stared until I stood up. "Why don't you take Ethan with you?"

I flipped her off as I walked out of the room.

As always, Emmy was right. I did feel better after a

few hours' sleep. And no, I hadn't followed through on her second suggestion.

Where was Ethan, anyway? He hadn't been around at breakfast, and I knew he wouldn't have left the house. I shuffled downstairs in socks and pyjamas to look for him. Not in the kitchen, not in the living room, not in the gym... I heard the faint sound of the piano coming from the direction of the music room. Emmy's husband was the only person who played it, unless...

I pushed open the door. Ethan sat at the keys, playing a song I'd never heard before. And with him was Eli.

Neither of them noticed me, and before I could step inside, Eli began to sing. Now, I'd heard his old recordings and the occasional drunk rendition at karaoke, but I'd never heard him sing live before and mean it.

His voice was pure sex, and Ethan's music was the bed for it. Yeah, I really shouldn't have been thinking that way seeing as Eli was almost a decade younger than me and also Tia's boyfriend, but there wasn't another description that would do it justice. Ethan's fingers glided effortlessly across the keys, and I leaned against the door jamb, eyes closed, lost in the song until it came to an end.

"Bravo. I think I'm having an eargasm."

They turned their heads, and Ethan blushed when he saw me. Shit. The man was a hot mess of sexy and adorable.

"That's not a proper word, Dani."

"I'm still claiming the ten points. Seriously, that was amazing. What song was it?"

"It hasn't got a name," Ethan said. "We just wrote

it."

Holy hell, that had "hit" written all over it. "You guys have to record that."

"We're just messing around," Eli said.

What had they been doing for the last three days? "Exactly how much messing around have you done?"

"About an album's worth," Ethan admitted.

I looked around the music room. Scattered notes covered the coffee table, accompanied by empty coffee cups, a pair of drumsticks, and a tambourine. Ethan's guitar, a Martin acoustic, sat on its stand next to Eli's favourite Gibson ES-295 and a Fender Stratocaster. Eli had brought his whole collection of guitars when he moved into Riverley a couple of months back. He'd even tried giving me a lesson, but my fingernails didn't mix well with the fretboard, and I'd quickly gone back to listening.

They *had* been busy, hadn't they?

"Can you play something else?"

Ethan moved across on the piano stool and patted the leather seat. I settled next to him, my thigh pressed against his, and my pulse began racing before they even started the next song.

A freaking love song.

I knew Eli was singing about Tia—the lines about an English rose and an artist's soul gave it away—but that didn't stop my heart from melting all the way to my freaking feet. And when Ethan switched to drums and Eli picked up the Fender, those feet wanted to get up and dance.

Yes, they'd written an album's worth. A platinum-selling, Billboard chart-topping, hit album's worth.

"I could listen to you all day." I looked at my watch.

"Oops, I actually have."

It was almost seven. Where had the time gone?

"And you haven't even heard Ethan sing yet," Eli said.

Ethan sang?

Maybe, but he also turned red and changed the subject. "Good thing you dressed up for the show."

"I'll remember to wear a cocktail dress next time."

"Don't worry. I've always been a big fan of the Simpsons."

My turn to blush. "Someone bought them for me as a joke. I'll change for dinner."

"Leave the pyjamas on. I get the impression nobody who lives in this house worries about that sort of thing."

So I did. Ethan wore a pair of distressed jeans, courtesy of Bradley, and a plain white T-shirt that contrasted with his darker skin. No hoodie, which was a definite improvement.

After dinner, we curled up under blankets in the basement screening room. I picked the movie, which I thought from the blurb was a lighthearted adventure but turned out to be a rather tragic tale of a boy searching for his parents. Each time I snuck a look at Ethan, he looked unhappier. First from the way he gripped the edge of the blanket, then from the tension that built up in his jaw, and finally, he bit that damn lip again.

"You want me to turn the movie off?"

He nodded.

"Ethan, what happened to you growing up?"

Mack hadn't been able to find a thing, not even a birth certificate, and it bugged the hell out of me.

Ethan's whole childhood had been erased.

Silence.

"Ethan?"

Nothing.

"It can help to talk about these things."

"I'll talk about anything but that. Please, just leave it alone."

"That's exactly why you should talk it through."

"Enough, Dani."

His answering growl should have been a warning, but I was too stupid to take the hint.

"But..."

He threw the blanket off, got up, and walked out. The sound of the door slamming behind him echoed as his footsteps grew quieter.

Good going, Dan. I sure could have handled that one better.

CHAPTER 38

WHAT WAS ETHAN hiding? Why wouldn't he talk about his early years? Apart from that one brief hint at trouble, when he told me he'd been alone through his teenage years, he'd given me nothing.

Why had I pressed him? The warning signs had all been there, and like an idiot, I'd ignored them. *Dammit, Dan.*

At times like this, I hated myself. And how did I deal with that self-loathing? That's right—I put on a party dress, fluffed up my hair, called for a car, and went to Black's.

"Been a while, Dan," the bartender said as he slid my first drink over. Double vodka, coke, no ice.

"Yeah, it has."

Because for a rare few weeks in my life, I'd enjoyed spending time with a man whose primary goal wasn't to get between my legs. And just look where that had left me.

Abandoned.

My mom always said nobody would want me, and I couldn't stand the thought of her being right. I didn't need a psychiatrist to tell me that was why I tried to prove, over and over again, that she was wrong.

And tonight, it didn't take long before the first willing piece of flesh walked over to me. A blond guy, tallish, vaguely attractive in that his eyes and mouth were in the right place. So was his wallet, because he kept buying me drinks.

After the fourth—or was it the fifth?—I let him help me down from the barstool. He wanted me, at least for the night, and that was enough.

Ethan didn't.

The blond's hand rested on my ass as he led me around the edge of the dance floor and out through the front door. Where were all the cabs? I just wanted to get out of there. The music was too loud, too insistent, and I began to feel a bit sick.

"Don't worry; I'll get an Uber."

The guy kept one hand around my waist, holding me up, as he tapped at his phone with the other.

Then I was torn away from him and lifted off the ground.

What the...?

"Who the hell are you?" my new friend asked, eyes wide as he gaped over my head.

My rescuer didn't answer. He was a man of few words. He was also Emmy's husband.

"Put me down!" I screeched at him.

"No."

I beat on his back, but it was pointless. The man was a mountain, huge and solid as rock.

He'd parked his Porsche Cayenne in the service alley at the side of the club, and I soon found myself dumped in the front seat.

"Stay," he instructed, then walked around to the driver's side.

There was no point in trying to run. I'd break an ankle in my pumps, and Black was faster than he looked. I stared out the window as he backed into traffic. The man he'd taken me from still stood at the kerb, on the phone, and I didn't know whether he was reporting my kidnapping or trying to find a replacement model.

"Why did you do that?" I asked Black.

"To stop you from making another mistake."

"I already made a mistake today. I was trying to fix it."

"With a meaningless fuck?"

"It helps."

"You'd have hated yourself in the morning."

What I hated even more was that he was right. I wiped at my eyes with my fingers, not caring whether my mascara smudged.

We drove back to Riverley in silence, with one brief stop for me to throw up the drinks I'd knocked back. My mouth tasted like an armpit when Black lifted me out of the car and carried me up to bed.

"Want me to get one of the girls for you?"

I shook my head. Another witness to my inadequacy? No thanks.

He told Emmy, though. I knew he would. They didn't keep secrets from each other. She knocked on my door just after eight with a glass of juice and some headache pills.

"How are you feeling?"

"Like shit."

"Same as usual, then. Swallow these and drink this. Georgia, Lara, and Mack are gonna be here in half an hour, and we need to have a meeting."

Suddenly, I was awake. "Did they find something?"

"Yeah. Get dressed."

When I got to the conference room, Ethan was already seated at the far end of the table next to Lara. He glanced over at me then quickly looked away. Great. I took the seat closest to the door and pretended to make notes. Anything to avoid eye contact.

Emmy sauntered in and peered at my legal pad.

"Why have you written 'strawberry cheesecake' six times?" she asked, sliding a cup of coffee in front of me.

"I'm just hungry."

"At least the strawberries are good for you."

Georgia and Mack hurried in with their laptops, and I could tell from Georgia's grin that they'd found something good. I sat up a little straighter, and cheesecake didn't seem quite so interesting anymore.

"Okay, so we pulled apart the accounting system," Georgia explained, "and looked in the most likely places for fraud. Journals, suspense accounts, fictitious employees, false supplier invoices. I think you can get a better deal on your office rent, by the way," she told Ethan. "Your landlord's screwing you over."

Trivial, in the great scheme of things.

"Did you find anything else?" I asked.

Why couldn't people get to the point?

"Yes, we did. It's actually quite clever. Every time a royalty payment comes in, it's followed by a separate invoice for twenty percent withholding tax, which the purchase ledger clerk dutifully pays at the end of every month after Harold authorises the payments."

Three blank faces stared at her—mine, Emmy's, and Ethan's.

She rolled her eyes. "The whole point of withholding tax is that it's withheld? Like, by the person who pays the royalty? They don't pay the whole lot then invoice for it separately. In this case, Spectre's ended up paying it twice."

"So Harry was doing the invoicing?" I guessed.

"The money goes to an offshore account in the Cayman Islands," Mack said. "He's the sole signatory."

"And what's the overall impact so far?"

Lara looked down at the papers in front of her. "It's been going on for almost ten years, so twenty percent on all the royalties paid through Spectre in that time, which comes to about $17 million."

"Fuck," Ethan whispered.

"Surely Ethan has tax advisors?" Emmy asked. "Why didn't they spot this?"

"Ah, now here's the clever bit," Mack said. "Every month, ten percent of the net transfers into the Cayman account get wired out to Puerto Rico. The receiving account is controlled by one Roland Harding."

Ethan turned pale. "Roland's the tax partner at the accounting firm I use."

"You've got to hand it to Harry," Emmy said. "It was a good little scam. Simple, elegant, easy money."

We all stared at her.

"Just saying. We're still going to fuck him over, obviously."

"Before what happened, I was thinking of changing accountants," Ethan said. "I thought Harding's fees were too high, and Ronan had met with a couple of other firms. Harold was trying to persuade me to stick with Harding. I guess now I know why."

"That's a good motive for somebody wanting you out of the way, don't you think?" I suggested.

He sagged back in his chair. "I can't believe he

would do this to me. I trusted him."

"Shitty people do shitty things to good people," Emmy said. "The question is, did he just steal money, or did he add murder to his repertoire?"

"We haven't been able to find an alibi for him on the night of Christina's death," Mack said. "His wife was at the opening of an art gallery, but he wasn't with her."

"You know what, normally I'm not a fan of the press or the police, but I vote we dump this back in their laps," said Emmy. "We give the cops the information on the theft, then we tip off the reporters, and that way the investigation can't be swept under the carpet. Let Harold's reputation get dragged through the mud. It might go some way to making Ethan's halo shine again."

She was right. The Virginia PD could do some proper work for a change. "It's trial by media nowadays. The courtroom part is almost incidental. I say we go for it."

"Ethan?" Emmy asked.

"I hate the thought of my face being everywhere."

"It already is, honey. This way, it just looks a little prettier."

If he kept biting his lip like that, there wouldn't be a lot left of it. Finally, he came to a decision.

"I'll go with whatever you think."

The sight of Harold being led from Spectre's offices did indeed make a compelling picture. Front page, above the fold. Officer Tenlow had been to the barber before he made the arrest and even ironed his uniform.

And in the scribblings underneath, the tide was indeed beginning to turn. A week after Georgia's discovery, the waters around Christina's murder were being muddied, and thanks to some well-placed leaks from Blackwood, doubt started to creep in over Ethan's guilt.

"This is good," I said to him, waving the paper.

"Is it? Now people see me as a victim again. Poor little Ethan, couldn't look after himself."

What did he mean by "again?" I had a horrible feeling he wasn't talking about recent events, but I didn't dare to press him on it. He'd begun speaking to me once more, small talk and careful, measured words, his eyes shuttered and his secrets safely locked away. Strained. I missed the carefree smiles from the music room. Ethan had another court appearance at ten tomorrow morning too, some preliminary motion, which added more stress to an already heavy load.

So I did the only thing I could. I backed off.

"I suppose that's not such a great thing, either."

That got me a tiny smile.

"Do you want me to come with you tomorrow?"

A nod.

Yes, we still had a way to go, but I counted that as progress.

But the day got worse after lunch when Tenlow called.

"Your man's singing like a canary about the fraud, but he's got an alibi for the murder."

I groaned. "What is it?"

"It's a she. Madame Felice. At the time your hooker was being stabbed, Styles was apparently..." Tenlow paused while he cleared his throat, "scrubbing Madame Felice's kitchen floor with a toothbrush. She knows this for sure because she was holding the other end of the leash he was wearing. And the squeaking from his rubber pants on the tile was really getting on her nerves."

I covered the mouthpiece while I burst into laughter. When I'd recovered enough to speak, I heard Tenlow chuckling away on the other end.

"Thought you might find that amusing. She supplied photos. Want me to send them over?"

"Oh jeez, yeah, why not?" Emmy would appreciate a laugh too. "But if Styles didn't actually kill Christina, maybe he hired someone?"

"We're working on that angle at the moment. He sure had enough money, but he's not admitting anything."

"Keep trying."

Tenlow's news wasn't the answer I'd been hoping for. It meant Ethan wouldn't get ripped off by that piece of pond slime anymore, but there was still a killer on the loose.

Ethan and Stefanie still weren't safe.

And my job wasn't over.

CHAPTER 39

"YOU KNOW YOU'RE going to court, right?" Emmy asked me the next morning. "Not a fashion show?"

Well, yes, of course I knew that. But I'd done my hair and chosen a suit that showcased my *ahem* assets because Jay would be there. And I also knew that would piss him off.

Ethan wore a suit too. Bradley had ordered it for him and put the screws on the designer to skip the wait for custom tailoring. I firmly believed that every man should own a made-to-measure suit, if only for the pleasure a woman got from peeling him out of it. I shoved my hands into my jacket pockets because they itched to reach for Ethan's buttons.

My phone buzzed in my hand, and I glanced at the screen. Trick? Guess Emmy wasn't answering right now, so he'd decided to try another option. Well, he'd have to wait.

"Ready to go?" Oliver asked.

He had an entire closet full of suits. Saville Row, mainly. He flew a tailor in once a year to measure up. Save for the occasional pair of shorts when he went running, Oliver never wore anything else.

Had I ever done the peeling thing with Oliver? No. Not because he wasn't hot—he was—but because he was fucked in the head, perhaps even worse than me.

And then he became a work associate, placing him firmly off-limits. Dancing the horizontal tango had the potential to end in disaster for both of us. Above all, I valued his friendship, and I'd never jeopardise that.

Today, he'd offered to come with us for moral support. He wasn't co-counsel, but I knew that even having him in the public gallery would bolster Lyle's confidence.

The plan called for us to arrive in the same car—Ethan, Lyle, Oliver, and I—run the gauntlet of fans and paparazzi waiting outside, walk in through the front door of the courthouse, and promise to answer questions afterwards. Except when the hearing was over, Oliver and Lyle would go out the way we came in while Ethan and I snuck out the back to a spare vehicle, thereby avoiding the press and their cameras. I'd used the tactic before with a degree of success.

Jay gave me a look of contempt when I walked in at Ethan's side, but his eyes widened when he saw Oliver behind us. Whoops, had I forgot to mention to Jay that his old nemesis was assisting us? Shame.

My plan to spring Oliver on him obviously worked because he wasn't his usual, smooth self while he tried to make his points. He stumbled over his words a couple of times and made so many objections that even the judge looked pissed off with him.

Lyle was nervous, but he'd worn his lucky tie, his lucky socks, and apparently his lucky boxer shorts too, and his time with Oliver paid dividends. He got through the hearing with barely a mark from Jay's claws. Bail was upheld. The case rumbled on.

But the court reporters waiting outside didn't care about Lyle. They'd spotted Oliver, and while Ethan might have been a star in the music world, Oliver was the undisputed king of this one. Even though he hadn't said a word inside, the instant he stepped out of the doors, they descended on him like the vultures they were.

Which gave me the perfect opportunity to flee for the rear exit with Ethan. And, as it turned out, Lyle.

"What are you doing here?" I asked him. "You're supposed to be giving a press conference."

"Did you see them?" He sucked in a breath. "No way am I going out there. They'll eat me alive."

"Oliver's gonna be pissed."

"I'd rather deal with Oliver than get knocked out by a microphone."

"Fine, come with us, then."

We seriously had to work on his resilience.

I went out first to check for reporters, and when there were none, I beckoned for the other two to follow me. Where was the damned car? One of the Blackwood drivers had dropped it off earlier, and I had the spare key in my purse.

"Black Ford Explorer guys. First one to spot it gets a cookie."

Why hadn't I got them to bring my Camaro instead? At least nobody could miss it.

A flight of steps led from the courthouse to the parking lot, and we'd just reached the bottom when a revving engine caught my attention. A black BMW, speeding towards us. What the...? Visions of Stefanie flew through my mind, and I backed up, pulling Ethan and Lyle with me.

Probably just me being paranoid. If someone wanted to run us over, they'd have waited until we were further from the steps, right?

Then the car slowed, and the rear window rolled down.

Oh fuck. Oh fuck!

The barrel of a gun poked out, and I had a fraction of a second to make a decision. Did I dive left or right?

Left. I went left.

I shoved Ethan behind a concrete planter and dove on top of him. As I looked back, I saw the confusion on Lyle's face for an instant, right before the back of his head exploded.

The chatter of an automatic weapon reigned supreme while I held Ethan down. As I'd been in the courthouse, I'd had to leave my gun at home so I couldn't even return fire. All I could do was lie there, helpless.

Glass shattered as the courthouse doors disintegrated, and concrete chips from the walls rained down on us. Splinters and leaves from the plants above filled the air.

The noise seemed to go on forever, but in reality, it could only have been seconds—the time it took to empty a magazine. Tyres squealed as the car took off.

Footsteps came running almost instantly, but it was too late. The shooter was gone, and Lyle was dead. And Ethan? Well, he wasn't moving, either.

Oliver appeared at my side and helped me up. "Are you hurt?"

"No, but I think Ethan is. And Lyle... Fuck."

Emmy insisted that every single person who worked for Blackwood took a first aid course, and Oliver was no exception. He crouched beside Ethan and checked his vital signs.

"He's breathing, and I can't see any bullet holes. There's a bit of blood, but I'm not sure it's his."

"It's not."

It was Lyle's, and I was covered in it too. I'd felt its warm stickiness spray over my back and smelled its distinctive tang.

"Ethan must have hit his head as he fell." Oliver twisted around and shouted for help. "We need a medic over here."

A crowd had gathered, court employees and passers-by hovering, unsure what to do. One woman retched into a bush, and I noticed even Jay looked ashen. The only people moving were the reporters, clicking away with their cameras. They seemed to have beaten the courthouse's own security officers to the scene.

Maybe not having my gun wasn't such a bad thing. Getting arrested for murder would be a definite inconvenience.

Ethan let out a low groan, his eyes flickering open.

"Thank goodness," I whispered.

He tried to sit up but flopped sideways instead. I put my hand behind his head so he wouldn't hurt it again.

"What happened?"

"Don't try to get up. We'll talk about it later."

"Dani, you're bleeding."

"I'm okay. Just stay still."

Where were the fucking doctors? I tugged my bag towards me and rummaged through it, looking for my phone.

I only needed to make one call, and that was to the emergency number for the central control room at

Blackwood's headquarters. The one call I'd hoped I'd never have to make.

"Go ahead, Dan," came the efficient voice of the shift supervisor.

"Man down. It's Lyle."

The Richmond branch office wasn't far from the courtroom, and our team of first responders arrived before the ambulance did. More would follow from our main base, which lay half an hour outside the city. There wasn't much they could do, but just having my own people beside me made me feel better.

"Did you see the shooter?" one of them asked.

"No. Just the gun, then I hit the deck. The car was a BMW 5-Series. Black."

"We'll put out an alert."

I knew they would, but it was pointless. That car was long gone. Dumped, burned out, or hidden away in a backstreet garage. It had probably been stolen in the first place.

The medics had checked Ethan over, and now they tightened the straps securing him to the spinal board. I followed him into the ambulance in a daze.

"You can't ride in here," the doctor said.

"Then you're gonna have to drag me out."

He shrugged and closed the doors.

Ethan had a mild concussion and cuts to his hands and face from his trip across the concrete. Apart from ripping my scabby knees open again, I'd gotten away with bruises. My pantyhose had been shredded, and I threw my suit in the trash before rubbing myself raw in the hospital shower to get Lyle's blood and brain matter off me. Now I was wearing a set of scrubs, but I still felt filthy.

In the ER, they'd given Ethan a paper gown and parked him in a cubicle to wait for yet another doctor. I hovered at the curtain until he held a hand out.

Such a sweet gesture, and it made my eyes prickle. I sat on the edge of the bed and curled my fingers around his.

"What happened?" he asked.

"Somebody shot at us. You slept through the drama again."

"Fuck." He closed his eyes and leaned back on the pillow. "Where's Lyle?"

I shook my head, trying to keep my tears from falling. It didn't work.

"Oh, hell," Ethan muttered. "Is this ever going to end?" He gathered me up in his arms. "I'm sorry I ever came into your life, Dani."

"Out of everything that's happened in this mess, that's the one thing I'm not sorry for."

I leaned back a little so I could see his face. Dammit, he'd gone all blurry. But our lips were just an inch apart, and the fragile part of me that fucked to forget was tempted to lean forward, just to see what he'd taste like. My heart hammered against my ribcage. Now, more than ever, I needed to find that oblivion I always craved. Should I? What if...?

The curtain behind me was ripped back.

"Right, tell me who I need to fucking kill," Emmy demanded in a harsh whisper.

I groaned and sat up. She always did have impeccable timing.

"I don't know. I hardly saw anything."

The nurse walked in behind her. "You two have to leave. The doctor needs to check on Mr. White."

"Now?" I asked. "Can't we just have a few minutes?"

She folded her arms. "Now."

Ethan reached out to squeeze my hand. "It's okay, Dani. I'm not going anywhere."

I trailed Emmy out into the hallway on shaky legs, pulse still racing as we walked past the two Blackwood guards stationed outside Ethan's room. She checked the rooms either side until she found an empty office. Messy, papers lay everywhere, probably a doctor's. I closed the door behind us.

"Well, what did you see?"

"A black BMW with a gun barrel poking out the back window, and then I was on the ground and the shooting started." I pinched the bridge of my nose between my thumb and forefinger. "Then Lyle died. Fuck, Ems, I let him die."

"Don't you dare blame this on yourself."

"He wasn't even supposed to be there. He was meant to be out the front with Oliver. Dammit! Why did he have to change the plan?"

"I don't know, but he *was* there, and we can't turn back time."

A choking sob clawed its way out of my throat, then another, and another. Emmy hugged me tightly as I bawled my eyes out. Fuck, this was embarrassing. I tried to pull away, but she wouldn't let me.

"Just let the pain go, Dan. It's the easiest way."

"Really? You think?"

"Better than bottling it up. Trust me. It took me fourteen years to learn that little trick."

I sniffled again and wiped my nose on my sleeve. "What am I supposed to tell Stefanie? She really liked Lyle, and that's two people close to her she's lost in as many months."

"You don't have to tell her anything. Oliver's on his way to her now. He's going to handle it."

Now that the shock had set in, I was shaking inside. "I could have saved Lyle. I had to make the choice between his life and Ethan's. It was like playing God."

"And if you'd saved Lyle, Ethan would be the one in the morgue."

That realisation made me go rigid. I tried not to think about it. Failed. "But what gave me the right to choose? Why did I pick Ethan?"

Emmy took both my hands in hers. "Because you love Ethan, honey. Everyone can see it except you."

I pulled back. "Oh, no no no no no. That's not true. It can't be true. Daniela di Grassi does not do love."

"I don't think your heart cares about that."

"But Ethan breaks all my rules."

"So write new ones."

She made it sound so simple when I knew it was anything but.

"What do I do now?" I whispered.

"You'll figure it out. Between you, you'll figure it out."

CHAPTER 40

THE ARMOURED LIMOUSINE that drove us back to Riverley weighed over two tons and handled like a barge, but it would give a small tank a run for its money. I wasn't taking any more chances with Ethan's life.

He gripped my hand across the seat, his whole body tense. He'd barely spoken a word to me or anyone else since our chat at the hospital, and I hoped he wasn't going to withdraw completely. The man seemed to handle tragedy by bottling it up and closing himself off, and like Emmy said, that wasn't healthy.

"Ethan, are you okay?"

"No."

Perhaps that had been a dumb question, but his answer didn't help. Damn this man and his mercurial moods and buried secrets.

He didn't let go of my hand when we pulled up outside Riverley, and when he climbed out of the car, I ended up scrambling across the seat to follow.

"You're cutting off my circulation here."

Nada. I stumbled up the steps after him.

"Ethan?"

Zilch.

I caught him off-balance and shoved him into the nearest living room, because I wasn't getting dragged all over the house like a bloody security blanket.

"Ethan, you can't keep this up. You need to talk to me."

"What am I supposed to say?"

"Anything. Everything. Just tell me how you feel. If you keep it inside, it'll poison you."

He rounded on me. "You want to know how I feel? You really want to know how I feel?"

I nodded, taking a step back. He stalked after me until my ass hit the wall.

Then he bent his head.

And then he kissed me.

There was nothing gentle about it. A harsh clash of tongues and teeth, bordering on desperation. My heart jackhammered against my ribcage, chipping away the wall I'd built to protect myself. His hands tangled in my hair, and I was helpless to do anything but kiss him back until he pushed me away.

"Happy now? That's how I feel. And your blood was this far..." he said as he pinched his thumb and forefinger together, "from being all over my hands today. Literally." Eyes flashing, he walked to the far side of the room, opening up the distance between us again. "And as it is, I'll never be able to scrub Lyle's off."

I followed him, stopping a few feet away, still breathless. "The only person with blood on their hands is the person who pulled the trigger."

"But I was the cause. I'm like a fucking curse."

"Don't talk that way."

"I'll talk how I want if it's true."

He strode past me and out of the door.

Slam.

Shit. I reached up and touched my lips. They still burned from his attack and all the passion and fire behind it. My legs trembled, and I had less coordination than a jellyfish. Holy hell, if he could do that with a kiss, what would it be like if he...?

I couldn't think that way. This wasn't happening.

Ethan needed some time to cool down, and I needed a drink, preferably a stiff whisky. I glanced at my watch. It was almost eight o'clock, so I was certainly entitled to it.

I walked into the next room, grabbed the Jack Daniels from the wet bar, and hustled to the kitchen for ice.

Except when I got there, I found Stefanie had already had the same idea, only her vice was gin. She looked up at me, trying to focus.

"He's dead, Dan. Did you know that? He's dead."

Yeah, I knew that. I fucking knew that. I ran shaky fingers through my hair. Was that a lump? Had I missed a bit? I grabbed the strands between my fingers and tugged until I felt a sting on my scalp.

"I know, Stef. I'm so sorry."

"He was the only man who ever treated me like a person and not a commer...commor...commodity."

How much had she drunk? If that bottle was full when she started, then too much. I slid it away from her.

"I know, sweetie. Lyle had a good heart."

She burst into tears daintier than mine. A delicate trickle rather than a flood. "He asked me out on a date last night," she sobbed. "He promised he'd take me ice skating. I always wanted to go, and I've never been."

I hugged her tightly, but it was difficult to soothe

her when I was crying too. What should I say? I couldn't tell her it would be okay because it wouldn't be. Not now, not ever. Nothing could bring Lyle back.

So instead, I made her a promise of my own.

"I'll find whoever did this, and I'll make him pay."

CHAPTER 41

IT WAS ALL very well me making that promise to find Lyle's killer, but where did I start?

Most of my initial suspects had fallen away, and I only had two left—the man who killed Christina and Christina's brother. I hadn't forgotten the crazed glint in Kevin's eyes at Harry's house; he'd undoubtedly want revenge for his sister's death. That, I could understand. It was just a shame he'd fixated on Ethan being the culprit.

And—plot twist—whoever shot at us also had an accomplice. The shooter was in the back of the BMW, and since nobody had perfected the concept of a driverless car yet, someone else must have been behind the wheel. Either our suspect was working with a friend, or he'd hired labour in.

Neither option filled me with joy, but it could make our job a tiny bit easier. Two suspects meant two people to slip up.

My phone vibrated, and Yoda informed me I had a message from the dark side. Thanks, Nick. He was always messing with my ringtones.

Trick: we need to talk to ethan.

Not now. Ethan had quite enough on his plate already.

Dan: He's a little busy at the moment. What's it

about?

Trick: music. its IMPORTANT

Right. Important like catching a killer was important.

Dan: I'll pass the message on.

I tossed the phone into my bag and headed for the car. This morning, I'd called a war meeting in the big conference room at Blackwood headquarters, fifty people at least. Emmy had given the okay to sling more resources at the problem. Although she was a businesswoman, she also had a strong sense of right and wrong, and she wasn't afraid to spend money in pursuit of justice.

Neither of us wanted more people to die.

Ethan had come to the meeting too, and now he sat at the other end of the table, studying his hands. Not once did he look at me. I'd have to tackle that problem later, but for the moment, I had a team to brief.

All eyes except Ethan's watched me as I explained my theories about Christina's killer, Kevin, and their desire for revenge against Ethan.

"Any questions?"

"What about Harold Styles?" one of my investigators asked. "Couldn't he have hired somebody in?"

"It's possible, and we're looking into it. But I'm just not sure he'd have the connections to contract somebody for a drive-by shooting. He doesn't run in those circles, and we've been keeping a close eye on his communications. We've also been over his personal finances, and there haven't been any unusual payouts."

"Other than more Botox for his wife," Mack muttered. "It's amazing she's capable of speaking at all."

"Could it have been random?" another guy asked.

"Unlikely. It would have been a huge risk for somebody to take."

"Mistaken identity?"

"Again, I don't think so. Ethan's face has been on every news channel lately." There were murmurs of agreement. "It's also possible that the same vehicle tried to run over Stefanie Amor, although we've got no evidence for that right now."

Then Emmy spoke up. "Just to make this job a bit more exciting, anyone who identifies the bastard gets a two-week, all-expenses-paid vacation. Happy hunting."

Blackwood paid well, but there was no harm in introducing a little extra incentive.

"Thanks, sweetie," I whispered.

She simply smiled.

The troops filed out to carry on with the hunt, but I still had one more difficult conversation to have, not counting the discussion with Ethan—and that wasn't so much difficult as futile when he wouldn't even make eye contact.

"Oliver, have you got a minute?"

"Sure."

We went into a smaller meeting room down the hallway. Nobody used it much, and the air smelled stale. I opened the window before I sat on the edge of the table.

Oliver leaned against the wall, watching me the same way a hungry lion might check out an antelope. His courtroom face.

"I have a feeling I know what you're going to ask."

"And if I asked it, what would your answer be?"

He sighed, and his features relaxed. "Nobody else knows this case like I do, and truth be told, I've missed it. When I watched Lyle up there today, I couldn't help wishing it was me."

"So will you take over?"

"Yes."

"Thank you. It means a lot."

"I know it does. To both of us." He gave me a tight smile. "I guess I'll see you in court."

Well, that was easier than I thought, but it still left me with one big problem. Except when I went to look for him, he'd disappeared again.

CHAPTER 42

AFTER I FOUND out from Leah that Ethan had gotten a ride back to Riverley with Emmy, I spent the morning on the street asking questions about the drive-by, but there wasn't much going on so early in the day. Things would come alive in the evening. When my phone rang, I was contemplating whether to go back to my apartment for a few hours' sleep or carry on. The receptionist from the Richmond office was calling.

"Dan, you've got visitors."

"I'm not expecting anyone." Which translated as, "Tell them to piss off."

"I can't just send them home. They're kinda cute in a scruffy sort of way."

Uh-oh. I had a bad feeling about this. Well, not bad, exactly, more wrong-time-wrong-place. "What are their names?"

"Stick, Fine, and Trace."

Close enough. And those kids were persistent little brats. If I didn't see them today, they'd be back. Might as well get it over with.

"I'll be there in half an hour. Would you do me a favour and put them in the conference room? And get them some drinks and sandwiches?"

Well, I could kiss my sleep goodbye. At least this time, Emmy wasn't there to make promises that would involve weeks of work, heartache, and confusion. I pulled a sweater over my cleavage before I went in, wondering what treats they had in store for me today.

"Hello, boys."

"All right?" Trick asked.

The other two just stared.

"What can I do for you?"

"We need to see Ethan. We saw you on the news with him yesterday, so we know you know where he is. Sorry about that dude, by the way."

"Yeah, it was shit," Vine muttered.

"Ethan's not having any visitors at the moment, I'm afraid."

"But it's an emergency."

"The music, right?"

What could possibly be so vital that it couldn't wait?

"Yeah, the music. The project with us kids."

"Can I help instead?"

"Doubt it."

"Why don't you try me?"

Trick folded his arms and stared. "Ethan's the only one that'll help."

"Look, I can take him a message. How about that?"

"You said that before, and you didn't, did you?"

Shit. "We were busy."

"I knew it. He'd have called back."

"I'm sorry, okay?"

"Why can't we just speak to him? He understands stuff."

At Trick's side, Race started sniffling. "She won't help. She's just like all the rest."

Oh, hell, what was I supposed to do with a crying child? I had enough trouble dealing with the adults. Then again, would it really be such a bad idea to let the boys see Ethan? He might not want to talk to me, but I'd like to see him blow off three sort of cute-ish kids in the same way. Trick and his stubbornness might be exactly what Ethan needed.

After all, it was just music. How bad could it be?

"Fine. I'll take you for a visit. A *short* visit. Ethan's been having a hard time lately, and he's not up to talking for ages."

Three faces broke into smiles.

"You're awesome!" Vine said.

Well, at least somebody thought so.

They quite liked my car as well. After a brief argument over who got to ride in the front, which Vine surprised me by winning, they all clambered in. Before long, we were driving through the gates at Riverley. I'd called ahead and asked Bradley to track down Ethan.

He was waiting in the hallway when I arrived, and the look of surprise followed by happiness that crossed his face told me I'd done the right thing by bringing the boys. They rushed over and hugged him, and he returned the favour.

"I've missed you guys. How's everything? How's the project? Are people still practising?"

"Yeah, we're all going, but that's the problem," Trick said. "Some dude's trying to close it."

"Yeah, he's shit," said Vine, whose vocabulary didn't seem to be all that comprehensive.

Fuck.

Why couldn't they have told me this? I thought they wanted to talk to Ethan about guitars or something, not dump more problems in his lap. For a moment, I considered shoving the three of them back into the car and driving them far, far away.

But Ethan didn't seem to mind. "Why don't you come through to the music room? We can talk in there."

"You want food?" Bradley asked, waltzing through the doorway.

The boys had to be full from the snacks they'd eaten at Blackwood, but they all nodded anyway.

I trailed behind them, keeping my fingers crossed that their news was an exaggeration. We had enough problems to deal with at the moment without adding the future of a teens' music club to the list.

Ethan got the kids arranged on the couch and sat down opposite them on the coffee table. "Now, what's going on? Who wants to close the project?"

"Some property guy," said Trick. "He wants to buy the whole block and build apartments and a shopping mall."

"What's he called?"

"Richard Carr."

"Yeah, Dick," Vine said.

Ethan shook his head. "I don't think that's right. Carr's been around for a while, and I spoke to him a few months ago. He told me he didn't have any plans in the near future."

"Well, he was lying," Trick said. "Shawn's mom works for the planning board, and she said he put in an application. He wants to knock, like, everything down."

He spread his arms wide for emphasis and nearly

knocked over his glass of cola. I snatched it out of the way just in time.

"Are you sure?"

"Yeah! So we need you to help us get rid of him like you did last time."

"What do you mean, last time?" I asked.

Trick turned to me. "Some guy wanted to take our building and turn it into a grocery store. Ethan fought him until he went away."

Dammit, Ethan. *Don't roll your eyes, Dan. Don't do it.* "And you didn't think to tell me this?"

"It happened three years ago. The corporation built its grocery store half a mile away instead."

"And this new guy?"

"The space we have for the project is big, and it's got good acoustics. It won't be easy to find another place like that, and Carr thought that because it was just kids, he could kick them out without offering a replacement. We had a chat, and he realised it wouldn't be so straightforward."

"Who owns the building?"

"The city, but the project's got a lease until next December with an option to extend for another three years. It's earmarked for regeneration at some point, but nothing's happened for years." He shrugged. "There's no spare money at the moment."

"And who pays the rent?"

"I do."

Somehow, that didn't surprise me. "So if you've got a track record of putting a wrench in the works when it comes to development, could it be possible that Richard Carr wants you out of the way for his own financial gain?"

Had another suspect just thrown his hat into the ring?

Ethan saw where I was going with this. "Don't you think framing me for murder would be a bit drastic?"

"Depends on his finances. If he was short of cash, it might have been an easy option."

"That's insane."

"And people have been killed over far, far less."

"I think you're on the wrong track. When I spoke with Carr, he seemed like a reasonable guy, just misinformed."

"How did you leave things with him?"

"We agreed that if he decided to pursue his plans in the future, we'd talk again, and he'd help us to find another home for the project. Probably an extension to the development, something purpose-built."

"Which adds to his costs."

"You're reading too much into this. He won't be out of pocket because I'd pay rent on the building. And he showed me pictures of two other places where he did something similar. One was a community theatre, and the other was a youth centre."

"Can you remember the details of those?"

"There's a brochure thing in my house." Ethan grimaced. "That doesn't help much, does it? But there've been at least six schemes like this over the years, and none of them have gone ahead." He turned back to the boys. "I'll go and have a word with him, see what's happening."

"No, you won't," I snapped. "You're not leaving this house. I'll speak to him."

"You can't go steaming in there and accuse a businessman of murder."

"I can do subtle."

He stared at me, radiating disbelief.

"Really, I can. I promise I'll behave."

"Fine, go." He reached over and picked up his guitar. "While you're here, guys, how about we play with some instruments?"

Ethan wasn't happy with me, but I didn't care. I wasn't having his safety compromised. It wasn't only Richard Carr that worried me but also the idea of Ethan driving around by himself in Richmond. So many chances for something to go wrong. Riverley was like a fortress, and as long as Ethan stayed within its walls, I had one less thing to worry about.

But before work, I needed some rest, so I left the boys to it and went to take an afternoon nap. If I couldn't have whisky or sex, sleep was the next best thing. Six freaking hours of sleep. Damn.

Back in the music room, Vine had a guitar, Trick was on drums, and Race strutted up and down with the microphone. I'd intended to take the boys home, but I stopped to watch instead. This was a side to Ethan I hadn't seen, happy and smiling as the kids belted out a mashed-up version of "Born to Run."

"They like rock?"

Ethan grinned up at me from the piano. "Rock, pop, rap. They'll try anything."

Trick was good, seriously good. I still wasn't convinced Vine would land a record deal unless Ethan offered him one out of sympathy, but he wasn't that bad. And Race? He came alive in much the same way Ethan did, dancing as he sang, a different person to the silent child I usually saw.

Ethan had turned himself into a father figure for

these kids, hadn't he? From what Trick said, none of them came from good homes, and the music project had brought some stability into their lives. They loved being with Ethan, not because he was the Ghost, but because he was the one grown-up who paid them any attention and let them have fun. Someday, he'd make a great dad.

And that was another reason I couldn't get involved with him.

I might have come to take the boys back to Richmond, but I just couldn't. Not yet. Not when they were all enjoying themselves, Ethan included. Instead, I grabbed my laptop and set up in the living room next door, listening to the music while I researched Richard Carr. I'd get Mack to do a more thorough search tomorrow, but I could do the basics myself this afternoon.

From what I was able to find, he'd been in Virginia for just over a year, renting a nice colonial on an acre lot in Rybridge. Not a million miles from Nick's place, and if Carr could afford to live in that area, money problems seemed unlikely. Before that, he'd moved around, renting close to whatever development he happened to be working on at that time. He catered towards the higher end of the market—enclaves of luxury houses and apartments with all the amenities. Idaho, California, Texas, upstate New York, Delaware...

Right now, Carr Property, Inc. was finishing up with Winter Pines, an exclusive retirement village twenty miles from Richmond. Sixty-three villas and condos set around an artificial lake with a community centre, walking trails, and even a garden of remembrance for those seniors who'd lost loved ones.

But with forty-six of the homes sold, according to the website, it stood to reason that Carr Property would soon be looking for a new project to get underway. Had Carr been telling the truth about his plans for Ethan's music centre?

I'd just finished reading about the company's environmental credentials—solar panels on all new properties and a fancy system to reclaim wastewater for the putting green at Winter Pines—when I realised the music had stopped.

Next door, Trick, Vine, and Race were laid out on the couch, sleeping, while Ethan tidied up the room.

"You wore them out," I said.

"They wore themselves out." Ethan put down the music stand he was carrying and walked over to me. "Thanks for bringing them."

"No problem. I'm glad you had a good time." He was close to me now. Too close, but I couldn't step back. My feet wouldn't move. "I'd better drive the boys back home."

"It terrifies me, you being out on your own with some head case on the loose."

His breath puffed over my cheeks. "I'll be fine, honestly. I'll take a gun."

"That's not making me feel any better, Dani."

Shit, my pulse was doing that stupid thing again. *Hop, skip. Hop, skip. Hop, skip.* Quick, change the subject. "Why do you call me Dani? Everyone else calls me Dan."

"You're too pretty to be a Dan."

Oh, nice move, Ethan. That really calmed my hormones down. "Uh, okay." Wow, that was eloquent. He'd robbed me of speech. "Well, I guess I should be going."

He bowed his head and his lips met mine. Just the merest brush of sweetness and warmth. Then he moved back.

"Take care of yourself, Dani."

At that moment, I wanted to take care of myself in a whole different way.

CHAPTER 43

I DROPPED ALL three boys home in turn, and thankfully Vine's mom was already unconscious, passed out on the stained couch with an empty bottle beside her. Vodka, the cheap stuff. I knew from experience she wouldn't wake up until morning, otherwise I'd have probably brought Vine back to Riverley again. Ah, Riverley. When I turned into the driveway, I could still feel the ghost of Ethan's lips on mine. If he came near me again tonight, I'd be on my knees begging for more. And possibly doing other things, since I'd be at the right height to...

Stop it, Dan.

No, it was far better if I kept my distance.

Not that I could sleep. I was already awake when Mack called at five, sounding far chirpier than I felt.

"I have news," she announced.

"Good news or bad news?"

Please don't let it be bad. I couldn't take much more of that.

"Sort of both."

"Go on."

"I found the guy who sent those vile letters to Ethan. You remember, the hate mail?"

"I'm not gonna forget it. Is that the good part or the bad part?"

"Well, I guess it's good that I found him."

"What's the bad part?"

"The asshole's on parole, and he's wearing an electronic tag. He wasn't anywhere near Ethan's house on the night of the murder. He was in Atlanta."

Well, it was good to rule him out, but it also meant we were running dangerously short of suspects.

"What was he in jail for?"

"Sending hate mail. Ethan was right—it doesn't look like anything personal. He sent it to everyone. Singers, TV stars, media moguls... The prosecution named seventeen different victims, and those were just the ones they could prove. At his trial, he blamed the entertainment industry for corrupting the youth of today."

Nice guy, upsetting people for the fun of it. Shame he didn't live nearer, or I'd have been tempted to show him a more creative use for a pen.

"Thanks anyway. I've got news as well—I've added another suspect."

She groaned. "Just when I thought we'd made the list shorter. Who is he?"

"Richard Carr." I gave her a quick rundown of what I'd found so far.

"Leave it with me."

The first thing I noticed when I pulled into Richard Carr's driveway, well, other than the ridiculously large house straight ahead of me, was the black BMW parked in front of the garage. I paused to look as I stepped out of the Camaro.

It wasn't the BMW from the shooting—this was a 7-Series rather than a 5-Series and the wheels were different—but could it be the vehicle Lavinia saw outside Ethan's place? A possibility.

The garden was beautifully kept, with ornate topiary and an array of flowers arranged in symmetrical beds. It matched the house, which was a delicate shade of peach with turquoise trim, a colour combination that shouldn't have worked but somehow did.

I climbed up four white marble steps to the front door and rang the bell. The sound of Mozart echoed through the house, but it took forever for anybody to come. Either the house was bigger than it looked, or Carr hoped I'd give up and go away.

Finally, the door swung open and a man peered out. He wasn't old, early thirties at a guess, but salt-and-pepper hair gave him a distinguished look.

"Richard Carr?"

"Yes? And you are?"

"My name's Daniela di Grassi. I'm an independent investigator, and your name popped up on one of my cases. I was hoping we could have a quick chat?"

He huffed a little and glanced at his watch. "Will it take long? I'm due at the tennis club, and my doubles partner gets annoyed if I'm late."

"Five minutes, maybe ten?" I smiled, hoping. "I promise not to take up too much of your time."

He led me into the living room, impeccably decorated to show-home standards. I hadn't seen any evidence of a wife, so either he was obsessive about tidying or he didn't spend much time in there.

"Forgive me if I don't offer you a drink. Take a

seat?" He waved towards a cream leather couch.

I sat, marvelling how a padded piece of furniture could still manage to feel like granite.

"So what 'case' are you talking about?" he asked.

"I'm sure you've seen it on the news lately—the death of Christina Walker."

"That poor prostitute who got killed by the DJ?"

Of course, the media had leaked her profession by now.

"Yes, except it's looking less and less like he's the culprit."

"Really? I saw the commonwealth's attorney on the news, and he seemed certain they'd got the right man."

"*Deputy* commonwealth's attorney. And he's not always right."

"I suppose that's why you're here, then. Because I had a meeting with Ethan White a few weeks before the incident? Well, I assure you I didn't pick up any strange vibes from the man. I'd have called the authorities if I did."

"What was your meeting about?" I already knew from Ethan, but I wanted to hear Carr's version.

"Oh, nothing much. More of a fact-finding mission than anything else."

"What kind of facts?"

"The man was running some sort of music club for children off the street." The look of disgust on his face when he said "off the street" left me under no illusions as to his thoughts on them. "I was curious to see exactly what he did there."

"With a view to closing it down?"

"With a view to possible relocation if I did ever develop in that area."

"So is development likely?"

"I'm never certain a development will go ahead until we break ground."

"I heard you've submitted plans."

"Only an outline. It's all very speculative."

"So do you have many outlines going through the process at the moment?"

He shifted in his chair. Uncomfortable?

"A few."

His eyes flicked left as he spoke. Liar.

"So, what did you think of Mr. White?"

"He seemed like an okay kind of a guy, but you never can tell, can you?"

Funny, that was exactly what Harry had said, and he turned out to be a lying bastard. I didn't trust Carr, although I couldn't put my finger on the reason why.

"No, you never can tell. What were his thoughts on your plans?"

"He was open to discussion. As long as the kids had somewhere to play with their instruments, I don't think he minded where it was."

What Carr said more or less matched Ethan's views, which was almost a disappointment because it meant he had no motive. But something about him rubbed me the wrong way.

He folded his hands in his lap, and I noticed the end of his right forefinger was missing. From the look of the skin, it had been like that for a long time. I quickly averted my eyes, but he still saw me looking. He held it up and gave a wry laugh.

"I had an accident in the kitchen when I was twelve. I learned the hard way not to play with knives."

Had he? Or was he just playing a sick game with

me?

"That must have hurt."

He shrugged. "I don't really remember. It was so long ago." He made a show of looking at the grandfather clock in the far corner of the room. "I'm afraid I really do have to go."

"So, just to confirm, if the development did go ahead, you'd help to relocate the project?"

"I'm sure we'd be able to sort something out. I may be a businessman, but I also believe in supporting the local community. Look..." He got up and fetched a pamphlet from a credenza on the far side of the room. "Here are the details of a facility for children with learning difficulties that my company sponsors."

The Carr Property Center of Excellence in Ohio. He did get around a bit, didn't he?

"Thanks."

"You're very welcome. But why all these questions on the community project? I thought you came to talk about Ethan White?"

"Of course. I just want to get a handle on White's frame of mind. Whether he was upset at that time."

"Well, he didn't seem that way to me. Are we done now?"

"Yes. I appreciate you giving up your time."

"Have you got a business card, just in case I think of anything else?"

"Sure." I handed one over. "Here you go."

Another hour, wasted. I didn't like Carr, but I didn't like plenty of people and most of them didn't turn out to be murderers.

Back to the office to work on plan B.

CHAPTER 44

PLAN B CONSISTED of sharing an entire package of chocolate chip cookies with Emmy and Mack, followed by a smoothie. We had to be healthy, right?

"So who do we have left on the suspect list?" asked Emmy.

"Nobody," I said, slumping dramatically over the table.

"Are you sure?"

"Ty's black and Lavinia thought the guy was white. Harry and the guy who sent the hate mail both have alibis. Ronan and the DJ are too short."

"And the property guy?"

"No motive. Unless being an asshole counts."

"We must be missing something." Emmy started pacing. I was with her in spirit, but I couldn't be bothered to get up and join in.

"If it helps, the property guy's having money troubles," Mack offered.

"What kind of money troubles? His house didn't smack of somebody who's on the breadline."

"He's three months behind on the rent."

"Interesting, but I'm still not sure how that would make him want to kill Christina. If the development went ahead, relocating Ethan's project would be such a tiny part of it."

"But why is he short of cash in the first place? I looked at his company accounts, and those developments are super profitable. Where did it all go? He's never been married, so there's no ex-wife who's taking alimony, and even living in a palace, he should have plenty to spare."

"Can't you see from his bank account?"

"He takes chunks out as cash."

"Drug habit?" Emmy suggested.

"I didn't see any evidence of that," I said.

He hadn't had any of the signs of a long-term user. I'd seen enough of them on the streets to know.

Emmy looked at Mack, Mack looked at me, and I looked at Emmy.

"Hookers," we said, all at the same time.

Could that be the answer? Had he met Christina?

"But there's nothing on his phone records," Mack said.

"Another phone?" I suggested.

"Maybe, but how do we find it?"

Emmy grinned. "Break into his house?"

Sometimes I think she actually preferred the illegal approach. Not that hacking the phone company's records was particularly legal either, but it somehow felt less invasive.

I groaned. "This is all just speculation. How do we know we're not just clutching at straws?"

"We don't," she said. "But in the absence of anything else to clutch at..."

"Let Mack try the rest of her searches first."

Emmy rolled her eyes. "Sometimes you're so boring."

Ethan was waiting in the hallway when I got back to

Riverley, and he leapt off the couch before I'd closed the front door.

"Bradley said you'd gone out to visit a suspect."

How did Bradley even know? Sometimes I swore he bugged the rooms more than Nate did.

"Yeah I did, and I was perfectly fine. I can look after myself. You have to learn to trust me."

Ethan didn't seem convinced. "What happened?"

"We've still got checks to do, but Carr's got no motive."

"I told you that already." He rubbed his temples. "Is this ever going to end?"

"One day. It has to."

He sighed, then made an effort to smile. "Do you want dinner? Mrs. Fairfax has been experimenting with Caribbean food."

"I need to look through the files again." His face fell. Dammit, I kept forgetting how sensitive he was. "Okay, just something quick. I can work afterwards."

He hesitated a second then took my hand. Thank fuck. Were we getting back to normal at last? Or at least, whatever passed for normal in this weird non-relationship we had going on?

In the kitchen, he held out a chair for me.

"Here, sit. I'll get your food."

Any other man who told me to sit like a dog would have felt my bite, but I kind of liked Ethan telling me what to do. The way he cared and wanted to look after me.

I sat.

Plus it meant I got to stare at Ethan's ass as he moved about the room, plating up jerk chicken and rice and getting us cutlery. Wherever Bradley had found those pants, he needed to go back and buy Ethan ten more pairs.

"Do you like hot sauce?"

"No, just hot men." Shit! It popped out before I could stop it, and Ethan stared at me. "Uh, hot man?" Dammit. "Just forget I said that part. Please?"

He leaned down, so close his lips brushed my ear. "Still having trouble keeping your mouth shut?"

Uh, yes? It hung open at the moment, and my tongue had rolled out. Ethan reached out and pushed my chin up then kissed the top of my hair.

"Eat the food, Dani."

I loved the way he used my name all the time, or at least his variant of it. It rolled off his tongue and shot straight between my legs. Did he talk in the bedroom? Or better still, sing? Eli said he sang, right?

He slid a plate in front of me, and I forced myself to concentrate on eating. Fork to mouth, chew. Fork to mouth, chew. It was official: Ethan White made me lose my freaking mind.

And the worst part in all of it? Having to admit that Emmy was right.

Ethan sat beside me rather than opposite, close enough for our knees to touch. With my nerve endings already on fire, every bump sent a shockwave through me.

"Food okay?"

"Delicious." I barely tasted it.

Ethan didn't say much, and I didn't trust myself to start a conversation. I'd probably blurt out something dirty and totally inappropriate and be forced to move into Emmy's other house. Not just because of the embarrassment, but in case I got tempted to act it out.

But words didn't matter. Just being in Ethan's company was enough.

"Do you have more work to do tonight?" he asked when I'd taken my last mouthful.

"Yes."

If there was one thing I could do for him, it was to solve this puzzle and get him his life back. I pushed my chair back and got up, and he did the same.

"Are you sure?"

He stepped forward and I held my breath, my heart thumping as his hand skimmed my hip.

No. "Yes."

He kissed me softly on the cheek. "Then I'll clear up here and see you later."

CHAPTER 45

ETHAN WALKED SLOWLY towards me, a towel wrapped around his waist. Drops of water glistened on his hard chest as he walked through a sliver of moonlight, and I licked my lips. I couldn't help it. He looked edible, and I longed to taste him. Every last inch.

My gaze dropped to the impressive bulge he sported under his towel. Oh yes, *every* last inch.

I slid one strap of my dress off my shoulder, and his eyes smouldered. The other strap followed, and the silky material pooled at my feet, leaving me standing before him in a pair of lace panties and diamond earrings.

"You're overdressed," I told him.

He closed the distance between us with four quick steps, then his mouth was on mine. Soft lips, and I couldn't resist biting the bottom one like he so often did. He groaned softly, and I swallowed the sound, licking along the seam of his lips until they parted. Red-blooded male with a hint of whisky. Delicious.

"Ethan."

His name escaped on a gasp as he brushed his fingers up the bare skin of my sides, so softly I could have imagined it. I shuddered, arching my back, and the movement pressed my breasts against him. His hand on my ass pulled me closer still, and his hard cock rocked against my stomach. I stood on tiptoes so it nestled between my legs, right where I wanted it to be. He lifted me effortlessly, and then we were both floating, floating...

Hold on, there was something wrong with this picture.

I woke with a start as Ethan's fingertips trailed across the back of my neck. Shit. I'd fallen asleep in the conference room. I froze, tempted to feign sleep so Ethan would keep touching me, but when I shivered involuntarily, he knew I was awake.

Great. I sat up and peeled a sheet of paper from my cheek. A couple of paperclips dropped onto the table after it. Shit. Nothing said sexy like the indent of stationery on a girl's face.

"Dani," Ethan whispered. "Time for bed."

He was right. It was. And as I shoved my chair back, I desperately wanted to drag him in there with me. And maybe take up Ana's suggestion about the handcuffs.

Half asleep, I stumbled back into him, and when he caught me, I knew at least one part of my dream was true. I could feel it at the top of my ass. He wrapped his arms around my chest, fingers brushing the underside of my breasts, and I relaxed then gave myself a mental slap. What was I doing?

Ethan was virtually a client. He was out on bail for murder, for fuck's sake. He didn't follow any of my rules. He knew my name. We'd had deeper conversations than, "Your place or mine?" Dammit, he knew *me*. He knew part of my history and some of my secrets. But did he know my desires?

Had he noticed my nipples straining against my bra? The goose bumps popping out on my arms? Did he realise my panties were soaking?

Time slowed down. All I could feel was his breath on my ear, his warm hands on my ribs, the beat of his heart against my back.

Fuck. Everything about this screamed "terrible idea."

Because I knew, I absolutely knew, that this was the one man I wouldn't be able to walk away from painlessly when the sun rose.

I closed my eyes as his lips brushed the skin under my earlobe. They were every bit as dangerous as I'd imagined. When I didn't move, he trailed kisses downwards, licking along my carotid artery. Could he feel my pulse? Did he know it was racing in time with his heart?

I twisted in his arms. I had a craving for a midnight snack, and only one thing would satisfy it. One man. Just like in my dream, his lips parted, but instead of whisky, I tasted orange juice. I ran my tongue along that perfect row of white teeth then tangled it with his.

Control was lost.

But was my heart gone as well?

I locked my arms behind his neck and pulled his head down as I pressed up against him, moulding myself to the length of his body. He held me tight, and the ferocity of his kisses scared me a little. Not because I was afraid he would hurt me, but because I was afraid the feelings pouring out of the crack in my heart would lead to me hurting myself.

But I couldn't stop. I needed this man inside me. I needed him to make the ache between my legs go away.

His hands were everywhere—my back, my ass, my breasts, tangled in my hair. I couldn't resist giving his butt a squeeze, and damn, the man had glutes.

I took a step backwards and my ass hit the table. Without pausing, he hoisted me up onto it, our lips never leaving each other's.

As he lifted, the smart dress I'd worn to meet Carr got bunched up, and now Ethan slid his hands underneath it, further, further, until his hands grazed the naked skin of my waist. I wrapped both legs around him and pulled him tight against me. He was rock hard now, and his cock had grown to a size that my subconscious had grossly underestimated. I released my arms to fumble with his belt, and I'd just gotten it undone when he pulled back and laid his forehead against mine.

"Dani, are you sure about this?"

In the dim light coming from my laptop screen, his eyes were endless black pools of emotion. Lust, hurt, and fear. It was like looking into a mirror.

"Sure? No, I'm not sure, but I don't want to stop."

He understood exactly what I meant.

"What about tomorrow? What happens then?"

"Tomorrow's tomorrow. Can't we live for tonight? Please, just give me tonight."

He closed his eyes, fighting an inner battle. Who would win? The child who feared being hurt again? Or the rebel that said, "Take a chance."

I closed my own eyes, fearful of watching his face in case I didn't get the answer I wanted. An age passed before I felt the pinch of his teeth on my bottom lip.

"Open your eyes, Dani. I want to see everything you feel."

I obliged, although the intensity of his gaze made me want to look away. For the first time, I saw right into him. And I knew he could see into me.

Right through to my twisted soul.

He arched his hips, and I writhed against him shamelessly.

"You feel how much I want you?" he whispered.

I nodded. It would be hard not to.

"How much do you want me?"

He soon got his answer as he pushed my panties to one side and slid a finger inside me. A half-smile, half-smirk appeared. Seeing some of the confidence this whole mess had knocked out of him return made my heart soar. Not to mention the fact that it made him look even sexier.

He drew his finger back and ran it along my centre, pausing on my clit then circling slowly. So maddeningly slowly. I sucked in a breath when he stopped, gripping him tighter with my legs.

"Please..."

"Please what, Dani?"

"Make me come."

He kissed me again, and I shuddered against him. Fuck. A bead of sweat ran down my spine as the room got hotter, and my skin sizzled as Ethan touched it.

He swapped out *that* finger for a thumb, and I jolted as he pressed. He played my body like his Gibson, strumming a sweet tune as I vibrated underneath him. Two fingers slid inside me, and that was enough. Stars burst behind my eyes, fire tore through me, and I slumped into his arms.

He held me tight as I melted against him. "You burn, baby," he whispered.

"You ignite me."

When I stopped shaking, my hands made their way downwards to complete what they started earlier. Ethan's belt already hung open, just a button and zipper to go. Then I could have my prize.

And what a trophy it was. I didn't know whether to touch it, taste it, or beg him to fill me with it. As it happens, I didn't have to make that decision.

Ethan groaned long and low as I stroked his length. "I don't have a condom. I wasn't exactly expecting to need any here."

Luckily, I spied my purse on the leather couch beside the door. Thank goodness I'd spent so long acting like a slut. I wriggled off the table and wobbled across the room on shaky legs.

"Got one! I'm always prepared for an emergency."

I clapped a hand over my mouth. Oh, shit. Why had I said that? Ethan knew he wasn't my first, but now was hardly an appropriate time to remind him of that. I wanted to sink into the floor, and my knees duly obliged. Ethan tried to walk towards me as I plopped onto the couch, but his pants were around his ankles, so he lurched forward in an ungainly hop instead.

We stared at each other, and I couldn't do anything but laugh.

"Could this be any more awkward?" he muttered.

Sure it could. We still had to get through the morning after part, and I'd spent my entire life avoiding that little issue.

I struggled to my feet and stepped forward, unsure, and he took another shuffle. We met in the middle and clung to each other.

"Can we just erase that part?" he asked.

I nodded, stifling a smile. He reached down and freed his legs then picked me up.

"Against the wall or on the table, Dani?"

"Table. We can do the wall later."

He set me down on the polished wood, ripped open the condom, then did the same with my panties. I'd never liked those ones anyway.

I wrapped my legs around him and locked his gaze with mine as he lined himself up. A little nudge and he slowly slid inside me, seating himself to the hilt. A gasp escaped my lips. It was most definitely a stretch.

His smile came back, that secret, cunning smile, and I grinned back like a bloody idiot. This was where I wanted him to be. It was where he was *meant* to be.

He drew back slowly, a man with far more patience than I had. When he pushed forward, a moan tore from my lips as every nerve ending tingled. What was happening to me? Sex never felt like this. So...so... volatile. Like I could explode at a moment's notice.

I wriggled, trying to get him to move again.

"Patience, Dani," he murmured against my lips. "Unless you want this to be over fast, you're gonna have to give me a minute."

"Fast is fine. We can do slow after."

"Fuck, baby."

"Yes. Yes! Fuck. Exactly that."

He gave up and slammed into me, again and again, and I screamed into his mouth as I came. Another second and I swallowed his cries as he let go as well. Holy freaking amazeballs.

All these years, I'd been doing it totally wrong. The old saying was true. Quality over quantity.

Hair fell into my eyes, and Ethan tucked it back

behind my ears. His body felt slick against my fingers as I traced the contours of his back.

"We're a mess," I murmured.

"In every possible way. And you know what? I don't care."

He kissed me softly, and my heart sang.

"You want to make a bigger mess?" I asked.

"The dirtier, the better. Shall we head somewhere more comfortable?"

I nodded. Fun though the table was, a bed gave us more options.

Ethan pulled his pants back on while I shimmied my dress down. The house was silent as we tiptoed through it, holding hands.

"Your room or mine?" he asked.

"Mine's closer."

We were already pulling each other's clothes off again as we fell through the door. If what happened downstairs was the warm-up, I couldn't wait for the main event. I clicked on the bedside lamp so I could see Ethan's face, and its soft glow showed he wanted this as much as I did.

That and his cock, already hard again despite its efforts downstairs. He lowered me to the bed, and I reached for the unopened box of condoms in the nightstand. I'd never brought a man back here before, but we'd be making quite a dent in those tonight.

What would happen come sunrise? I pushed that thought to the back of my mind.

Just enjoy tonight for what it is, Dan.

Ethan didn't waste any time. Despite what he'd said about slow, our thrusts soon turned frantic. There was an undercurrent of need, an intensity that I'd never felt before, and it bordered on terrifying. Did Ethan feel it too?

I didn't dare to ask.

After he'd spilled into me for the second time, he relaxed a little, and I lay back, boneless, as he went exploring. Fingers, lips, and tongue. Thank fuck I got waxed last week. Then it was my turn, and he tasted every bit as delicious as I'd imagined. My very own lollipop, sweet as sugar.

We played for hours, and the moon was already dropping when my eyes began to close. Ethan gathered me close, and I nestled against him as I drifted off. Safe. Wanted. Content.

But for how long?

CHAPTER 46

ETHAN STIRRED ME from a hazy sleep with kisses the next day, starting at my neck and peppering down my collarbone until he got distracted by my breasts. I moaned in pleasure as he licked and sucked my nipples into peaks before continuing his journey south.

He paid particular attention to my belly button, but rather than heading to the sweet spot, he trailed a digit along my belly.

I froze, fully awake now, a cold finger of fear tracing along the path he'd just taken. The sun was high in the sky, a beam cutting across my bare stomach. And that meant he could see what I always kept hidden with dim lighting or strategically placed clothes.

"Stop." It came out barely audible, and I tried again. "Ethan, stop."

Those blue eyes stared up at me, kindness turning to confusion, and I began shaking as I scrambled away from him.

"You need to go. Please."

Hurt replaced the confusion, and Ethan's shoulders slumped.

"Dani, what's wrong?"

I shook my head, struggling to hold back the tears building behind my eyes. "I can't."

"Tell me what I did, and I'll fix it."

"Nothing."

And I was still naked in the bright light. *Wrong, wrong, wrong.* I fled into the bathroom and slammed the door. It was only once the lock clicked that I dissolved.

Fuck, fuck, fuck.

"Dani?" Ethan's voice sounded muffled through the door. "I don't know what just happened, but please don't do this."

I didn't speak. I couldn't. My legs gave way and I slid down the wall to the floor as a wave of old emotions crashed over me. Fifteen years, and the wounds were still as raw and painful as the day I woke up in hospital with Emmy by my side.

My phone rang in the bedroom, but I ignored it. Leah could deal with the problem, or Emmy if it was important enough. Today, I needed the time on my own.

Time to weep for the son I'd never known. I ran my own finger along the stretch marks that still showed up when the light was right. Fifteen years, and they'd faded from an angry red to pale silver, but they'd always be there as a reminder of what I'd lost.

Why had I let things go so far with Ethan last night? I'd been selfish, taking what I wanted, and now I'd hurt both of us in the process. Far better to spend a few hours with a faceless hookup who wouldn't remember my name in the morning.

Now I was in a world of trouble, and I needed to dig myself out. What should I say to Ethan? How did I break the news that I wasn't relationship material? That one night was all I could offer? A simple "sorry" just wouldn't cut it.

An hour passed as I shivered in my bathrobe, then two, and I still had no clue. Words were totally inadequate in a situation like this.

I crawled over to the door. "Ethan?"

Nothing, so I tried a little louder.

"Ethan, are you there?"

Silence. He'd gone. Of course he'd gone. What kind of man would sit outside a bathroom for two-and-a-half hours waiting for a crazy woman to come to her senses?

I opened the door, and Ethan fell backwards and landed at my feet.

"What are you still doing here?" I snapped. "Why didn't you answer?"

The hurt that crossed his face made my chest spasm. "Because you wouldn't have come out, would you?"

I folded my arms over my chest as he stood up. His gaze dropped, and I realised my tits were bulging out of my bathrobe. I quickly tugged it shut.

"Would you?" he repeated.

"No, but I told you to leave."

"You were upset. Still are upset. What kind of man would I be if I'd listened?"

"I'm fine."

"The hell you are."

"Please, just leave me alone."

I put my hands on my hips and glared. Normally that would be enough to send a man running for the hills, but Ethan stepped forward, pushing me backwards until his hips trapped me against the bathroom vanity.

"I spent most of last night inside you, and this morning you flip out and want me to leave? Well, I'm not going to, not until you tell me what's wrong."

My carefully rehearsed speech flew from my mind. "It was a mistake," I croaked out, gripping the edge of the marble until my knuckles went white.

"Once, we could have written off as a mistake, Dani. Twice, even. But not six times. Six times you screamed my name and came apart around me. Six times you made me feel like no other woman has before. So get this, I'm not fucking leaving until you talk to me, and I don't mean some bullshit about this being a mistake."

I thought I'd cried all my tears, but it turned out I was wrong. As one after another ran down my cheeks, Ethan kissed them away, and when the stream became a river, he wiped it with his thumbs. Then he held me.

"Those marks on my stomach," I whispered. "They're stretch marks. The kind women get when they're pregnant."

He tried to look at me, but I turned my head away.

"You have a kid?"

I couldn't answer. All I managed was a strangled cough.

"Dani? You have a kid?"

I quickly shook my head. "He was stillborn."

Ethan held me tighter and didn't let go even when I tried to push him away.

"When?" He spoke close to my ear.

"He would have been fifteen next week."

"How are you old enough to have a fifteen-year-old son?"

"I'm thirty-one."

He quickly did the math. "Fuck, baby, you were sixteen. That wasn't even legal."

"I know."

I took a deep breath, remembering the night I lost my little boy. The same night I'd met Emmy. She'd been the one to take me to the hospital, the one who'd covered my medical bills and given me a place to live afterwards.

My eyes got wetter. "But a good kicking took care of the problem, and I can't have another child."

Now Ethan would leave, right?

Wrong. His fingers dug into the tops of my arms. "Who was he? I might not have killed anybody before, but it's not too late to start."

"It's dealt with. Even back then, Emmy was somebody you didn't want to mess with."

His grip loosened, and he hugged me tightly instead. "Dani, I'm so sorry. That a man did that to you. That you lost your baby."

"My son. I lost my son."

Sobs wracked my body as the pain that had been festering inside me for over a decade leached out. Pain and guilt and sadness and anger. And Ethan took it all.

"Is that why you run?" he asked, finally.

I nodded. Not many men would stick around through what he'd just witnessed.

"I'm gonna tie your fucking feet together, then."

I giggled. Seriously, giggled. I couldn't help it. "Won't that make a repeat of last night a little difficult?"

"On the contrary, the added friction can be extremely pleasurable."

As could the warmth coming from his smile.

"Really, Mr. White?"

"Allow me to demonstrate."

And so it was that Ethan stopped me in my tracks.

CHAPTER 47

EARLY AFTERNOON, AND my lunch had consisted of Ethan. I'd even gone back for seconds. My stomach grumbled, and I knew we should get up for some proper food, but neither of us had the energy to move.

Ethan spooned me, one arm wrapped around the stomach I'd hated for so long. As the sun climbed higher in the sky, he'd kissed every inch of it, erasing my fears and melting the last of the ice around my heart.

And the Queen Bitch was totally on the money. Usually, I hated when Emmy was right, but this time I couldn't get upset. I loved Ethan, no matter how much I might try to deny it.

My fingers wrapped around his, holding his hand against my heart. I was trapped, and what was more, I wanted to be.

His breath tickled the back of my neck, and my eyes were closing when he began to speak.

"I was born in Minneapolis."

I froze. Was Ethan finally going to open up to me? Let a little of his own pain out? I held my breath until he continued.

"My name wasn't Ethan White back then. It was Ethan Briand."

Holy fuck! That was why Mack had never been able

to find him.

"Like you, I never knew my real father, but I had a replacement. His name was Frank White, and I was nine years old when my momma met him."

Ethan's breathing turned rough, heavy, and I felt the agony in his voice.

"You don't have to do this," I whispered.

"Yeah, I do." His tone had a finality about it, a man who'd accepted his fate. "They never married, but after a few months, Frank moved in with us. There was no way I could ever be mistaken for his real son, but he treated me like one. It was him who taught me piano and guitar. I still hear his voice speaking to me as I play."

It hadn't escaped my notice that he talked about Frank in the past tense. "What happened?"

Ethan's arms tightened around me, a far cry from his reaction last time I'd asked that question. "Kids at school weren't very kind. First, I was the mixed-race boy with two white parents, and second, I wasn't great at reading. Frank tried to help, but nobody had ever taught him properly either. I got the crap beaten out of me at least once a week by the older kids, and back then, the teachers did nothing to stop it."

He paused for breath, chest shuddering. Should I turn around? Comfort him? Or would having to look at me make him clam up again? I couldn't take that chance, so I just kissed his palm instead.

"One Tuesday, I came home early because the worst group of bullies had stolen my shoes. Frank took one look at me and said enough was enough. He marched out of the house to go and complain to the principal, and that was the last time I ever saw him."

"He died?"

"They killed him. The kids. The same ones who hurt me. They were smaller than him, but there was a whole gang of them, and they hit him and kicked him until he died. The witnesses who had the guts to come forward said they accused him of being in league with the devil for bringing up a black man's child."

We were both crying by that point. I'd known kids could be cruel—hell, I was bullied myself—but I'd never experienced such outright hatred.

"Did they catch the children that did it?"

"They got sent to juvie. The ringleader got two years. Two years for a man's life."

I understood now. "Your sentence lasted a lot longer than that."

I felt him nod.

"What happened afterwards? Did school get any easier with them gone?"

"No, because I never went back."

"What about your mom? Didn't she make you?"

"Momma told me Frank's death was my fault. That if I'd learned to stick up for myself better, it never would have happened."

"Was she crazy?"

"A little. Mostly drunk. She told the truth once she hit the vodka. Told me I was the biggest mistake of her life. That was when I left."

"And you were twelve?"

"Almost thirteen by then."

Fuck. How could somebody say that to a twelve-year-old child? *Her* twelve-year-old child. I couldn't think of words to describe her. She made my mom look like a damn saint.

I twisted around in Ethan's arms and cupped his face. "That's why you wore the mask, isn't it? Because you were ashamed of yourself? Of your skin?"

He nodded.

Shitting hell. That bitch had fucked him in the head for years.

I kissed him on both cheeks, then his lips. "You've got a beautiful face. Don't ever let anybody tell you different."

"Maybe one day I'll believe that."

"You'd better, because I'm gonna remind you every day for the rest of our lives."

It was his turn to stiffen. "You still want to be with me?"

"Yeah, I do." I managed a smile. "Although sometimes I'm not sure why when you act all frustrating."

He hugged me tightly against him and squeezed the breath out of me. "I'm never letting you go."

"Not even for lunch?"

"Not yet."

"So, how did you get to where you are now?"

"When I left home, I took Frank's old Martin guitar, and I started busking. I had to keep moving around in case someone called social services, but I made enough to eat. And in the evenings, I went to the library and pretended I was doing school assignments. Taught myself to read properly and do math and all that other bullshit even if I never got a piece of paper to say so."

"Where did you sleep?"

"Anywhere I could."

Shit. I hugged Ethan back and wrapped my legs around his waist for good measure too. When I first met him, I never imagined how much pain lurked under the surface, and now I knew, I was kind of in awe of everything he'd done.

"Ethan, I'm so fucking proud of you." He didn't say anything, but a minute later, I felt dampness in my hair. "What's wrong?"

"Nobody's ever said that to me before."

Oh, hell. We were such a mess. A big, wet, sloppy, teary mess. And after we'd had wet, sloppy, teary sex, I wiped Ethan's cheeks dry and he did the same for me.

"Dani, the past is the past, and we can't change it, but for the first time, I'm looking forward to the future."

"Me too. But you know what I want now?"

"What?"

"Food. I'm starving."

Eventually, Ethan and I untangled ourselves and put some clothes on. My stomach was grumbling worse than Nate by the time we sat down for a meal that was too late for lunch and too early for dinner. What would you call that? Dunch? Linner? Eating spaghetti with one hand was quite difficult, but Ethan hung onto the other in a death grip.

Emmy walked in as I tried to catch a forkful with my tongue, and she looked down at our joined hands.

"Oh, bollocks. You did it, didn't you?"

Ethan went still beside me. I gave a tiny nod and Emmy sighed.

"Shit, I had next Thursday. I never win these fucking things."

She grabbed a carton of orange juice and stomped out.

"What was she talking about?" Ethan asked.

"It appears they were running a pool on when we would sleep together."

His eyes widened. "Who does that?"

"My friends. They bet on everything from office romance to beach volleyball."

We got interrupted again, this time by Bradley. "Before or after midnight?"

"Bradley, can't you leave us alone for five minutes?"

He put his hands on his hips. "No, it's important."

"Well, I don't know. I had better things to do than check my watch."

Bradley just stared at me. Clearly, that wasn't the answer he'd been seeking.

I turned to Ethan and gave him a helpless look. "Any ideas?"

"Uh, I'd just finished watching the eleven o'clock news bulletin when I woke you." He shrugged. "Didn't take long after that."

"Yes!" Bradley shouted, pumping his fist in the air. "And I am fifty bucks richer."

He skipped out of the kitchen, leaving us in peace once more.

"Is it always like this?" Ethan asked.

"Yeah, pretty much." I squeezed his hand. "Does that bother you?"

He stared out the window for a few seconds, then shook his head. "This place is special."

"What do you mean?"

"Everyone's different, but everyone's the same. It doesn't matter whether you're black or white, rich or poor, old or young, gay or straight. Nobody differentiates."

I chuckled, because he was right. "Unless you're an asshole. Nobody likes an asshole."

Except... I clenched my butt cheeks together. No, it was too soon for that.

Ethan let go of my hand and wrapped an arm around my shoulders, pulling me close to kiss the top of my head.

"Eat your food, Dani. I'm getting hungry again."

CHAPTER 48

AFTER A DISCUSSION that lasted all of two seconds, Ethan moved his things into my room. I'd wasted enough of my life waking up alone, and I didn't intend to keep making the same mistake.

I'd thought that giving myself over to a man would feel wrong, based on the fact that the longer I'd spent with every man in the past, the more awkward it felt. What I hadn't realised was that when I found the right man, the opposite would happen.

I couldn't get enough of him.

The next morning, Ethan woke me with his tongue. Not so much a kiss but making love to my mouth, deep, hot, and utterly satisfying. That led to more, and I didn't roll out of bed for another hour. Screw my first meeting. I'd just have to be a few minutes late. It was only a catch-up with Emmy and Black, and I'd spent ages laughing at them for the exact same thing, so I figured I'd be getting a dose of my own medicine today.

I figured right.

The jokes carried on when I got to the office and opened my drawer. Some enterprising asshole had rigged it with a spring mechanism to fire half of the Trojan factory's morning output at me. There were hoots of laughter as I got showered, but I had to join in. At least that would save me from buying any more condoms for a week.

When I got my laptop out, I found Nate had changed the screensaver. Instead of the Blackwood logo, Ethan and I sailed down The Tunnel of Love in an oversized pink swan while the speakers played "I'd Do Anything for Love (But I Won't Do That)" by Meatloaf. The sentimental old git. Nate, not Meatloaf.

Before I jumped into work, I paused by Mack's desk. "I need another favour."

"Honey, you're so deep into the red with favours, I'd go so far as to say you're bankrupt."

"Just one more," I pleaded. "It's more of a personal one."

"All right, but it'll have to wait until I've finished this report for Nate."

I gave her a grateful smile. "Can you look up this name for me? In Minneapolis?"

She glanced down at the piece of paper. "Ethan?"

I nodded.

"I'll do it as soon as I can, okay?"

It was midafternoon when she handed me a memory stick. Her already pale face had turned ashen.

"Holy fuck. No wonder he's messed up. How much of this has he told you?"

"I'm not sure, which is why I asked you to take a look. I want to know what I'm dealing with."

"Whatever help you guys need, just say the word. I'll be there. We all will."

She leaned down and gave me a hug.

"I know, and it means the world to me."

Hand on heart, I didn't want to look at the files, but I had to. Navigating Ethan's psyche still felt like tiptoeing across a minefield, and I needed all the assistance I could get. Like a PhD in psychology, Sigmund Freud as my sidekick, and a whole truckload of the lucky four-leaf clover charms Bradley had brought back from his trip to Ireland last year.

The first article came from the *Star Tribune*. A scanned copy, a little yellowed around the edges. I squinted at the date. Eighteen years ago last month.

There was drama in the Midtown neighbourhood yesterday as local carpenter Frank White was beaten to death in broad daylight just yards from the gates of the school attended by his girlfriend's son, Ethan Briand.

Unconfirmed reports suggest a gang of youths followed him along the road for several minutes beforehand, screaming and yelling, before the brutal assault took place. White died later in the hospital from internal bleeding after his liver ruptured.

"There was a whole gang of them," one eyewitness said. "Shouting and throwing things. All little boys. I recognised some of them. Nobody's safe anymore."

Although both Frank and the gang members were reported to be white, several of the taunts were believed to concern the ethnicity of Ethan. Police are treating the crime as racially motivated and are appealing for any further witnesses.

The photo below showed Frank on stage, a guitar slung over his shoulder, one hand working the frets and the other outstretched. He gazed at the audience with the kind of confidence those pint-sized shits had stolen from Ethan. A caption underneath said Frank had played lead guitar for a blues band, The Blue Mondays.

I sat back in my chair, hollow. Little boys? Monsters more like. Further articles detailed Frank's injuries, Ms. Briand's grief, and the mayor's denial that racism was a problem in his fine city.

Then came another article in the *Star Tribune*.

Police today confirmed that twelve minors have been charged in association with the horrific attack on local man Frank White last week. While no names have been released, it's understood that the boys are aged between 13 and 16, and all attended the same school as Ethan Briand, a boy neighbours say Frank considered to be his son. According to Ethan's mother, he was bullied at school, although the school denies this.

We spoke to Janice Freeman, the school principal, who refuted the allegations, saying, "Recent news coverage has painted a false picture of Fillmore High. Our school may not be perfect, but there is certainly no bullying culture. We're confident that pupils feel safe with us, and it's a shame that some parents are trying to claim a wider problem rather than addressing issues with their own children."

However, one mother, whose son was in Ethan's class, spoke on the condition of anonymity and told a different story. At least three times in the last month, she claims to have seen the young boy being physically assaulted on the way to the bus stop, but was too fearful of retaliation from other parents to intervene. Not only that, her son allegedly witnessed Ethan being dragged into the bathroom and having his head flushed down the toilet while teachers stood by and ignored his cries.

What kind of world are our kids living in?

The mother of one of the boys arrested said her son is a quiet child, just easily led. "It was the others that did it. My boy was just in the wrong place at the wrong time."

Maybe so, but that will be of little comfort to Frank White and the family he left behind.

A photo accompanied the article, taken at the funeral. Ethan's mother was a sour-faced woman, thin as a rail, dressed in black and surrounded by a crowd in similar attire. A small boy stood at her side. It must have been Ethan, but even then he was staring at the ground, his face hidden.

Two final articles gave details of the trial.

Twelve young boys sat on raised seats in court this morning, sandwiched between social workers as the prosecution summed up their case. Individually, the accused boys all deny the manslaughter of Frank White, choosing to blame each other instead.

The assistant DA claimed that the boys intended to kill Frank or cause him serious injury, that they acted jointly throughout the attack, and that they knew what they were doing was wrong. But throughout the trial, the defence argued that the tragedy was an ill-judged prank, a game with unintended but deadly consequences.

The case has split the community, with one local mother saying, "Boys will be boys."

And two days later...

It only took the jury nine hours to come to their

decision in the Frank White case: guilty on all counts.
Sentences varied from three months to two years, and
many parents left the court in tears.

Today marks the end of an ordeal, not just for
Sarah and Ethan Briand, but for the whole
neighbourhood. Racial tensions have been high, with
several clashes outside the gates of Ethan's former
school. Now that the trial is over, Midtown can finally
move on.

Move on? For Ethan, the nightmare had only been
beginning. The kids who killed his father got social
workers, but Ethan got no help from anyone, least of all
his mother. I'd spend the rest of my damn life making
up for what other people had done to him.

I clicked on the next folder and found Mack had
managed to get the juvie records. They were supposed
to be sealed, but she had her ways. Twelve cropped
mug shots of twelve little boys. Ethan's was the
thirteenth life ruined on that heinous day.

I scanned the screen, taking in their features,
looking for commonality. What made a person lust for
blood? Why did they join the pack, ready to prey on the
innocent? The kids were all white, but that was the only
feature they shared. Chubby, gaunt, blue eyes, brown
eyes, blond hair, brown hair—it didn't matter.

Then one face made me pause.

The eyes. It was the eyes that caught my attention,
but the name bore a similarity as well.

I hurried to open the other files Mack had sent,
searching for another photo, something, anything that
would prove I was right.

Two minutes later, I found it in another prison mug

shot, this one dated a year later. A handwritten note at the bottom said he'd been transferred to another holding facility.

In this picture, one cheek was bruised, and his pale blue eyes, which a year earlier had been smug and arrogant, were now filled with an anger so cold I wanted to turn my screen off. But that wasn't what got my pulse racing.

Lower down in the photo, where he held the board with his name and number, the forefinger on his right hand sported a bandage. The end was stained with blood, and that finger was obviously an inch shorter than it should have been.

An accident in the kitchen, my ass.

His nose looked different now, narrower, and he'd lost the buck teeth, but both of those things were easy enough to change with an application of money. It was the same guy.

I hit the conference button on my phone, calling Emmy then Mack. "I've got him. The prime suspect's name is Richard Carr, but when Ethan first met him, he was called Ricky Carter. I want him brought in, and I don't care how we do it."

"The property developer?" Mack asked.

"Yes, the lying shit."

We'd worked together for so long that neither of them questioned me.

"I'll get a team together. Half an hour," Emmy said. "You can brief us on the way."

"Mack, can you get us more details on the house?"

"I'll get whatever I can."

Half an hour might not seem like long, but Emmy and her team had spent years training for every eventuality. They could have launched a coup in a small country with that much time to spare. While she assembled weapons and manpower, I pored over the documents Mack fired at my inbox.

Ricky Carter, now thirty-four years old, had gotten two years in juvie and seemed to have treated it as a learning experience rather than a punishment. He'd lost the finger in a knife fight. His opponent lost an eye. While he was locked up, his mother had married an ageing poker player who died the year after Ricky walked free. It seemed that was where Richard Carr got the seed money for his property business.

He'd hidden his dark side under a veneer of respectability and a cloak of money, but once a bloodthirsty freak, always a bloodthirsty freak. If he'd killed Christina, and I very much suspected he had, we were up against Satan's protégé.

Emmy materialised beside me, Ana trailing behind. For once, I was glad she was coming.

"Ready to go?"

"Just let me grab my gun."

Ana snicked open the tanto blade on her Emerson CQC-7, closed it again, and stowed it on her belt. "Perhaps a knife would be more appropriate."

"Be my guest."

Twelve of us packed into the back of a specially modified truck, painted to look like a furniture delivery van from the outside. Carr's gates had been open last time, and if that was the case again, our driver would pull up in front of the garage and ring the front doorbell. That distraction would allow us to sneak out the far side of the truck and surround the house.

If the gates were shut, we'd just park outside and go

in over the walls. Simple, dirty, and quick. According to Mack's research, the family to the left were in Hawaii for three weeks, and the neighbour to the right worked all day while his wife played hide-the-salami with her golf instructor.

Far from looking like a SWAT team, we wore civilian clothes and our weapons were concealed. Ana still channelled her inner bitch, but Emmy could be mistaken for a soccer mom with her perky ponytail and designer sportswear. I'd brought a few religious pamphlets with me as cover. *Knock knock. Do you believe in the afterlife?*

Even if a neighbour noticed us and called the cops, we'd be gone before they arrived. Mack would keep an ear out on the police band and warn us if we got spotted. We'd pulled this stunt at least a dozen times before, no problem.

Except today, things didn't quite go according to plan.

"Gates are open," our driver informed us over the radio.

So far, so good.

"But there's no car in the drive."

"Maybe it's in the garage?" I said, hoping.

"Place looks deserted. I'll try the door."

We spread out, but five minutes later, there were still no signs of life from the house.

"Do we want to wait? Come back?" Ana asked.

"No, we don't. We could be waiting forever," I said.

I had a horrible feeling my visit had scared Carr off.

Emmy agreed. "Let's see what's in the house."

"Look but don't touch," I reminded everyone. "The cops are gonna need this place for evidence at some point, and we don't want to jeopardise any prosecution."

There were murmurs of agreement while I picked the lock on the back door and Emmy did the honours at the front.

Inside, the still air and signs of a hasty departure told me we were too late. Clothes were strewn across the bed in the master suite, and half the toiletries were missing from the bathroom. A hideous watercolour print hung askew over a concealed safe. The door was locked, but I'd bet my Camaro the safe was empty. Carr had gone.

"Rest of the place is tidy," Emmy said, opening and closing drawers with gloved hands. "The bastard even loaded the dishwasher. He'll certainly get his security deposit back if the landlord can find him."

I cursed myself for allowing him to escape. "Why didn't I think to put a surveillance team on him after my visit?"

"You didn't know, honey. He hid his true colours well."

"But..."

"Stop it. We'll get him. It might just take a bit more time than we hoped."

The worst part of the day was having to explain things to Ethan. He'd tried so hard to bury his past, so finding out it was alive and kicking back big time would undoubtedly hurt.

Not only that, I'd have to admit I'd been snooping on him, and I didn't imagine he'd be too happy about that, either.

I'd planned to down a stiff drink, change into an outfit that didn't make me look like a door-to-door saleswoman, and maybe wallop a punchbag a few times before I fessed up. But today was jinxed in its entirety, and Ethan was waiting in the hallway at Riverley when I walked in. He paced up and down on the tiled floor while Stefanie watched him from one of the high-backed couches at the edge of the room.

As soon as I crossed the threshold, he grabbed me and kissed me. "Nobody would tell me what was going on. Are you okay?"

Well, that was a "welcome home" I'd never had before. "I'm fine. What makes you think otherwise?"

"I called the office, and your assistant said you were in a meeting with Emmy."

"I was." Sort of.

"But Bradley called Emmy's other assistant, and she said Emmy had gone out to pick up a package."

Also true. "She did."

"Oh. I didn't know what to believe. So nothing happened today?"

Might as well get this over with. "Some stuff happened. But it all went so quickly, and I wanted to explain in person rather than over the phone."

"Did you find him?"

"We think so."

Stefanie stepped forward. "Oh my goodness, who?"

"Ethan, it's someone from your childhood."

He went rigid, then paled so much I led him over to the seat Stef had just vacated and pressed him down onto it. She perched beside him and put an arm around his shoulders while I crouched in front.

"You know him as Richard Carr. The property developer. But back then he was called Ricky Carter."

Ethan started shaking, and I added my arm to Stefanie's.

"But I met him," Ethan said. "How did I not recognise him? Ricky Carter was the worst of all the kids. I knocked his glasses off by accident once, and from that moment on, he was out to get me. One time, he got the others to hold me down while he poured a can of white paint over my face."

Red hot anger flooded through me, and I forced myself to unclench my teeth before I needed dental work.

"He doesn't wear glasses now, and he looks very different. Cosmetic surgery, I think. I only knew for certain it was the same guy because the end of his finger was missing. He lost it in juvie."

Now Stephanie turned ashen. "Which finger was missing?"

"The tip of his right forefinger."

"Do you have a picture of him? Do you?"

I pulled up his driver's licence photo on my phone and showed her. With hindsight, that was a bad idea because she crumpled over sideways. Ethan sat her up, and I pushed her head between her knees.

As soon as she came around, she said, "I'm gonna be sick," and retched all over the floor.

Fuck.

"What's going on?" Oliver asked, walking into the hallway.

"I'm not sure yet, but we're gonna need a bucket, tissues, and disinfectant."

"I'm on it."

"Stef, what's wrong?" I asked her.

"I slept with him," she whispered, looking more like a ghost than Ethan ever had. "He was a client."

Holy shit. "When?"

"Over a year ago. He wanted to do things I didn't do, but I knew Chrissie did, so I suggested he give her a try. Oh, hell, this is all my fault."

She burst into big, messy tears.

Well, I guess we'd established a connection between Carr and Christina, although in the worst possible way.

Oliver came back with supplies, and I transferred Stef to him while I cleaned up. He looked a little worried, and I couldn't exactly blame him. He didn't sign up for hysterical females when he took on the case.

I was still on my hands and knees when Emmy walked in. "What did I miss?"

Chapter 49

I FEARED AFTER my confession that I'd been researching his past, I might get angry Ethan, but what I got was sad Ethan. Come to think of it, I hadn't yet seen him lash out at anybody. He just walked away instead. All his hate seemed to be directed at himself, which was something we'd need to work on.

That night, he made love to me with a care bordering on reverence, and I treasured every touch and every caress. He made me *feel* with every nerve ending. I could have spent the rest of my life never moving from his bed, and I'd have spent it happy.

They say love is found in the most unlikely places, but I can honestly say a super-max prison wasn't one I'd considered. Until it happened.

My sweet little jailbird, just waiting to be set free.

After a shower the next morning, which took longer than it should have because Ethan joined me, I was eager to get on with the search for Carr, but I couldn't, not straight away. I had to stop by the police precinct first to give an extended statement on the shooting outside the courthouse, which was something I didn't look forward to re-hashing.

Still, at least it would be over with. Ethan had already made the same trip with Oliver yesterday morning. Just a formality, they said.

Oliver was waiting downstairs for me, looking rough around the edges, which was unusual for him.

"Sorry about yesterday," I said. "I mean, I kind of foisted Stef on you."

"Don't worry about it. This house sees more drama than a courtroom, so it was only a matter of time before I got sucked in. You ready to go?"

I gave him a twirl in the suit Bradley had picked up for me yesterday. "Think so."

"Very professional. Glasses?"

"Yeah. Do ya think they make me look smarter?"

He laughed. "You'd probably let the air out of my tyres if I said no."

"You got that right."

Neither of us were laughing in the interview room a little later while two cops asked the same questions six times over, just phrased in different ways. Three hours of our lives, wasted.

No, I didn't see the shooter.

Yes, I was sure the car was a BMW.

No, Ethan hadn't received any specific threats that suggested something of that nature was going to happen.

By the time they'd finished, both my caffeine levels and my patience were running dangerously low. Oliver looked like I felt. Guilt over Lyle still gnawed away at me, leaving me hollow.

"Coffee?" I asked, though it wasn't a suggestion; it was a necessity.

"Place by your office?"

He knew that was my favourite.

Or at least it had been. I thought back to my run-in with Jay. The drinks from that place would be forever tainted with the taste of his foul temper.

"How about we just go to Starbucks? It's closer."

"I'm easy."

"Tell me something I don't know."

The barista was drawing pretty patterns in the froth on my flat white when the receptionist at Blackwood's Richmond office called me. What now?

"Your little visitors are back. At least, two of them are."

Oh, great. Just when the day couldn't get any better. "What do they want?"

"They won't talk to me. They seem kind of agitated, though."

"Give me fifteen minutes." I turned to the guy behind the register. "Could you give me a bag of cookies to go, please?"

When we got back to the office, Trick was sitting in one of the grey leather chairs, his left leg stuck out in front of him. Vine bounced on his tiptoes, eyes darting from side to side.

When he saw me, Trick scrambled to his feet, wincing as he did so.

"What's up?" I asked. "What've you done to your leg?"

He waved a hand at me. "Just fell off a wall, that's all. It's nothin', except I can't run now. That's not the problem."

"Then what *is* the problem?"

"We can't find Race."

"What do you mean, you can't find him?"

"We got chased by these bigger kids last night, and they were catching us, so we split up. And now we can't find him."

"Could he have gone home?"

"Vine went round. His foster mama said he ain't there."

"Can you think of anywhere else he might have gone?"

"We got a few places. Vine checked a couple, but I don't want him on his own, not if them kids are still about."

"Fine. Give me the list and I'll go."

I looked at my watch. How long would this take? Not more than an hour, surely? I could do with some air before I ended up glued to my laptop screen again. Yes, I needed to hunt for Carr, but half the company was on the case, and Race was just a child. He shouldn't be roaming the streets.

"We'll come with you," Trick said.

"No, you won't. You'll stay here while I get our doctor to check out the damage to your leg."

He looked like he was about to argue, but he must have been in pain because he acquiesced. "Vine can go."

"No, he stays here too." I wasn't going to babysit as well as traipsing around on what could very well be a wild-goose chase. "I go alone, or I don't go at all."

Oliver watched our little exchange with amusement. Well, I was glad he found my life funny.

"Oliver here would love to take you out for milkshakes after your checkup. Wouldn't you, Oliver?"

I gave him a gritted smile.

"What, uh..." Two faces looked up at him hopefully, and he glared at me. "Yes, fine. We'll go for milkshakes."

Oh boy, I was going to pay for that one.

I left in a hurry, clutching a pad filled with Trick's scrawled diagrams. The first place I had to check was a tumbledown shed on a mothballed building site.

I ignored the "keep out" signs and climbed over the fence, ripping a pair of Calvin Klein pants as I did so. Bradley was going to love me for that.

The door hung ajar, and I gingerly pushed it open, only to leap back as a spider the size of a dinner plate swung out at me, its fat legs twitching. I fucking hated those eight-legged freaks. Where was a can of hairspray when I needed it? Or even a gun? I'd shot one of the bastards once when I was with Emmy, and she'd never let me forget it.

Attila the spider descended to the ground and scuttled away, so I pushed the door again. There was nothing in there but more arachnids and a few beetles, and I beat a hasty retreat.

Next up was an abandoned tunnel next to the rail line. *Please, don't let there be any more spiders.*

Good news! There weren't, but only because the rats must have eaten them. Beady yellow eyes stared at me from the shadows then one of the little bastards ran over my foot. I kicked out, and a kitten heel went flying into the darkness. Fuck. Cursing worse than Emmy, I shone the flashlight from my purse into the gloom. My shoe had landed in a corner full of trash, and I had to fish through mouldy fast food boxes to retrieve it.

The boys came here to hang out? Seriously? Life at home must be even worse for them than I thought.

Ethan's building was next on the list. According to Trick's scribbles, there was a lean-to at the side where dumpsters were stored, and on days when the refuse had been recently removed, the stink wasn't too bad, so they sat in there to keep out of the cold.

I scraped something nasty off my other heel and climbed back into the car. Dumpsters I could cope with. Anything was better than spiders and rats.

The Camaro engine roared into life, and five minutes later, I parked in the service alley outside Ethan's building. There was the storage cupboard, right where Trick said, but he'd grossly underplayed the smell. The stench was vile, like a week-old corpse in the tropics. Perhaps I'd been wrong about the rats.

Surely nobody could stand to be in there for longer than a second? I held my breath and pushed the door open. Nothing but overflowing trash. I had one place left to try—a woodland den in the local park. I hadn't been there since I chased that bail jumper, and—

Hold on. Why was the door to the building open? It swung ajar in the breeze, the padlock hanging off the hasp. Could Race have decided to hide out in there? It certainly looked like a better choice than any of the options so far.

I pushed the door open and peered inside. Who had unlocked it? Had the cleaner been slacking or was somebody inside? I reached for my purse then cursed when I realised I'd left my gun in my desk drawer. Dammit. Ethan made me lose my freaking mind. All I had was the knife in my pocket and a smile.

A short hallway led to a flight of stairs, and I tried not to let my heels click on the tile as I climbed them. There was a lot to be said for carpet. Or sneakers. Or both.

Photos of the kids covered a notice board on the second floor, some holding instruments, some in song, a few perched at a mixing desk that looked enormous next to their tiny frames. I recognised Trick, strumming away at a guitar, and started to look for Vine and Race before I reminded myself I didn't have time for that.

When things got back to normal, I hoped to come to a session or two myself. I admired what Ethan was doing, and if there was any way I could support him, I'd be standing in line to volunteer.

I reached a door and peered through the glass panel near the top. This was the main music room, by the looks of it—there was a low stage at the far end with a drum kit and a piano. Screens either side were decorated with drawings and photos, hundreds of them. What else was in there? I was hoping for a small child.

The door creaked as I pushed it open. Movement caught my eye, but before I could turn, I heard a pop, quickly followed by the sensation of termites running through my veins, eating me from the inside out while I got beaten thirty times a second by a baseball bat.

I knew I'd been hit by a Taser—it wasn't the first time—but my muscles spasmed then locked up, and while the juice kept flowing, there wasn't a damn thing I could do about it. The volts from a cop's Taser lasted five seconds, but this must have been the civilian model because it carried on far longer than that.

Carr walked towards me, but I lay helpless. When the pulses finally stopped, I felt a stab in my thigh, and I recovered just enough to see the needle sticking out of it before everything went black.

CHAPTER 50

WHEN THE HAZE began to clear, I tried to get up, but I couldn't move. As I wiggled my arms behind me, something chafed at my wrists, rough and raw. I came to my senses enough to realise that I was tied to a chair. How fucking original.

And it wasn't only my arms. My feet were bound to the front legs and, just for good measure, there were a couple of coils around my waist as well.

"Well, this wasn't quite the result I was hoping for, but I guess it'll have a similar effect." Carr's voice jarred my brain, harsher than I remembered.

"Yourrrr crassshy," I slurred.

Fuck, I couldn't even speak properly. What had he given me?

"No, darling, crazy people go to jail. I'm just... adventurous."

Oh, shit. He was fucking nuts.

"You're gonna...go...to jail."

Every word was an effort.

He laughed, a hideous cackle that would have done any movie villain proud. "No, I don't think so. I'll be long gone by the time anyone realises what's happened. Fires aren't that quick to put out."

For the first time, the vague smell of diesel fumes registered in my brain. Oh fuck, no. Tell me this wasn't happening.

He flicked the lighter in his hand and laughed again. "I see you've realised your fate. It's always more fun when the victim sees it coming, don't you think? Ethan White was a bit of a shame in that respect."

"Why? Why are you doing this?"

"Two years I spent inside because of that little bastard and his family. They chopped off my fucking finger, did you know that? And that wasn't even the worst of it."

He walked closer, circling me, just out of reach even if my arms had been free. "Do you know what it's like to get fucked up the ass until you bleed? To be forced to take a man's cock in your mouth until you choke on it and gasp for air?"

I shook my head. Those were two things I'd managed to avoid.

"Well, I do. And it's all because of that half-caste cunt, tattling to his pretend daddy."

The guy was whacked. Properly whacked. He carried on talking, no doubt pleased to have a captive audience.

"Years I spent looking for him. Years! And one day I walked in here and there he was, sitting right in front of me. Somebody was smiling down on me that day. Finally, I could ruin his life the way he ruined mine."

Carr stopped a foot away and bent over, his face mere inches from mine. "And then you came and wrecked it, you little bitch," he yelled, spit peppering my face.

"Sorry."

I wasn't, but I didn't have much else to say.

"No, you're not." He stood up again. "But it doesn't

matter. I'd only planned to burn the building today, then I was going to come back for Briand when the heat had died down, if you'll excuse the pun." Carr smiled to himself, twisting his mouth into a malevolent grin as he checked my bonds. "But I can ruin his life by taking yours instead. I saw the way he looked at you outside the courthouse. It was all over the news."

He flicked the lighter again and stared into the flame, mesmerised.

Slowly, slowly, my brain began to function again. Logic said I should stall Carr, although I didn't know how that would help. Only Trick, Vine, and Oliver knew I'd come here, and they were most likely choosing milkshakes right now.

"Why Christina?" I asked.

Carr waved his hand with a dramatic flourish. "Why not Christina? If it hadn't been her, it would have been any other one of those greedy whores looking for a man to pay their way. Christina's affections were directly proportional to the amount of money she received, but at least she was more honest than most about her prices."

"Do you not think stabbing her so many times was overkill?"

"No such thing, dearie. Have you ever driven a knife into a young girl's flesh? Felt that moment where the skin stretches and gives way with a quiet pop? When the blade slips through the muscle and sinew on its way to the hilt? Let me tell you, there's nothing like it. It becomes an addiction."

Was he telling me what I thought he was telling me? "She wasn't your first, then?"

Another peal of the laughter I hated so much

bounced off the walls. "Of course not. I've learned a lot over the years about how not to get caught."

I felt sick, and not just because of my own predicament. "How many?" I asked, my voice flat.

He rubbed his chin. "Now, there's a question. I tend to lose count. Fifteen, maybe sixteen? Something like that. They all start to look the same after a while."

Fuck. We'd suspected Christina wasn't his first victim, but sixteen other women, dead? The man was a monster, more so than we'd ever imagined.

"Why the shooting?" I asked. "Wasn't that a bit of a departure from your usual methods?"

For a second he looked puzzled, then the lines in his forehead disappeared. "That thing outside the courthouse?"

I nodded.

"Oh, that wasn't me. You give me too much credit. I'd like to shake the hand of the person who did it, though. I watched that snivelling little attorney from the public gallery one day. He deserved to be put out of his misery."

Confusion reigned in my already addled mind. Carr hadn't been behind that? Then who the hell had?

To my left, the monster looked at his watch. "Would you look at the time? I'll miss my flight if I don't get a move on. Nice talking to you, Miss di Grassi. Enjoy the show."

Without further ado, he turned his back on me and walked towards the door, his leather-soled wingtips slapping on the tile as he jogged down the stairs.

The only consolation I had, as I heard the *whoomph* of the fire catching hold below me, was that Emmy would one day find that man and kill him.

CHAPTER 51

I ROCKED BACKWARDS and forwards, trying to get my arms free, but the bindings had no give whatsoever. The best I could manage was to shuffle the chair a few inches to the side, but the only way I knew to get out of the building was the way I'd come in, and even if the fire wasn't raging downstairs yet, it sure would be by the time I got there.

With nothing else to lose, I hurled myself sideways, hoping the chair might break on impact with the floor. It didn't, but I thought my shoulder might have as pain shot along my arm.

An involuntary tear rolled down my cheek when I thought of what I was about to lose. All my life, I'd been waiting for Ethan to come along, and I'd had just a few precious days with him as my lover. If there was someone up there watching over us, he sucked.

And it wasn't just Ethan. I'd never see Emmy, Mack, Oliver, or the rest of my friends again either. We'd gone through so much together, and in my final minutes, I'd be without any of them.

I jerked my legs, hoping the knots would loosen, but Carr must have been a Boy Scout. He'd even looped the rope around the struts of the old wooden chair so I couldn't slide it off the bottom of the legs.

Was there anything in this room that could help? I

twisted to look—a row of guitars, comfy armchairs, a foosball table. Even a TV in one corner. Nothing useful but plenty to burn.

Smoke gathered overhead, black plumes billowing near the ceiling. Carr had left the door open, and I saw the light from the flames dancing on the walls as they inched closer, burning all those precious pictures on the walls.

I wished I'd stayed upright, that way I could have inhaled the deathly clouds and put myself out of my misery faster. As it was, I'd have an extra minute or so as the veil of darkness crept ever closer.

Fuck my life.

Did angels exist? If they did, would my son be up there waiting? I let out a heavy breath. I'd probably never see him even if he was because I'd be going to hell, both metaphorically and literally.

I was about to close my eyes so I wouldn't have to watch the inevitable when I caught movement by the stage. Was I seeing things? I squinted through the smoke as a tiny figure wriggled out from underneath it.

"Race," I screamed.

He froze, unsure what to do.

"Come here," I begged. "Please!"

"Is that man gone?"

"Yes, he's gone." On his way to a non-extradition country, no doubt.

Race scuttled over and crouched in front of me. "What do I do, lady?"

"Can you untie me?"

He crawled behind me, and I felt his fingers working at the knots.

"They're too tight. I can't do it!"

"That's okay; we'll try another way. There's a knife in my right-hand jacket pocket. You need to get that out and cut through the rope."

"Which is right?"

"The top one."

He slipped his hand inside and came out holding my Emerson CQC-7B. I'd "borrowed" it from Emmy a few weeks back. It was her knife of choice, and she bought them in bulk.

And with its tanto blade, it went through the cord binding my hands like a hot poker through an eyeball.

As soon as my hands were free, I took the knife back and made short work of the rope around my waist and legs. Beside me, Race bent over and started choking, coughing up phlegm onto the polished floor.

Flames danced in the doorway, and I half lifted him towards the windows at the front. If I broke one with a guitar...

Race dug his heels in and yanked my hand. "This way, lady."

"But—"

"Come on!"

He pulled me over to the stage, and behind a screen to the side of it was a door I hadn't realised was there. Was it locked? No, just sticky. Race gave it a shove, we sped through, and I slammed it behind us to keep the smoke at bay before we ran along a dimly lit hallway lined with doors. They all looked the same to me, but Race didn't hesitate. Thank goodness one of us knew where we were going. Race led me through a virtual maze then shoved the bar on a fire door, letting us out onto a metal balcony. I hung onto the railing and doubled over, gulping in great lungfuls of air. Race's breathing was ragged, and he collapsed to his knees.

"You okay?" I asked, dropping down beside him.

He managed a nod, his eyes still wide with fear. I hugged him and squeezed his hand, crying silent thanks for the tiny scruff of a miracle that had just rescued me.

Sirens sounded in the distance, and I tried to gather my thoughts, which had scattered like smoke on the breeze.

Phone home, that's what I needed to do.

Only I couldn't. My cell was broken where I'd landed on it when the chair tipped over. At least I still had my keys, as well as a nice bruise from where they'd stabbed me in the leg.

"Do you have your phone?" I asked Race.

He shook his head. "Got taken."

"Can you climb down the ladder?"

A nod.

I went first, keeping him in front of me so if he fell, I'd catch him. I needed to get back to Blackwood. Carr was about to board a plane.

Luckily, my Camaro was still in the alley where I'd left it. Thick smoke swirled all around, but otherwise it was untouched. Carr's arrogance had worked in my favour this time—he didn't think I'd escape, so he hadn't burned my car or even punctured a tyre. Still wheezing, I got Race strapped into the front seat and took off just as the first fire truck turned the corner. I'd listen to the reports of myself fleeing the scene later.

It was only a fifteen-minute drive to Blackwood, but every second put Carr closer to take-off. I floored it, past caring about speeding fines or stop signs or traffic lights. Emmy could apologise on my behalf later.

The tyres squealed as I sped into the underground parking garage and plucked Race out of the car, staggering towards the elevator in the corner. It crawled upwards slowly, oh-so-slowly, until I finally burst out on the third floor.

"Call Emmy," I sputtered. "Check the airports. Carr's about to get on a plane."

Strong arms gripped under my armpits as my knees gave way, and someone pulled me onto a chair. That was the last thing I remembered before everything turned black again.

CHAPTER 52

I WAS ONLY out for a minute or so, but it was long enough for Dr. Stanton to appear by my side. I tried to push her away.

"Check him," I said, pointing at Race.

"I'll check both of you." Her tone left no room for argument.

She gave me an oxygen mask to hold over my nose and pressed the business end of a stethoscope against my chest. I gave in and let her. I didn't have the strength to object. It was only when she prodded my shoulder that I let out a yowl.

"You need to go to hospital with that."

"Later. Just strap it up, would you?"

I wasn't going anywhere until someone gave me some news on what was happening with the search for Carr.

"There's every chance it's broken."

I tried a smile, although it probably came out as more of a grimace. "Would you be a sweetheart and give me some painkillers? The good stuff."

"I'll bring Advil and an ice pack until we know what we're dealing with."

"Advil? Fucking Advil?"

She pursed her lips. "Codeine might help with the pain, but it won't do anything for the inflammation.

Advil is the best thing. As I said, you need to get to the hospital."

"Yeah, yeah, in a minute." I trundled the chair over to the nearest desk and picked up the phone. "Mack? Tell me what's going on."

An hour later, Race had been pronounced fit by Kira, but I'd insisted he get checked out at the hospital too. Mack had tracked Carr's departure to Richmond International, and his booked flight to Orlando had just departed. We didn't know yet whether he'd made it onto the plane, and if he had, where he planned to go after that. Mack was busy hacking into airline records when Emmy strode across the floor, grinning like the Cheshire fucking cat. Ana and Fia weren't far behind, and even Ana didn't look totally miserable.

"You got him?"

"Yeah, we got him. Beat him to Richmond International. If you ever say anything about my driving again..."

"You bitch. Why didn't you call?"

She dropped the remains of her phone into the trash. *Another one bites the dust.* "Thought I'd tell you in person. Besides, it was messy."

"Messy how?"

"I stun-gunned him in the terminal and he pissed himself. Fia shot him up with ketamine, Ana borrowed an airport uniform and one of those golf carts they use for VIPs so we could get him to the car, and now Black's Cayenne needs valeted."

"Thank fuck. I'll pay for new upholstery."

Emmy gave me a high-five then a hug, and I almost forgot about my shoulder until a bolt of pain shot through me.

"Yeouch!"

"Fuck, I'm sorry." She pulled back and stared. "You're filthy and not in a good way."

"So are you now."

Grey splodges covered her white shirt, and I started laughing. I couldn't help it. I'd nearly died this afternoon, and all I could think of was Bradley's face when he saw the state of us.

Emmy joined in, and we snorted until tears ran down our cheeks.

The men looked on nervously. "Should I call the doctor back?" one of them asked. "She went to the ER with the kid."

I held a hand up, stopping him. Eventually, our hysterics subsided and we grew serious again.

"Ems, tell me you've got codeine."

"Fia?"

"Codeine, hydrocodone, oxycodone, meperidine, morphine, fentanyl. Take your pick."

Fuck. "Morphine."

If I couldn't twist Carr's balls off in a vice, at least I could get high.

"Two minutes."

"Where does she get all that shit?" I asked Emmy as Fia disappeared.

"Best not to ask. So, did you speak to Carr?"

"Yeah. The freak loves the sound of his own voice."

"Did he have anything useful to say?"

I lifted my glasses off and handed them to her. "Want to watch?"

When I'd seen the pair of high-res camera-glasses Nate had made for Emmy, I'd wheedled and cajoled until he gave me a pair too. He'd sighed and handed them over yesterday. I'd only worn them to record my police interview for posterity, but I'd forgotten to press the "stop" button, and it turned out that was one of the best moves I'd ever made.

Emmy grinned at me. "I love home movies."

"Where's Ethan?" I asked. "I need to see him."

"He's at Riverley, climbing the walls. He knows something's happened, but I wasn't going to give him the details until I'd seen you."

"Can you take me over there?"

"Don't you think you should go to the hospital first?"

Fia chose that moment to stab me with a needle.

"Nope, I'm good. We can go right after."

Emmy rolled her eyes. "Fine. We'll be at Riverley in no time."

"Please make it a little longer than no time. I've had enough excitement for today."

"Slow enough?"

Emmy made a show of letting a minivan beat her Corvette away from a traffic light, but I barely noticed.

"Fine."

"Okay, what's up? You've been quiet for at least five minutes, and that's not like you."

Everything was confused in my head, and I had no idea what to tell her. Or Ethan. I'd nearly met my maker today, and on the inside, I was shaking. On the outside too, at least, I would have been if I hadn't gripped the edges of the seat.

"Dan?"

"I'm fine."

"Bullshit." Three seconds later, she'd done a J-turn and the car was pointing in the other direction. "I'm taking you to the hospital."

"No!" I closed my eyes and leaned back against the headrest. "I'm just scared, okay?"

"You got Tasered, escaped from a burning building, drove all the way to the office while practically unconscious, and *now* you're scared?"

"I'm scared of this thing with Ethan."

I hung on as Emmy spun the car again, then she drove into a grocery store parking lot and put the brake on.

"What scares you?"

"I don't know. Everything?"

"Can you narrow it down just a little?"

"It's all happened so fast. I mean, three months ago, I spent my nights partying or hunting criminals, and now I have this weird urge to curl up on the couch with a cup of cocoa and a painfully shy guitarist. We're from two totally different worlds, but no matter how hard I try, I can't imagine my future without him in it."

"Then don't. He's crazy about you."

"What if it doesn't work out? I mean, women throw panties at him."

"They throw all sorts of underwear at Eli, and Tia copes."

"But what if we're just too far apart?"

Emmy began ticking off on her fingers. "Okay, we've got Xav and Georgia—a hitman and a senator's daughter. Then there's Quinn and Ana, and Fia and Leo. And Jed fell in love with a scientist, for fuck's sake."

"But—"

"And then there's me and Black."

"But you're perfect for each other."

Emmy closed her eyes and screwed her mouth up the way she did when she was deciding something. Five seconds passed. Ten.

"When I first met Black, he was obviously a billionaire, and I was a stripper."

"I'm sorry, you were a *what*?"

"You heard. And if you tell anyone, I'll kill you. I mean that."

"B-b-but... I thought you worked in a gym?"

"I also worked in a gym, but stripping paid better."

"Black knows?"

"Of course he knows. I was dressed up like a slutty schoolgirl when I nicked his wallet."

"Holy fuck." I doubled over with laughter then quickly regretted it. "Ouch, that hurt."

"So you see, people don't have to be perfect on paper to be right for each other. And even if you try and it all goes wrong, surely that's better than not even taking the chance?"

"I guess. But it's not just Ethan. It's the kids too. I always avoided spending time with children because I thought it would hurt too much, and it does hurt, but I also kinda like it."

"If you like it, then just enjoy it. Don't keep second-guessing yourself."

"Why do you always have to be right?"

Emmy's smile was so smug I wanted to sandpaper it right off her face.

"I just can't help it. Are you ready to head off? Because seriously, if you don't go to Riverley right now,

I'm definitely taking you to the hospital. You've gone a horrible colour."

"Okay, go. Let's get this over with. What should I tell Ethan?"

"The truth. That Carr was crazy, but you're fine, and it's done. You perhaps want to gloss over the smoke inhalation part, though."

"I love you, you mental bitch."

"Stop getting all emotional, you silly cow."

I followed Emmy's advice and told Ethan a condensed version of this afternoon's adventures.

Went looking for Race.

Found Carr.

Teensy fire.

Found Race.

Lost Carr.

Drove back to work.

Found Carr.

All good, couldn't be better.

Ethan took the news of my ordeal worse than I did, and his mouth set into a thin line.

"Sorry," I muttered, then shrieked as he caught me by surprise with a hug.

Stars burst behind my eyes, and I'd probably have fainted if Ethan hadn't been holding me up. The effects of Sofia's little gift were no match for two strong arms.

"Dani? What's wrong?"

"Uh, I have a small problem with my collarbone. It might be a little bit broken."

He sprang back, and I bit my lip as another band of

pain pulsed through me.

"Fuck. I'm never letting you out of my sight again." He squeezed my hands in his. "Never."

"That suits me, but you'll have to come to the hospital. I need to get an x-ray."

"Why couldn't I have fallen in love with a nice, normal girl? One who likes baking cookies and going to movies with friends."

I went rigid. It was kind of like being Tasered, except without the feeling I was going to wet myself. "You love me?"

He smiled that sweet, shy smile. "Yeah, I love you."

I buried my face in his chest, squeezing him as tightly as I could with my good arm. "I love you too."

"Sorry, I didn't quite catch that."

I looked up at him. "I love you too."

He grinned. "Nope, still didn't hear it."

"I love you too. What, do you want me to tattoo it across my forehead?"

"Now that you mention it..."

Dr. Beech met us at the hospital entrance with a wheelchair. Thanks to Blackwood's regular donations to his fundraisers, we never had to wait in line.

"Ouch. That looks nasty, Daniela. Tennis injury?"

"Something like that."

Blackwood had a lot of tennis injuries. Sometimes golf.

"Perhaps we should give you some painkillers. Morphine?"

"Thanks, that's—"

"No," Emmy said. "She's fine with Advil."

Bitch.

Ethan hovered in the hallway while I got x-rayed then sat on the side of my bed while we waited for the results. Emmy disappeared for fifteen minutes and came back with coffee.

"I bought another one of those incubator things. That should keep us good for a while."

"Incubator things?" Ethan asked.

"For the baby unit."

"Just Emmy showing her philanthropic side," I told him. "She's good like that."

Dr. Beech returned before my coffee was cool enough to drink and put the X-ray of my shoulder up on the lightbox. Oh, shit. Even I could see the break.

"The bad news is that you've fractured your scapula. You'll need to wear a brace so the bones knit together in the proper alignment."

"Is there good news?"

He glanced sideways at Emmy. "You get six weeks off work."

She just smiled. "Six weeks with Ethan, honey. Enjoy them. I did say that whoever caught Carr could have a vacation."

Okay, when she put it that way...

We had our first date that evening. Dinner and a movie. Well, Mrs. Fairfax's homemade burgers and a special showing of Psycho, part II.

Nate hooked up the glasses I'd been wearing earlier to the big screen in Emmy's movie theatre, and I settled back onto the couch beside Ethan. He'd gone tense again, but when I pressed my lips against his cheek, he relaxed a little.

"Lucky you didn't spend longer dying," Nate said. "The battery was almost drained."

Sympathy wasn't one of his strong points.

"I'll make sure battery life is at the forefront of my mind next time I get tied to a chair by a madman."

Oliver settled on the other side of me, legal pad and Montblanc pen in hand. Even now he still wore a suit, although he had taken his tie off.

"Did you bring the popcorn?" Emmy asked him, earning herself an eye roll.

Bradley skidded in, bowls in hand. "Here I am. Popcorn, M&Ms, and I'll just fetch the bubbles." He held out a hand to Race, who was squashed on the other side of Ethan. "Hey, let's get some juice. Do you like Disney?"

Yes, Race. After the fire, he'd been shaken, even quieter than usual. I'd wanted to take him home, but he'd clung to Ethan and begged me not to. He thought he'd get into trouble.

Well, I'd told so many fibs in my life, one more wouldn't hurt. I called his foster mom and explained that the boys were putting on an impromptu music show. Would she mind if Race stayed out for the evening?

"One less mouth to feed," she said.

"Is it okay if he stays overnight occasionally?"

"Long as I get my cheque from the state each month and the kids keep out of my hair, I don't care what they do."

How sad that this woman had the greatest gift of all —children—and she treated them like an annoyance, or worse, a meal ticket. I stopped feeling guilty after that.

But I didn't want Race to watch the video. Yes, he'd

seen the live version, but one dose of Richard Carr was quite enough. And now, as he silently followed Bradley up to the small TV room on the second floor, I stuck by that decision.

"Ready?" Nate asked.

"Go for it."

I watched for the second time as Carr ranted like the lunatic we knew him to be. Now my adrenaline had stopped flowing and I had time to analyse his words, I felt properly sick.

Ethan didn't look so good either, and he gripped my thigh so tightly I had to ask him to ease off.

"And people say I'm crazy," Emmy said when the video ended with me falling out of the elevator at Blackwood. "How did that man manage to go undetected for so long?"

"Moved around a lot, I imagine," Nate said. "How long do you think he'd been at Ethan's building?"

I'd already spoken to Race about that. "A couple of hours." The poor kid had been lying under the stage for that long. "Race found the door unlocked and went in, then heard Carr coming up the stairs with the gas cans and hid. After that, Carr spent a while pacing and muttering until I arrived."

Emmy's husband stretched out his legs, and I detected a faint aura of relief around him today. Relief that, for once, it wasn't his wife getting into all manner of trouble. And now he asked the fifty-thousand-dollar question.

"So, what next?"

I'd thought about that too. "One, we need to make sure Carr stays locked up. Two, we should look for unsolved murders wherever he's had construction projects. I'll bet we could attribute some of them to him."

"I'll file a motion to dismiss in the morning," Oliver said. "No grand jury in their right mind would touch Ethan after this."

At least one good thing had come out of today. Ethan would be free to get on with his life without that cloud hanging over him. Over us.

But there was still one more storm on the horizon. It had almost been lost on me in all the drama.

"Carr said the shooting outside the courthouse wasn't him."

"What if he was lying?" Ethan asked. "He lied to you before."

"No, not this afternoon. This afternoon, he was bragging. He admitted to killing fifteen or sixteen women without missing a beat, plus Christina, and he wouldn't have missed the opportunity to add another victim to his tally."

"So if it wasn't him, who was it?"

"It had to have been the brother," Oliver said. "He's the only other person with a good motive."

"Kevin had an alibi," Emmy said. "While you were tied up this afternoon, I was on my way back from visiting him. The afternoon of the shooting, he was in a college lecture with thirty other witnesses. He works at a burger place for twelve bucks an hour, so he didn't have the cash to hire outside help, and we couldn't find any connections on the street."

"Where there's a will, there's a way."

"He didn't have the will either. In fact, he asked me to apologise to Dan and Ethan for his behaviour outside Harold's house. Said he realised it made him as bad as the guy who killed his sister."

"You think he was being straight up?"

"Hard to be a hundred percent sure, but I'd put money on it."

"So, who does that leave?"

Emmy shrugged and turned to Ethan. "You pissed anyone else off lately?"

A cold feeling of dread came over me. "No, he hasn't. But I have."

CHAPTER 53

ETHAN STILL HAD no idea about Jay and me. I suppose some stupid part of me had been hoping that if I pretended it never happened, it would all go away.

But it hadn't gone away. And what if it never did?

Jay had a fierce temper, and he wasn't renowned for his reasonableness. But was he heartless enough to order somebody's murder?

If I was forced to answer one way or the other, I'd have to go with yes.

I closed my eyes, half wishing I'd suffocated this afternoon. Because at least then I wouldn't have to see the look on Ethan's face when I told him I'd once slept with the man who'd tried to send him to the electric chair.

"I had that argument with Skinner," I said, still with my eyes shut.

"The bust-up after Ethan made bail, or another one?" Emmy asked.

"Just that one."

Nate groaned, and I couldn't blame him. He'd been present for the aftermath of Skinner round one, and it wasn't pretty. "How bad was it?"

"Some shouting, some yelling. He threatened to rip me apart and I threw a macchiato at him."

"Smooth, Dan, real smooth."

"I couldn't help it, okay? He just knows all the right buttons to push."

Silence. I cracked an eyelid open, and Ethan was looking at me funny.

"How does he know which buttons?"

I couldn't meet his eyes. "I dated Jay for a while. Back in a time when I'd lost my mind."

Ethan's arm fell away from my leg. "What?"

"He can be charming when he puts his mind to it, but underneath his smart suit and his fake tan, he's a troll."

"Skinner wears fake tan?" Emmy asked.

"He got a full-body spray every week."

She wrinkled her nose. "Didn't he get that horrible smell?"

"He covered it up with expensive aftershave."

Ethan's mouth flattened into a thin line. Shit. Okay, perhaps he didn't need to know those details.

"I'm sorry," I whispered. "I should have told you before. I just didn't want you to look at me the way you're looking at me now. Believe me; I know how stupid I was."

He stayed silent, hurt etched across his face. *Oh, please say something.* And not "it's over" because I wouldn't survive that.

Finally, he spoke. "Just so I don't get any more surprises, are there any other assholes in your past I should know about?"

I let out the breath I'd been holding. "No. Only Jay and the guy Emmy put in the hospital."

Ethan gave my hand a squeeze. "I hate knowing you got hurt twice. It won't happen a third time."

There were signs of relief from around the room,

not least of all mine.

Emmy pointed her pen in his direction, "Dan, keep that one."

"So, what about Jay?" Nate asked.

"Money, connections, and motive—he's got all three," Emmy said. "I vote we take a good look at him." She gave a sudden grin. "Even if he wasn't responsible for Lyle, I'm sure there's something we can find that he doesn't want us to."

I nodded my agreement. "Nothing would give me greater pleasure than digging it out."

CHAPTER 54

WITH THE STRONG possibility that someone out there wanted to kill one or the other or both of us, Ethan and I were still at Riverley two weeks later. Whoever had been involved in the shooting, whether it was Skinner or someone else, had covered their tracks well. There was nothing.

Not only that, Skinner had started his campaign for the commonwealth's attorney position, and every time I saw a newspaper or pamphlet featuring his smarmy mug, I wanted to barf.

At least all the charges against Ethan had been dropped, and he had access to his property once more. The first thing he'd done was put the house on the market.

"I don't ever want to set foot in there again. I'll hire people to pack my stuff up."

"Where will you live?"

"Anywhere but there. In a hotel if I have to."

A nervous shiver ran through me. As a confirmed commitment-phobe, I couldn't believe I was about to ask what I was about to ask. "How about my place?"

He wrapped his arms around my waist. "Are you serious?"

"We're together all the time anyway. Might as well make it official."

"You've just made me the happiest man alive."

The significance of the last word in that sentence was not lost on me.

We celebrated in our manner of choice—naked, slow, and sweet. We'd both discovered the joys of a relationship that lasted longer than an hour. Every night, we learned more about each other's bodies, and I'd go so far as to say Ethan knew mine better than I did now. He sure made it rock. And me? I knew the taste of every inch of him, the way he shuddered when he came, the quiet sigh he gave when he released into me.

I'd never get enough of him.

The only thing he wasn't keen on was my job, but he also understood I'd never quit. I'd discovered when I was a teenager that private investigation was what I'd been born to do, and if a man ever tried to make me choose between him and my career, well, he wasn't the one for me.

Ethan knew that, and he accepted it. It didn't stop him from worrying every time I went out the gates, though. This morning was no different. He kissed me goodbye with a lot of tongue and told me he loved me— the best three words in the English language.

At least my caseload was approaching normal now, or as normal as it could be with my stupid shoulder brace on. And while I went to Blackwood, Ethan would do his time in the gym then head to Spectre with Eli. Their messing around in the music room had turned more serious, and I'd heard whispers of a comeback. I'd also heard Ethan sing, and his husky voice did funny things to my insides. If they did decide to put out a Ghost-slash-Red Bennett album, I'd have to invest in new speakers for my apartment plus a pair of waterproof panties.

Right now, Ronan and his friend Reena had stepped in to manage Elastic Trickery and a few other acts while Ethan hunted for a replacement for Harold, easier said than done with Ethan's standing in the music industry. Only an old hand with the right connections would do. But ol' Harry had been right about one thing: no publicity was bad publicity. Ethan's studio was booked solid through next year, and he had stars the world over clamouring to work with him.

Ethan, in turn, had reevaluated his priorities.

"The kids are coming to the studio tonight," he told me over breakfast. "They want to work on a cover of Bruce Springsteen."

Trick, Vine, and Race had been to Spectre a couple of times. After I saw the places they were hanging out— the tunnel, the shed, the bin store—I wanted to help them, and Ethan did too.

I'd already spoken to Race's foster mom, so I did the grown-up thing and visited the other so-called parents. That experience made me want to spit. First came Trick's mom, who was tolerable. She worked two jobs and spent most of her spare time with her boyfriend.

"Could I have a quick chat about Trick?" I'd asked her.

She sighed. "What's he done now?"

"Nothing. It's just that my boyfriend's a musician and Trick and a few other kids have been hanging out in our apartment to learn how to play the guitar. I just wanted to check you were okay with that."

"Oh, sure, that's fine." She patted me on the arm.

"Just let me know if he bothers you, and I'll tell him to stop coming around."

Fair enough.

Then I'd shaken Vine's mom out of her alcohol-induced coma on the couch, whereupon she'd told me to fuck off unless I had more vodka. I gladly did so, taking Vine with me.

Honestly, it was a miracle those kids had turned out as good as they had.

After that, we'd come to an arrangement. If they went to school, passed whatever tests they had and did their homework on time, they could come to my place or Riverley or the studio whenever they wanted. They all knew the drill—call the Blackwood control room for a car and don't go walking in dodgy areas where big kids took their phones.

So far, it seemed to be working out.

Or so I thought.

I'd just ordered an Americano at my new favourite coffee place when Blackwood's receptionist called.

"Your fan club's here again."

"The kids?"

"All three of them."

"I'll be there soon."

Dammit, why were they skipping school? We'd talked about this.

It all felt kind of odd, spending time with them, but now I'd learned to live with Caleb's death, it turned out doing kid stuff was actually quite fun, at least when they behaved.

"Can you add a blueberry muffin, a chocolate chip cookie, and a glazed donut to that order?" I asked the guy behind the counter.

"You get real hungry, miss," he said with a grin.

I knew the kids' favourites now. Call me a soft touch.

But where were their smiles? Three serious faces greeted me when I walked into the Blackwood lobby.

"What's up, boys?"

"We got news," Trick said, his face grim.

"Yeah, it's shitty," Vine added.

I was trying to improve his vocabulary, but it wasn't easy, especially when Emmy meandered past and turned the air blue. Perhaps I should get him a Scrabble set? Out of the bedroom, that was my new favourite game, especially since Ethan had started writing me little messages with Scrabble tiles and leaving them all over the apartment.

Race said nothing, just stared at me with his big aqua eyes. One day, he'd grow into them. Sometimes I was convinced he was a mini-Ethan. As well as the eyes, they shared the same skin tone and the same quiet demeanour. He clutched a plastic bag in his lap, his knuckles white.

"Go on, hit me with it."

"Ethan said he couldn't start the project properly again until the dude that shot at you got caught."

"That's right, I'm afraid. It's just not safe for him."

Thanks to the publicity about Carr, the city had found Ethan a new space to use. The old building needed to be demolished, which ironically was what Carr had wanted in the first place. The funding to run the project was already in place, jointly from Ethan's pocket, mine, and Emmy's pet charity, The Blackwood Foundation. Meanwhile, the forty or so kids who attended were bored as hell, according to Trick, who seemed to know everybody in Richmond.

"Yeah, we get that," Trick said. "So all of us from the project decided we'd look for the dude with the gun, then we can have our instruments back."

Oh, heaven help me. "Boys, you can't do that. It's just not safe."

"Well, we did. Now we found the asshole, can you arrest him or something?"

What? "You're saying you found the person who shot at us?"

"Yeah, and the one driving, but it wasn't his deal."

Shitting hell. I didn't know whether to hug them or lock them up in a padded cell. Instead, I bit back the lecture I wanted to give and buzzed Emmy on the intercom.

"Meet me in the conference room, would you? You're gonna want to hear this."

The three boys tore into their snacks like they'd been starved for a month, which I knew wasn't the case because Ethan and I had taken them out for pizza the evening before. By the time Emmy arrived with fresh coffee, they'd devoured everything.

"Okay," I said. "Can you start from the beginning?"

Trick started talking, gesturing with his hands as was his habit. "So one of our buddies heard this rumour that some fancy attorney wanted some chick killed."

"That was you," Vine elaborated.

I'd assumed as much.

"Anyway, you know the Skrills?"

I nodded. They were a gang from the worst area of the city. The territory they controlled, about six square blocks, was a no-go area unless you had a death wish. Emmy and I used to dare each other to ride through there on our motorbikes when we were younger. I'd been shot at more than once.

"So one of them was gonna get done for assault. He robbed this guy in a shop and landed him in the hospital. Anyway, the attorney said he'd make the charges disappear if the Skrills did him a favour."

"And I was the favour?"

"Yeah, exactly."

"Do you know who was in the car?" I asked.

Trick nodded. "The one with the gun was called Screw, and the driver was Lock."

I knew of both of them, but only by reputation. It would require a small army to get them out of their lair. Good thing Emmy had one.

"Guess we'll be having an evening out," she said. "Maybe I should order new body armour first."

"I don't suppose you know the lawyer's name?" I asked.

A quick shake of the head. "Nobody knows that, only Screw. But Screw isn't stupid. Nobody trusts lawyers, so he recorded the conversation when the guy did the deal. We got that."

"Can't you do some magic computer shit and find out who it was?" Vine said.

"Hang on—you've got a lawyer ordering a hit on tape?"

"Yeah, sounds like a real dick."

Race held out his little bag to me. I took it and found a digital recorder inside.

"How the hell did you get this?"

"That's why we call him Race," Trick explained. "'Cos he gets in places then gets out real quick."

EPILOGUE

ETHAN LOOSENED HIS black tie and slid it off from around his neck. Lyle's funeral had been a sombre affair, and the simple cremation had been overshadowed by a team of Blackwood bodyguards and the crowd of photographers and fans hanging around outside the chapel, still fixated on the Richard Carr case.

Ghouls, the lot of them.

Ethan had kept his head down until the service was over. Guilt ate away at him, not just because of his involvement in the whole affair, but because today should have felt like the end and instead it felt like the beginning. The first day of his new life.

This morning, he'd signed the papers to sell his house. Once it had been his home, but not anymore. He'd thought nobody would want to buy it with its grisly history, but the freaks had been out in force. One weirdo even asked if he could leave the bloodstained carpet in place. Screw that. He'd sold the property to a developer who wanted to level it and build six apartments. A fitting end for a place he'd once loved but now couldn't bear to look at.

But he loved his new home. Not just the apartment, but the person he shared it with. Dani. His Dani. The woman who'd believed in him, fought for him, and almost died for him. He owed her everything, and he'd spend the rest of his life giving it to her.

And now she appeared in the doorway of the walk-in closet, wearing a black wraparound dress that showed nothing but hinted at everything.

"Do you want to go out for dinner, or shall I cook something?" she asked.

"Neither." Dani still wore a shoulder brace, and she should be resting. "I'll cook. You can sit down and watch TV."

She hit him full-beam with a smile, something that still made his heart swell up to bursting point. Dani was just so damn pretty, not that she cared. He stood in the doorway, slowly unbuttoning his shirt as she slipped her dress off and laid it over a chair. His cock twitched. Those curves got him every time, even when she covered them up with a pair of cartoon pyjamas. Some men liked lace and satin. He got hard for Wonder Woman.

"What do you want to eat?" he asked, mentally cataloguing the contents of the fridge. "Lasagne?"

"No."

"Chicken?"

"Nope." She took a step closer.

"Meatballs?"

"Getting warmer."

"Salad?"

"Colder."

"I give up. Tell me."

She dropped to her knees and reached for his zipper. How the fuck had he ever gotten this lucky?

"Don't stop. Don't stop!"

Ethan didn't, but Dani's phone ringing once, twice, three times with the theme song to *Mission: Impossible* while they made love nearly killed his mojo. In the end, she put her hands over his ears and kissed him hard, murmuring her filthy thoughts into his mouth as she often did. One final thrust and she came, then he shot his load inside her, bare and messy as fuck, but he wouldn't change it for the world.

"Love you, Dani."

She released her legs from around his ass. "Love you too, Ethan."

Then the damn phone rang again.

He rolled off her, reached out to the nightstand, and grabbed it, passing it over when what he really wanted to do was toss it out of the penthouse window.

Dani fumbled and pressed the speaker button.

"Oliver? What do you want?"

"Are you watching TV?"

"No, we're...we're not watching TV."

"Then switch it on."

"What? Why?"

"Just do it."

"Which channel?"

"The news."

Ethan already had the remote, and it didn't take long to see what Oliver was talking about. The glorious sight of Jay Skinner being led out of his office in handcuffs would be a memory to treasure. The assistant commonwealth's attorney's furious expression when an officer shoved him into the back of a squad car and slammed the door was an image Ethan wanted to frame and hang over the mantelpiece for posterity.

"Couldn't have happened to a bigger asshole," Dani muttered.

"Lock and Screw gave their statements from their hospital beds, and they were surprisingly forthcoming," Oliver said. In the end, it had taken a couple of weeks to dig them out of their hole safely. "Skinner approached Screw while he was in the police precinct. Talk about brazen."

"He thought he was untouchable. Did Lock and Screw say much else?"

"Apparently, they promised Nate they'd confess to anything as long as he kept Emmy and Ana away from them."

"All's well that ends well," Dani said. "I'm just glad the worst part's over."

The police were still looking for the missing girls Richard Carr claimed to have killed, and Dani and Mack were helping as a macabre sort of hobby, but the hard work was done.

"Yes. Mostly."

"Mostly?"

Oliver hesitated momentarily. "The state attorney general asked me to switch sides and prosecute Skinner. He's concerned that the commonwealth's attorney's office is tainted, at least in the public's eyes."

"Are you gonna do it?"

"I think so, yes. And also Carr. I've spoken to Emmy, and she's practically shoving me back inside a courtroom."

"Well, she's been saying for years you're wasted on her corporate stuff."

"It'll feel strange being on the other side."

"This time, it's the right side."

"Yes." Another pause. "It is. Guess I'll see you in court."

Oliver hung up, and Dani settled back on the bed, stretching her good arm above her head.

"Did you notice anything odd with Oliver and Stefanie yesterday?" she asked.

"What, at the funeral?"

"Yeah."

"No, why?"

"Oliver smiled at her, and she glared back at him. They used to get on okay. Unless..."

Ethan saw where she was going with that. "You don't think...? Oliver and Stefanie? Really?"

"Maybe." Dani's lips flickered into a cute little smile, and she nodded to herself. "Be interesting to see where that goes."

Ethan and Dani finally got dressed by midafternoon. The day after the kids turned up with the smoking-gun tape, Emmy had told Dani to take six weeks off, that they'd manage without her, but Dani's life of leisure had lasted about three days. On day four, she went through her voicemails, and by day five, she had her laptop open at the kitchen counter. Day six, and Ethan had given in and driven her to Blackwood.

Being honest, he'd missed the studio too, and each of them spending a few hours a day doing what they loved was a compromise that worked.

Down in the parking garage, Ethan got Dani settled into his new vehicle. Not another Mustang—Dani already had her Camaro, and they needed something roomier to shuttle the boys around. This time, he'd bought a Maserati Levante SUV.

A little ostentatious, perhaps, but the court had released his assets now. The cops had made noises about trying to get some of his money back from Harry, but Harry's offshore account had mysteriously drained itself overnight. The same night $12 million had appeared in Ethan's own bank account. Mack and her husband denied all knowledge, but Ethan knew damn well it had been them.

So, he'd splashed out on his new car.

At some point, he wanted another house as well, a home for Dani and him with a basement for his personal recording studio. Maybe a pool too, and one of those big brick grills. Two things he'd never needed before, but with the kids visiting every week and all Dani's friends, plenty of outdoor space seemed like a smart idea.

Funny how those kids had grown on him. When he first started the project, he'd hated every second. Since Frank died, he'd avoided groups of teenagers, but he told himself that if he could stop just one child from turning out like Ricky Carter and his gang, it would be worth it. Seven years on, he'd watched several of his group go on to be musicians, and the others had mostly kept out of trouble. Until he met Dani, they'd been his family.

"Busy today?" he asked her as he started the engine.

"I'm working with Ana to trace a missing toddler."

"She still make you nervous?"

Dani had confessed her feelings about Emmy's partner in crime.

"I think she'll always make me nervous, but she's damn good at what she does. You're taking the boys to the studio, right?"

"Just for an hour or two, but after I've dropped them home, I might be late back—there's a song stuck in my head, and I want to get it down."

"Sure. Leah brought in more books for Vinnie. Can you come in and get them?"

Now they'd gotten to know the boys better, they'd found out Vine's actual name was Vinnie. They also found out he was dyslexic, which was why his name had got shortened in the first place. He'd fallen behind at school, so Ethan and Dani were doing their best to help him catch up, although he got frustrated as hell when his classmates called him stupid. Bradley, as enthusiastic as ever, had spent the last week researching dyslexia to help out with books and teaching aids.

In the atrium at Blackwood's headquarters, Dani paused halfway to the reception desk and greeted a girl with a mop.

"Hey, you're new, right?"

The girl went full deer-in-headlights, much like Ethan used to do when a stranger introduced themselves.

"Th-th-that's right."

"I'm Dan. I work in investigations, and this is Ethan. He's just visiting."

"I'm Taylor."

"Nice to meet you, Taylor."

Ethan shook her hand, and she looked at her feet. Well, she'd landed up in the right place. At least at Blackwood, she mattered.

"Can I go on drums?" Trick asked.

He always asked that, and the answer was always yes. The kid had natural talent, and even at fifteen, he was better than eighty percent of the session musicians Ethan worked with. Rhythm, flair, a good memory for each track—he had it all. Plus ambition. Trick would go places, and Ethan wanted to take him there.

Was it fair for him to work at such a young age? Well, he was drumming anyway, just not getting paid for it. Ethan had started out busking at twelve, and music was the only part of his life he hadn't hated back then. He really needed to speak to Trick's mother.

But not today. Today, he had another problem to solve.

"Katie's gone sick," Ronan said.

Shit. So much for getting that track down.

"Is it serious?"

"Her roommate says she's puking everywhere."

"We still need a pianist."

"You?" Ronan suggested, plucking a few chords.

Without Harold throwing his weight around, Ronan had stepped out from behind his desk and picked up a guitar again.

"Somebody better than me."

"Julius is on vacation. I'll try to find a replacement for tomorrow."

Six months ago, a missing pianist would have been

a major headache. Harold would have been blaming everyone from God to Katie's gut bacteria, Ronan would have made himself scarce, and Ethan would have spent the next two nights creating a backing track out of nothing to keep the old man happy.

But today? It didn't matter so much anymore. The last couple of months had taught Ethan all about priorities, and he was coming to believe that shit happened for a reason.

"Hey, Race. You wanna sing?"

"Can Vine play guitar?"

Dani called him a soft touch, but he'd bought new instruments for the boys. And bicycles. And he may have also started a college fund, although they didn't know it yet. He owed those kids a lot, and he intended to repay every cent, but it was more than that. He liked them. They made him laugh, and their enthusiasm was infectious.

"Sure, Vine can play guitar."

With three tired boys dropped off at home, Ethan headed for Riverley. Apparently, Emmy was holding some kind of get-together, and Dani needed moral support.

Ethan heard the music as soon as he turned into the driveway. It was one of his tracks, a chart topper from last year. But why was somebody playing it loud enough to perforate an eardrum?

Bradley rushed out of the house the instant Ethan parked outside, which went some way to explaining things.

"Ethan! Welcome to the party! We've got food and games and loads of champagne."

Dani shuffled out sheepishly behind him, mouthing, "Sorry."

This was like immersion therapy, right? Dani had told him all about Emmy's fondness for that.

"We don't have to stay long," she muttered.

Bradley took them by the hands and led them through to the ballroom. "We've got champagne pong, karaoke, a treasure hunt, and loads of party games."

Ethan leaned close to Dani. "Is that a Skinner-piñata?"

"Yup. And we've got Carr-piñatas too."

Bradley overheard. "We've saved you the best one, and a really big stick."

This new life sure had turned out to be interesting.

Three hours later, Ethan and Dani snuck out of Riverley's side door. They'd both drunk too much to drive, Ethan was inexplicably horny, and Dani had the bright idea of sneaking over to Emmy's other house to get some alone time.

Good plan.

Or at least, it was until they walked in the front door.

"Who's that playing the piano?"

"Akari. It's a long story, but she's related to Black."

Ethan followed the sweet sound of Beethoven along the hallways, listening intently. Akari never missed a note, every bar in perfect tempo as she played through the tricky third part of the Moonlight Sonata that Ethan had messed up so many times yesterday.

He'd get down on his knees to have that woman in his studio.

The door to the music room hung ajar, and Ethan paused, letting the notes flow over him as the Asian lady playing them swayed gently in time, eyes closed. Then he took several rapid steps backwards as the giant cat lying next to the piano raised its head.

"What the fuck?"

Dani stood her ground as the monster stalked towards them. "Oh, it's just Kitty. He's Akari's pet."

"Kitty? That's not a kitty. That's a...that's a..."

"A jaguar," Akari told him. "Don't worry. He's eaten today."

The cat raised a giant paw, and Ethan took another pace back. Dan just laughed and high-fived the beast.

"Honestly, he's fine. He thinks he's a dog, anyway. Most of the time he lives in a big enclosure out back, but sometimes he comes in the house."

"Are you sure he's safe?"

"As long as you don't get on the floor and wrestle with him."

"There's no danger of that."

Akari walked towards them. She was a dainty lady in her early thirties with black hair cut into a bob and the fingers of a fucking angel.

"Ethan?"

He nodded, and she reached one of *those* hands out. Suddenly, he felt like teenage Ethan again, all awkward and tongue-tied.

"I heard what happened. I'm so sorry."

"Akari's studying music in Boston," Dan said. "At the Holborn School."

Studying it? She was a fucking maestro. *Say something, Ethan.* "Uh..."

"Ethan's got a studio in Richmond. You should visit

while you're here. Maybe you could record something for your folks back home? That would be okay, right, Ethan?"

"No problem."

Yet another reason he loved Dani. She gave him everything he wanted, sometimes without even realising it.

"Tomorrow?" Dani asked.

Ethan nodded.

"Tomorrow's okay," Akari said, her accent a strange mix of American and Japanese.

"Great. We can all go. Have you heard Eli sing yet? And there's this kid, Trick, who Ethan's been working with. He plays the drums, and..."

Yeah, shit definitely happened for a reason.

A week later, Ethan sat at his mixing desk with Dani on his lap. Bringing her with him sure slowed things down, but yesterday, she'd sucked his cock while he worked, and he'd never be able to hear that track again without picturing her head between his legs.

And now she nibbled on his earlobe. "Want me to twiddle your knobs today?"

Fucking hell. He groaned, feeling his cock twitch. "Baby, I need to get this song finished."

Akari had done three sessions for him, one on her own, and two with Eli, Trick, and Ronan. The final track they'd laid down would be the first record Eli had released in years, and rumours were already flying about their collaboration.

Let them fly.

Once, Ethan would have skulked in darkness to avoid the media, Eli as well, but life was too short to keep hiding. Neither of them planned to go out of their way to court publicity, but they'd discussed it at length and decided a few photos were something they could both live with now.

A soft knock at the door was followed by Trick's head poking around it. What was he doing here? Good thing Ethan hadn't given in to his earlier urges.

"Can we come in?"

"Sure. I thought you were going to the movies this evening?"

"We were."

The three boys filed into the studio, their expressions ranging from solemn to glum. Ethan knew those looks. He hated those looks.

"What's up?"

"Race's mom is sending him back."

"What?"

"He punched his foster brother, and she says she don't want troublemakers."

Dani crouched down in front of Race. "Is that true?"

He nodded.

"Why did you punch him?"

"He broke my drumsticks."

His foster brother was fifteen to Race's eleven, and it wasn't the first time the boy had done something nasty like that. He was also a devious little asshole who managed to blame everything on Race.

"They're sending him upstate where there's space," Trick told us.

Dani had already gone into fight mode. "The hell they are." She turned to Ethan, and he saw her bottom lip quiver. "We can't let them do that."

Ethan wrapped his arms around her waist. He knew how much that boy meant to her. Not only had he saved her life, he made her smile every day with his antics.

"I'm with you all the way, Dani."

They took the boys out for pizza, trying to stay positive, but by the time they climbed into the elevator up to their apartment at the end of the evening, Dani looked like Ethan felt. Exhausted, shell-shocked, kind of pale, but still determined.

"What do we do now?" he asked. "Will the state let us become foster parents?"

"What do we do?" She pulled out her phone. "Now? We talk to Black."

Ethan hadn't spent much time in Black's company, and quite frankly, the man intimidated the hell out of him. Not just his physical size, but his dark eyes. Eyes that bored right into a man's soul and mentally eviscerated him.

Like they were right now.

"So, you want to foster a child? Big step."

Dani shook her head. "Not foster. Adopt. He's been passed around nine homes already, and he's only eleven years old. He needs stability."

"What about your job, honey?" Emmy asked. "Would you quit?"

"No! I love my job, and other people at Blackwood make it work. Nate's got a son, and Ana's got a daughter."

Ethan's turn. "We'd share the childcare. Race comes to the studio after school with me, anyway."

"How about when you travel?" Black asked him. "You were playing gigs all over the world."

"I don't care about the gigs. Maybe I'll play one occasionally, and we can turn it into a vacation. At the moment, I'm in demand as a producer, and if people want to work with me, they'll just have to come to Richmond."

Sure, the glitz and glamour of touring had been exciting to start with, but the novelty soon wore off. The reality—living out of a suitcase, being stuck in a hotel room while fans screamed outside, sneaking around so he didn't get recognised—was far from fun. Going home to Dani each night had the star-studded lifestyle beat hands down, and the idea of having a bigger family... Yeah, he liked that. He liked it a lot.

"It would be a huge change," Black said.

"Look, I grew up without a father, and I don't want the same to happen to Race."

Black settled his dark gaze on Dani. "Are you sure this isn't just guilt talking? The boy saved you, and now you want to return the favour?"

A tear leaked out of her eye, and Ethan tightened his arm around her waist.

"No. Well, I guess a bit. I mean, I owe him everything, but that's not why I'm doing this. I never thought I'd have a child, and more than anything, I want to be Race's mom."

"Caleb."

Dani went rigid. "What?" she whispered.

Black pointed at the closed file on the coffee table in front of him. "Caleb's mom. Race Melliton's birth name is Caleb."

"Fuck."

Now Dani sobbed properly, and Emmy reached out and squeezed her hand, stroking her thumb over the knuckles.

"Her son was called Caleb," she whispered.

Oh, Dani. Ethan kissed her hair, wishing he could take some of her pain. She'd lost so much. He wanted to give her the world, starting with that little boy.

Black knelt in front of her and took Dani's other hand in both of his.

"You're sure about this?"

She nodded.

"Then I'll fix it."

Whatever else Black might have been, he was quick and he was thorough. The first batch of paperwork was completed in record time. The adoption was going through as a two-stage process, with a single-parent adoption followed by a second-parent adoption, and three weeks later, Dani walked into the apartment with her son, now officially Caleb di Grassi.

Ethan hoped to change that to Caleb White in the near future, but he'd take things one step at a time.

Dani led Race into his new bedroom, the second biggest, now furnished with a double bed and two bunks so his friends could sleep over too. Bradley had been involved in the decorating, so as well as the closet and the chest of drawers, Race had a state-of-the-art silent drum kit and a TV the size of Texas.

"How long can I stay here?" he whispered, and Dani

got all sniffy.

Ethan sat on the bed, bringing him to eye level. "This is your home now. Wherever we live, you live."

"Can I put up posters?"

"Any posters you like."

"Is there any food?"

"Why don't we help Dani to cook dinner? She still can't chop things up with her bad arm."

He wrinkled his nose. "Will she make us eat vegetables?"

"A few. But I'm sure we can find some chocolate too."

That evening, Ethan leaned back on the couch with one arm around Dani's shoulder and Race squashed in between them. In four short months, Ethan had gone from rockstar DJ to family man, and that should have scared the shit out of him but somehow it didn't. Everything about this felt right—his girl, his soon-to-be son, and the new direction of Spectre.

The good balanced out the bad. The horror of Christina's murder, Lyle's death, having to confront the demons of his childhood—nothing could erase them, but hope could ease the hurt.

Everything happened for a reason.

What's Next?

So, what's going on with Oliver and Stefanie? I wanted to know too, so I wrote them their own story.

Rhodium

Lawyers. Stefanie Amor's had enough of them to last a lifetime. One left her heartbroken, the other left her in bed and did a runner. But as the witness in a murder case, she's got no choice but to cooperate with defence attorney Oliver Rhodes, a great white shark who gets his kicks from chewing up lesser mortals and spitting out their sorry remains.

Oliver has two passions in life: money and winning. Stefanie's a shiny new toy he's not supposed to have, pretty to look at but so easy to break. Playtime's fun, but what happens when the game isn't a game anymore?

WARNING - Rhodium's dirty!

Find out more here: www.elise-noble.com/rhodium

And the Blackwood Security series continues with *Sphere*, a fun novella starring Emmy, Bradley, and the girl squad, and *The Scarlet Affair*, a full-length romantic thriller...

Sphere

When Emmy Black's personal assistant forces her to take a day off from saving the world and go to an amusement park, he promises it'll be a fun day out for her and the Blackwood girl squad. But it turns out the escaped monkeys are just the beginning, and before Emmy has even finished her first cocktail, she finds herself planning perhaps the most unusual rescue operation she's ever been involved in. Thank goodness she brought her duct tape...

Find out more here: www.elise-noble.com/sphere

The Scarlet Affair

Eight dead men. Eight grieving widows...

After a series of particularly nasty home invasions, Blackwood Security is hired to catch the killers. With the company's reputation at stake, everyone on the team is desperate to solve the mystery, unaware that there's a traitor in their midst.

Cade Duchamp's eager to help, but a minor indiscretion with the wrong girl leaves him banished to undercover duty. He's always liked motorbikes, but he doesn't like being a biker. Uncomfortable leather, an itchy beard, a lack of soap—need he say more? Cade wants to be back at head office, hunting down the real bad guys. At least, he does until five-year-old Scarlet turns up. The daughter he never knew he had.

Taylor Hancock likes to fade into the background. As an office cleaner, she can come to work, do her job, and avoid those dreaded social interactions. But nobody says no to Emmy Black, and as Scarlet's new nanny, Taylor's forced way out of her comfort zone into a world of shopping trips, parties, and playdates.

The only problem?

She's the traitor.

Find out more here: www.elise-noble.com/scarlet

If you enjoyed *White Hot*, please consider leaving a review.

For an author, every review is incredibly important. Not only do they make us feel warm and fuzzy inside, readers consider them when making their decision whether or not to buy a book. Even a line saying you enjoyed the book or what your favourite part was helps a lot.

Want to Stalk Me?

For updates on my new releases, giveaways, and other random stuff, you can sign up for my newsletter on my website:
www.elise-noble.com

Facebook:
www.facebook.com/EliseNobleAuthor

Twitter: @EliseANoble

Instagram: @elise_noble

If you're on Facebook, you may also like to join Team Blackwood for exclusive giveaways, sneak previews, and book-related chat. Be the first to find out about new stories, and you might even see your name or one of your ideas make it into print!

And if you'd like to read my books for FREE, you can also find details of how to join my advance review team.

Would you like to join Team Blackwood?

www.elise-noble.com/team-blackwood

END OF BOOK STUFF

I knew from the moment Dan walked into Albany House in Pitch Black that she'd have her own book someday, and I hope White Hot didn't disappoint. At first, Ethan was going to be a rock star, because I can imagine Dan at a concert climbing up on random men's shoulders to get a better view, but after I introduced the Ghost as a little red herring in Red Alert, I started wondering about the man behind the mask. And I figured Dan would share that curiosity.

Research for Ethan was fun too—I was totally in the dark about how mixing desks work, but luckily, I found a guy who works in a factory that makes them and he gave me a tour. Kind of fascinating, and some of them cost more than a house!

The other characters who intrigued me were Stefanie and Oliver. I've been deliberately vague about Oliver in previous Blackwood Security books, but if you imagined Emmy's lawyer was a crusty old dude in a baggy suit, then you were totally wrong. Oliver might have grey hair in a young-Richard-Gere sort of way, but he's hot and he's filthy.

Filthy.

I normally hold back a touch with the dirty bits—Carbon is my grubbiest story to date—but that wouldn't do Oliver justice. So I decided to write his story in the

Elements series. And I know people in my family are going to read it (including my mum) so if you'll excuse me, I'm just gonna go and die of embarrassment before its publication date.

You can think of Rhodium as an extended epilogue to White Hot, if you like. It covers the Carter and Skinner trials as well as what happens between Mr Rhodes and Miss Amor. But before I wrote Rhodium, White Hot had a different ending, one where Emmy didn't make it to the airport on time and Carter managed to escape.

Just for fun, here's what happened a few weeks after that...

"You were right about the fuel tank," Emmy said to Ana *as they peered over the edge of the cliff. The outlines of the few trees that had found life clinging to the steep, rocky slope were lit up from below by the glow of the burning car.*

Ana smiled. "Always a shame when somebody falls asleep at the wheel, isn't it?"

Emmy's answering grin was a mirror of Ana's. "Especially when it means the waste of a perfectly good BMW. That thing had an awesome sound system. It almost drowned out the asshole shouting in the trunk."

Even while on the run in Colombia, Ricky Carter had still gone for his first choice of vehicle. A BMW 5-series with all the bells and whistles.

"I liked your idea of using curare to incapacitate him rather than scopolamine," Ana said. "It was a nice twist, him being awake all the way down, just unable to move."

"Eduardo taught me about it. He's been cultivating the vines in his garden for years. I've taken a few home with me for the greenhouse at Riverley. You never know when they might come in handy, although Sofia stole half of them."

Ana's stomach grumbled, and she glanced at her watch. "Speaking of Eduardo, we should head back to his place. It's late and I'm getting hungry."

Emmy took one last look at the flames before swinging her leg over the sleek black motorbike. Ana climbed onto the pillion seat and wrapped her arms around Emmy's waist.

"You're right," Emmy said. "I could do with something to eat as well. What are we having?"

"Barbecue."

Anyhow, back to the real world where Carter's awaiting trial and Oliver's busy pissing Stef off and Stef's dealing with money trouble and blackmail and her dysfunctional family back in Georgia... I hope you'll join me for Rhodium if you like your books a little dirtier.

Huge thanks to my team as always—Amanda for editing, Abi for the cover, Lizbeth, John, and Dominique for proof reading, and Harka, Cecilia, Jeff, Quenby, Renata, Nikita, Helen, Lina, Musi, David, Stacia, and Jessica for beta reading. You guys rock!

OTHER BOOKS BY ELISE NOBLE

The Blackwood Security Series
For the Love of Animals (Nate & Carmen - prequel)
Black is My Heart (Diamond & Snow - prequel)
Pitch Black
Into the Black
Forever Black
Gold Rush
Gray is My Heart
Neon (novella)
Out of the Blue
Ultraviolet
Glitter (novella)
Red Alert
White Hot
Sphere (novella)
The Scarlet Affair
Spirit (novella)
Quicksilver
The Girl with the Emerald Ring
Red After Dark
When the Shadows Fall
Pretties in Pink (TBA)

The Blackwood Elements Series
Oxygen

Lithium
Carbon
Rhodium
Platinum
Lead
Copper
Bronze
Nickel
Hydrogen (TBA)

The Blackwood UK Series
Joker in the Pack
Cherry on Top (novella)
Roses are Dead
Shallow Graves
Indigo Rain
Pass the Parcel (TBA)

Blackwood Casefiles
Stolen Hearts
Burning Love (TBA)

Blackstone House
Hard Lines (2021)
Hard Tide (TBA)

The Electi Series
Cursed
Spooked
Possessed
Demented
Judged (2021)

The Planes Series
A Vampire in Vegas (2021)

The Trouble Series
Trouble in Paradise
Nothing but Trouble
24 Hours of Trouble

Standalone
Life
Coco du Ciel (2021)
Twisted (short stories)
A Very Happy Christmas (novella)

Books with clean versions available (no swearing and no on-the-page sex)
Pitch Black
Into the Black
Forever Black
Gold Rush
Gray is My Heart

Audiobooks
Black is My Heart (Diamond & Snow - prequel)
Pitch Black
Into the Black
Forever Black
Gold Rush
Gray is My Heart

Printed in Great Britain
by Amazon